Lynne Graham was born in Northern Ireland and has been a keen romance reader since her teens. She is very happily married, to an understanding husband who has learned to cook since she started to write! Her five children keep her on her toes. She has a very large dog, which knocks everything over, a very small terrier, which barks a lot, and two cats. When time allows, Lynne is a keen gardener.

Louise Fuller was once a tomboy who hated pink and always wanted to be the Prince—not the Princess! Now she enjoys creating heroines who aren't pretty push-overs but strong, believable women. Before writing for Mills & Boon she studied literature and philosophy at university, and then worked as a reporter on her local newspaper. She lives in Tunbridge Wells with her impossibly handsome husband Patrick and their six children.

Discover more at millsandboon.co.uk.

CINDERELLA'S DESERT BABY BOMBSHELL

LYNNE GRAHAM

BEAUTY IN THE BILLIONAIRE'S BED

LOUISE FULLER

MILLS & BOON

First Published in Great Britain 2021
by Mills & Boon, an imprint of HarperCollins*Publishers* Ltd,
1 London Bridge Street, London, SE1 9GF

www.harpercollins.co.uk

HarperCollins*Publishers*
1st Floor, Watermarque Building,
Ringsend Road, Dublin 4, Ireland

Cinderella's Desert Baby Bombshell © 2021 Lynne Graham

Beauty in the Billionaire's Bed © 2021 Louise Fuller

ISBN: 978-0-263-28257-3

08/21

MIX
Paper from
responsible sources
FSC® C007454

This book is produced from independently certified FSC™ paper
to ensure responsible forest management.
For more information visit www.harpercollins.co.uk/green.

Printed and bound in Spain
by CPI, Barcelona

CINDERELLA'S DESERT BABY BOMBSHELL

LYNNE GRAHAM

MILLS & BOON

CHAPTER ONE

THE HEIR TO the throne of the Middle Eastern kingdom of Alharia, Prince Saif Basara, frowned as his father's chief adviser, Dalil Khouri, knocked and entered his office with a charged air of importance and the solemn bearing of a man about to deliver vital information.

In recent years Saif had heard every possible story relating to his father's eccentric dictates and views. He was thirty years old, his difficult parent's successor, and the courtiers of his father's inner circle were now routinely playing a double game—nodding with false humility at his father's medieval dictums and then coming to Saif to complain and lament.

The Emir of Alharia was eighty-five years old and horrendously out of step with the modern world.

Of course, Saif's father, Feroz, had come to the throne in a very different age, a feudal ruler in an unstable era when a troubled country was overwhelmingly grateful to have a safe and steady monarch. Oil had then been discovered. Subsequently, the coffers of Alharia had overflowed and for decades everyone had been happy with that largesse. Unhappily for Feroz, the desire for democratic government had eventually blossomed in his people, as well as the wish to modify cultural rules with an easier and more contemporary way of life. He, however, remained rigidly opposed to change of any kind.

'You are to be married!' Dalil announced with so much throbbing drama that Saif very nearly laughed until he registered that the older man was deadly serious.

Married? Saif stiffened in surprise, well aware that only his father's misogyny had allowed him to remain single for longer than most sons in his position. After four failed marriages in succession, Feroz had become deeply distrustful of women. His final wife, Saif's mother, had inflicted the deepest wound of all. An Arabian princess of irreproachable lineage, she had, nonetheless, abandoned both infant son and elderly husband to run away with another man. That she had then married that man and become joint ruler of another small country and thereafter *thrived* in tabloid newspaper photographs enraptured with her beauty had definitely been salt rubbed in an open wound.

'Married to a very *bad* choice of a woman,' Dalil completed with regret, mopping his perspiring brow with an immaculate linen handkerchief. 'The Emir has turned his back on all the many respectable possibilities both in Alharia and amongst our neighbours' families and has picked a foreigner.'

'A foreigner,' Saif repeated in wonderment. 'How is that possible?'

'This woman is the granddaughter of your father's late English friend, Rodney Hamilton.'

As a young man, the Emir had undergone a few months of military training at Sandhurst in England, where he had formed an unbreakable friendship with a British army officer. For years, the two men had ex-changed letters and at least once there had been a visit. Saif dimly recalled a whiny, weepy little girl with blond pigtails appearing in his nursery. His future bride? Was that even possible?

Dalil dug out the mobile phone he kept carefully hidden from the Emir, to whom mobile phones were an abomination. He flicked through photos and handed it to Saif, saying, 'At least she is a beauty.'

Saif noted that his father's adviser took it for granted that he would accept an arranged marriage with a stranger, and he swallowed hard, shocked by the apparent belief that he was required to make that sacrifice. He stared down unimpressed at a laughing, slender blonde in an evening gown. She looked frivolous and wholly unsuited to the life that he led. 'What do you know about her?' he prompted.

'Tatiana Hamilton is a socialite, an extravagant party girl...not at all the kind of wife you would wish for, but in time...' Dalil hesitated to avoid referring to the reality that the Emir's failing health would not conserve the ruler for ever. 'Obviously, you would divorce her.'

'It is possible that I will refuse this proposition,' Saif confessed tautly.

'You *can't*...it could kill your father to go into one of his rages now!' Dalil protested in consternation. 'Forgive me for speaking so bluntly, but you do not want that on your conscience.'

Saif breathed in slow and deep as he faced the truth that he was trapped. He banked down his anger with the ease of long practice, for he had grown up in a world in which personal choice about anything was a rare gift. He had been raised to be a dutiful son and, now that his parent was weak and ailing, it was a huge challenge to break that conditioning. It didn't help that he also understood that it would be very painful for his traditional parent to be confronted by a defiant son. Arranged marriages might have been out of fashion for decades in Alharia but, at heart, the Emir was a caring father and Saif was not cruel. He was also very conscious that he was indebted to his father for the loving care he had practised in an effort to ensure that his son was less damaged by his mother's abandonment.

Consequently, he would wed a stranger, he acknowledged, bitterness darkening his stunning green eyes.

'Why would a spoilt English socialite want to marry me and come out here?' he demanded of the older man in sudden incomprehension. 'For a title? Surely not?'

A look of distaste stamped Dalil's wrinkled face. 'For the money, Your Royal Highness. For the lavish dowry your father is prepared to pay her family,' he replied in a tone of repugnance. 'They will be greatly enriched by this marriage and that is why you will wish to divorce her as soon as possible.'

Saif was aghast at that statement. It gave him the worst possible impression of his future bride and filled him with revulsion. He knew that he would find it very hard to pretend any kind of acceptance of such an unprincipled woman…

'George has just asked me to marry him!' Ana carolled, practically dancing out of the bathroom where she had been talking on the phone to her ex-boyfriend. 'Isn't that typical of a man? It took me to come to Alharia and be on the very brink of marrying another man to get George to the point!'

'Well, it's a bit foolish, him asking you this late in the day,' Tati opined with innate practicality as she studied her beautiful and lively cousin with sympathetic blue eyes. 'I mean, we're here in the *royal* palace and you're committed now. The preparations for the wedding are starting in less than an hour.'

'Oh, I'm not going through with this stupid wedding now—not if George wants me to marry him instead!' Ana declared with sunny conviction. 'George has already booked me on a flight home. He's planning to pick me up at the airport and whisk me away for a beach wedding somewhere.'

'But your parents…the money.'

'Why should I have to marry some rich foreign royal because my father's in debt to his eyeballs?' Ana interrupted with unconcealed resentment.

Tati winced at that piece of plain speaking. 'Well, I didn't think you should have to either, but you did *agree* to do it and if you back out now, it'll plunge us all into a nightmare. Your father will go spare!'

'Yes, but that's where *you* are going to *help* me play for time and ensure that I can get back out of this wretched country!' her cousin told her without hesitation.

'Me? How can I help?' Tati argued in bewilderment, because she was the most powerless member of the Hamilton family, the proverbial poor relation often treated as little more than a servant by Ana's parents.

'Because *you* can go through these silly bridal preparations pretending to be me, so that nobody will know that the bride has scarpered until it's too late. I mean, in a place as backward as this, they might try to *stop* me leaving at the airport if they find out beforehand!

I bet it's a serious crime to jilt the heir to the throne at the altar!' Ana exclaimed with a melodramatic roll of her big brown eyes. 'But, luckily, no member of the groom's family has even seen me yet and Mum's certainly not going to be getting involved with these Alharian wedding rituals, so the parents won't find out either until the very last minute, by which time I'll be safely airborne!'

Tati dragged in a ragged breath as her cousin completed that confident little speech. 'Are you sure this isn't an attack of cold feet?' she pressed.

'You know I'm in love with George and I have been...*for ever*!' her cousin stressed with strong feeling. 'Didn't you hear me, Tati? George has finally proposed and I'm going home to him!'

Tati resisted the urge to remind her cousin how many other men she had been wildly in love with in recent years. Ana's affections were unreliable and only a month earlier she had claimed to be excitedly looking forward to her wedding in Alharia. Back then, Ana had been as delighted as her parents at the prospect of no longer being short of cash, but of course, that angle would no longer matter to her, Tati conceded ruefully, because George Davis-Appleton was a wealthy man.

'I can understand that you want to do that.' Tati sighed. 'But I don't think I want to get involved in the fallout. Your parents will be furious with me.'

'Oh, don't be such a wet blanket, Tati! You're *still* family,' Ana declared, impervious as always to her cousin's low standing in that sacrosanct circle. 'Mum and Dad will get over their disappointment and they'll just have to ask the bank for a loan instead.'

'Your father said that he'd been refused a loan,' Tati reminded her gently.

'Oh, if only Granny Milly was still alive…she would have helped!' Ana lamented. 'But it's not my problem… it's Dad's.'

Tati said nothing, only reflecting that their late and much-missed Russian grandmother had had little time for her son Rupert's extravagant lifestyle. Milly Tatiana Hamilton, after whom both girls had been named, had controlled the only real money in her family for many years. Tati had been surprised at her uncle getting into debt again because she had assumed that he had inherited a sizeable amount after his mother's death.

'Sadly, she's gone.' Tati sighed heavily.

She did not, of course, point out that she had a vested interest in her aunt and uncle remaining financially afloat because she felt that that would be utterly unfair to Ana. She could hardly expect her cousin to go through with a marriage that would be abhorrent to her simply for Tati's benefit. In any case, Ana appeared to have no idea that her father paid for his sister Mariana's care in her nursing home. Tati's mother, Mariana, had lived there since her daughter was a teenager, having contracted early onset dementia.

'So, will you do it?' the beautiful blonde demanded expectantly.

Tati flinched because she knew that she shouldn't risk angering her aunt and uncle lest they withdraw their financial support from her mother, but at the same time, she was as close to Ana as a sister. Ana was only two years older than Tati's almost twenty-two years. The pair of them had grown up on the same country estate and had attended the same schools. Regardless of how different in personality the two women were, Tati loved her cousin. Selfish and spoilt Ana might occasionally be, but Tati was accustomed to looking after Ana as though she were a young and vulnerable sister because Ana was not the sharpest tool in the box.

The whole 'marrying a foreign prince sight unseen to gain a fat dowry' scenario had never struck sensible Tati as anything but ludicrous. Naturally, her cousin should have had the sense to refuse to marry Prince Saif from the start because Ana was not the self-sacrificing type. But at first, Ana had seen herself as a heroine coming to the aid of her family. Furthermore, the tantalising prospect of increased wealth and status had soothed an ego crushed by George's refusal to commit to a future with her. Sadly, now that reality had set in, Ana was ready to run for the hills.

For a split second, Tati felt rather sorry for the bridegroom, whoever he might be, for he had no presence whatsoever on social media. Alharia seemed to be decades behind in the technology stakes—decades behind in most things, if she was honest, Tati had reflected after their drive through the desert wastes to the remote palace, which was an ancient fortress with mainly Victorian furnishings.

'All that money and no idea how to spend it or what to spend it on,' her aunt Elizabeth had bemoaned in envious anguish, soon after their arrival. And it was true: the Basara royal family might be oil billionaires, but there was little visible sign of that tremendous wealth.

Ana had met someone who had sworn blind that Prince Saif was 'absolutely gorgeous' but, as even Ana had said, how much faith could she place in that when people tended to be more generous when it came to describing rich, titled young men? Even if the poor chap were as ugly as sin, most would find something positive to say about him.

Tati knew all about that approach and the accompanying unkind comparisons, having grown up labelled a plain Jane beside her much prettier and thinner cousin. Of course, Tati was the family 'mistake' being illegitimate, something which might not matter to others, but which had seriously mattered to the uptight Hamilton family and had embarrassed them.

Both girls were blonde, but Tati had blue eyes and Ana had brown and Ana was a tall, slim beauty while Tati rejoiced rather more simply in good skin, a mane of healthy hair and curves. Well, she had never exactly *rejoiced* in her body, she conceded ruefully, particularly not after her only serious boyfriend had taken one look at her cousin and had fallen in love with her to the extent that he had made an embarrassing nuisance of himself, even though Ana had not had the smallest interest in him.

'Have you even thought of how you're going to get back to the airport?' Tati asked her cousin when she returned to the bedroom they were sharing.

'Already sorted,' Ana said smugly. 'You don't need the lingo to get by here. I flashed the cash, pointed to a car and it's downstairs waiting for me already.'

'Oh…' Tati whispered in shock as she watched her cousin scooping up her belongings and cramming them back into the suitcase she had refused to allow the maid to unpack. 'You're definitely doing this, then?'

'Of course, I am.'

'Don't you think it would be better to face the music

and tell your parents that you're leaving?' Tati pressed hopefully.

'Are you joking?' Ana exclaimed. 'Have you any idea of the fuss they would make and how bad they would make me feel?'

Tati nodded in silence because, of course, she knew.

'Well, I'm not putting myself through that for anybody!' Ana asserted. 'Now, you be careful. Don't let them realise that you're not the bride for a few hours… that's all I'm asking you to do, no big deal, Tati! Come on, give me a hug and wish me well with George!'

Tati rose stiffly and hugged her, because she knew how headstrong Ana was and that nothing short of a nuclear bomb would alter her plans once she had made her mind up. 'Be happy, Ana,' she urged with damp eyes and a sense of dread she couldn't shake.

Tati hated it when people got angry and started shouting and she knew that the moment her aunt and uncle realised that their daughter had departed there would be a huge scene and furious raised voices. They would blame *her* for not telling them in advance. At the same time, though, she understood her cousin's fears. Ana's parents were so set on the marriage taking place that they were quite capable of following her to the airport and trying to force her to return to the palace. How could she subject Ana to that situation when she no longer wanted to marry the wretched man? After all, nobody should be forced to marry anyone they didn't want to marry.

Ana departed with the utmost casualness, a gormless servant even carting her luggage for her without a clue that he was assisting the Prince's bride to stage a vanishing act. Tati sat on the edge of a seat in the corner of the bedroom, panicking at the very thought of allowing people to credit that she was her cousin and the bride-to-be. She supposed that that meant she was a coward and she felt ashamed of herself for being so weak. Deception of any kind was usually a complete no-no for Tati, whose birth father had gone to prison for financial fraud. Her mother, Mariana, ashamed of the character of the man who had fathered her daughter, had raised her to be honest and decent in all situations. And what was she doing now?

While Tati was struggling with her loyalty to her cousin, her anxiety about her mother's continuing care and her troubled conscience, someone knocked on the door and entered, a brightly smiling young woman, who greeted her warmly in English. 'Tatiana? I am the Prince's cousin, Daliya. I am a student in England, and I have been asked to act as your interpreter.'

'Everyone calls me Tati,' Tati told her apprehensively, thinking how silly it was that she didn't even have to lie about her name because she and her cousin were both officially Tatiana Hamilton, thanks to her rebellious mother's obstinacy. Tati's mother and uncle had never got along as siblings. When Mariana's brother, Rupert, had named his child after his mother, his sister had seen no reason why he should claim that privilege and she should not. Of course, back then, her mother could never have foreseen that she would end up living back at her birthplace and that there would be two little girls rejoicing in the same name.

'I am sure you are wondering about the importance my people put on the bridal preparations,' Daliya assumed. 'Let me explain. This is not typical of weddings in Alharia because it is no longer fashionable. But you are different because this is a *royal* wedding. All the women who will attend you here today consider this a great honour. Most of them are from the older generation and this is how they demonstrate their respect, loyalty and love for the Basara family and the throne.'

'I shall feel privileged,' Tati squeezed out between clenched teeth, the guilt of being an impostor on such a solemn occasion cutting her deep. The pretty brunette's explanation had made her want to die of shame where she sat. The very least she could do was be polite and respectful...until the dreadful moment when people realised that she was *not* the right Tatiana Hamilton. Inwardly she was already recoiling in horror from the thought of that dramatic unveiling.

'All the same, I'm sure the unfamiliar will feel strange, and it may possibly intrude on your privacy to accept these diverse customs,' Daliya suggested, her intelligent brown eyes locked to Tati's face. 'You are very pale. Are you feeling all right? Is it the heat?'

'Oh, it's just nerves!' Tati exclaimed shakily as the other woman showed her out of the room and down a corridor. 'I'm very robust in the health stakes.'

Daliya laughed. 'The elderly women obsessed with your fertility will be delighted to hear that.'

'My f-fertility?' Tati stammered helplessly in her incomprehension.

'Of course. Some day you will be a queen and the natural hope is that you will provide the next generation to the throne.' Daliya frowned in surprise as Tati stumbled in receipt of that explanation.

For a split second, Tati had almost divulged the truth that she was not the right Tatiana, because it seemed so wrong to deceive people at such an important event. But they were already entering a very large room crammed with older women, some of whom wore the traditional dress but most of whom sported western fashion like her young companion.

Aware of being the centre of attention and ill accustomed to that sensation, Tati flushed just the way she used to do at school when the bullies had christened her 'Tatty Tato,' mocking her for her shabby second-hand uniforms and worn shoes. Her uncle's generosity in paying her school fees had not extended to such extras, and why should it have? she reflected, scolding herself for that moment of ingratitude. Tati had adored her loving mother growing up, but sometimes she had been embarrassed by her parent as well. Mariana Hamilton had never stood on her own feet and had never done anything other than casual work when it suited her. Relying on other people to pay her bills had come naturally to Tati's mother and that had made Tati both proud and independent. Or as proud and independent as one could be when forced to live in her uncle and aunt's country house and be at the family's beck and call while working for barely minimum wage.

All those thoughts teemed in Tati's busy brain while she calculated how many hours she would need to play the bridal role to allow Ana to make her getaway, and that introspection got her through the hideous public bathing rite she endured. Herbs and oils were stirred through a steaming bath and then she was wrapped in a modesty sheet, just as if she were entering a medieval convent, and settled into the water to have her hair washed. Keeping up an air of good cheer was hard. Daliya lightened the experience with explanations of the superstitions that had formed such rituals and cracking the occasional discreet joke.

'You are a very good sport,' Daliya whispered in quiet approbation. 'It is a good quality for a member of the royal family. I think all the women were afraid that you would refuse their attentions.'

Tati contrived to smile despite her discomfiture because she knew for a fact that nobody would have got to roll Ana in a sheet and steep her in a hot herbal bath that smelled like stewed weeds. Ana would have flatly refused any such ritual, too attached to her own regimented beauty routine and too afraid that her hair would be ruined. Unfamiliar with such routines, Tati had told herself that she was having a treat, a rather exotic treat admittedly but pretty much a treat for a young woman who generally washed, cut and styled her own hair. What little she earned only kept her in clothes and small gifts for her mother when she was able to visit her.

'You are very brave,' Daliya told her as her hair was being combed out.

'Why do you say that?'

'You are marrying a man you have never seen, never spoken to…or have you and the Prince met up in secret?' she prompted with unconcealed curiosity.

'No, we haven't. Isn't that the custom here? The sight-unseen thing?' Tati queried.

Daliya laughed out loud. 'Not in Alharia now for generations. We meet, we date. It is all very discreet, of course. Only the Emir follows old cultural traditions, but with the Prince you need have no fear of disappointment. Had His Royal Highness desired to marry any sooner, he would have been snatched up by any number of women.'

'Yes, I believe he's quite a catch,' Tati remarked politely.

'Saif is of a thoughtful, serious nature,' Daliya murmured quietly. 'He is very much admired in our country.'

Tati had to bite her tongue on the flood of curious questions that she wanted to fire at the brunette. It was none of her business. Even the Hamiltons knew next to nothing about the Crown Prince, for none of them had cared about the details. That the marriage should take place and the dowry be given had pretty much encompassed the extent of her relatives' interest and that awareness shamed Tati, because everything that her present companions took so seriously had been treated with scornful indifference by Ana and her parents.

At that point, Daliya contrived to persuade their chattering companions that the waxing technician could take Tati into the giant bathroom with its waiting treatment couch alone. Tati had never been so grateful for that small piece of mercy in the proceedings. Discovering that she was only an hour and a bit into the lengthy bridal preparations, she heaved a heavy sigh, knowing that her cousin needed longer to make good her escape from Alharia. She felt worse than ever about her deception.

After the waxing, the preparations moved on to a massage with scented oils. Her nails were painted and then henna patterns were drawn on her hands. Mentally exhausted, Tati drifted off into sleep and when she was wakened gently by Daliya, she sat up and was immediately served with a cold drink and a tasty little snack while all the women hummed some song around her. Her watch had disappeared, and she had no idea what time it was. Daliya was now telling her that she had to leave for a little while but would be back with her soon.

That announcement plunged Tati into an even deeper dilemma. She had originally planned to share her true status and the reality that the bride had fled with the chatty brunette, but she was painfully aware that Daliya had been very kind to her. As the only English speaker she might well receive considerable blame for not having registered the fact that the bride was not who she was supposed to be. After all, everybody was likely to get very worked up once the truth emerged. Tempers would be fraught, angry accusations would be made. Uneasily, Tati decided to wait for a less personal, more *official* messenger before confessing that she was a complete fraud in the bride stakes.

A long silk chemise garment was displayed for her benefit and it was evidently time for her to get dressed. She would be making her big reveal very soon, Tati acknowledged, sick at the prospect, her tummy hollowing out. But she had to be clothed to do anything, she reflected wretchedly, and she stood in silence while she was engulfed like an Egyptian mummy in layers of tunics and petticoats and her hair was combed out and a cosmetic technician every bit as slick as the type Ana used at home arrived to do her work. By the time Daliya reappeared beaming, Tati was ready to nibble her nails down to the quick, only she couldn't because they too had been embellished and she didn't want to offend anyone. And even that thought struck her as ridiculous, considering how offended everyone would be when the awful truth came out.

'It's time,' Daliya informed her cheerfully.

Tati feared she might throw up, so knotted were her

insides by that stage, and the brunette's reappearance didn't help because she honestly didn't want to involve Daliya in her disaster. And it would *be* a disaster, she thought wretchedly. However, her aunt and uncle were the proper people to be told first that their daughter had fled. As they were to be witnesses to what Ana had described with a sniff of disappointment as a very *private* ceremony, she was sure to see Ana's parents very soon in the flesh.

A posse of chattering women walked her through the palace, down stone staircases, across inner courtyards, through endless halls and corridors until finally they reached a set of giant ornate double doors set with silver and glittering gems and guarded by two large men in traditional dress brandishing weapons.

'We must leave you here…but we will see you soon,' Daliya smilingly told her, exchanging a brief word with the guards that had them springing into action and throwing wide the double doors…

CHAPTER TWO

ONLY A SMALL number of people awaited the bride's arrival in the ancient splendour of that giant painted and gilded room, which was surrounded by elaborate carved archways and pillars. A regal elderly man was stationed by the side of another, taller figure shadowed by the archway below which he stood. Another pair of older men hovered beside a table, and across the room stood Rupert and Elizabeth Hamilton, Tati's uncle and aunt, glaringly out of place in their fashionable Western attire.

Rupert Hamilton frowned the instant he saw Tati and he strode forward. 'You're not supposed to be here for the ceremony. Where's Ana?'

Tati's mouth ran very dry. 'Gone,' she croaked.

'Gone?' the older man thundered. 'How can my daughter be gone? Gone where?'

Saif watched with keen eyes from the sidelines and wondered what was happening. Seemingly the bride had arrived, but her father was angry and that word, *gone*, was remarkably explanatory in such circumstances. Who on earth was the woman who had arrived in her place dressed as his bride? Saif almost laughed out loud with relief and amusement at the confirmation that the

Basara family's bad luck with wives was continuing into his generation. Beside him, he could feel his father bristling with impatience, and he translated that single word for his benefit. 'The bride is gone,' he murmured in their own language. 'This is a different woman.'

'Gone to catch a flight back home. She'll be airborne by now,' Tati explained in a rush. 'She didn't want to go through with this.'

'You bitch! You helped her to run away!' her aunt Elizabeth shrilled at her in a tempestuous bout of annoyance, stalking across the room and lifting her hand as though to slap Tati.

'No...there will be no violence in the Emir's presence,' another voice intervened—male, accented, dark and deep in pitch.

Tati looked up in shock at the very tall young man who, for all his height and build, had approached so quietly and quickly that she hadn't heard him. He had caught her aunt's hand before it could connect with Tati's face, and he dropped the older woman's wrist again with a chilling air of disdain at such behaviour. And Tati's first thought was foolishly that Ana would be raging if she ever saw a photo of the bridegroom she had abandoned, because there were few women who appreciated a handsome man more than her cousin.

The big, well-built man towering over them, sheathed in an embroidered traditional tunic and trousers in opulent shades of brown silk worn with boots, was absolutely gorgeous. He had unruly black hair, eyes that were a startlingly unexpected and piercing green and lashes long enough to trip over, set deep below slashing ebony brows. He had skin the colour of creamy coffee whipped with cinnamon and stretched taut over spectacular bone structure, with a straight nose, a strong jawline and a wide sensual mouth. He was so good-looking that Tati's tongue was glued to the roof of her mouth and she simply stared at him as if he had suddenly materialised in front of her like an alien dropped from a spaceship.

'Be quiet, Elizabeth!' Rupert Hamilton snapped to silence his wife's ranting accusations. 'How long has it been since Ana left the palace?'

'It was hours ago,' Tati confirmed reluctantly.

The elderly man at the front of the room erupted into an angry speech in his own language. Saif shot a highly amused glance down at the bride who was not a bride. A sense of regained freedom and strong relief was now powering through him. She was tiny and she had huge blue eyes and a mass of wheat-blond hair that almost reached her waist…if she had a waist. The women had put so much clothing on the fake bride that she closely resembled a small moving mound of cloth. It was possible that she was rather round in shape but equally possible that she was built like a twig…and it didn't matter either way to him now, did it?

'And who are you?' he prompted with what he felt was excusable curiosity.

'Ana's cousin, Tati.'

'Which is a diminutive of?'

'Tatiana.'

'The same as the bride who is…*gone*?' Black lashes swooped down low over his glittering gaze and his mouth quirked. 'Is there a shortage of names in your family?' he enquired with complete insouciance, apparently untouched by the angry outbursts emanating from everyone else in the room.

A determined hand closed over her elbow, pulling her away from the silk-clad Prince. 'I want a word with you,' her uncle told her angrily. 'Here you are clearly *desperate* to take your cousin's place! That's why you helped her, isn't it? The temptation was too much for you. The thought of the clothes, the jewels and the holidays you'd be able to enjoy…the rich lifestyle that you've always dreamt of having and now, with Ana out of the way, it can *all* be yours!'

'Keep your voice down,' Tati pleaded with the older man because the Prince was only a few feet away from them.

She was absolutely horrified by her uncle's accusation that she had deliberately schemed to step into her cousin's shoes, that unspoken but deeply wounding suggestion that she must always have been envious of Ana and her superior financial prospects. 'Of course, I'm not trying to take Ana's place. Right now, you're upset—'

Dalil Khouri was endeavouring to explain to the enraged Emir that although a bride had arrived, she was not the chosen bride, she was a substitute even if she was another grandchild of the Emir's late friend. 'Well, then, let the ceremony proceed!' the old man commanded impatiently.

Saif, repelled by the brutal condemnation he had heard the uncle aim at his niece, made an attempt to reason with his exasperated parent, but his father could not move beyond the perceived affront of his precious only son and heir being jilted by his bride. The Emir could not accept that outrage. He felt it too deeply, chiming in as it did to his own unhappy past experiences with the opposite sex. 'I will not have my son left without a bride when the entire country knows he is to be wedded today,' he told his adviser with barely leashed anger. 'That is an insult we cannot accept. The other girl will do.'

Saif's brows shot up and he encountered a pleading look from Dalil, which almost made him roll his eyes. *'The other girl will do?'* Why not go out onto the street in Tijar, their capital city, and grab the first single woman they saw? Was he expected to marry *any* available woman? The volatile temperament that Saif usually kept restrained was suddenly flaring with raw, angry disbelief. What kind of insanity was his father proposing now? If the bride had run off, goodbye and good riddance was Saif's response, as he was no keener on the marriage taking place than evidently she had been. But, tragically, his father was reacting with very real wrath to what he saw as a loss of face and an insult to the throne of Alharia.

Dalil aimed a powerless glance of regret in Saif's direction and crossed the room to speak to the Englishman. Saif twisted to attempt to reason with his father and then registered that the Emir was tottering and swaying where he stood. With a shout for assistance, he supported the frighteningly pale older man, and a guard came running with a chair.

'I am fine… I am good,' the Emir ground out between gritted teeth.

'Allow me to call Dr Abaza,' Saif urged.

'Unnecessary!' the Emir barked.

Dalil returned. 'It is your wish that the ceremony proceeds?' he prompted his ruler, while Saif thought in disgust of the mercenary young woman he was to be cursed with.

'Why else am I here?' the Emir demanded on a fresh burst of annoyance.

On the other side of the room Rupert Hamilton was cornering his niece. 'The Emir simply wants his son married off.'

'Why? What's wrong with him?' Tati questioned with a grimace.

'Well, you should be happy that all that needs to be altered on the paperwork is your birthdate,' her uncle told her, as though what he had suggested were a perfectly reasonable change. 'You will be marrying him in Ana's place.'

Tati stared up at the older man in disbelief. '*I'm* not willing to marry him!' she snapped half under her breath for emphasis.

Rupert Hamilton gave her an offensive smile. 'So you say,' he said, clearly unconvinced.

'I didn't seek this development,' Tati argued in a low, desperate undertone.

Her uncle shrugged. 'Then think of this as a long-overdue repayment for my family's generosity towards you and your idle, feckless mother,' he told her thinly. 'You owe us, Tati. You haven't put a bite of food in your mouth since you were born that hasn't come from this family. Now your mother's draining our resources like a leech…all these years in that overpriced nursing home—'

'She can't help that!' Tati exclaimed chokily, shaken at being confronted by his heartless resentment that her poor mother had not yet seen fit to die of the disease that had already robbed her of memory, physical health and enjoyment of life.

'If you want her to stay on there, you *will* marry the

Prince,' her uncle told her callously. 'And if you don't marry him, she can go on welfare benefits and move to some council place where she'll be a damn sight less comfortable!'

'That's a horrible threat to make,' Tati whispered shakily. 'You can't still hate her that much. She's a frail shell of the woman she once was.'

'You made your choice. For whatever reasons, you *helped* Ana skip out on us…now *you* can pay the price!' her uncle slammed back at her bitterly.

For a split second, Tati lingered there, frozen to the spot as she stared into space. But she knew she didn't have a choice. The mother who had loved and appreciated her throughout her childhood deserved to be contented for what remained of her life. Dementia patients found any sort of change in their routines distressing and if Mariana Hamilton were moved to another home, she would very probably decline at an even faster rate. Tati neither liked nor respected her uncle, but she was willing to concede that perhaps he needed the dowry he was to receive from the marriage to help maintain her mother in her current home. He had called her mother a leech and apparently regarded his niece in the same light. That hurt, when she had spent the past six years industriously cleaning, cooking and fulfilling her relatives' every request to the best of her ability in repayment for her mother's care. Her work had begun while she was still at school and had eaten up every free hour, becoming a full-time job once she had completed sixth form.

'I'll do it,' she breathed stiffly. 'I don't have any other option.'

'Good.' Squaring his shoulders, her uncle walked

over to the table and nodded at the older man. 'Well, let's get this over and done with.'

Barely able to credit that she was in such a position, Tati followed the older man across the room. The Prince approached the table but kept his distance, which suited her fine because she was already wondering what was amiss with him that his father could be so eager to marry him off that even a last-minute change of bride didn't dim his enthusiasm. Maybe he was a lecher and marriage was aimed at making him appear more respectable.

Good grief, he couldn't be expecting a *real* marriage, could he? Real as in sex and children? Ana had never actually discussed much relating to the marriage with Tati because in recent years Ana had spent most of her time in the family apartment in London. And when her cousin had come home to the country she'd often brought friends with her and Tati had not liked to intrude. Ana had once remarked that Tati couldn't clean and cook and then expect to socialise with her cousin's guests because that would be too awkward. Tati breathed in deep and slow to counter the pain of rejection that that recollection reawakened. Well, she guessed it would be quite a while before she had to cook and clean for her relatives again...if ever. And all of a sudden, her biggest apprehension assailed her, and she put out a hand and yanked at the Prince's sleeve to grab his attention.

'I have to be able to fly home regularly to visit my mother,' she told him apprehensively. 'Will that be allowed?'

I may be buying you, but I don't want to own you or

be stuck with you round the clock, Saif almost replied before he thought better of being that frank.

'Of course,' he confirmed flatly, his attention on his seated father, who had regained his colour and his temper now that everyone was doing what *he* wanted them to do. Just as quickly Saif despised himself for even having that ungenerous thought.

Yet never had Saif more resented the reality that his father's state of health controlled him and deprived him of the options he should have had. His fierce love for his ailing parent warred against that resentment. Had he not had the fear of the Emir succumbing to a second heart attack after his first small attack some months earlier, Saif believed that he would have refused to marry a stranger. As it was, he dared not object. And what the hell was a sophisticated English socialite likely to find to do with herself in Alharia?

Why had his father selected such an unsuitable wife for him? Saif lifted his chin in wonderment at that question while the marriage celebrant droned on. He would organise tutors for his bride, Saif decided, ensure that she studied their language, culture and history. If she wanted to be his wife so badly, if she was *this* determined to be rich and titled, then she would have to learn to fit in and not expect others to accommodate her. If he were to be cursed with a wife he could neither like nor respect, he would not allow her to also be an embarrassment to him.

'Sign your name,' he urged as he scrawled his own name on the marriage contract and handed his bride the pen.

Her palm perspiring, Tati scrawled her signature in

the indicated spot. 'Is that it? I mean, when will the ceremony take place?'

'It's done,' Saif told her grimly. 'Excuse me.'

That was it? That was them *married*? Without even touching or indeed speaking? Tati was shaken and taken aback by his immediate departure.

'Are you happy now that it is done?' the Prince asked his father.

'Very,' the Emir confirmed with a nod of approval. 'And I hope that soon you will be happy as well.'

'May I ask why you wanted this for me?'

His elderly father regarded him with a frown. 'So that you will not be alone, my son. I am unwell. When I am gone, who will you have? I could not stand to think of you being alone.'

Saif swallowed the sudden unexpected thickness clogging his throat, stunned by that simple explanation and the strong affection it conveyed, acknowledging that he had misjudged his father's intentions. 'But why…an Englishwoman?'

'I had no good fortune with the wives I married and yet they were all supposedly wonderful local matches. Like to like didn't work for me and I sought a different experience for you. It is my hope that your lively and sociable bride will make you relax. You are a very serious young man and I thought she might help you have some fun.'

'Fun,' Saif almost whispered, barely crediting that such a word could have fallen from his strait-laced father's lips.

'And provide you with company. Like you and unlike me she is westernised and sophisticated and you should have more in common.'

Saif was now ready to groan out loud. His father believed that he was westernised and sophisticated because he had spent five years abroad studying business and working while the Emir had only spent a matter of months out of Alharia and had never gone travelling again. Saif, however, had spent more time working to gain the necessary experience than in clubs or bars.

Tati went through the hours that followed in a daze. Men and women were segregated in the celebrations, but Daliya was very keen to assure her that that was the habit only in the Emir's household and that no such segregation was practised by the Prince or anyone else in Alharia. 'The Emir is as old as my great-grandfather,' Daliya told her in a polite excuse for what she clearly saw as an embarrassing practice.

In the all-women gathering where she was very much the centre of attention, Tati watched her aunt, Elizabeth Hamilton, partake of drinks and snacks and ignore her niece. Tati's rarely stirred temper began to spark at that point. She had learned the hard way to be hugely tolerant of other people's rude behaviour, but being studiously ignored by her aunt when her marrying Prince Saif had won her relatives a large amount of money left a bitter taste in her mouth.

She thought of all the humble pie she had eaten at Elizabeth's hands over the years and simmered in silence, too accustomed to restraint to surrender to the anger building inside her, the resentment that, *once again*, she was the fall guy even though she had not enjoyed even one day of the expensive lifestyle her aunt, uncle and cousin took for granted with their designer clothes and glamorous social lives. She and her mother had always scraped along, living cheap, never living well and never ever enjoying the choices and outings that the better off took for granted.

'It's time for you to leave,' Daliya whispered quietly. 'You have scarcely eaten, Your Highness.'

Your Highness, Tati thought in disbelief as she was escorted from the room and down all the endless corridors and up the staircases and across the halls to a totally different giant bedroom, where the maid who had unpacked her luggage in the room she was sharing with Ana already awaited her. Daliya and the maid together assisted her in removing the tunics and petticoats until at last she was down to the final layer, the sort of lingerie layer, she called it, and she finally felt as though she could breathe freely again.

'Where am I going now?' she enquired of Daliya.

'To Paris,' the brunette informed her with a beaming, envious smile. 'On your honeymoon trip.'

Oh, joy, Tati reflected, the angry resentment stirring afresh as she rustled through her slender wardrobe to extract clothing of her own in which to travel and tugged out a pair of leggings and a loose top, neither of which, she could see, satisfied Daliya, who, after asking permission with an anxious look, resorted to fumbling through Tati's case herself in search of something fancier.

'I don't have many clothes,' Tati muttered, mortified for the first time ever by that admission. Of course, she had a dress she had packed in case she got the chance to go to the wedding reception, she recalled wryly, but that slinky, glittery gown, which had originally belonged to Ana, wouldn't be remotely suitable for travelling.

'It is fine, Your Highness. It is more sensible to travel in comfortable garments,' Daliya assured her kindly.

Just as Tati was about to change, a knock sounded briefly on the door and it opened without further ado, framing Prince Saif—all flashing green eyes and what Tati inwardly labelled 'temperament and volatile with it'—who stalked into the room. He instantly dominated his surroundings and her pair of companions muttered breathless apologies for their presence and immediately took themselves off.

My husband, Tati conceded in shock. *The stranger I have married...*

'Now here we are at last with no more barriers between us,' Prince Saif pointed out curtly.

All his bride wore was a silk shift. She *had* a waist, a tiny one, and curves, distinctly sexy curves, Saif noted unwillingly, for he was determined to see no saving grace in the wife who had been forced on him, although he could not help admiring that long wheaten-blond hair that rippled down her spine like a sheet of rumpled satin. Nor could a thin silk slip hide the firm thrust of pouting breasts and prominent nipples or the luscious shape of her highly feminine bottom. Involuntarily Saif hardened and he clenched his teeth against the throb of arousal, a natural response for a man whose sex life was, by virtue of necessity, non-existent in Alharia. Only when Saif travelled could he indulge his sensual appetites and that amount of restraint did not come naturally to a young, healthy man, he allowed wryly.

Any reasonably attractive woman would turn him on at present, he assured himself, but, at the same time, Tatiana *was* his wife and that made quite a difference, he registered, wondering why that aspect had not occurred to him from the first. Yes, he could definitely do with a wife in that department. And what was more, the substitute was infinitely more to his taste than the original bride put forward. Unlike her cousin, Tati wasn't artificially enhanced to pout like a pufferfish on social media. Her lips had a naturally full pink pucker. She had a handful of freckles scattered across the bridge of her undeniably snub nose, but her face was still remarkably pretty, shaped like a heart with big blue eyes the colour of pansies.

Tati gazed back at him, heart starting to hammer inside her chest, breathing suddenly a challenge. 'Why are you staring at me?' she asked tightly.

'Why do you think? How many gold diggers do you think I meet and marry in the space of the same day?' Saif enquired with a lethal chill in his dark drawl, his shrewd green eyes glittering with sheer antipathy. 'And I am disgusted to find myself married to a woman willing to sell herself for money!'

Utterly unprepared for that attack coming out of nowhere at her, Tati whirled away from him, stabbed to the heart by his scorn. Of course, she hadn't thought beyond meeting her uncle's demands to ensure her mother's needs were met. Ridiculous as it was, she had rushed in where angels feared in too much of a hurry to consider what she was actually doing in marrying Prince Saif of Alharia for the wealth that would protect Mariana Hamilton's continuing care. But even as her shoulders drooped, they as quickly shot up again, roused by the fiercest anger she had ever felt.

'How dare you try to stand in judgement over me?'

Tati launched back at him angrily. 'I did not sell myself for money and I am *not* a gold digger.'

Grudgingly amused by the way she straightened herself and stretched, as if she could magically gain a few inches of more imposing height just by trying, Saif regarded her coldly. 'From where I'm standing—'

'Yes, standing with your mighty dose of sexist prejudice on show!' Tati condemned wrathfully. 'You don't know what you're talking about because you don't know anything about me.'

'As you know nothing about me. You married me for cold, hard cash…or was it the title?'

'Why the heck would I *want* to be a princess? I wasn't one of those little girls who dressed up as one as a kid! And for that matter, if you're so darned fastidious and critical, why did you agree to marry a total stranger?'

'That is my private business,' Saif parried with a regal reserve that was infuriatingly intimidating.

A furious flush lit Tati's cheeks at that refusal to explain his motivation. 'Well, then, my reasons are my private business too!' she snapped back at him. 'I don't have to explain myself to you and I'm not going to even try. I'm quite happy for you to think of me as a gold digger, but I'm not selling myself or my body for cash! Be assured that there will be two blue moons in the sky and pigs flying before I get into a bed with you!'

Saif was outraged. He had never been exposed to such insolence before and her attitude came as a shock. Somehow, he had expected her to be ashamed when he confronted her, *not* defiant. 'If the marriage is not consummated, it is not a marriage and will be annulled,' he pointed out for no good reason other than the pride that would not allow her to believe that when it came to sex she could have any form of control over him.

'Is that some kind of a threat?' Tati yelled at him, barely recognising herself in the grip of the anger roaring through her slight body. She had simply been pushed around too much for one day. She was fed up with being forced to do what she didn't want to do, first by Ana refusing to face her own parents and then being bullied and threatened by her uncle. Now it seemed that the Prince, her *husband*, was trying to do the same thing. And she wasn't having it! In fact, she was absolutely done with people ordering her around and never saying thank you, taking her loyalty and gratitude for granted, acting as though they were the better person while they blackmailed and intimidated her!

Saif stilled, a very tall dark man who towered over her like a building. 'It is not. I do not threaten women. I simply voiced facts.'

'Right… OK.' Tati hovered, fighting to compose herself again when she had the most extraordinary desire to cry and shout and yell like an hysterical woman at the end of her tether. And that wasn't her, had never been her, she reminded herself. She had always been the calm, practical one compared to Ana, who flung a tantrum when she didn't get her own way and sulked for days. But for Tati, it had been a truly horrible long strain of a day and it was not done yet, and she did not feel that just then she had the necessary resources to cope with Saif's antagonism on top of everything else.

'I hate you,' she told him truthfully, because no guy that good-looking, who had *chosen* to marry her, had the right to tell her that she disgusted him. He was gorgeous to look at, but he had no manners, no decency and no sense of justice. If she were to blame for marrying him, he was equally to blame for marrying her. 'You're just one more person trying to blame *me* for *your* bad decisions!'

CHAPTER THREE

THE BRIDE AND the groom dined at opposite ends of the cabin.

A private jet, Tati acknowledged, covertly admiring the pale sleek leather and gleaming wood fitments in the cabin while telling herself firmly that she was not impressed. There were a lot of stewards on board as well. The level of contemporary luxury on the jet was not even remotely akin to the Victorian grandeur of the palace. A bundle of glossy fashion magazines was brought to her. She was waited on hand and foot and the meal that duly arrived was amazing. Only then did she appreciate that she was starving because she had barely eaten all day.

That terrible looming apprehension that had killed her appetite had drifted away, but the anger still lingered. Her face burned afresh at the recollection of being labelled a shameless gold digger. But wasn't that kind of woman what Prince Saif of Alharia deserved in a wife? After all, he had agreed to marry without demonstrating the smallest personal interest in his bride. He had not bothered to engineer a meeting or even a phone call with her cousin before the wedding! So, if he was displeased with the calibre of wife he had acquired, it

was all his own fault! Still fizzing with resentment, Tati
shot a glance down to the far end of the cabin where her
husband was working on a laptop, once again showing
off his indifference to the woman he had married. She
wasn't one bit sorry that she had told him she hated him!

But my goodness, he was, as her mother would have
said, 'easy on the eye.' Black hair tumbled across his
brow, framing his hard, masculine profile. Those ridiculously long ebony lashes were a visible slash of darkness even at a distance and the curve of his shapely
mouth was as obvious as the dark stubble beginning
to shadow his jawline. Annoyingly, he kept on snatch-
ing at her attention. And she didn't know why he interfered with her concentration. Well, that was a lie,
she acknowledged ruefully. A guy that gorgeous was
kind of hard to ignore, especially if you had just married him, even though there was absolutely no way it
would ever be a *real* marriage.

By the time the jet landed, Tati was smothering
yawns. She was too incredibly weary to do more than
disembark from the plane and climb into the limousine
awaiting them without comment. The Prince was silent
as well, probably busy brooding over the sheer indignity
of being married off to a money-grubbing foreigner, she
thought nastily. She had assumed they would be staying in a hotel, so it was a surprise when the limousine
purred to a halt outside what appeared to be a rather
large three-storey house in an affluent tree-lined street.

A little man in a smart jacket ushered them into a big
opulent hall with a chandelier hanging overhead that
was so spectacular she suspected it was antique Vene-
tian glass. And she only knew that because her aunt
Elizabeth had once had one made to look as though it

were an antique and had regularly passed it off as such to impress her guests. Saif addressed the man in fluent French.

'Would you like a meal? A snack?' he then enquired politely of her.

'No, thanks. I just want to sleep for about a week.' Her face flamed as she belatedly realised that it was their wedding night and she stiffened, averting her attention from him in haste, although she didn't think he had any expectations whatsoever in that field. The look the Prince had given her when she had earlier told him she wasn't going to have sex with him should have frozen her to death where she stood. He had been outraged, but at least he hadn't argued. There was a bright side to everything, wasn't there?

'We will have to share a bed tonight,' Saif informed her in an undertone. 'We were expected to remain in Alharia until tomorrow. This place will not be fully staffed until then and only one bedroom has been prepared. Marcel is already apologising in advance for any deficiencies we may notice.'

The concept of having to share a bed with the Prince almost made Tati groan out loud. But she was too tired to fight with him. She didn't think he would make any kind of move on her. She was quite sure that she could have located linen and made up a bed for herself, but she was in a strange house, wary of treading on domestic toes and too drained to make a fuss. 'I'm too exhausted to care.'

It went without saying that she was not accustomed to such luxurious accommodation. Her aunt and uncle's home, Fosters Manor, was a pretty Edwardian country house but, as such houses went, it was not that large and it was definitely shabby. When her grandmother had still been alive, it had been beautifully kept, but maintenance standards had slipped once her uncle took over and dismissed most of the staff.

'It has been a long day,' Saif gritted, relieved she hadn't thrown a tantrum over the bed situation. He wasn't in the mood to deal with that.

Yet after the way he had confronted her with his opinion of her, it was little wonder that she had lost her temper with him, he conceded grudgingly. He had been insanely tactless when he had told her the truth of what he thought of her. It would have been more logical to swallow his ire because he was trapped in their marriage until such time as he was able to divorce her. On the other hand, he *could* take the annulment route, he reasoned thoughtfully. But that would upset his father, who would feel responsible for the whole mess because he had insisted that the wedding go ahead with the substitute bride.

He wondered if the little blonde beside him and the cousin who had taken flight had planned exactly this denouement. Clearly, her uncle had suspected her of that duplicity. Who would know her nature better than her own flesh and blood? Furthermore, anyone with the smallest knowledge of his father's character would have guessed that he would do virtually anything sooner than accept his son and heir being jilted. The Emir loathed scandal and he was very proud and touchy about any issue that might inflict a public loss of face on the throne. It seemed rather too neat that the original bride had vanished at the eleventh hour and her stand-in had appeared in her place, dressed as a traditional Alharian bride. He needed answers, Saif acknowledged, because now that she was his wife, he wanted to know precisely who and what he was dealing with. How calculating was she? How greedy? Could he make her less of a problem simply by throwing money at her? It was a distasteful idea but one he was willing to follow through on if it granted him peace.

Marcel cast open a door at the top of the stairs into a superb bedroom suite. Saif was reluctantly amused by the opulent appointments, thinking fondly that his half-brother, Angelino Diamandis, certainly knew how to live in luxury. Having worked hard to put any personal issues with his deserting mother behind him, he had gained sufficient distance from that betrayal to seek out his younger half-brother. A smile illuminated his lean dark features, softening his set jawline. If he was honest he occasionally envied his brother, Angel, for his freedom and independence, but he was not prepared to lose his father and step up to the throne to attain that same lack of constraint.

Barely able to credit how a single smile could light the Prince up to reveal ten times the charisma he had so far shown her, Tati got all flustered and heard herself ask, almost as if it were normal to speak to him civilly, 'Does this house belong to you?'

'No, it belongs to my—' Saif hesitated and swallowed what he had almost revealed, because he couldn't trust her with that information lest it reach the wrong ears. 'It belongs to a relative of mine. He offered it to me because he was unable to attend the wedding.' Well, at least *not* in his official capacity, Saif adjusted with a winning smile of satisfaction, for he had contrived to spend almost an hour with his brother that same afternoon. 'I prefer this to the anonymity of a hotel.'

'It's a fabulous place…from what little I've seen,' Tati adjusted awkwardly, moving past him to scoop up her toiletries bag and nightwear from the case that a maid had already begun to unpack, just as another had embarked on Saif's luggage. *Two* maids and yet supposedly the household was understaffed this evening?

As she bent down Saif stared, focused hungrily on her curvy bottom and the bounce of her full breasts as she straightened again, blond hair flaring like polished silk round her heart-shaped face, big blue eyes skittering off him at speed. She wouldn't meet his eyes. He didn't like that. It made him wonder what she was thinking, what she could be planning. The more he considered the manner in which she had immediately stepped into her cousin's shoes, the more suspicious he became of her every move. He winced at the current of lust still trying to pull him in a dangerous direction. Possibly an annulment would be the path to take if he could sell the idea to his father without shocking him too much. In the interim, he definitely needed to keep his hands off his bride.

Through an open door Tati could see a bathroom and she hastened into the sanctuary it offered. She didn't really need a bath but she ran one just the same, determined to make the most of her time alone. She took off the make-up, cleaned her teeth before finally lying back in hot, scented water and striving to relax. But how the heck could she relax with *him* out there? Ana would have charmed him out of the trees by now, she reflected ruefully. Men adored her cousin for her looks, her smiles and her flirtatious ways. Tati had never had that light, fluffy, girly vibe. She was sensible, practical, blunt. Life had made her that way, forcing her to be responsible. She loved her mother, but she had also learned very young that *she* had to look after her only parent, rather than the other way round.

Having a man in her life had been the least of her ambitions. Mariana had had a whole raft of unsuitable boyfriends, among them drunks, abusers and cheats. After Tati's first serious boyfriend, Dave, had ditched her to chase Ana instead, Tati had decided that men drummed up way too much drama in a woman's life. Once or twice, she had wished that she had got a little more experience out of the relationship and had tried out sex with Dave, because sometimes still being a virgin at her age made her feel out of step with the world she lived in. But the attraction had just never been strong enough for her to experiment with Dave and once he had succumbed to her cousin's allure, she had been relieved that she had held back.

An hour later, Tati emerged, flushed and soaked clean from the bathroom. Saif, casually clad in jeans and a black shirt, twisted round from his laptop to glance at her. His bride wore nothing suggestive, nothing even slightly sexy, so evidently seduction did not feature in her current plan. Saif strove to feel suitably relieved by that reassuring reality while wondering how the hell pink and white shorts with little bunnies on them and a plain white vest top could offer such dynamite appeal. It was all about shape, he reasoned abstractedly, a mathematical arrangement of feminine proportions in the exact combination that most appealed to the average male.

Evidently he was very much an average male, he decided, attention lingering on the smooth upper slopes of the soft firm breasts showing above the top, the shadow of the valley between, her tiny waist and the pleasing swell of the pert derriere that the clingy shorts enhanced. A pulse kicked up in his groin and he swung back to his work with a curse brimming on his lips.

'What are you working at?' she asked to break the taut silence, her face still flaming from his lengthy appraisal.

'I'm checking figures. I manage Alharia's investments,' Saif murmured tautly.

What had that long look of his been about, for goodness' sake? Tati supposed that she should have worn a dressing gown, but she hadn't packed one. Her inclusion in the trip to Alharia had been very much a last-minute thing, an added expense loudly objected to by Ana's parents. Ana, however, had said she could not go through with the wedding without Tati's support and that had got Tati on the flight, her case packed in a rush and not even full. She had left behind several items which she should have brought.

'Is the bathroom free now?' Saif enquired without turning round again.

Momentarily, Tati froze, mortified by her thoughtlessness: she was a bathroom hog. 'I'm sorry, I should've thought that you might want—'

'There must be a dozen such facilities in this property. Had I needed to do so, I could easily have found another.'

In silence, Tati nodded. 'Goodnight,' she said in a muffled tone and dived below the duvet.

Strange little creature, Saif decided, glancing at the bed, seeing her curled up in one small corner, only a tousled mop of blond hair showing above the duvet. If he hadn't known what he did know about her he might've thought that she was shy. He smothered a laugh at that ridiculous idea, shut down the accounts he had been working on and started to undress.

Tati peered out from under her hair and watched the jeans hit the polished floor in a heap. So, he was untidy as well as obnoxious, she thought without surprise, as he left them lying there and the shirt drifted down to join the jeans. He stretched in a fluid movement and for an instant she saw him standing there, naked but for a pair of boxers, every muscle flexing and pulling taut... and he had an awful lot of muscles enhanced by coffee-coloured skin that resembled oiled silk. Tati stared, remembering the ghastly charity calendar of half-naked men her mother had once put up on the wall. Mariana had accused her daughter of being a prude when Tati had said it embarrassed her.

But it *had* been an embarrassment to have that hanging in the kitchen, particularly after Ana had seen it and had told everybody at school. Tati had had to live through a barrage of sniggering 'dirty girl' abuse for weeks afterwards. Compared with Ana and her mother, she *was* a prude because, from what she had seen of their experiences, a more adventurous approach to men and sex more often led to hurt and disappointment than happiness.

Now watching Saif stretch and muscles ripple across his hard, corrugated abdomen and down the length of his smooth brown back, Tati reminded herself that it was just a body, truly a more blessed body than most men rejoiced in but simply a body, an arrangement of bones, flesh and muscle that every single living person had. Only that very grounded outlook did not explain why she was still staring and why she had a hot, tight, clenched sensation tugging at the junction of her thighs. She had stared because he was beautiful, and she hadn't realised that a man could be beautiful that way. *Really, Tati*, she mocked her excuse. All that Adam and Eve stuff in the Bible hadn't tipped her off about that essential attraction? Cheeks hot enough to fry eggs on, she rolled over and buried her face in the cool pillows, trying not to listen to the distant sound of water running in the shower.

Saif was unaccustomed to sharing a bed and his bride's every movement disturbed him, reminded him of her existence and pushed rudely past his wall of reserve. He couldn't ignore her, he couldn't forget the allure of those eyes with the velvety appeal of a flower, her pale slender thighs or her surprisingly full breasts. That failure to maintain his usual mental discipline only made him even angrier with her. As he lay awake, he came up with a plan as to how to keep her occupied and marvelled at its simplicity. He could send her out day after day…

Tati wakened in the early hours because she felt cold. As she flipped over, she discovered the reason: the duvet had been stolen. That fast, she remembered that she was sharing a bed and she dug two hands into the bedding and yanked her side of it back with violent determination. Saif sat up with a jerk and flashed on the light.

'I was cold,' Tati announced in a snappish tone of defence and she hunched under the section of duvet she had reclaimed, turning her back on him.

Saif thought with satisfaction of the bride-free day ahead of him and lay back down. Even hunched in the bedding, she contrived to look unbearably alluring. How could she make him want her so much? Were a few sexless weeks sufficient to make him desperate? He lay there thinking of the many sensual ways he could have raised his bride's temperature without recourse to warmer bedding. Just considering those pursuits, indeed leafing through them with the intensity of an innate sensualist, left Saif as hard as a rock and it was dawn when he finally gave up trying to rest and rose to start work again.

The maid bringing her breakfast wakened Tati. She sat up while the curtains were being opened and registered that she was alone in the bed and expected to eat there. Pushing her hair off her brow, she accepted the tray, setting it down again once the maid had gone and scrambling into the bathroom to freshen up before she ate.

While she was enjoying her cup of tea and a buttery, flaky, delicious croissant, the Prince strode in. Saif emanated pure sophistication and sleek good looks in his perfectly tailored dark business suit. Involuntarily, her mouth ran dry, her tummy fluttering, responses she struggled to suppress. Expensive fabric outlined and enhanced his wide shoulders, his narrow hips and long, strong legs. He was very well built...as she had cause to know after ogling him while he undressed the night before, she reminded herself irritably. He was also infuriatingly calm and in control while she still felt as though her life had lurched off track without warning and fallen into a very large, very deep pothole.

As she sat there, Tati was extremely tense, her fingers locked tight to her china cup. It had occurred to her for the first time that she had overlooked one very obvious point of dissension between them. Saif had expected to marry her glamorous, sexy cousin and had instead ended up with her dull, plain and unsexy substitute. Of course, he was disappointed; of course, he was angry. No man would choose Tati in place of Ana, she reflected painfully. 'I'll sort out another bedroom for me to use tonight,' she proffered stiffly, meaning it as an olive branch of sorts in the aftermath of the duvet tussle.

In the sunlight slanting through the windows, the brilliant green eyes locked to her were as jewelled and intense as polished emeralds. All of a sudden, a bizarre level of annoyance was gripping Saif. Evidently it was one thing for him to want to be rid of her, but another thing entirely when she appeared to return the compliment. 'That will not be necessary,' he began before he could question the far from sensible reaction steering him off course.

Tati tilted her chin. 'It's necessary,' she pointed out. 'I don't think either of us could have got much sleep last night.'

Saif discovered that he did not like being told what was necessary by *her*. It set his even white teeth on edge and brought out a self-destructive edge of pique he had not known until that instant that he possessed. 'We will *continue* to share the same room.'

'But why on earth would we?' Tati exclaimed with incredulity.

'You wanted this marriage… *Live with it!*' Saif spelt out without apology or, indeed, further explanation. Even had he tried to do so, he could not have explained the gut instinct that was driving him because he did not know what had roused it or even what it meant.

'You know…' Tati began, her chest heaving with a

sudden dragged-in breath, furious that he appeared to be taking out his disappointment that Ana wasn't his bride on her…as though it were *her* fault. Did he think that? And shouldn't she know by now what he was thinking? The lack of communication between them was only adding to their problems. 'Sometimes, you make me want to hit you!'

'I noticed the streak of violence in your family when your aunt attempted to slap you. Make no attempt to assault me. There is no reason in the world why we should descend to such a degrading level,' the Prince asserted.

His mind was wandering again, questioning how she could utter such a threat while still looking so fresh and tempting. It was first thing in the morning as well and her hair was tousled and she had utilised not a scrap of cosmetic enhancement that he could see. Indeed, in harsh daylight her porcelain skin had an amazingly luminous quality that confounded his every expectation. She might be a substitute; she might be everything he despised in the wife he had not wanted in the first place, but one truth was inescapable: she was much more of a beauty than he had initially been prepared to acknowledge.

'You don't even have a sense of humour, do you?' Tati gasped, staring accusingly at him.

'I have made arrangements for your entertainment today,' Saif informed her smoothly, refusing to react in any way to the charge of a lack of humour. Certainly, he found nothing about their current situation worthy of amusement.

'How very kind of you,' Tati muttered tautly, wondering what was coming next.

'I have hired a team of personal shoppers to give

you a tour of the best retail outlets in Paris,' the Prince completed.

Send the little woman out shopping, Tati thought furiously. He simply wanted her out of his hair. And what did you do with a gold digger when you wanted peace? Throw money at her! And when you had more money than a gold mine, throwing money was the easy option. Tati clamped her teeth together hard on a sarcastic response. She recalled her Granny Milly telling her that you caught more flies with honey than vinegar. But sheer rage rippled through her in a heady wave that left her almost light-headed because she wasn't some greedy tramp the Prince could tempt, control and ultimately debase with cold, hard cash!

'How wonderful,' Tati told him with a serene smile. 'I shall feel as though all my Christmases have come at once. Do I have a budget?'

Saif interpreted the glitter in her big blue eyes as pure avarice. 'No budget,' he retorted with a flashing smile of reassurance.

He was giving her a free ticket to spend, spend, spend and she would be sure not to disappoint him. After all, if ever a guy deserved to have his worst expectations met, it was Saif, and she would *enjoy* playing the gold-digging bride, she told herself fiercely. If anything, he would learn to know better than to send her out shopping in one of the most expensive cities in the world without a budget.

She put on her jeans. Her brain could still not quite encompass the reality that the Prince was now *her* husband instead of her cousin's. He didn't even act as a husband would, did he? Well, like a very reluctant one, she decided ruefully. Possibly he hadn't wanted to get married either.

My goodness, maybe that could even explain why he had been married off in the first place…was it possible that the Prince was gay? And that he had been married off to conceal the fact? But if that were true, why, given the opportunity, wouldn't he have wanted to claim a bedroom of his own?

Tati frowned and conceded that Saif was a mass of confusing contradictions. He insisted they *had* to share a bedroom. For the sake of appearances? Did he want their marriage to look normal even if it wasn't? Out of pride or out of necessity? If he was gay and if it was impossible for his father to accept him as such, their crazy marriage made sense. Of course, understanding didn't make her like Saif any better for the way he had accused her of being a gold digger.

In fact, she hated him for that. Tati had spent her entire life being pushed around and put down by those who had more power than she had. Her own relatives had done that to her and, even before her mother had succumbed to dementia, Mariana had urged her daughter not to 'rock the boat' by defending her. Sadly, swallowing her pride and turning the other cheek had never improved matters in the slightest for Tati. In fact, that attitude, both at school and at home, had only made the bullying worse. And she wasn't prepared to settle for that again, for being abused when she hadn't done anything wrong, for being insulted simply because she was poor and had fewer options than other people. Her head came up, her chin lifting. No. No way was His Royal Highness the Crown Prince of Alharia about to get away with doing her down as well!

Thirty minutes later, Tati stepped into a long cream limousine containing three very ornamental and chatty women. At first glance, she could see that she was a surprise, a disappointment, in that she wasn't as decorative as they had expected and, as it was normal for her to want to please people and she fully intended to spend, spend, spend as directed by her bridegroom, she said, 'I need a whole new wardrobe!'

And the smiles broke out, betraying the visible relief that she was likely to be a keen buyer. Presumably, her companions worked on commission and why shouldn't they profit from her pressing need for clothes? Starting with nightwear and lingerie, she required everything. It was one thing to be proud and independent, another thing entirely to be the most poorly or inappropriately dressed person in the room. And she had no plans to start washing and drying her knickers in the nearest bathroom any time soon. In fact, she had to suppress a giggle as she attempted to picture the Prince's reaction. She doubted that he had ever been exposed to that kind of common touch.

The first stop on their trip was the Avenue Montaigne, a tree-lined thoroughfare packed with high-end fashion outlets. Aside from the uneasy acknowledgement that her cousin, Ana, would have truly revelled in such an opportunity, Tati concentrated on the practicalities of buying as much as she possibly could without ever consulting a price tag lest it send her into shock. She strayed from one designer boutique to the next with her companions, having by then established her preferences, working hard to locate the casual and formal items she specified. They moved on to the Boulevard Saint Germain, where she found chic dresses aplenty and the shoes and bags to team with them. She eventually succumbed to the temptation of putting on a new outfit. They visited a trendy rooftop café, where she enjoyed the spectacular views of the city and drank champagne. Of lunch there was no sign and only a handful of nuts came her way.

Mid-afternoon, she was professionally made up and equipped with enough cosmetics to provide a makeover for half a city block. Perfume specially mixed for her came next and she loved the perfume as much as the professional jargon of the scent world, which talked of hints of jasmine and spice, redolent of hotter climes. She allowed herself to be talked into buying a new phone and a new watch as well.

The guilt of enjoying herself while being wildly extravagant soon engulfed her in a tide. She had spent, spent, *spent* to hit back at Saif for his condemnation of her when in truth he knew nothing about her and evidently didn't care to find out anything about her either. But only on the drive back to the house, while her companions were cheerfully breaking out the champagne again to celebrate a successful day of shopping, did she ask herself how meeting every one of Saif's worst expectations of her character could benefit her in any way. She refused the champagne because she wasn't in the mood to rejoice.

What had she done? Why had she let her raging resentment at her position and his attitude take over and drive her? Why had she set out to prove that she was every bit as greedy as he had assumed she was?

A severe attack of the guilts gripped Tati as she watched a procession of staff march through the echoing hall to deliver the boxes and bags of her accumulated shopping upstairs to the bedroom. There they would proceed to unpack and organise her many, many purchases before storing them in the empty drawers and closets. She flopped down on an opulent couch in the drawing room, her face burning with mortification as she pictured the sweater she had bought in *four* different colours. The cringe factor was huge because in all her life she had never made an extravagant purchase before.

When would she contrive to wear a sweater in a desert kingdom? Presumably, she would wear the winter garments when she went home to visit her mother, she reasoned weakly. As for the fancy dresses, the high heels and all the elegant separates, where was she planning to wear them? Observation currently suggested that the Prince she had married would be in no hurry to take her anywhere, particularly now that she had shown what he would no doubt deem to be her true colours. And yet she had *needed* clothes, she thought wretchedly, for not only had she packed very little to fly out to Alharia for what she had assumed would be a very short stay, but she also had nothing much worthy of packing back home. The kind of casual wear she had worn to run her aunt and uncle's household wouldn't pass muster in her current role.

But neither of those facts excused her extravagance. She could have gone to a chain store to cover her requirements and only bought the necessities, she conceded unhappily. Instead she had shopped and spent recklessly in some of the most exclusive designer shops in the world.

Marcel brought her tea and tiny dainty macarons on a silver tray. She glanced up when she heard a step in the hall and saw Saif still in the doorway. He had shed his jacket and tie and his sculpted jawline was shadowed with stubble. His gorgeous green eyes clashed with hers and she felt hot all over as if she had been exposed to a flame. She went pink and shifted uneasily on her seat, her mouth running very dry.

Saif was trying very hard not to gape at the blonde beauty on the opulent sofa. Like a fine jewel once displayed in an unworthy setting, she had been reset and polished up to perfection since their last meeting. A dark off-the-shoulder top clung to her like a second skin, lovingly hugging pert full breasts and skin that looked incredibly perfect and smooth. A short skirt in some kind of toning print exposed slender knees and shapely calves leading down to small feet shod in strappy heels. Off the scale arousal inflamed Saif as fast as a shot of adrenalin in his veins. An uncomfortable throb set up an ache at his groin.

Tati gazed back at him, dismay and a leaping hormonal response that unnerved her darting through her tense body. She found it utterly impossible to look away from Saif. His raw desirability was that intense from his tousled black hair to the rich green deep-set eyes fringed with ebony lashes that magnetised her.

'We have to talk,' she told him awkwardly. 'We have to sort stuff out.'

His half-brother, Angelino, the consummate playboy, had once told Saif that the minute a woman mentioned the need to talk, a sensible man should go straight into avoidance mode. Saif collided warily with huge blue-pansy-coloured eyes and parted his lips to shut her down.

'Please,' Tati added in near desperation. 'Because right now, everything's going crazy and wrong.'

'Is it?'

He did not know why he questioned that statement when he should have agreed because the arousal afflicting him was both crazy and wrong. He *had* to remain detached and in control. Nothing good could come from giving in to his baser instincts; nothing good could come from him backing down when confronted with her feminine wiles. And those flowery eyes of hers were shimmering with what might have been tears, her full lower lip quivering. The sight stabbed him to the heart, and he strode forward, a forceful, instantaneous urge to fix whatever was wrong powering him.

'Tatiana,' he began, determined to continue the conversation in private where they could be neither overheard nor seen. It was second nature for Saif to consider appearances, raised as he had been in a palace swarming with staff where keeping secrets was an almost impossible challenge.

'Nobody calls me that,' she told him in a wobbly voice.

'Except me. I will not call you Tatty like your relatives. It is an insult and I don't know why you've allowed it.' Without another word, Saif bent down and scooped her off the couch as if she were no heavier than a doll.

'What are you doing?' she exclaimed in stark disconcertion.

'Taking you upstairs where we may be assured of discretion,' the Prince countered, striding out across the hall with complete cool as if carrying a woman around were an everyday occurrence for him.

'Why on earth would we need discretion?' Tati queried nervously. 'You can put me down now.'

'You were becoming distressed... *Crying!*' Saif pointed out with a raw edge to his dark, deep drawl.

'I wasn't crying!' Tati protested, highly offended by the charge. 'I don't cry. You could torture me and I wouldn't cry! Just sometimes my eyes flood when I'm upset—it's a nervous thing but I don't start crying, for goodness' sake! I'm not a little girl!'

'No, definitely *not* a little girl except in height,' Saif quipped, pushing through the bedroom door to set her down on the big bed. 'Now tell me, why are you upset?'

'Because I let you *goad* me into behaving badly today and I'm furious with myself and with you!' Tati told him roundly. 'I went out today and spent a fortune on clothing because—'

'I urged you to...how is that bad behaviour?' Saif prompted, his gaze locked to the beautiful eyes angrily fixed to him, his fingers rising to brush back the silky blond hair rippling across her cheekbone. The long strands fell over his wrist, pale wheaten gold against his skin.

That light touch that seemed perilously close to a caress made Tati shiver while her skin broke out in goosebumps of awareness. 'You don't understand...'

'The only thing I understand right now is that I want you,' Saif breathed in the driven tone of harsh sincerity, his beautiful jewelled eyes smouldering as she looked up at him.

'Me? You want...*me*?' Tati almost whispered in disbelief and wonderment.

'Why wouldn't I want you?' Saif turned the question back on her in equal surprise. 'You are a remarkable beauty.'

That was a heady compliment for a woman who had

never been called beautiful in her entire life, who had always been in the shadows, either unnoticed or passed over or summarily dismissed as being unimportant. Tati stared at him in astonishment and she was so blasted grateful for that tribute that she stretched up and kissed his cheek in reward.

As her breasts momentarily pressed into his chest and the intoxicating scent of her engulfed him, the soft invitation of her lips on his skin burned through Saif's self-discipline like a fiery brand and destroyed it. Without any hesitation, he closed her slight body into the circle of his arms and brought his mouth crashing down on hers with a hunger he couldn't even attempt to control.

Oh, wow, Tati thought abstractedly, *wasn't expecting this, wasn't expecting to feel* this...

CHAPTER FOUR

AND THIS WAS the amazing sign that Tati had always been waiting and hoping to feel in a man's arms: electrified, exhilarated, physically aware of her own body to the nth degree. Only until that moment she had honestly believed that that kind of reaction was simply a myth, something that some women chose to exaggerate, which didn't truly exist. But with that single kiss Saif had knocked Tati right out of her complacent assumptions, knocked her sideways and upside down and just at that moment, regardless of whether it made sense or not, her stupid body was humming as fiercely as an engine getting revved up at the starting line.

'So…er…you're not gay,' Tati commented weakly as he released her mouth and dragged in a shuddering breath. 'Obviously.'

Saif gazed down at her in complete astonishment. 'Why would you think I was gay?'

'Your father marrying you off like that, not caring that I was a substitute for the bride that he had chosen,' Tati pointed out breathlessly. 'It seemed like he didn't care who you married as long as a marriage took place.'

'It *was* like that. All of Alharia knew that it was my wedding day. My father viewed the bride's disappearance as an absolute humiliation and an outrage against the throne itself. He could not accept that shame. As long as a wedding took place and he could cover up what really happened, he was appeased,' Saif explained, a lingering frown drawing his sleek dark brows together.

'I didn't appreciate how far-reaching the effects of Ana running away would be,' Tati admitted. 'I didn't understand that it would be such a crime and an embarrassment in your father's eyes either... I was stupidly naïve.'

'Kiss me again,' Saif husked, his attention locked to the full pink lower lip she was worrying at with the edge of her small blunt teeth.

'I'm not sure that we should.'

'Nothing that tastes as good as your mouth could be wrong,' Saif told her.

'Quite the poet when you want to be,' Tati whispered, barely breathing as she looked into those stunning green eyes of his and felt the flutter of butterflies in her tummy and the wicked heat of anticipation. A 'what the heck?' sensation that felt unfamiliar but somehow very, very right was assailing her. Other people took risks all the time, but she never did and the acknowledgement rankled.

'We are married.'

She wasn't thinking about that, all she was thinking about was how he made her *feel* and that felt wildly self-indulgent, something she never allowed herself to be. But what were a few kisses? No harm in that, no lasting damage, she reasoned with determination. Why did she always stress herself out by trying to second-guess stuff? Why did she take life so seriously and always behave as though the roof were likely to fall on her if she deviated from her set path of rectitude? In a resentful surge of denying that fretful and serious habit of generally looking on the downside of life, she tipped her head back and said tautly, 'So we are...'

Saif tasted her soft pink mouth, which had all the allure of a ripe peach, and then he yielded even more to the hunger storming through his tall, powerful frame, nudging her back against the pillows, a lean hand gliding up from a slender knee to skate along the stretch of her thigh.

Tati gasped, her hips rising, her thighs clenching on the sudden ache stabbing at the heart of her. It was terrifyingly intense. 'You make me want you... I don't know how!' she exclaimed helplessly, every nerve ending in her body on the alert.

Saif smiled down at her, green eyes aglow with energy below well-defined brows. 'You know how...you're not that innocent.'

But she was, she *was*, she conceded uneasily, because absolutely everything felt so novel and fresh and exciting for her. And why wouldn't it when she had never felt that way before? He shifted over her, one long, strong leg sliding between hers, and her breath snarled in her throat, her tummy fluttering with an incandescent mix of nerves and craving that left her light-headed. He kissed her again, parting her lips, delving between, his tongue flicking across the roof of her mouth, making delicious little quivers circulate through her lower body.

The weight of him against her, the clean, musky, all-male scent of him engulfing her, the way he plucked at her lower lip and teased it with the edge of his teeth. It all drove her a little crazy, igniting an insane impatience that made her fingers spread and dig into his shirt-clad back, needing to touch the skin below the cotton, clawing it up to finally learn that he was every bit as hot in temperature as his kisses promised. She squirmed up into the sheltering heat of him and he pressed his lips to the slender column of her throat, discovering yet another place that was extraordinarily sensitive, tracing it down to the valley between her breasts.

Saif pulled her top over her head and cast it aside. His big hands spread to cup the full swell of her breasts cupped in lace-edged silk. His thumbs found her prominent nipples, stroked, and an arrow of heat speared down into her groin, making her hips rise. The bra melted away and she barely noticed because the feel of his hands on her naked skin sent literal shivers of response through her. He lowered his head over the pouting mounds and employed his mouth on the straining peaks, and she discovered a new sensual torment that utterly overwhelmed her as his tongue lashed the swollen buds and set up a chain reaction inside her that increased the ache tugging between her thighs.

He brushed away her last garment and her whole body rose as he finally touched her *there* where she had the most powerfully indecent craving to be touched. A light forefinger scored across the most sensitive spot of all and her spine arched, a gasp parting her lips. Her hand travelled up from his shoulder into his ruffled black hair and rifled through the silky strands to draw him back down to her again.

He nuzzled her parted lips, plucked at the full lower one with the edge of his teeth, teasing and rousing while he traced the damp, silky flesh between her thighs. She moaned and shifted her hips, the fiery pulse beating at her core rising in intensity in concert with her heartbeat. As he circled the most tender spot, the sizzling desire thrumming through her took an exponential leap and her fingers dug into his scalp as she fought for control. She wanted more, she *needed* more, she wanted him inside her to sate the tormenting hollow ache. She didn't recognise herself in the blind hold of that overwhelming craving.

Indeed she was at the agonising height of anticipation when Saif suddenly stopped dead and stared down at her with green eyes glittering with frustration. 'I don't have contraception here.'

'I'm on the pill…it doesn't matter!' Tati gasped.

'I have not been with anyone since a recent health check.'

Unaccustomed to such sensible conversations even while accepting that they were necessary, Tati could feel the heat of embarrassment burning her already flushed cheeks. 'I haven't been with anyone either,' she hastened to assure him.

Relief flooded his expressive gaze. 'I wasn't expecting this…*us*,' he admitted tautly, rearranging her under him, unzipping his trousers.

The instant she felt the satin-smooth touch of him against her entrance she tipped her legs back, hungry for the experience. He pushed into her slowly and she tensed at that strange sensation, closing her eyes tight and gritting her teeth momentarily when the sting and burn of his invasion broke through the barrier of her virginity. It hurt but not as much as she had feared it might. In fact, if there was such a thing, it was a *good* hurt, she reasoned abstractedly, her ability to concentrate still utterly controlled by that overriding hunger for the fulfilment that only he could give her.

Pleasure skated along her nerve endings as he bent her further back and drove deeper into her needy depths. Excitement climbed as he picked up his pace and her heart began to thump inside her, her breath catching in her throat. The whole of her being was caught up in the tightening bands of tension in her pelvis that merely pushed the craving higher and then the storm of gathering excitement coalesced in one bright, blinding instant. Like fireworks flaring inside her, it was electrifying. The excitement pushed her over the edge in an explosion of incredible pleasure that engulfed her in a sweet aftertide of blissful release. She tumbled back into the pillows, winded and drained but feeling light as a feather.

Saif achieved completion with a shuddering groan of relief and quickly pulled away from her, afraid of crushing her tiny body beneath his weight. He flung himself back and whispered, 'I've never had sex without a condom before. That was…unexpectedly…much more exciting than I ever dreamt…but you…you were *amazing*,' he stressed, locking brilliant green eyes to her burning face with sensual appreciation.

Tati's light-as-a-feather sensation was fast fading and the regrets were kicking in even faster. 'How did this happen?' she whispered shakily. 'We don't even like each other—'

'Speak for yourself. I like you very much indeed at this moment,' Saif countered with dancing eyes of amusement.

Tati was remarkably disgruntled by that light-hearted comment. There he lay, confident, calm and absolutely in control, while she felt as if she were falling to pieces inside herself. She couldn't believe that she had had sex with him, didn't want to accept that she had urged him on like a shameless hussy. A strand of nagging anxiety pierced her.

'Did you…er…withdraw?' she mumbled in mortification, ashamed that she hadn't noticed, hadn't thought to suggest, hadn't acted on a single intelligent thought.

'Why would I have done that when you are protected by contraception?' Saif enquired.

Tati said nothing but she paled. She had left her contraceptive pills behind in the rush of packing for Alharia and could only wonder how effective those pills would be when she had already missed a couple of doses. She had never had to worry about anything like that before because she was only taking the pills in the first place to ease a difficult menstrual cycle.

Saif sat up. 'I need a shower… I'll use the one next door.' He sprang out of bed, stark naked and unselfconscious. 'We could share it…it's a big shower.'

'I don't think so,' she said flatly, downright incredulous at the suggestion that they could share a shower.

He didn't need to be self-conscious with his lean, athletic physique, she thought ruefully, but, personally speaking, she would not be getting out of bed in front of him without sucking her tummy in to the best of her ability. As she watched, he flipped through drawers and brought out fresh clothing to pull on trousers and a fresh shirt and stride out of the room.

How on earth could she have been stupid enough to have sex with him? How the heck had that happened? She hadn't been her usual self, she reasoned ruefully—she had been angry, guilty and upset about the situation she was in and ashamed of her extravagance. But then *somehow* curiosity and desire had combined to blow all common sense out of the water, she reflected unhappily as she darted out of bed and raced into the dressing room to extract fresh underwear before speeding into the bathroom.

Where would she be if she fell pregnant? She had just had unprotected sex and she knew the risks. Her parents hadn't conceived her by choice. She had been an accident, conceived at a party with a man with whom her mother had had only a casual relationship. In every way, never mind her birth father's eventual arrest for fraud, Tati had been a mistake even if her mother had made the best of her arrival and had always assured her daughter that she had no regrets whatsoever.

As he stripped again next door, Saif was thinking that he would buy his bride something special as a mark of his appreciation. She deserved a handsome gift for not holding against him the cruel accusations he had made. He had been harsh and much less generous but that *had* to change, he acknowledged ruefully, because Tatiana was his wife and, for as long as they were together, she had a right to both his respect and his care. Just as he was about to switch the water on, he noticed the streak of blood on his thigh and he stopped dead with a frown.

When Tati emerged from the bathroom, she was fully dressed and unprepared to find that Saif was waiting for her. His impact stole the breath from her lungs. Black hair still damp from the shower, his lean dark features unnervingly grave, he was strikingly handsome. Tailored black trousers outlined his long powerful thighs and his plain white shirt was open at his throat. He was the very definition of casual, elegant sophistication.

'Is there something wrong?' she prompted, striving to appear more composed than she indeed felt.

'Before I showered, I noticed that there was blood on me… I must know—did I hurt you?'

Tati's face flamed crimson because she was utterly unprepared for that question. 'A little, but it's par for the course, isn't it…the first time, I mean?' she completed awkwardly, trying to pass it off casually, wishing he simply hadn't noticed anything amiss.

Saif froze in astonishment. 'You *were* a virgin?'

'Yes. Let's not make a fuss about it,' Tati urged tightly.

'It is not something I can ignore… I am guilty of having made assumptions about you, assumptions that clearly have no basis in fact,' Saif breathed tautly, far less comfortable after she had made that confirmation.

Tati breathed in deep and slow, but it still didn't suppress the rage hurtling up through her. 'So, because I was greedy, I also had to have been… What do we call it? Around the block a few times?' she paraphrased with a grimace.

'At twenty-four most young women have some sexual experience,' Saif countered, standing his ground on that score.

'But I'm not twenty-four. I'm twenty-one… Within a few weeks of my next birthday, but not quite there yet,' Tati filled in thinly, her spine rigid as she moved to the door. 'Perhaps you should find out a little more about me before you start judging.'

'I am not judging you,' Saif countered with measured cool.

'You've been judging me from the moment you met me, and it stops here and now,' Tati told him, lifting her chin in challenge, her accusing blue eyes bright as sapphires. 'Clearly you weren't any keener on this marriage than I was, but I'm done taking all the blame for it! I've been pushed around and used by my cousin and then by my uncle and aunt but I'm *not* going to accept being pushed around and used by you as well!'

With that ringing assurance, Tati stalked out of the room, her short skirt flipping round her slender knees, her breasts taut and firm and highly noticeable from the rigid angle of her spine. Challenged to drag his attention from her, Saif swore under his breath, rebelling at the temptation to follow her and argue. He didn't do arguments with women. He didn't do drama. He didn't believe that he had ever pushed around or *used* any woman. He had been force-fed his father's deep suspicions of the opposite sex from an early age and had done his utmost to combat that biased mindset with his intelligence.

Yet he had never wanted to fall in love and run the risk of giving up control of his emotions to a woman and trusting her. The rejection dealt by the mother who had deserted him had cut him deep down inside. He had learned to live with that reality, though, by burying his sensitivity on that issue.

And life experience had made him more cynical. He had been used by women, used for sex, for money, chased and feted by those in search of status and a title. Once or twice when he was younger and more naïve, he had been hurt. As a result, he was *not* prejudiced, he was *wary*, he reflected grimly.

CHAPTER FIVE

AS TATI REACHED the foot of the sweeping staircase without any idea of where she was going, she was intercepted by Marcel and shown across the hall into a dining room with a table already beautifully set for a meal. She took a seat with alacrity because she was more than ready to eat. She had been hungry even before she got into bed with her prince, she thought wildly, although she had done nothing there worthy of the excuse of having worked up an appetite. That belated reflection birthed a host of insecurities. She had lain there like a statue, she thought in dismay, as much of a partner as a blow-up doll. The slow-burning heat of mortification crept up through her like a living flame and it was not eased by Saif's sudden entrance into the dining room.

'I forgot about dinner,' he said almost apologetically.

'I didn't get lunch either,' she hastened to admit.

'Why not?' Saif queried, his startlingly light eyes bright against his olive skin.

'Nobody else seemed to be interested in eating.' Tati shrugged, still fascinated by those eyes of his.

Saif frowned as Marcel arrived with little plates. 'It was for you to say that you wished to eat,' he told her gently. 'You were the client. You were in charge.'

Stiffening at that veiled criticism, Tati looked down at her plate and shook out her napkin. 'I usually go with the majority vote and endeavour to fit in.'

As Tati shifted awkwardly in her seat, in the silence the dulled ache at the heart of her almost made her wince, and recalling exactly how she had acquired that intimate ache made her flush to the roots of her hair. In haste she began to eat, struggling to suppress the over-whelming memory of his lean, powerful body sliding over and inside hers, the heart-thumping excitement that had gripped her and the sheer unvarnished plea-sure of it.

As Marcel arrived with the main course, she glanced up, desperate to distract herself from such thoughts. 'Your green eyes… So unexpected, so unusual,' she heard herself remark gauchely, inwardly cringing from the surprise that lit up those extraordinary eyes of his.

'I inherited them from my mother,' Saif proffered, amused by her embarrassment and how little she was able to hide it from him. 'I don't know where she got them from or if anyone else in her family shares them because I have no contact with her family.'

'Why's that?' Tati pressed, unable to stifle her in-terest.

'You really don't know anything about me, do you?' Saif registered. 'My mother ran off with another man six months after my birth, deserting me and my father. Her family took offence when my father spoke his opin-ion too freely of her behaviour.'

'My goodness, that was tough for both of you. What was it like growing up, torn between two parents? I pre-sume they divorced?'

'Yes, there was a divorce. I have no memory of her,

though, and I was never torn between them. She never asked to see me. She wiped her first marriage out of her life as though it had never happened.'

Tati grimaced. 'That was very sad for you.'

'Not really,' Saif countered, his jawline stiffening as he made that claim. 'I had three very much older half-sisters, who devoted themselves to my care in her place.'

'How much older?'

'They were born of my father's first marriage and are in their sixties now. I was spoiled as the long-awaited son and heir,' Saif told her quietly. 'I have much to be grateful for.'

He had dealt with his troubled background with such calm and logic that she was slightly envious, conscious that she had more often been mortified by her own. She dealt him a wry glance. 'You notice that we're talking about everything but the elephant in the room.'

'I didn't want to give you indigestion by mentioning our marriage,' Saif delivered straight-faced.

Tati stared at him, entrapped by those striking eyes as green as emeralds in his lean dark face, and then her defences crumbled as she spluttered and then laughed out loud, grabbing up her water glass to drink and ease her throat. 'So, you *do* have a sense of humour.'

'Yesterday was trying for *both* of us,' he pointed out as he pushed away his plate and leant back fluidly in his chair to give her his full attention.

'Why did you agree to go ahead with the marriage?'

'My father has a serious heart condition. I didn't want to risk refusing to marry you and stressing his temper,' Saif admitted grimly. 'He needs to remain calm, which is often a struggle for him.'

Tati was disconcerted by that admission. It had not

occurred to her that he might have an excuse as good as her own for letting the ceremony proceed. That knocked her right off the moral high ground she had been unconsciously hugging like a blanket while silently blaming him for being willing to marry her.

He hadn't had a choice either.

'You must've been disappointed that I wasn't my cousin, Ana,' she said uncomfortably.

'Why would I have been? She was a stranger too.'

'Yes, but she's much prettier than I am and she's sophisticated and lively. I'm none of those things. Ana's one of the beautiful people… I'm a nobody.'

'How a *nobody*?' Saif framed, his nostrils flaring with distaste. 'She is your cousin. I assume you have led similar lives.'

Tati breathed in fast and deep as Marcel arrived with a mouth-watering selection of desserts. 'Not for me, thank you,' she said in creditable French.

'Saif,' she said quietly once Marcel had departed. 'You married the poor relation, not the family princess. I'm illegitimate and my birth father, whom I never met, was imprisoned for fraud. He's dead now.'

'Why are you telling me this?' he demanded.

'You need to know who I am. I grew up in a cottage on my uncle's estate. My mother and I were never welcome there because my uncle didn't get on with my mother and viewed the two of us as freeloaders. I received the same education at the same schools as my cousin but only because my grandmother insisted. This is only my second trip abroad…'

Saif was watching her closely. 'I'm listening…' he told her.

'When I was about fifteen my mother began getting

forgetful and confused. Eventually she was diagnosed with early-onset dementia. She was only forty years old.' Tati looked reflective, her eyes darkening with sadness. 'I looked after Mum for as long as I could but eventually she had to go into a nursing home. She's been there for almost six years and it costs a fortune. My uncle pays for her care—'

'Which is why you married me,' Saif assumed, slashing ebony brows drawing together in a frown. 'So that you could take care of her yourself.'

'I didn't receive that dowry for marrying you or whatever it's called,' Tati told him immediately. 'My uncle got that. He has debts to settle. That was why Ana was originally willing to marry you, because she has never worked and she's reliant on an income from her father.'

'So, what changed?' Saif pressed.

'Out of the blue, her ex got back in touch and asked her to marry him on the phone while she was here. That's why she ran back to England at the very last minute, leaving me to face the music... She asked me to pretend I was her to give her enough time to leave Alharia. She was afraid her parents would try to prevent her going. I really didn't enjoy deceiving your relatives into believing I was the bride, but I didn't truthfully expect any lasting harm to come from my pretence. I certainly *didn't* realise that I would end up married to you instead!'

'Then why did you agree?' Saif asked bluntly.

'Uncle Rupert threatened to stop paying my mother's nursing home bills. I couldn't let that happen,' Tati murmured heavily. 'She's happy and settled where she is—well, as happy as she can be anywhere now.'

'Will you excuse me for a moment?' Saif asked tautly as he stood up and left the room.

Out in the hall he pulled out his phone and contacted the private investigation agency he often used in business. He wanted information and he wanted it fast. He needed to know everything there was to know about the woman he had married. Ignorance in such a case was inexcusable and had already got him into trouble. The last-minute exchange of brides had plunged him into a situation in which he was not in control and he refused to allow that state of affairs to continue.

Alone in the dining room, Tati felt like dropping her head into her hands and screaming out loud. Why had she told him all that personal stuff? What was the point? She might even be giving him information about herself that he could use as another weapon against her. Saif was not a man she could trust. She cringed at the recollection of what she had said about herself, as if she was apologising for who and what she was, as if she was openly admitting that she was something less than he was just because she hadn't been born into either wealth or status.

Her pride flared at that lowering image and it shamed her, even more than he had already shamed her with that outrageous shopping trip. She had fallen head first into that nasty trap, she conceded painfully.

As Saif strolled back into the room, dark head high, green eyes glinting with assurance, Tati's small hands flexed into claws, that family trait of violence he had accused her of harbouring leaping through her instantaneously. 'You sent me out shopping so that you could snigger behind my back when I met all your worst expectations!' she condemned furiously. 'And I was mad enough at you to allow you to goad me into behaving badly!'

'I don't know what you're talking about,' Saif countered with unblemished cool. 'I do not snigger.'

Pansy-blue eyes now as hard as diamond cutters, Tati tossed her head back, soft, full mouth rigid. 'I'm done with talking to you. I'm done with telling you the truth and letting you judge me for what I can't help or change. You set me up to get me out of your hair and to make a fool of myself and I played right into your hands!' she condemned.

'I didn't set you up when I sent you shopping,' Saif retorted crisply. 'I arranged the outing to entertain you.'

'Like hell you did!' Tati raged back at him.

'And if you played right into my hands, surely that is your own fault?' Saif drawled smoothly.

'Oh, you...*you*...!' The exclamation was framed between gritted teeth. Tati's hands knotted into fists because she wanted to swear at him and she didn't swear, not with the memory of her Granny Milly telling her that only people with a weak grasp of language needed to use curse words. 'I've never been in shops that exclusive in my life. I've never owned clothing such as I'm wearing now. I went shopping to punish you.'

'Why would you have wanted to punish me?' he enquired in wonderment.

'I thought you deserved to have a spendthrift wife after labelling me a gold digger! I know it doesn't sound like much of a punishment right now but at the time... *at the time*...it made sense to me,' she confided in an angry challenge that dared him to employ logic against her. 'But then I got tempted by all those beautiful fabrics and designs and how I looked in them. I started to actually enjoy myself…and I'll never *ever* forgive you for that, for tempting me into wasting all that money.'

'I arranged for you to go out shopping and I would not describe the outfit you are currently wearing as a waste on any level,' Saif asserted softly. 'You look amazing in it.'

'And do you seriously think that *your* opinion makes any difference to the way I feel?' Tati flung back at him furiously. 'Well, it doesn't! I hardly brought any clothes with me to Alharia. Why would I have? As far as I knew I was only staying for forty-eight hours and I certainly didn't factor in marrying you and being swept off to Paris!'

'In other words, you *needed* to go shopping,' Saif interpreted with an unshakeable calm that simply sent her temperature rocketing again because it was infuriating that the more she freaked out, the calmer he became. 'I don't understand why you're so upset.'

'Because I could have bought ordinary cheap clothes and proved to you that I'm *not* a greedy gold digger!' Tati yelled back at him.

'You're my wife and entitled to a decent wardrobe. I wouldn't want you swanning round in what you describe as "cheap" clothes,' Saif pointed out with distaste.

'For heaven's sake, I'm not your wife!' Tati fired back at him in vehement disagreement.

'From the instant you shared that bed with me, and an annulment became an impossibility, you also became my wife in law *and* in my eyes,' Saif informed her with fierce conviction. 'You were a virgin. While you urged me not to make a fuss about that fact, it did make a difference on my terms. Perhaps that is old-fashioned of me, but you do now feel very much like my wife and all this nonsense about how much you spend on the clothes you needed is pointless now.'

'I'm not your wife,' Tati argued in a low, tight voice. 'If you wanted an annulment to end this marriage then you didn't want a wife and we could still apply for an annulment. We could *lie*.'

Her prince threw his handsome dark head back and surveyed her with narrowed, glittering green eyes. 'I do not tell lies of that nature and, now that the marriage has been consummated, neither will you. For the moment, we will make the best of our situation until such time as our circumstances change and we are free to go our separate ways. In the meantime, you are entitled to a very healthy allowance as my wife and I will take over the cost of your mother's nursing care, so let us have no more foolish talk about how you shouldn't spend *my* money.'

'I would lie to get an annulment,' Tati told him stubbornly. 'I don't normally tell lies but in this instance I would be prepared to lie… Just putting that out there for you to consider.'

'I have considered it and I reject it,' Saif stated curtly. 'I—'

'No, there's no need for another moral lecture,' Tati hastened to assure him. 'I do know the difference between right and wrong but I *also* know that neither of us *freely* agreed to marry the other.'

'And yet you gave your virginity to me.'

Tati's face burned red as fire. 'I didn't give you anything… Well, I did, but not the way you make it sound! I was attracted to you and we had sex. Let's leave it there.'

'But where *does* that leave us exactly?' Saif demanded impatiently.

Tati winced at his persistence. 'You can't put a label on everything.'

'I need to know where I stand with you,' Saif breathed with driving emphasis. 'You have to put *some* kind of label on us.'

'Friends…hopefully eventually,' Tati suggested weakly. 'Maybe friends with benefits. Wouldn't that be the best description?'

In the tense silence that gradually stretched, a slow-burning smile slowly wiped the raw tension from Saif's expressive mouth and his vaguely confrontational stance eased. His extraordinary eyes clung to her blushing face. 'Yes. I could work with that,' he murmured in a husky tone of acceptance. 'Yes, I could definitely work within those parameters.'

'I'm really sleepy,' Tati mumbled, putting a hand to her mouth as if to politely screen a yawn, a potent mix of embarrassment and confusion assailing her. 'May we call a halt to the post-mortem for now?'

'It's been a long day,' Saif agreed, deciding to look into whether or not that phrase 'friends with benefits' encompassed what he thought it did.

Naturally, he had heard the expression before. He knew there was a movie by that name but he had never watched it and had never entertained the concept of attempting so spontaneous and casual a relationship with any woman. Although he was close to some of his female cousins, he was mindful of his position and there was no one in whom he confided. He had only once had a female friend. He had been a student at the time and his supposed female friend had suddenly announced that she was in love with him and everything had become horribly awkward from that point on. His sole sexual outlet was occasional one-night stands and that kind of informal never led to a misunderstanding.

At the same time, he marvelled at his bride's audacity in making such a suggestion. He had always assumed that there was truth in that old chestnut that women generally wanted more than sex and friendship from a man, but obviously there were exceptions to every rule. Possibly his own outlook was a little out of date, he thought uneasily, wondering darkly if his father's rigidly traditional attitudes could have coloured his views more than he was willing to admit. Even so, if he and his bride had no choice but to remain together for the present, why shouldn't they make the best of it in and out of the bedroom?

Bearing in mind his distrust of committed relationships, formed by his inability to forget how easily his mother had walked away from him and his father, he suspected that being friends with benefits might be an excellent recipe for temporary intimacy.

Tati sped back upstairs as if she were being chased because she was reeling in shock from what she had accidentally said to Saif, and the manner in which he had received what had undoubtedly struck him as an *invitation*. Her face burned afresh as she got ready for bed, every movement reminding her of what had occurred earlier because the ache of her first sexual experience still lingered with tingling awareness. And, strangely, so did the hot curling sensation she experienced deep down inside whenever she thought about it.

Not strange, she adjusted, simply normal. There was nothing weird about sexual chemistry and Saif had buckets of sex appeal. Even moving across the room, all loose-limbed grace and earthy masculinity, he entrapped her gaze and when she collided with those startling green eyes of his she felt light-headed. So, no mystery there about what had led to her downfall, she told herself plainly. She had never been affected like that by a man before, certainly not to the extent that he interfered with her brain and her wits and smashed through her every defence.

She even *said* the wrong things around Saif, she acknowledged unhappily. She had been desperate to hide how deeply affected she had been by their intimacy, desperate to keep up an impenetrable front. After all, Saif had taken the sex in his stride without betraying any emotional reaction whatsoever. She had wanted it to look as though she took such steps with equally bold panache, so she had seized on the chance the friends idea offered with alacrity and had added in that ghastly *benefits* tag to coolly attempt to dismiss the reality that they had already got far more familiar than mere friendship allowed. She had been referring to the past, *not* to the potential future. Was it any wonder that he had seemingly got the wrong message? And was she planning to disabuse him of the idea that she was willing to continue their relationship as a friend with benefits?

Her head beginning to ache with her ever-circling thoughts and a growing sense of panic that she had let her life get so out of control when she was normally a very calm and organised person, Tati slid into bed, convinced that she had not a prayer of sleeping. And yet moments later, odd as it seemed to her the following morning, sheer emotional and physical exhaustion sent her crashing straight into a deep sleep.

Saif went to bed in a totally distracted manner far

from his usual style. His wife, that much-maligned bride of his, had without warning become a *real* wife. It might be a casual bond, it might not be destined to last for very long, but he was much inclined to believe, even though he had yet to receive concrete facts in an investigation file, that Tatiana was telling him the truth about herself.

Saif was a shrewd observer and he trusted his own instincts. His assumptions about her had been laid down from Dalil Khouri's first reference to her as a fortune hunter, an adventuress, a gold-digging socialite with expensive tastes, who could find no wealthier husband than a Middle Eastern prince from an oil-rich country like Alharia. That might well be true of the woman he *should* have married, the one they called Ana. She was the daughter of the grasping uncle and aunt. He had himself witnessed their threatening behaviour towards their niece with their raised hands, angry voices and devious looks, he conceded grimly. Now he believed that those original allegations were *not* true of the woman he had actually married.

The very beautiful, sensual woman he had married, Saif repeated inwardly as he glanced at her, sound asleep on the pillow beside his, long wheaten hair tumbled across the linen, soft pink mouth relaxed, porcelain skin flushed. He had stayed up late watching *that* film. It had struck him as fashionable and he didn't do, or certainly never before had done, 'fashionable.' But the creeping, unpleasant suspicion that he could be as much of a dyed-in-the-wool traditionalist as his father, unable to adapt to the modern world or to a modern woman, had cut through him like a knife and hammered his pride.

So, although it went against his *every* instinct, Saif

was determined to do the 'friends with benefits' thing even though the movie had already demonstrated the pitfalls. After all, he would not be emotionally vulnerable, would he? He did not have the habit of attachment, he reasoned with resolve, he had never been in a proper relationship and had always kept his distance from that level of involvement. He would not be guilty of attaching feelings to sex. He knew all about sex. They would be friends, *sexual* friends. A pulse beat at his groin stirred at the mere thought of repeating that encounter with her.

Even so, he would exercise caution, he told himself fiercely, scrutinising her delicate profile and feathery eyelashes, noting the tiny group of freckles scattered across her nose, the gentle curve of her pink lips. He wanted to see her smile for a change. And why not? She was his wife, deserving of respect and consideration, regardless of how casual and temporary their alliance was. He might not be cutting-edge trendy, as she appeared to be, but he believed that with the exercise of a little imagination and research, he knew how to treat a woman well…

CHAPTER SIX

TATI STUMBLED AS she walked away from the giant Ferris wheel on the Place de la Concorde. Her head was still spinning from the experience and the fabulous views of Paris. Saif's hand shot out to steady her and she glanced up at him with a huge grin. 'My goodness...that was amazing!' she exclaimed.

Saif gazed down into her glowing face and the bright blue eyes lit up with enjoyment and he bent his head and crushed her mouth hungrily under his. That hunger speared through Tati like a flame striking touchpaper. Her knees wobbled and her hands closed into his sleeves to keep her upright. The urgent plunge of his tongue formed a pool of liquid heat in her pelvis and she gasped.

Saif jerked his head up, momentarily disconcerted to discover that he was in a public place, his bodyguards all politely looking away and probably astonished by his behaviour. In the crush of tourists and cameras flashing, he clenched his jaw hard. A very faint darkening scored his high cheekbones as he closed a hand over his wife's and walked her in the direction of the picnic lunch awaiting them on the Champ de Mars. He felt vaguely as though she had intoxicated him.

'The Louvre was exhausting.' Tati sighed as she sank down on the rugs already laid across the springy grass for their comfort. She imagined that going sightseeing with Saif was very different from the usual tourist trek. They didn't queue, they didn't wait anywhere for anything and everything that they required was instantly provided. Her elegant black sundress pooled around her feet and she tugged off her high heels to curl bare pink toes into the grass beyond the rug.

'We did only do the highlights tour. I spent months working in Paris and I went to the Louvre several times,' Saif imparted with amusement, watching the way the sunshine bathed her luxuriant mane of hair in gold. He wanted to touch her again and the temptation entertained him because it was a novelty.

Usually, one taste of a woman was sufficient for him and he would move on. Sex, however, was a great leveller, Saif allowed cynically and, clearly, he hadn't enjoyed enough of it for too long because around Tatiana he was on the constant edge of arousal and it was a challenge to resist her appeal. Yet, only a few yards away, young lovers were lying in the grass kissing passionately with their bodies entwined and their mouths mashed together. The Crown Prince of Alharia, however, had always known that he was not able to practise that kind of freedom and he told himself that he was too disciplined to give way to so juvenile a display. Yet he had kissed her in the street, utterly forgetting where he was, *who* he was.

'I'm not really into art. Mum was,' Tati confided. 'She could look at a picture and make those highbrow comments the way people do, but then she went to art college and originally planned to train as an art historian.'

Dainty little bites of food were set out on a low table in front of them along with china plates and wine glasses in an elaborate spread.

In terms of an outside space, it was a picnic, but not quite the kind of picnic Tati had naïvely envisaged when Saif had first mentioned it. The Prince, she was starting to realise, didn't truly know what informal or casual was. He was far too accustomed to top-flight silent service. Marcel had arrived laden down with hampers and his spry companion, who was an Alharian, had served them, moving forward on his knees with a bent head as though even to meet the eyes of the Emir's heir would be a familiarity too far. A lot of people were watching the display but Saif seemed no more aware of that scrutiny than of the presence of the plain-clothes police hovering beyond the ring of their personal protection team, keeping a watchful eye over a foreign royal. But then why would he be aware? she asked herself ruefully. Presumably, this was Saif's world as it always was, surrounded by security and hemmed in by tradition and formality.

'Why didn't *you* go to college?' Saif asked softly.

'Further education wasn't an option for me after Granny died. Uncle Rupert was covering the cost of the nursing home and I was already living below their roof because, when Mum went into care, my uncle needed to rent out the cottage we had been using to set against the bills and I was too young to live alone,' Tati explained wryly. 'I felt obligated to help around the house because they couldn't afford full-time staff and I was able to plug the gaps.'

'Your relatives should not have allowed you to make such a sacrifice,' Saif opined, impressed by the sacrifices she had made on her mother's behalf. When he had been younger, he had been much more curious about his absent mother, particularly after her death. He might even have initially sought out his brother to find out more about the woman who had brought him into the world and then walked away. Angel had told him all he needed to know about his absent parent, had satisfied that empty space inside him.

'She's my mother and she was a loving one. It was my duty to do what I could to pay my uncle back,' Tati contradicted gently. 'If I'd gone to college I would have built up thousands of pounds in student loans and it would have been years before I was in a position to make a decent financial contribution. I'm only twenty-one. I've still got loads of time to study and focus on a career.'

'That was a mature decision,' Saif acknowledged, wryly recalling the party girl he had assumed he was marrying while conceding that, undeniably, her cousin made a far more appropriate wife for a man in his position.

Tati nibbled at the delicious finger food on the plates and quaffed her wine.

'We have one personal topic which we haven't yet but *must* touch on,' Saif murmured in a low voice, and he topped up her wine glass, impervious to the shocked appraisal of the server hovering only yards away, keen to jump at the smallest sign of either of them having any need for attention.

Smooth brow furrowing, Tati glanced at him, thinking how incredibly good-looking he was with sunshine gleaming off his black hair and olive skin, lighting his eyes to a sea-glass green shade. 'And what is that?' she prompted abstractedly.

'Yesterday I was negligent in my care of you. As the experienced partner, all the blame on that score is mine. But that recklessness must not be repeated. In our position, the potential consequences would bring complications we would not want to deal with,' Saif framed in a taut undertone of warning.

It took a rather long moment for Tati to grasp what he was talking about. *'Negligent in my care of you... consequences...complications...mustn't be repeated...'* And then the penny of comprehension dropped with a resounding thump and her tummy curdled in dismay. He was referring to their lack of contraceptive common sense the day before. What else could he be talking about? He hadn't used birth control and she had reassured him, it only occurring to her later that her contraception was scarcely reliable when she had already been off it for a couple of days because she had left her strip of pills behind in England. Losing the rosy colour in her cheeks, she paled and swallowed down her misgivings before sipping her wine while studiously not looking in *his* direction.

There was no point worrying him ahead of time when really...what were the chances that she would conceive the very *first* time she had sex? She gritted her teeth, anxiety flashing through her as she reminded herself that she was not a naïve teenager, thinking that that should be sufficient to keep her safe. There was a chance, *of course*, there was when, even with precautions, no form of contraception was foolproof.

'We need to be responsible,' she said, proud of the steadiness of her voice until it occurred to her that, once again, she was throwing up a green light for further such intimacy.

And she shouldn't be doing that, of course, she shouldn't be. Even though she had *enjoyed* the experience? Her cheeks hot, she argued with herself inside her head. If they were careful going forward, there was no reason why she shouldn't be intimate with Saif again. She was an adult woman capable of making that choice on her own behalf. There was nothing morally wrong about having a sexual relationship, she reminded herself irritably, as long as the same consequences that had derailed her mother's life did not assail her.

Sadly, unplanned pregnancies sometimes extracted the highest price from the female partner, she reflected ruefully, because a man might have to contribute to his child's maintenance, but that did not necessarily mean that he took on any share of the childcare or indeed had any further interest in the child involved.

Her father had been of that ilk, indifferent from the day that her mother had informed him of her pregnancy. Even after his release from prison, he had pleaded poverty when pursued by the law for child support payments. She had never met her reluctant father in the flesh. As a teenager she had once written to him asking for a meeting but, even though the courts had verified her paternity, he had only responded with the denial that she was his child. That had hurt, that had blown a giant hole in her secret hope that he was curious about her as well.

'Yes,' Saif agreed, relieved, it seemed, by her attitude, which only made her feel even guiltier for not being fully honest with him from the outset and just admitting that there was a risk, admittedly, she *hoped*, a very slight risk that conception was a possibility.

Only telling the truth would make her sound like

such an idiot, she conceded ruefully. She had told him it was safe. She had told him she was on contraception, only to recognise when it was too late that the pill method only worked if taken on a consistent schedule.

'We're attending a party tonight,' Saif murmured, disconcerting her with the ease with which he flipped the topic of conversation. 'You should enjoy it. I believe it's usually quite a spectacle.'

'Fancy, then,' Tati assumed, mentally flipping through her new wardrobe and realising with some embarrassment that she had bought so much that she couldn't remember all of the outfits without the garments being physically in front of her. That was not a problem that she had ever thought she would live to have, she acknowledged ruefully.

'Very,' Saif confirmed lazily, watching her with eyes that were sea-glass bright green seduction in the sunlight, his gaze enhanced by dense black spiky lashes. He wasn't touching her, he didn't *need* to touch her, she acknowledged in wonderment, he just had to look at her a certain way and that certain way was, without a doubt, incredibly sexy and potent.

Heat rose at the heart of her, butterflies fluttering in her tummy. Dragging her gaze from his, she sipped at her wine, reminding herself afresh that she was an adult woman, able to make her own choices…and right now, she thought, dizzy in the grip of that sensual intoxication, her choice was *him*.

Ana had always told Tati that she was very naïve about men. Her cousin prided herself on being as ruthless as any male in taking what she wanted from a man and then moving on, regardless of how the man felt about it. Ana often left broken hearts in her wake. Tati not only didn't *want* to leave broken hearts behind her, but also didn't think she would ever possess the power her cousin seemed to have over the opposite sex.

No, she couldn't compare herself to Ana, Tati acknowledged back at the magnificent house while she browsed through her wide selection of gowns. She was not and would never be a heartbreaker, but she rather suspected that Saif fell into that category. He emanated that cool, sophisticated air of unavailability that her cousin found so attractive in a man, so it was rather ironic that he had ended up married to Tati instead. Tati, unrefined, clumsy…and so angry from the moment he had met her.

Tati had never argued and fought with anyone the way she had with Saif. And where had all that rage come from? She supposed it had built up over the years below her uncle and aunt's roof where she had been consistently bullied and reminded of her lowly place in life on a daily basis. The smallest request for a wage that would at least fund her bus trips to visit her mother and little gifts for the older woman had been viewed as an offence of ingratitude. That she was a 'charity' child dependent on the goodwill of others for survival had been brought home to her hard and often and that label had ground her pride into the dust. Her mother's troubled past, her care bills and even the family embarrassment caused by Tati's illegitimate birth had often been used as a stick to beat Tati with and keep her down. Her uncle would not have dared be so offensive had her mother been around still possessed of her cutting tongue.

At the same time, her grandmother had had no idea what went on in her own house and Tati had shielded the frail old lady from the ugly truth. Even so, her Granny

Milly had once taken the trouble to assure Tati that her mother would *always* be looked after, and Tati had prayed that sufficient money would be laid aside in the old lady's will to cover the nursing home costs. Unhappily, though, her late grandmother had forgotten that promise and had remembered neither her daughter Mariana nor Tati in her last will and testament.

That oversight had hurt, Tati conceded ruefully, because she had been deeply attached to her grandmother. In addition, the soothing knowledge that her mother's care was secure would not only have meant the world to Tati, but would also have released her from her virtual servitude in her uncle's home. But she had long since forgiven the old lady, who had been quite ill and confused towards the end of her life.

Shaking her head clear of those disturbing recollections of the past, Tati tugged a silvery-grey evening gown out of one of the closets. The delicate lace overlay was cobweb fine and it shimmered below the lights. She had fallen in love with the elegant dress at first sight, thinking comically that it was a princess dress for a grown-up, it not occurring to her that she was, technically speaking anyway, now a princess, thanks to her marriage to a prince. The modest neckline and long sleeves might not be eye-catching, but the gown had a quiet, stylish elegance that appealed to her.

As she emerged fully clad from the bathroom, her make-up applied in a few subtle touches, Saif stilled halfway out of his shirt. Tati paused as well, reluctantly enthralled by the expanse of muscular bronzed chest on view. He was beautifully built from his broad shoulders to his narrow waist and long, powerful thighs. For a split second she remembered the weight of him over her and she was suddenly so short of breath she almost choked, her cheeks flaming as she coughed and croaked, 'Sorry, wasn't expecting to see you!'

'That dress is spectacular on you,' Saif breathed appreciatively, because that particular shade of grey enhanced the deep blue of her eyes and lent a glow to her porcelain skin while the tailoring of the dress sleekly outlined the feminine curves of her lush figure.

'Seriously?' Tati queried, her head lifting high again.

'Seriously,' he confirmed, strolling across the room to indicate the gift boxes on the highly polished dressing table. 'These are for you.'

'Presents? It's not my birthday yet,' Tati told him, lifting a gift box with the certainty that such packaging could only contain jewellery and uncomfortable at the prospect.

'As my wife, you need to wear jewels. It's expected,' Saif said smoothly.

Tati dealt him a suspicious glance before opening the boxes to reveal a diamond necklace and earrings. 'These are…spectacular,' she whispered truthfully, a fingertip reverently stroking the rainbow fire of a single gleaming gem. 'But I *shouldn't*—'

'No. These are family jewels that my father once gave to my mother. My mother left everything behind when she left Alharia and it would please my father very much to know that his gifts are being worn again.'

'Is your mother still alive?' Tati asked gently, detaching the necklace from the box, feeling the cool of the beautiful gems against her skin as her reluctance to wear the diamonds melted away.

'No, she passed away about three years ago in a helicopter crash with her husband,' Saif explained.

'Did you ever meet her again after she left your father? Or even see her?' she prompted, intrigued by his seemingly calm attitude to his abandonment as a child.

'I was devastated when I heard of her death,' Saif heard himself admit, disconcerting himself almost as much as he surprised Tati with that declaration. 'While she was alive I could toy with the idea of looking her up and getting to know her—should she have been interested—but once she was gone, that possibility was gone for ever.'

'I know what you mean,' Tati murmured wryly. 'I wrote to my father when I was a teenager asking him to meet me and, even though it had been proven in court that I was his daughter, he wrote back telling me that he wasn't my father and didn't wish to hear from me again. It hurt a lot. My mother had tried to warn me that he wasn't interested, but I was too stubborn to listen.'

'My father told me that he didn't think that my mother had many maternal genes. Some women don't, I believe, and presumably fathers can suffer from the same flaw. Let me help,' he murmured, crossing the room to remove the necklace from her fingers and settle it round her throat, his fingertips brushing the nape of her neck as he clasped it, sending a faint quiver of awareness through her.

Awesomely conscious of his proximity and the familiar scent of his cologne, Tati struggled to behave normally as she donned the earrings and finally turned to let him see her.

'Perfect,' Saif pronounced.

'I'll wait downstairs for you,' Tati told him breathlessly, not sure that she could withstand the desire to watch him while he undressed, and mortified by the temptation. It was as though Saif had cast some weird kind of sex spell over her, she conceded shamefacedly as Marcel offered her a drink in the grand main salon.

It was normal, healthy lust, Tati supposed of her fixation and her growing obsession with Saif's extraordinary eyes, Saif's hands, what he could do with them, how it felt when he touched her…

Enough of this nonsense, she mentally screamed at herself. She was behaving with all the maturity of a schoolgirl with a first crush. None of it was any big deal, she told herself bracingly, deciding that she was only so bemused and off balance because she was a decidedly late starter when it came to the opposite sex. All over again, she wished she had acquired some of her cousin's glossy cool and confidence. But, marooned on a country estate without money and with few social outlets, Tati had not enjoyed her cousin's opportunities to meet men and date. In reality, Tati thought with regret, she probably *was* as naïve as an adolescent.

When she climbed into the limo with Saif she was, momentarily, tempted to pinch herself before accepting that the designer gown, the incredibly handsome man by her side and the opulent mode of travel could figure in *her* new lifestyle. It was even more ironic to know that her uncle and aunt would now be furious that *she* was the one benefiting from the marriage rather than their daughter. They had needed her to marry the Prince to gain access to that dowry, but it would still outrage them that their niece was now living in luxury. And for the first time, Tati acknowledged that she was grateful to have escaped her relatives' demands, relieved to know that in many ways she was finally free and that her mother's residence in her care home was secure. She would eventually be able to look towards her own future, unfettered by the limits imposed on her by others.

'You're very quiet this evening,' Saif remarked as they crossed the pavement to the large illuminated mansion with its classic gardens that were equally well-lit to show off glimpses of women in elaborate dresses and men in dinner jackets, their necks craned as they watched the glorious fireworks shooting and sparkling across the night sky in a rainbow of colour and illumination.

'Gosh, these people know how to party,' Tati commented, hugely impressed by her surroundings as they stepped into a brilliantly lit hall and a crush of little groups of chattering people. And everybody, literally *everybody*, looked as though they might be a celebrity of some kind. In such company, neither her gown nor her magnificent diamonds could ever look like overkill. 'Are the hosts close friends of yours?'

'No. I owe this invitation to the relative whose house we are using,' Saif admitted. 'But I have no doubt that I will see familiar faces here.'

'Yes. I suppose you get to meet a lot of people.'

'Because the Emir doesn't travel. I take care of Alharia's diplomatic interests in his place. It entails attending formal receptions and dinners. You'll be accompanying me to some of them,' he declared, startling her.

'*Me?*' Tati stressed in a low mutter of disconcertion as he curved a guiding hand to her taut spine.

'The joys of marrying a crown prince,' Saif murmured teasingly, his breath fanning her cheekbone. 'Some of that kind of socialising is boring but, equally, sometimes it's fascinating.'

'I should've realised that there would be…er…duties

to carry out in this role.' Tati sighed. 'It all happened so fast, though… One minute Ana was running for the airport and the next we were married.'

In the midst of that speech, Saif was hailed by two men, who addressed him in another language. It wasn't French and it wasn't English, and she was introduced and served with a drink of champagne by a passing waiter before they moved on into a room. 'Could we go out and see the fireworks?' she pressed once they were alone again.

Saif glanced down at her in surprise, for in his experience women in their finery avoided the outdoors like the plague. The unhidden eagerness brimming in her upturned gaze, however, made him laugh and for a moment she seemed much younger than her years. 'Why do you want to see them?'

'Mum was so terrified of fireworks that I never got to see them properly as a child. When she was young she witnessed a dreadful accident, which injured a friend at a firework event, and it put her off them for life,' she explained. 'Every Bonfire Night, we sat indoors with the curtains closed and then, the next day, Ana would tell me how much fun she had had at whichever party she had been invited to and I would feel madly jealous.'

Saif's expressive lips quirked. 'Naturally.'

They stood on the paved terrace watching the display until a low murmur of a comment made Tati turn her head. A very tall brunette in a startlingly see-through dress was stalking towards them. For a split second, Tati was guilty of staring, taken aback by a woman revealing that much flesh in public, showing off her bare breasts and her nipple rings below the thin white chiffon gown. Truly, however, Tati was forced to admit, the woman had a *superb* body. In haste she turned her head away from the conspicuous beauty, only to stiffen in astonishment when the woman appeared in front of them and greeted Saif with the kind of familiarity that no woman wanted to see her male companion receive in her presence.

'Saif!' she carolled, followed by a voluble gush of French as she walked her long, manicured fingertips up over his chest in a very inviting gesture.

'Juliette,' Saif murmured with rather more restraint. 'May I introduce you to my wife, Tatiana?'

'Your *wife*?' Juliette gasped in consternation while walking her fingers down over his flat muscular stomach in unmistakable invitation.

Tati couldn't stop herself. In a knee-jerk reaction, she reached out and pushed the brunette's hand away from Saif. 'His wife, sorry,' she said with a smile that she was sure was unconvincing.

A split second later, Juliette having languorously taken the hint and strolled away, Tati was shattered by her own possessive and wholly inappropriate reaction to another woman touching the man she had married. Saif didn't belong to her in the usual sense of married people. They weren't in love either. She had come up with the label of friends with benefits but even that wasn't a fair tag for them, because people in that kind of relationship were generally those who had had a reasonably long and close friendship before intimacy developed and she and Saif didn't fit into that category either. The intense colour of mortification swept her cheeks and she felt as though she were burning alive inside her own skin.

'I'm sorry... She was annoying me,' she said uncomfortably.

'It was unseemly for her to touch me in that way,' Saif murmured, appraising her with gleaming green eyes fringed by black lashes. 'There is no need for an apology.'

But regardless of what he said, Tati felt very differently. She had shocked herself with that little show of possessive behaviour. After all, she wasn't entitled to be that territorial with Saif. She should not be experiencing any prompting to react as though she were jealous of another woman touching him. Of course, she wasn't jealous or possessive of him, she told herself fiercely.

'And it was sexy,' Saif murmured in a husky undertone, gazing down at her with potent green eyes of appreciation. 'Very, very sexy.'

Stunned, Tati looked back at him in wonderment and then she couldn't help herself—she laughed, and all her discomfiture was washed away as though it had never been. Evidently, Saif took a very different view of her attitude, but as the evening wore on she continued to marvel at the way she had behaved. Clearly, she *was* possessive of Saif. Was that simply because she had gone to bed with him?

Brow furrowing, she attempted, during all the chatter, the dancing and the eating that comprised the lively party atmosphere, to pin down what she was feeling about the man she had married. It was surprisingly difficult. She had travelled at speed from raging resentment and frustration over her powerlessness to grudging acceptance that Saif had had little more choice than she had in their marriage. And somewhere along the line she had begun lusting after him, *liking* him, appreciating his calm, measured approach to life. It certainly didn't mean that she was developing any kind of mental attachment to him, she assured herself confidently.

She wasn't so naïve that she would confuse lust and love, was she? Admittedly, she was enthralled by the fluid movement of his hips against hers on the dance floor, the pulsing ache building between her thighs and the provocative awareness that she was having the *same* physical effect on him. Unlike her, he couldn't hide his response. She was insanely conscious of his arousal. And that sheer reciprocity thrilled Tati because it made her feel powerful and seductive for the first time in her life, no longer a weak pawn in someone else's game, but an equal. She was finally making her own choices and doing what pleased her, rather than someone else.

'So, you and Juliette?' Tati whispered as she stretched up to Saif. 'Do share…'

Saif tensed, wondering why on earth she would ask such an awkward question before reminding himself that women were often morbidly curious about a man's past. His three older sisters had taught him that, always prying where their interest was least welcome.

'Was she your girlfriend?' Tati prompted.

'No. It was a casual connection.' Saif shrugged in emphasis, hoping that her curiosity concluded there, long brown fingers skimming soothingly down the side of her face. 'I can't keep my hands off you,' he breathed with a sudden raw edge to his dark, deep drawl that sent a responsive shiver of delight down her taut spine.

'It's mutual,' she whispered.

Even so, she was still assailed by a sudden perverse attack of guilt and discomfiture because, try as she might to be a bolder version of her old self, being bold still felt sinful and brazen. She would have to work harder on that outlook, she told herself firmly, because being quiet, accepting and the person others preferred her to be had only served to deprive her of her freedom and her choices in life. Wanting Saif, allowing herself to succumb to that sizzling chemistry that went way beyond anything she had ever experienced, was probably the most daring thing she had ever done. And one of the best things about Saif, Tati reflected happily, was that he hadn't known her as she used to be and, with him, she could be entirely her true self.

He curved an arm round her in the limousine on the drive back to the house. She was gloriously aware of the strength of his lean, powerful frame up against her and the subtle musky, fragrant scent of him that close. Her heart was pounding in her chest when he stopped on the landing halfway up the fabulous staircase of the town house and hauled her up against him to kiss her with all the fierce hunger she craved. The lancing touch of his tongue inside her mouth set her on fire and a choked moan escaped low in her throat.

Her whole body was surging with wild anticipation and, lifting her, he cannoned into the bedroom, pushing her back against the wall and pinning her there afresh to crush her lips hungrily beneath his again. Her heart was thumping, her pulses thrumming because that rocketing passion of his took her over and thrilled her to death. It was the exact match of her own, a wild, seething need that drove out every other logical thought, leaving only the wanting behind.

Saif turned her round to run down the zip on her dress, pushing it off her shoulders, stroking it down her arms until it dropped round her feet. Kicking off her shoes, heartbeat accelerating, she stepped out of the dress. His lips traced the line of her shoulder and every nerve ending in her body leapt to attention as she pressed back into the heat of him, breathless and bone-less with need.

'I like the lingerie,' Saif husked with appreciation as he carefully lifted her and lowered her down onto the well-sprung bed. 'But I think I'll like you even better out of it.'

Flushed and wide-eyed, her eyes very blue in her face, Tati watched Saif shed his tailored dinner jacket and bow tie, standing over her while he unbuttoned his dress shirt, smouldering emerald-green eyes locked to the silvery-grey cobweb-fine bra and panties she sported and the firm, soft curves they enhanced. 'Your eyes are so unusual,' she whispered, and then wanted to cringe at herself for saying it just at that moment.

'As I said, my only inheritance from my mother,' Saif muttered, his shirt fluttering to the floor, exposing an impressive bronzed torso composed of chiselled abs and a flat, taut stomach and the intriguing little furrow of black hair that ran down below his waistband. 'But I didn't like being different as a child when everyone else's eyes were dark. You occasionally see blue eyes in the desert tribes but never this shade.'

Something clenched almost painfully in Tati's stom-ach as she looked up at him. He came down on the bed beside her, naked and aroused and, oh, so sexy to her riveted gaze. 'I *like* your eyes,' she framed unevenly, her chest lifting as she dragged in a sustaining breath.

His expert mouth toyed with hers while he released her bra and explored the pouting swells and hard tips eager for his attention. He trailed his lips down to tease those rosy, sensitive crowns and her hips rose and she gasped, her entire body shimmying on an edge of gathering anticipation, desire twisting sharp as a knife inside her, tensing every muscle. He skimmed away the panties, parted her thighs and she trembled, feeling shy, tempted to say no but too aroused to have that discipline.

And then he employed his tongue on her and exquisite sensation flooded her. He dipped a finger into her tight channel and her spine arched, the craving climbing again. Melting heat liquefied her pelvis, excitement gripping her taut, and before she could even work out what was happening to her, she became a creature only capable of response, so worked up to a peak that she could only moan and gasp while her body moved in a compulsive rhythm. When she reached a climax it was fast and furious, ripping through her quivering length in an explosion of raw heat and ecstasy, leaving her flopping back against the pillows, limp as a noodle.

Saif dug into the cabinet beside the bed and donned protection. 'We will take no further risks,' he murmured with a slanting, charismatic smile.

Relief filled Tati because she had been thinking that perhaps she ought to go out and look for an English-speaking doctor and ask for replacement pills. But wouldn't Saif's precautions be sufficient until she went back to England to see her mother and reclaimed her possessions from her uncle's home? Convinced that she no longer needed to worry on that score, Tati wrapped her arms round him as he came down to her again. Her body was still pulsing with the aftermath of satiation and highly sensitive.

'I've been thinking about this moment all day and

all evening,' Saif groaned, startling green eyes alight with desire.

'*All* day?'

'Yes.'

'Then why did we wait this long?' she whispered as he shifted against her tender core, sliding into her in a sure rocking motion that sent her heart rate flying.

'You tell me,' Saif urged thickly, awash with surprise at the sheer mutuality of sex with Tatiana.

With a twist of his lean hips he pushed deep and fast into the tight, damp welcome awaiting him and he listened with satisfaction to his bride moan with a pleasure that only echoed his own.

His hard, insistent rhythm enthralled her in the wild ride that followed. Excitement roared higher for her with his every thrust. She moved against him, lost in the experience as her excitement rose higher and higher, the need tugging at her every sense pushing her to a frenzied peak where only mindless sensation controlled her. When the glorious wave of excitement tipped her over the edge, she cried out in writhing delight before the last of her energy drained away, leaving her limp and winded.

Saif thrust away the bedding and fell back from her. 'I'm hot…'

Tati grinned and rolled closer, a possessive hand smoothing down over his heaving chest. 'Yes, *very* hot.'

Saif sat up and pulled her to him. 'And you're joining me in the shower.'

'Why? I'm not fit for anything else right now,' she protested, shy about getting out of bed naked in front of him and knowing how silly that was after what they had shared.

'I'm not ready to let go of you yet,' Saif told her truthfully, his fertile imagination already arranging her in erotic positions round the marble bathroom and seeing possibilities everywhere. *Cool off*, his brain told him, *step back, regain control*, because he suddenly felt as though he were in dangerous territory, a territory without rules or boundaries and not his style at all.

That uneasy feeling, that sense of wrong, stabbed at him because Saif liked everything laid out neat and tidy, nothing left to chance. And yet here he was with a wife who wasn't a genuine wife, a lover who wasn't a simple lover and a friend who wasn't a real friend. Where was he supposed to go next? What was his end goal?

And even though Tati knew in her heart of hearts that she shouldn't go there, she was too curious to silence the question brimming on her lips. 'And when will you be ready?'

Having switched on the shower, Saif swung back to her, startlingly handsome with his black hair tousled, his green eyes very shrewd, sharp and bright, his strong jawline defined by black stubble. 'Ready for what?' he queried.

'Ready to let me go?' she almost whispered in daring clarification, sliding past him to take refuge behind the tiled shower wall where he could no longer see her.

Saif froze. 'You're asking how soon we can decently go for a divorce without unduly surprising anyone?' he murmured flatly, unprepared for that sudden far-reaching question and wishing she hadn't asked before he had even had the time to decide on the wisest approach to their predicament. 'Possibly six months…a year? I don't really know yet. We *should* make it look as though we've given the marriage a fair chance before throwing in the cards.'

Six months to a year, Tati mused, thinking what a very short space of time that was. A mere blink and their relationship would be over, done and dusted, ready for the archives. Her tummy hollowed out and sank while she busied herself washing her hair, her movements slowing as she became aware of the little muscles she had strained and the ache between her thighs, the inescapable reminders of their intimacy. Friends with benefits, she reminded herself doggedly, but that tag no longer enjoyed the same exhilarating ring of daring that it had first seemed to have. Indeed, all of a sudden that style of thinking seemed a little sad and immature, she acknowledged ruefully. Saif was making it very clear that what they currently had was a casual fling with an ending scripted in advance.

An ending written and decided at the same instant they had married, she reminded herself. There was nothing personal about his decision, she reasoned, determined not to take umbrage. Saif could never have planned to stay married long-term to the bride his father had picked for him and she could hardly blame him for that, could she? Saif was way too sophisticated to settle for an arranged marriage with a stranger. And when the stranger was also an unsuitable foreigner, a divorce was a fairly predictable conclusion.

Of course, *she* wanted a divorce as well, Tati assured herself. Naturally, she wanted to reclaim her own life again. Yet it was a challenge for Tati to consider a future that she had never been free to consider before. And *would* she be free?

After all, for how long would her marriage to Saif ensure that her uncle would continue paying her mother's expenses? Now that he had got the money he wanted, it was difficult to have faith in the older man's word. Perhaps her mother *would* eventually have to be moved to a cheaper care facility, Tati reasoned unhappily. Beggars couldn't be choosers. There were worse options, she reminded herself impatiently. Whatever happened, she would handle it and she would help her mother to handle it too. Although, had Saif meant it when he had said that from now on *he* would handle her mother's care bills? But, for how long would he be prepared to do that? Would there be a divorce settlement that covered that need?

Tomorrow, she decided, she would phone the nursing home to check on the older woman. She would also ring her mother's cousin, Pauline, who lived only yards from the care facility and who, as Mariana's only other visitor, always had a more personal take on Mariana's condition. She would discuss the possibility of a move with Pauline.

How could she possibly accept *more* money from Saif? Neither she nor her mother were his responsibilities. They could not acknowledge on the one hand that theirs was not a real marriage and then behave as though it were when it came to money. She had to grow up and stop looking to other people to support her, Tati told herself in exasperation. Saif didn't owe her anything!

CHAPTER SEVEN

ALMOST THREE WEEKS into their stay, the bridal couple were viewing the catacombs beneath Paris.

Saif was uncomfortable with his surroundings. He had done all the tourist stuff without complaint for his wife's benefit. He had taken her for a cruise on the Seine and they had climbed the Eiffel Tower at night when it was an illuminated beacon of golden light across the city. He had even dutifully snacked on macarons at the famous Ladurée, while treacherously thinking that they could not match similar Alharian delicacies. But the catacombs were proving a step too far for him because he felt claustrophobic below the low ceilings, and the skulls and remains of six million souls stacked up to make artistic patterns in the walls did not improve his mood. Tatiana might enjoy the morbid atmosphere, but it spooked him.

Tati sidled up behind Saif, forcing his bodyguards to back away, and stretched up to cover his eyes with her hands. 'I'm a zombie… *Run!*' she whispered in the creepiest voice she could contrive.

Saif whirled round and gazed down into her lovely smiling face as she giggled, eyes dancing with mischief. It was one of those occasions when she made him feel twice her age, yet it was also one of those times he cherished because she brightened his days like sunshine while simultaneously turning the darker hours into sensual experiences of indescribable pleasure. He valued a bride, blessed with such advantages, obviously he valued her greatly.

That wasn't something he thought about much, though, because she had been with him round the clock since their marriage. He did know, however, that he wasn't looking forward to her departure the following day for a trip back to England to see her mother. She had refused the offer of his company, saying it was unnecessary. He should have been relieved by that breezy dismissal because he had a duty to return to Alharia and see his own parent, not to mention needing to deal with at least a dozen tasks he had been unable to tackle from a distance. For the first time he was acknowledging how much he missed his father and how lucky he had been in the older man's reliable care. Yet Tati's regular references to her mother and her deep attachment to her often made him wonder what he had missed out on.

As a further complication for Saif, there were the worrying irregularities uncovered by the investigation agency he had initially hired to provide him with a background check on his bride. As yet he had no idea what those anomalies meant, and he didn't want to upset Tatiana with concerns that might yet prove to be groundless. He wished to handle that matter in person, rather than allow a member of his staff to deal with such a confidential matter, but if the agency's suspicions *were* true, there *would* be criminal charges brought, he thought with angry disgust.

'Sometimes…you are way too serious,' Tati scolded

softly, a fingertip gently tracing the firm sculpted line
of his full lower lip.

'But I have you to remind me of the lighter side of
life,' Saif countered, closing an arm round her to move
her on. 'Let's get out of here…we're eating out tonight.'

'It's sort of our last night,' Tati muttered abstractedly, small fingers toying with the magnificent emerald that hung on a chain round her slender neck as they
emerged back into the sunshine, the light momentarily
blinding her.

Saif had somehow contrived to talk her out of returning to England the week before and she wasn't quite
sure how he had done it, because she did miss that
regular connection with her mother, slender though it
was. It was true that her mother didn't look for her if
she was absent. Indeed, Mariana had to be introduced
to her daughter at every visit because she no longer recognised her. The time for producing the family photo
albums and reminding Mariana was long past because
it only confused and upset the older woman now to be
confronted with faces and events she had forgotten.
So, Tati was accustomed to a mother who greeted her
each time as a stranger. And every time, it broke her
heart a little more.

For dinner, she picked a dress from her array of
choices that she had been saving for a special occasion. It was a cerise-pink print with slender straps and
that whole summery vibe somehow encapsulated the
holiday spirit of freedom that she had revelled in since
her arrival in Paris. Saif, she thought ruefully, really
knew how to show a woman a good time. Although
he spent several hours a day working, he had devoted
more time to ensuring that she enjoyed herself. And

whether they had been admiring the gorgeous cathedral of Sainte-Chapelle or wandering hand in hand around Saint-Germain-des-Prés, where she had explored intriguing little shops full of wonders or sat outside cafés watching the world go by, Saif had made a praiseworthy and highly successful effort to entertain her. She had gathered a handful of little gifts that would make her mother's eyes sparkle but she felt guilty as hell for not returning sooner to England.

She had worried too when she hadn't heard anything more from Ana and her texts had failed to receive a response. She was beginning to suspect that the beach wedding that her cousin had been so excited about hadn't happened because Ana documented the big moments in her life with photos and she would definitely have sent at least one photo. Sadly, Tati was reluctant to contact her uncle and aunt to check on Ana's well-being because of the way they had behaved at the wedding in Alharia. She would be staying in a hotel near the care home because she wasn't sure that her relatives would even be willing to offer her hospitality.

'I'll have to pack up and collect my stuff from my uncle's house while I'm in England,' she sighed over dinner in a sophisticated bistro in possession of several Michelin stars that evening.

'No, that would be unwise. You should *avoid* visiting Fosters Manor,' Saif startled her by intoning with a harsh edge of warning to his dark drawl.

'Why on earth would you say that?'

Saif studied her. She was pretty as a picture in her dress, blond hair gleaming below the low lights, soft blue eyes politely enquiring, so naturally lively that she exuded a positive glow of vibrance, but she was also so

trusting that she would be innately vulnerable to anyone wishing her ill.

As Saif looked, a stab of lust pulsed in his groin and
he almost winced at his own predictability. *That* was
beginning to bother him and make him think that the
absence of his bride for a week would do him good. He
couldn't afford to want Tatiana too much or too often,
nor could he allow himself to depend on her for anything when she was only passing through his life. It was
the first time he had ever had a longer, more intimate relationship with a woman and he told himself that it was
excellent practice for the future when he would surely
find a more lasting partner. Unhappily, however, Tatiana, with all her little individual quirks and inherent
sensuality, didn't feel like a practice run for *any* other
woman. Even so, he knew that he didn't have Tatiana
to keep and he acted accordingly.

'Why did you say that?' Tati pressed again, her
smooth brow furrowing.

'Your uncle and aunt are hostile towards you, and I
don't trust them,' Saif told her truthfully.

'You think they might murder me and bury me below
the floorboards?' Tati teased.

'Safety concerns are not a joke, Tatiana,' Saif sliced
back, pushing away his serving of Baba au Rhum with a
frown as his appetite died. 'If you *do* choose to visit your
relatives, keep your bodyguards with you at all times.
But there is no need for you to visit their home merely to
collect your possessions. That can be arranged for you.'

'I don't want my aunt Elizabeth going through my
belongings,' Tati said with distaste. 'And that's what
would happen if I don't go myself. Are you serious
about bodyguards accompanying me to England?'

'Of course. You are my wife, the Crown Princess of Alharia, and as such require security measures,' Saif parried without hesitation. 'It's not as though you wear a label saying that you are not my "real" wife, as you are so fond of telling me…or as though anyone wishing me harm would even believe that.'

Tati reddened and shifted uncomfortably in her chair. That was a comment she had regularly made as much for her own benefit as his, because there had been several occasions of late when she had felt that they had crossed boundaries that she had not foreseen at the outset of their agreement. For a start, Saif could not be dissuaded from buying her gifts, not least the huge emerald currently nestling above her breasts.

He seemed to be the sort of guy who liked to buy things for women, and time and time again he had surprised her. She had a gorgeous silk scarf that had cost the earth, designer shoes that looked as though they had been sprinkled with stardust and a diamond bracelet that was blinding in daylight. On her twenty-second birthday, he had engulfed her in gifts and treats and that lavish desire to spoil her rotten had touched her to the heart. There had been a whole host of presents from flowers to little trinkets she had admired. He was ridiculously generous and totally out of touch with what being friends with benefits should encompass—that being, in her view, a much looser and more casual connection.

Only she could hardly criticise Saif when she had been shamelessly, wantonly hogging his attention whenever she got the opportunity. There was nothing casual about her behaviour, she allowed guiltily. They had had sex on his office desk the day before because she was turning into a stage five clinger who found it hard to keep her distance when he was working for several hours.

'Will you promise me that you will be careful of your security while you are away from me?' Saif pressed gravely. 'Even though you think that my concern is unnecessary.'

Tati nodded hurriedly, disconcerted by his reading her so accurately, something he often did and which she found unnerving. The sea-glass brilliance of his eyes made warmth pool in her pelvis, sent her pulse racing, made it difficult for her to catch her breath.

'You haven't eaten much this evening,' Saif commented.

'I probably ate too much all day,' Tati quipped, reluctant to explain the very slight sense of nausea that had afflicted her when the scent of meat assailed her nostrils. She wasn't actually sick and didn't think that she was falling ill, but her usual enthusiasm for food had recently dwindled. Possibly it was the result of eating too many rich, elaborate meals, she reflected ruefully, thinking how easily she had become accustomed to being thoroughly spoiled on the gastronomic front. Now she was clearly getting fussy, craving salad when there were barely any cold options on offer.

An hour later, she walked into the dressing room off their bedroom to check the case she had already partially packed.

'The staff could have taken care of this,' Saif told her from the doorway, moving forward to glance down into the case with a frown. 'You don't seem to be taking very much.'

'At most I'll be away a week and I won't be going any place where I need to dress up,' Tati proffered.

A week. A kind of relief engulfed Saif. A week was no time for a man accustomed to living without a woman although it was astonishing, he acknowledged, how quickly he had become used to her presence and how rarely she irritated him. He was reserved, a loner, and had always suspected that marriage would be a challenge for him, but Tatiana was accepting rather than demanding and took him as he was. He ran an appreciative fingertip over the porcelain pale expanse of her back, caressing the soft silky skin.

'Need some help getting out of this?' Saif husked, tugging on the strap of the dress.

Tati stifled a grin. 'Go ahead...'

The zip went down, and the dress floated to her feet. She stepped unhurriedly out of her heels, superaware of the fine turquoise silk bra and panties she wore and the intensity of Saif's appraisal. When she glanced up, his stunning green eyes glittered like emeralds and butterflies took flight in her tummy, her body's programmed response to that appreciation as natural as her need to breathe.

Lifting her out of the folds of cloth on the floor, he pinned her slight body to his, a large masculine hand splayed across her bottom to hold her close. His tailored trousers could not hide the hard heat of his erection, and as she felt the raw promise of him against her stomach, fierce desire flashed through her like a storm warning. Her arms snapped round his neck as his mouth came crashing down on hers with a ravaging, smouldering hunger that matched her own.

Somewhere in the background a vaguely familiar

snatch of music was playing, and her brain strove to rise to alert status again. There was a reason why she should know that sound, only it didn't seem important with her fingers raking through Saif's silky black hair while her heart was racing and her body was pulsing with insane arousal. He was tumbling her down on the bed with scant ceremony when she realised that that sound was her mobile phone ringing and that there were very good reasons why she always leapt to answer it on the rare occasion that it rang. Consternation gripping her, Tati broke free of that kiss and rolled over, almost falling off the bed in her haste to reach her clutch bag and the phone within it.

Half-naked, she sat on the floor clutching the silent phone and checked the call that she had missed. It was from her mother's nursing home as she had feared. Within the space of a minute she was ringing back, identifying herself, listening with an anxious expression to what the manager was telling her and asking apprehensive questions, all beneath Saif's frowning gaze. Assuring the older woman that she would be returning to England as soon as she could arrange it, she sat silent, tears prickling her eyes and stinging them before slowly overflowing to drip down her cheeks.

'I should have gone back last week. I should have known better. If anything happens to Mum, I'll never forgive myself for neglecting her,' she whispered brokenly.

'You haven't neglected her. Even the most dutiful daughter is entitled to a holiday.' Saif crouched down in front of her. 'What's happened?'

'Mum has a chest infection…she's had a few of them but they think she'll have to go into hospital this time,'

Tati muttered wretchedly. 'I should've visited her last week, Saif.'

'That wouldn't have prevented her illness,' Saif pointed out shrewdly. 'You will want to return to England as soon as possible. I will make the arrangements.'

While he engaged in phone calls, Tati stayed on the floor, rocking slightly in self-comforting mode as she thought with a shudder about how horribly selfish she had been. She had always placed her mother's needs first…until *Saif* came into her life. And then everything in her world had changed. Saif had turned her world inside out and upside down. Emotions had come surging in a colourful explosion: anger, excitement, attraction, a shocking awakening to all the feelings she had no reason to feel before. And, unforgivably, she had stopped putting her mother first because Saif had turned her head and made her as irresponsible as a teenager.

'I will come with you,' Saif informed her gravely.

'No…no, that's not necessary,' Tati said sharply, reluctant to expose her fragile mother to a stranger, even though she knew that Saif would be kind and respectful. But that protective instinct was hard to combat and, what was more, she didn't want the temptation of Saif being with her in England when she needed to focus solely on her mother.

'I think it is necessary when you will need my support,' Saif overruled.

'If I hadn't been forced to stay abroad, I would never have been away from her for so long,' Tati argued, knowing she was making a veiled and unjust accusation but wanting to punish him as much as she wanted to punish herself. 'Mum's had these infections before. I don't want anyone with me. She gets upset if she sees a strange face, particularly male ones. I don't need you.'

Tati watched his lean, darkly handsome face freeze in receipt of that ungenerous response and her conscience smote her. She didn't need him, couldn't afford to need him, had to persuade herself that she didn't *need* Saif in any corner of her world. Why was it that only at the moment she realised that she *did* crave his support she grasped why it would be even more foolish to rely on him?

Because they weren't a *real* couple or a *real* husband and wife where such troubles as family illness were shared. They were friends with benefits at most, casual lovers at the least and in that type of relationship people didn't get involved in the commitment of deeper problems. And she couldn't afford to forget that because very soon, perhaps sooner than she even believed, she and Saif would be separating, their intimacy at an end. That was what her future held and wanting anything more was nonsensical and unrealistic...

CHAPTER EIGHT

'GO ON,' URGED PAULINE, Mariana Hamilton's cousin, as Tati hovered at the foot of the hospital bed, torn by indecision. 'Your mum's sleeping peacefully. This is the time to go and take care of other things.'

Tati thanked the older woman warmly. In recent days, she had been very grateful for Pauline's unflagging support and affection for her parent. Her mother's chest infection had exacerbated, and she was still in hospital and upsettingly weak. The medical staff seemed to doubt that her mother *could* recover, which had made Tati afraid to abandon her vigil because she didn't want her mother to slip away without her. Lack of sleep had drained her complexion and etched shadows below her eyes.

She had phoned her uncle to update him on her mother's condition but his lack of interest in his sister's state of health had been unhidden. She had explained that she would be calling to collect her possessions and had asked after Ana, relieved but a little surprised to learn that her cousin was currently back at home. If that was true, why on earth hadn't Ana responded to her texts? Tati suppressed her disquiet, which was, after all, only one of several worries haunting her and giving her sleepless nights.

Having initially assured Saif that she would only be away a week, she had now been absent for almost three. He had suggested that he join her, had offered his assistance, had, in short, done everything a committed partner could be expected to do in such circumstances, but Tati had held him at arm's length. After all, their marriage was only temporary, and he had no obligation towards her mother. But at heart, Tati had a far stronger and more personal reason for avoiding Saif: the pregnancy test awaiting her in her hotel bathroom. If her worst fears were proved to have a solid basis in fact, she didn't know what she would do or even how she would face telling him.

Was sheer cowardice the reason that the test had sat unopened for a week? She was ashamed of her lack of backbone but at the same time she was dealing with the awful awareness that her mother's life was slowly and inexorably draining away. For the moment that was sufficient to cope with.

As she settled into the limousine that Saif had insisted she utilise, she nervously fingered the emerald on the chain that hung beneath her silk shirt. It had become something of a talisman through the dark days of stress and loneliness. She missed him *so* much. Her breath caught in her throat as she stifled an angry sob because she was so furious with herself for failing to keep her emotions under control.

When had she begun caring about Saif, needing him, wanting him around? Those feelings had crept up on her without her noticing in Paris and, now she was deprived of him, those longings and the sense of loss inflicted by his absence had only grown stronger.

She had been in England for only a couple of days when she'd registered that her period was very late. At first, she had blamed that on stress. Eventually, she had acknowledged that the smell of certain foods made her tummy roll and that the coffee she usually enjoyed now tasted bitter. Her breasts were tender and bouts of nausea troubled her at odd times of the day. The fear that she could be pregnant had made her very anxious, but it had still taken time for her to muster the courage to buy a pregnancy test. She would do the test once she got back to the hotel, she told herself ruefully. No more putting it off!

Pulling up outside her uncle and aunt's home, Fosters Manor, Tati was enormously conscious that she was making a swanky arrival in a limo accompanied by a carload of diligent security men. As she climbed out, she straightened the light jacket she wore teamed with neat-fitting cigarette pants, a silk top and high heels. Yes, her life and her appearance had certainly changed, she reflected ruefully, heading for the front entrance rather than the rear one that she had once used.

'You can wait for me in the car,' she told the men standing behind her. 'I'll be an hour at most.'

Not one of them moved an inch into retreat, she noted without surprise. They all became uniformly deaf when her requests contravened Saif's instructions, which seemed to encompass keeping her in physical view at all times. Her aunt answered the doorbell wearing a sour expression.

'It won't take me long to pack up,' she assured the older woman quietly.

'It's been done for you,' Elizabeth Hamilton asserted, indicating the dustbin bags messily littering a corner of the dusty hall.

'Oh, thanks,' Tati said stiffly, forcing a fake polite smile and advancing on the collection, leafing through the pile for the only items of value in her care. 'Mum's jewellery box doesn't seem to be here. It's probably still sitting on the dressing table,' she remarked.

Elizabeth's face froze. 'What would you want with that old thing?'

'I want it because it's Mum's. I'll go and fetch it,' Tati said decisively, directing her companions towards the pathetic collection of bags and asking them to put them in the car.

As she started upstairs, her aunt said thinly, 'That box contained some of Granny Milly's pieces.'

'Yes, and they belong to my mother,' Tati retorted crisply. 'They were given to her by *her* mother.'

'I think you and my sister have done well enough out of this family,' Rupert Hamilton informed her from a doorway, his big bluff form spread in an aggressive stance. 'The jewellery should stay with us where it belongs.'

'No,' Tati argued, lifting her chin. 'Any dues my mother or I owed were paid in full in Alharia.'

'Call off your watchdogs!' her uncle instructed with a scowl as two of her protection team followed her upstairs.

Ignoring him, Tati continued up another two flights to her small bedroom. It wasn't quite in the attic, but it was close enough and in bygone days it *had* been a maid's room. It was a relief to see her mother's jewellery box on the dressing table but when she opened it, she found that it contained only the inexpensive costume pieces. A pearl pendant and earrings and a rather distinctive diamond swan brooch were missing. She tucked the box under her arm, wondering what to do next, reluctant to stage a showdown with her relatives that there would be no coming back from, wondering what Saif would advise because he had a cool head.

'Well, well, well, you're looking…*different*.' Ana selected the word with a sneering curl of her lip as she leant against the landing wall. 'Very fancy.'

'Ana!' Tati responded in cheerful relief at seeing her cousin again. 'Why haven't you called me or answered my texts? Did you change your number?'

'Why would I call you when you stole my bridegroom?' Ana asked with wide eyes, shattering Tati with that absurd question.

'What happened with George?' Tati asked gently.

Ana contorted her lovely face into a grimace. 'He only proposed to stop me marrying someone else. He wasn't willing to set a wedding date once I was home again.'

'I'm so sorry,' Tati said truthfully.

'Oh, I'm sure you're not… How could you be?' Ana demanded thinly, her voice a rising crescendo of complaint. 'My departure worked out *very* well for you. You married a billionaire and now travel around in a flippin' limousine with bodyguards! You robbed me of what should have been mine!'

Mindful of the presence of the protection team, Tati winced. 'Let's talk downstairs in private,' she suggested.

'I don't want to talk about it,' Ana told her stridently.

'I want you to step aside, agree to a divorce and give me back the future you stole from me!'

Tati frowned at that preposterous suggestion. Ana talked as if Saif had no will of his own and as though Tati had entered the marriage freely, which she had not. 'It's not that simple, Ana,' she responded quietly.

'It can be as simple as you're willing to make it. I mean, the Prince would be getting a far superior bride in me. I'm a beauty, classy and educated, the perfect fit for a royal role, which you are not!' her cousin proclaimed as she stomped down the stairs in Tati's wake. 'And I saw a picture of him in the papers.'

Tati faltered. 'A picture?'

'Yes…a photo of you with *him* in Paris,' Ana told her bitterly. 'He's wasted on you. He's absolutely gorgeous! I'd never have walked away had I seen him first!'

'That's…unfortunate,' Tati remarked, although she was terribly tempted to laugh out loud. If George had gone ahead and kept his promise to marry her cousin, Ana would have abandoned all thought of Saif, but because George had disappointed her Ana was looking back with regret to what might have been.

'It's more than unfortunate, Tati!' Ana almost spat at her in her resentment. 'It's wrong and unforgivable that you, a member of my own family, should have taken this opportunity from me!'

'Ana…' Tati's voice was reduced to a discreet whisper. 'I married him in your place because your father threatened to stop paying for my mother's care home. Let's please stick to the facts.'

It amazed Tati how calm and unintimidated she now felt in the face of her relatives' animosity. She rather suspected that Saif's attention and support had contributed to the stronger backbone she had developed.

Her cousin gave her a stubborn, stony appraisal and went on downstairs ahead of her. Tati reached the hall with relief, eager to be gone. The box tucked below her arm, however, slid out of her precarious hold and fell on the rug. In that instant as she stooped down to retrieve it, the emerald round her neck swung out from beneath her shirt into view and glittered in the light.

'Good grief!' Ana exclaimed, reaching forward and almost strangling Tati in her eagerness as she yanked her closer to get a better look at the jewel. 'Is that real? A real emerald *that* size? And there're diamonds all around it!'

Tati's fingers closed over the chain to stop it biting into her neck. 'That's enough, Ana…'

One of her bodyguards stepped forward. 'Let the Princess go before you hurt her,' he told Ana curtly.

Disconcerted, Ana dropped the emerald and took a step back. 'I *feel* like hurting her!' she snapped back in a sudden burst of spite.

'You don't mean that,' Tati said gently, but she was taken aback when her cousin slanted her a look of open resentment.

Sadly, she knew and understood Ana well enough to comprehend her feelings. Ana envied what she saw as Tati's good fortune and believed that Tati had moved up in the world at her expense. She took no heed of the reality that Tati had not wanted to marry Saif in her cousin's place. She chose to forget that she had not been willing to marry Saif sight unseen and had opted to turn her back on the marriage. All she saw now was how handsome Saif was, and the designer garments and the valuable, opulent emerald that Tati wore that had ignited Ana's avaricious streak. Ana felt cheated even though she had chosen to walk away.

Unexpected and unwelcome tears stung Tati's eyes as she climbed back into the limousine to be driven back to the hotel. She had always been very fond of her cousin and until now she had had a much warmer relationship with Ana than she had ever had with her uncle and aunt. Rupert Hamilton and his wife had looked at their niece as though they hated her too and she couldn't understand why.

Did she remind her uncle so strongly of her mother? What had she ever done to them to deserve such treatment? Hadn't she done them a favour by marrying Saif when their daughter ran away? Hadn't that been what they wanted her to do? And now that her mother was so ill, couldn't her brother have some compassion and forgive and forget the petty resentments he had cherished throughout his life?

As for her mother's missing jewellery, what was she planning to do about that? It had to be returned. Those were family keepsakes she valued. She would have to phone her uncle and speak to him once tempers had hopefully settled.

Entering the luxury suite that had been put at her disposal, thanks to Saif, who saw no reason why his wife should sleep in one single room when she could have a giant lounge and two bedrooms all to herself, she went into the bathroom to freshen up and the first thing she saw was that wretched pregnancy test. Gritting her teeth, she picked it up, wondering why she was hesitating when she had to find out one way or another. After all, she might be worrying about nothing!

Ten minutes later she sat staring at the result, her tummy flipping at the confirmation she had received. She had told Saif she was on the pill and, whether she liked it or not, that had been a lie when she had accidentally left her contraceptive supply behind in England. After the test she had planned to acquire a fresh prescription with which to return to Alharia, but that precaution would be wasted when she had already conceived.

For an instant her despondency lifted and a sense of wonder filled her while she allowed herself to imagine a little boy or girl, who would be a mix of her genes and the genes of the man she loved. And she *did* love him, she thought ruefully. There was little point telling herself that it was an infatuation that would soon dissipate when she had fallen head over heels for Saif in Paris. Sizzling chemistry had first knocked her off her safe, sensible perch and scrambled her wits, but the connection had turned into a much deeper attachment on her side. They had shared a magical few weeks, and all her common sense had melted away in the face of Saif's charismatic appeal. But there would be nothing magical about his reaction to the latest development, she reflected unhappily. Saif had warned her that a pregnancy would be an undesirable consequence, a *complication*. She shivered at the memory as she changed to return to the hospital.

And how would he feel about having a child with a woman who wasn't a permanent part of his life? With his own history of maternal abandonment, might it not make his reaction even more emotive?

That evening, her mother passed away without ever regaining consciousness. Tati had fully believed that she was prepared, but when it happened shock flooded her. As she left the hospital again, Pauline gave her a consoling hug before heading for the exit that lay closest to her home. When Tati turned away again in search of the limousine, she saw Saif striding towards her across the car park. Her steps quickened. Her gut reaction was to run to him. She had never been more grateful in her life to see anyone. She was at her lowest ebb and Saif had arrived. Without even thinking about it, she flung herself at him.

'You should've let me join you sooner,' Saif scolded, holding her fast, so strong, so reliable, so reassuring.

A stifled sob rattling in her throat, she allowed him to tuck her into the car drawing up. 'I didn't ask you to come and yet here you are.'

'I've been keeping in touch with the hospital, following the situation. I'm so sorry, Tatiana,' he breathed, his deep dark drawl hoarse with sympathy. 'I would have flown over last week, but you were insistent on doing this alone.'

'I've always done stuff like this alone…apart from Pauline, and she only moved here after her husband died, and began visiting Mum a couple of years ago,' she muttered shakily. 'I'm so tired, you wouldn't believe how tired I am.'

'It's anxiety and exhaustion. And you have been skipping meals, which won't have helped,' Saif remarked with disapproval.

'Sometimes I haven't been hungry… How do you know that?' And then comprehension set in. 'The protection team…my goodness, they're like a little flock of spies, aren't they?'

'It is their job to look after your well-being in my

absence. I also believe you visited your aunt and uncle today and that there was an unpleasant scene,' Saif breathed in a driven undertone. 'I did ask you to stay away from them.'

'Later, Saif,' she sighed, her face buried in a broad shoulder as he kept his arm round her and she drank in the warm familiar scent of him. 'We can talk about it later.'

Afterwards, Tati barely remembered returning to the hotel. She did recall having a meal set in front of her and Saif encouraging her to eat. She had the vaguest recollection of her determination to have a bath and although she recalled getting into the warm scented water, she did not recall getting out of it again. She wakened alone in the bed and, in reliving the day's sad events, suddenly felt a fierce need for Saif's presence. She slid out of bed and padded out to the lounge where he was working on his laptop while watching the business news.

'Sorry, I just collapsed, didn't I?' She sighed. 'Now I have arrangements to make.'

'Those arrangements are being dealt with by my staff. The care home manager permitted me access to your mother's wishes with regard to her interment. I believe she wrote her instructions before she even entered the home,' Saif told her, striving not to stare at her in the fine cotton top and shorts he had put her in after he had lifted her fast asleep out of the bath.

Days of watching her mother's slow decline had marked her, bringing a new fragility to her delicately boned face and shadowing her eyes but in no way detracting from her luminous beauty. He shifted where he stood, uncomfortably aroused. He had pretty much stayed in that condition since he'd found her asleep in the bath and, in the circumstances of her grief, he was anything but proud of his susceptibility.

The weeks without her had been long and empty. For the first time, small foolish things had annoyed him: stodgy courtiers, petty squabbles, long boring meetings. Usually he took such issues in his stride as part and parcel of his life as his father's representative, but recently his temper had taken on a hair-trigger sensitivity and he had had to watch his tongue. His father's adviser, Dalil Khouri, had infuriated Saif by drawing the Emir's attention to a photograph in the newspapers of that stupid kiss in Paris, using it as ammunition in his eagerness to show Tatiana to be an unsuitable wife, who lacked the formality and restraint Dalil believed a royal wife should have. Of course, Dalil had only been trying to do Saif a favour by encouraging his father's disapproval in the belief that it would enable Saif to request a divorce sooner. It had been unexpectedly funny, however, when the Emir startled them all by chuckling and telling his son that he had hoped he would have fun in Paris and, by the looks of it, he *had*.

Tatiana was grieving for her lost parent in a way he himself had never had the chance to do, for how could he have grieved for a woman he had never met, a woman who had walked away while he was still a babe in arms? For that reason he was keen to give his wife all the support he could during so testing a time.

'Thanks,' Tati said in a wobbly voice. 'You know, I thought I was prepared for this.'

Saif set down the laptop and rose fluidly upright, very tall and dark and breathtakingly handsome in the open-necked black shirt and jeans he now wore. Her heart skipped a beat, her mouth ran dry as she thought of what she was hiding from him and instinct almost made her hand slide protectively across her still-flat stomach. She resisted the urge while wondering if she ought to be afraid.

How big a complication would her pregnancy prove to be? Would he ask her to consider a termination? Although he had no hope of persuading her into that choice, she conceded ruefully. She wanted her child even if it hadn't been planned, even if that was an inconvenient preference. But at the same time, she also wanted her child to have a father, because she hadn't had one of her own and knew how much that could hurt.

She would tell him about the baby once they had returned to Alharia, she decided, when life had calmed again, when she had recovered from the first vicious onslaught of loss and felt more able to cope with the stress.

'Tell me about your visit to your relatives,' Saif prompted.

Tati winced. 'Actually, I wanted your advice about something,' she admitted, and she told him about her mother's jewellery. 'She was given the pearls on her eighteenth birthday and the diamond brooch on her twenty-first and I want them back because they have great sentimental worth and Mum loved them.'

'Leave the matter with me. I will handle it,' Saif assured her.

Tati breathed in deep. 'I didn't…er…want to get a solicitor or anything involved,' she warned him. 'When all is said and done, they are still my family.'

'Even when a family member assaults you?'

Tati paled. 'It *wasn't* an assault! The emerald simply attracted Ana's attention and she wanted a closer look at it.'

'If you say so,' Saif sliced in, even white teeth flashing against his bronzed skin, his spectacular green eyes unimpressed by that plea and cool as ice. 'But I say that you are not safe in that house and that you will not be returning there unless I am with you.'

And she thought that that protective instinct of his was one very good reason why she had fallen in love with him. After all, nobody had ever tried to protect Tati before. When she had been oversensitive as a child her mother had simply talked to her about the need to grow a tougher skin. At school she had been bullied and the bullying had been even worse in her uncle's house. Saif, however, stepped right in to help and protect on instinct. And that drew her, of course, it did, particularly when she was feeling vulnerable and raw. Yet she was equally aware that normally she cherished the concept of independence and was keen to make her own decisions, options that her mother's illness had long denied her.

Saif extended a hand to her and drew her down on a sofa beside him. 'Now share your happiest memories with your mother with me...it will help you to keep them alive and turn your thoughts in a better direction. I have no memories whatsoever of my mother, so make the most of what you have left.'

Tears burned and brimmed in her eyes and she blinked them away, digging deep for self-discipline before speaking.

In the early hours, she climbed into bed, lighter of heart and having talked herself hoarse. Saif emerged from the en-suite bathroom still towelling himself dry, black hair ruffled, green eyes very bright against his bronzed skin. Her gaze strayed down the long length of his body, grazing wide shoulders, corrugated abs, a taut, flat stomach, and turbulent warmth tugged at the heart of her, shocking her with its urgency. She lay down and closed her eyes.

'My life felt dull without you around,' Saif breathed in a driven undertone.

Heartened by that admission, Tati slid her hand across the divide between them and closed it over his. 'You can't expect ordinary routine to live up to three sunny weeks in Paris,' she teased.

'It's not a matter of comparisons. You're not always going to be a part of my life and I must adjust to that,' Saif pronounced very seriously.

For a split second it was as though he had plunged a knife into her heart with that reminder and then her natural spirit rallied. 'But I'm here right now,' she pointed out daringly.

'Yes, you are,' Saif conceded huskily as he tugged her closer. 'And nobody has the ability to foretell the future.'

'That's right,' she agreed, frustrated when he made no further move.

'You must be tired.'

'Not since I slept the evening away,' Tati told him, leaning over him and then slowly, gently bringing her lips down to his, because there was a great driving need in her to reconnect again and to make the most of every moment left with him.

Saif lifted a hand and framed her flushed face. 'I assumed touching you would be inappropriate. I didn't want to get it wrong.'

'I want to forget the last three weeks,' she confessed. 'I don't want to think.'

He circled her lips with his and hauled her down to him without any further ceremony, tasting her soft lips with a scorchingly hungry kiss. While he kissed her, he dealt with removing her pyjamas with ruthless expertise. He rolled her under him, parting her legs and sliding his lean hips between her thighs. Her entire body stimulated, she quivered, momentarily mindless with desire, her fingers curling convulsively into his smooth back as he drove into her in one masterful stroke. Jolt after jolt of pure pleasure coursed through her as the excitement mounted. All the tension that had held her taut was now locked in her pelvis and when the exhilaration peaked and she almost passed out from the intensity of her climax, she held fast to him in the aftermath, lost in the blissful wash of relaxation.

'I almost forgot to use a condom.' Saif laughed as he rolled back, carrying her with him. 'You get me so worked up I can still be careless.'

And that was the instant that she should have spoken up. She recognised it as the moment immediately and froze, the truth of her condition clawing at her conscience, but her lips remained stubbornly sealed. Her confession might well lead to an angry confrontation and more distress and worry and right then she couldn't face it.

Reality reminded her that she had entered an intimate relationship in which conception was forbidden from the outset. She had acted without due consideration or concern because the risk of pregnancy had not crossed her mind. Saif might joke that she made him careless, but *she* was the one who had been thoughtless and had chosen not to speak up at the time her oversight occurred. She had conserved her pride rather than lose face and she had simply hoped for the best.

And the price of that silence had now truly come home to roost and there would be no escaping the fall-out. Saif would hate that she hadn't warned him. He would hate how long it had taken for her to come clean and own up. He would hate the whole situation and maybe by the end of it he would hate her as well...

CHAPTER NINE

TATI STUDIED SAIF over breakfast in the sun-dappled courtyard, around which their wing of the old palace was built. Her surroundings were beautiful, and she was very much at peace there. Colourful mosaic tiles covered the ground around the softly playing fountain that kept the air fresh and cool. Palm trees and mature shrubs provided shade from the hot sun above while a riot of exotic flowers tumbled round the edges of the dining area.

Saif was checking the business news on a tablet, black hair flopping over his brow, lustrous black lashes shading his spectacular eyes.

'I need to talk to you this evening,' she mustered the courage to announce, because if she mentioned that necessity in advance she couldn't then weaken and back out of it again.

'What about?' Saif sent her an enquiring glance from glittering light green eyes that riveted her where she sat and sent entire flocks of butterflies fluttering inside her.

'Just something important that we need to discuss,' Tati extended uneasily.

Saif did not like to be kept in suspense. 'What's wrong with right now?'

Like the answer to a prayer, Dalil Khouri appeared in the doorway opposite, bowing his head deferentially as he greeted them and addressed Saif. Saif rose with a determined smile to greet the older man. His unfailing courtesy in the face of the constant demands on his time never failed to impress Tati. He was very tolerant. She hoped he brought that tolerance to the fore when she admitted that she was carrying his baby. But she needed the rest of the day to work out the right words with which to frame that admission and that was why Dalil's interruption had been timely.

Tati had learned that the royal palace was always a frantically busy place. Everyone had a role and a schedule, even her. She was currently attending language classes every morning while also enjoying the benefits of a tutor employed to give her a crash course on Alharia's history and culture.

'You cannot be left so ignorant of our country that you will be embarrassed,' Saif had told her. 'People ask questions at the events we attend. I hope you won't object to being effectively sent back to school.'

And she had merely chuckled and shaken her head while wondering what the point of such lessons was intended to be when she wasn't likely to be Saif's wife for longer than a year at most. But at a dinner she had attended with him at an embassy earlier that week, she had been grateful for the ability to join in on a discussion relating to Alharia's current dealings with one of its neighbours.

Only two weeks had passed since her mother's funeral. Her uncle and aunt had not put in an appearance, which had very much shocked Saif's sense of propriety. That evening while she was packing, Saif had gone out for a couple of hours and when he had reappeared he had handed her two worn jewellery boxes that were familiar to her. In wonder she had studied the pearl set and the swan brooch that had belonged to her late mother and she had looked at Saif and asked, 'How on earth did you manage to get hold of them?'

'I simply told your uncle that your mother's possessions should be returned to you. He apologised and blamed your aunt for taking the items. He said she was like a magpie with jewels. I believe that your relatives were so used to taking advantage of your good nature that they assumed they could get away with their behaviour... Now they know different,' he had completed with satisfaction.

'Thank you... Thank you so much,' Tati had told him, relieved that he had understood how precious her mother's former possessions now were to her.

Back then, on the brink of a return to Alharia, it hadn't occurred to her that she might struggle to find the optimum moment in which to tell Saif that she was pregnant. Unfortunately, work had engulfed him in long working hours when they had first come back, and he had been very much preoccupied. They were only ever reliably alone in bed, but she had shrunk from destroying those brief moments of trust and relaxation with a shock announcement. Only now, after almost two weeks of procrastination, was it finally dawning on her that there *was* no right moment for such a revelation. As if the timing were likely to influence his attitude!

Thoroughly exasperated by her apprehensions, Tati thrust away her plate impatiently and leapt up, stepping away from her chair. Her head swam sickly and she tried to grab the stone table as everything swam out of focus, but the darkness rushed in on her and she folded down onto the ground in a heap.

She surfaced groggily to discover that she was lying on her bed with an older man gazing down at her. 'I'm Dr Abaza, Your Highness, the Emir's personal physician. May I have your permission to examine you?'

'Is that necessary?'

'It's necessary,' Saif asserted, stepping forward out of the shadows to make her aware of his presence. 'I would prefer you to have an examination. You passed out. It's possible that you have caught an illness.'

Registering the gravity stamped on his lean, dark features, Tati subsided, quietly responding to the doctor's polite questions and realising too late the direction in which those questions were travelling. Bearing in mind that she was on the very brink of telling Saif the truth, she could not lie, and as she answered she could not work up the courage to look at him. Dr Abaza completed a brief physical examination and smiled at her. 'I will carry out a test later to be sure, but I am almost certain that you are pregnant. Certain distinct signs characterise a first pregnancy. Low blood pressure most probably caused you to faint. It is a common issue in the first trimester but, naturally, you must guard against it lest you injure yourself in a fall.'

The silence seemed to stretch into every corner of the room and back again and Tati could hardly bring herself to draw breath. She heard Saif thank the doctor. Ice trickled through her veins as he closed the door again.

'How long have you known?' The simplicity of that first question startled Tati.

'I… I—'

'When the doctor told you, it was obvious that you

were not surprised. You were already aware of your condition,' Saif conjectured with disturbing discernment. 'For how long have you known?'

'Well, I suspected weeks ago but I sort of…sort of chose to ignore my suspicions.'

'You *ignored*?' Saif emphasised in open disbelief.

'I didn't think it was very likely and I was coping with Mum's illness. I didn't do a test until just before you arrived in England,' she recited breathlessly as she dug in her elbows and sat up.

'But that was over two weeks ago!' Saif exclaimed.

'I was planning to tell you this evening.'

'You should have told me the instant you had grounds for concern,' Saif grated, striding away from her only to swing back, green eyes iridescently bright with anger in his lean bronzed face. 'You have been less than honest with me.'

In receipt of that condemnation, Tati lost colour and slid her legs off the side of the bed. At least he hadn't outright labelled her a liar, she thought ruefully. But she also wondered if his own mother's desertion had made him so wary of women and pregnancy that he expected the very worst of her.

Saif made a commanding staying motion with one hand. 'Don't stand up until you're quite sure that you're not dizzy.'

'Telling you sooner than this that I was pregnant wouldn't have changed anything.' Tati argued her case tautly, still perched on the side of the bed.

'Regrettably, nothing you have yet shared tells me *how* this happened,' Saif framed grimly. 'I believed we had taken every possible precaution.'

'I know that I told you it was safe that first night

in Paris. I *was* on the pill, but then I had to pack in a hurry to fly to Alharia for the wedding and I forgot to bring the pills with me. So, I wasn't *lying* when I said there wasn't a risk… I just hadn't thought the situation through properly,' she explained uncomfortably. 'It was only afterwards that I realised I'd left the pills behind in England and that I'd already been off them a couple of days before we…er…got together…and that that was dangerous. It was a genuine oversight, but just then it didn't seem like much of a risk.'

'How did unprotected sex fail to strike you as a risk?' Saif shot at her with raw incredulity.

Tati reddened at his tone and then she shrugged. 'It was only the once and I assumed I would still be semi-protected by the pills I had already taken that month. You were very careful after that, so I thought we would be all right. I didn't see any reason to worry you when there was probably going to be nothing to worry about.'

'You should have told me. I had a right to know,' Saif breathed in a driven undertone as he paced in front of the doors that led out to a balcony.

'Yes, but the only option at that point would have been me taking a morning-after pill and I didn't feel comfortable with that option,' Tati admitted bluntly.

'I would not have suggested that, but I dislike the fact that you chose to keep me in the dark when I am *equally* affected by this development!' Saif shot back at her crushingly.

It was a fair point and she didn't argue. 'Well, at least you know now,' she pointed out, feeling forced into the role of Job's comforter.

'I should think that half the palace is now aware of Dr Abaza's diagnosis!' Saif retorted drily. 'He will have reported straight back to my father and I would imagine others will have overheard sufficient to comprehend.'

'For goodness' sake…' Tati groaned in embarrassment.

'Why? It's not as though it is something that you could keep a secret for much longer.' Saif subjected her to a long intense appraisal. 'You're carrying my child. That is very big news in Alharia so we could not hope to keep it to ourselves. I very much doubt that you currently appreciate how much this development will impact our situation, which is naturally why I tried to ensure that it didn't occur.'

Tati stood up and lifted her head high, rumpled blond hair rippling round her shoulders, blue eyes mutinous. 'Oh, do stop talking in that deadly tone, as though it's the end of the world. It's a baby…and I love babies! I mean, we didn't plan this, and I know you like to plan stuff in advance, but how much difference can one little baby make to our *situation*, as you call it?'

Saif dealt her a bleak appraisal. 'A huge difference. I would never have chosen to conceive a child in a marriage that is not intended to last. I *know* what that situation is like from my own childhood. It is unfair to our child and will likely affect his or her emotional well-being and sense of security.'

'Don't talk to me as though I'm stupid, Saif,' Tati countered angrily, her eyes flaring with temper. 'Neither of us planned this. Both of us tried to be careful. Yes, I agree it's *not* perfect, but neither of us had perfect when it came to parents and *we* survived!'

'It's clear to me that you have still not thought through the ramifications of this development and the effect it will have on *your* freedom,' Saif grated, raking lean brown fingers through his black hair in a gesture of unconcealed frustration. 'My mother didn't want this sort of life in Alharia and she walked away from it. How will you be any different? The main point I would make is that although you grew up without a father and I grew up without a mother, neither of us was torn between two opposing households and cultures.'

'Parents do successfully work together to raise children after a divorce,' Tati protested. 'We're not enemies. We're both rational, reasonable people.'

'If you give birth to a boy he will be an heir to the Alharian throne and he will have to spend the majority of his time in *this* country, which will naturally have an influence on where you choose to live,' Saif spelt out.

'Why would he have to spend the majority of his time here?' Tati demanded with a frown.

'How else could he prepare for his future role? He must grow up amongst our people, with the language and the culture. His education and future training would be of the utmost importance and could not be achieved if his main home were to be in another country. And if you have a girl, she may well be the next ruler because I have every intention of changing the constitution when I ascend the throne. It is what our people want and expect in these days of equality,' Saif completed, his darkly handsome features troubled and taut. 'I would not want to see my child, girl or boy, only occasionally or for visits. That would bother me.'

Tati was tense. 'It would bother me as well. So, you're saying that to share a child I would have to make a home for myself in Alharia.'

'Yes. Becoming parents will make a clean break impossible,' Saif delivered heavily. 'I appreciate how much that would detract from your independence.'

Tati was almost paralysed by the pain of hearing Saif refer to the option of 'a clean break.' In that scenario, after a divorce he would never have had to see her again and obviously that would have been his preference. Yet the same concept devastated her even as she finally grasped the obvious truth that the birth of a child would entangle their lives for a long time and that, self-evidently by his tone, was not what Saif wanted. He didn't *want* to share a child with an ex who lived elsewhere. How could she hold such honesty against him? But why did he have to be such a pessimist about the future? Why couldn't he make the best of things as she was striving to do?

'Your attitude annoys me,' Tati told him honestly. 'I tend to believe that the mixing of two cultures and lifestyles is more likely to enrich our child.'

'In an ideal world,' Saif slotted in grimly. 'But we don't live in one. If this *were* an ideal world, I would be able to openly acknowledge to my father that I have a close relationship with my half-brother, Angelino Diamandis.'

'You have a brother?' Tati exclaimed in complete surprise, disconcerted by that sudden revelation from a man who could, at the very least, be described as reticent.

'He is two years younger than I, born from my mother's second marriage. I sought him out years ago, but I think initially I wanted to meet him to see what he had that I didn't because my mother stuck around to raise him,' he pointed out curtly, the darkening of his bright eyes the proof of how emotive that topic was for him.

'Instead I discovered that my half-brother had enjoyed little more mothering than I had and I was surprised at the depth of the bond that developed between us. That relationship, however, had to remain a secret because I did not want to upset my father. He was devastated by my mother's desertion and the wound never really healed because after her second marriage she was rarely out of the newspapers. She was a great beauty and she revelled in publicity,' Saif explained ruefully. 'Children born across the divide of divorce are often placed in difficult positions out of loyalty to their respective parents. Step-families are created and other children follow. The experience may strengthen some, but it injures others.'

'That relative of yours who owns the house in Paris. Is that your brother?' Tati prompted with sudden comprehension.

'Yes, that house belongs to Angel. He also attended my wedding incognito and I got to spend some time with him before he had to leave again,' Saif told her. 'I value my relationship with my younger brother although it shames me to keep it a secret from my father. However, I cannot mention my mother or her second family to him without causing him great distress, which I obviously don't want to do when his health is poor.'

'He must really have loved her to still be so sensitive… Or is he just bitter?' Tati questioned with open curiosity.

'No, she was truly the love of my father's life, but the marriage was always destined to fail,' Saif opined fatalistically. 'She was too young and worldly, and he was too old and traditional. When you consider the very public social whirl she embarked on after deserting her husband and son in Alharia and her complete lack of regret for what she had done, you realise that they were ill-suited from the start. Whatever else he may be, my father is a most compassionate man. Had she given him the opportunity he would have given her a divorce and there would not have been a huge scandal. But the Emir was not the only one to suffer her loss… I did as well and spent many years wondering why she couldn't have stayed for my benefit.'

'That's very sad,' Tati acknowledged reflectively. 'But not really relevant to us. I'm not planning on deserting anyone, least of all my child, nor am I the sort of person attracted to the idea of publicity.'

'Who can tell what you will be enjoying in a few years' time?' Saif said with sardonic bite, his sheer cynicism infuriating her.

'You are such a pessimist!' Tati exclaimed. 'Do you always expect the very worst of people?'

'I'm a realist, not a pessimist. I would be foolish to ignore the truth that you will be a young and very wealthy divorcee and that inevitably you will remarry, have other children and change from the woman you are now,' Saif breathed, untouched by her criticism.

'I bet that, right now, you are really, *really* regretting that you consummated our marriage!' Tati accused tempestuously.

'My only regret is that I wanted you so much that I went along with that "friends with benefits" idea even though I *knew* from the outset that it was absolute madness!' Saif flung back at her in a raw-edged tone of self-loathing.

Tati froze as though she had been slapped and lost colour. It was clear that Saif could not get onboard with her conviction that they should make the best of her pregnancy. He hadn't planned the conception; he hadn't agreed to it and he seemed unlikely to move on from that position. But it was even worse to be confronted with the truth that he now regretted their relationship in its entirety.

'Madness,' she repeated through taut, dry lips with distaste, feeling totally rejected.

'What else could it be in our circumstances? This relationship of ours is insane and you know it!' Saif condemned harshly. 'Once we had both acknowledged that we didn't want to be married, we should have abstained from sex.'

Tati reddened. 'You weren't a great fan of abstinence either,' she reminded him accusingly.

'I am not solely blaming you,' Saif countered grittily. 'I was also tempted, and I gave way to that temptation, but it is exactly that self-indulgence that has landed us both into this predicament. A divorce is out of the question for the foreseeable future.'

'But why?' Tati prompted in stark disconcertion at that statement.

'It is far too soon for us to separate and I refuse to seek a divorce from a pregnant wife. I should be with you during your pregnancy, offering whatever support I can. I feel equally strongly that for the first crucial years of our child's life we should remain together, trying to be the best parents we can be for our child's benefit,' Saif explained heavily. 'It would be selfish to only consider our own wants and needs. I wouldn't ever want our child to know the pain of not being wanted by a parent.'

His outlook made Tati feel wretched and like the most selfish woman in the world. She stood up to move towards the door, saying, 'I have a language lesson in ten minutes, and I don't want to miss it. We can talk later, and it might help a lot if you could come up with something positive rather than *negative*.'

Saif swore under his breath as she left the room. So fierce was his frustration that he was tempted to punch the wall, but bruises and a loss of temper would not change anything, he reflected with grim resignation. His wife was planning to leave him just as his mother had left his father and her son. Saif, however, was determined not to lose either of them. There was also a very real risk of his losing his child because Tatiana was, he surmised, a great deal more maternal than his mother had been.

In a different scenario he would have been overjoyed at the news that he was to become a father and he was angry at being deprived of that natural response, but it was, sadly, an issue clouded by his own experiences. Being abandoned by his mother soon after birth had hurt and changed his attitude to childbirth and parenthood because he already knew that he could never leave his child as his mother had done.

Yet how could he celebrate the birth of a child in a marriage that was a fake? A marriage that had been deemed over before it even properly began? Tatiana had never given him a fair chance, not one single chance. She had not budged an iota in her attitude since their first day together. She expected and wanted a divorce as her recompense for agreeing to a marriage that she had been blackmailed into accepting. And during the weeks they had been together she had frequently alluded to the prospect of that divorce and was obviously perfectly content with that outcome. And, even more revealing, she had refused Saif's support when her own mother was dying. She had in every possible way treated Saif as though he was superfluous, merely a casual sexual partner in a fling without a future. What she had never done, he thought painfully, was treat him like a friend.

And how much could he blame her for her attitude when he had become her first lover? Tatiana had had a difficult life with little liberty, even less money and few choices, he reminded himself. Furthermore, although she had yet to find it out, she had been ruthlessly used, abused and defrauded by relatives who should have cherished her, most especially after her mother fell ill. Saif frowned, wondering if he should tell her the truth about her grandmother's will and her uncle's wicked greed, but he had withheld what he knew on the basis that the police were in charge of the investigation now and the truth would come out soon enough when arrests were made. Saif had no desire to be the person who broke that bad news and hurt her.

Naturally, that revelation would adversely affect Tatiana because she remained blindly, ridiculously attached to those relatives of hers. From her teenaged years she had depended on them, and they had been all she had once her grandmother died and her mother sank into dementia. She had even excused their greed to Saif by explaining that her uncle had always been hopeless with money and had married an ambitious woman with grand expectations. How would she feel when she appreciated that they had lied and cheated to deprive her of her inheritance and had been busy ever since overspending *her* money as fast as they could?

When that grievous knowledge was unveiled, his bride would be even keener to enjoy the freedom she had never had. The freedom *he* didn't *want* her to have, Saif reflected bitterly. Was it any wonder that he was such a cynic?

Tati struggled through the language lesson with tears burning the backs of her eyes while she fought to relocate some seed of concentration. She struggled to dwell on the positives rather than the negatives of her plight. Saif wanted their baby and was already anxiously considering the potential effect of a divorce on their child. Why didn't he thread her into that problem and realise that if he *stayed* married to her, he wouldn't have to worry about their child's security? Obviously because he didn't *want* to stay married to her, Tati reflected miserably. Why was she set on beating her head up against a brick wall?

And what would it be like to continue living with Saif for another four or five years? Wouldn't that simply make the whole process of breaking up more agonising? It would drag it out and place her under heavier stress. She would always be waiting for the moment when he decided they had stayed together long enough and were in a position to separate. How could a future like that appeal to her?

It would freeze her life and prevent her from moving on. How could she truly move on if she were to be forced to live in Alharia for her son or daughter's sake? The prospect of standing on the sidelines watching Saif with other women, having to share her child with those same women, made her shudder. No, that wouldn't work for her. He would have to come up with a better, more bearable solution. When her mother was ill, she had accepted that being bullied, being forced into a position she didn't want, was a situation she could not escape. But life had changed for her and she herself had changed, she reflected ruefully. Ironically, Saif had made her realise that she was much stronger than she had ever appreciated. With regard to future arrangements between them for their child, she was prepared to be reasonable, but she wasn't a martyr. She would get over him at some stage, but how was she to achieve that if she was still forced to live with him?

Saif spent an hour that afternoon listening to his father wax lyrical about the joys of fatherhood. Thinking of the disappointments the older man had suffered in the wife department convinced Saif that Tatiana had been right to denounce his pessimistic outlook. Somehow, it would all work out, if they both made an effort, if he controlled the urge to lock her up and throw away the key, not because he was a controlling creep, but because, try as he might, he kept on thinking of the way his mother had just abandoned ship and run for greener pastures. Might not Tatiana also choose to bolt if he put too much pressure on her? She was pregnant and she couldn't be feeling well when she was fainting, he reasoned worriedly.

A man famed for his cool, logical approach to problems, he wondered how it was that in a moment of crisis he had said and done everything wrong. He had *told* Tatiana that they would have to stay married for years longer. He had *told* her that she would have to live in Alharia. How could he have been that clumsy, domineering and stupid? And he hadn't *once* mentioned how excited he was about the baby they had conceived.

It was at that point in his ruminations that Dalil

Khouri joined Saif to announce that his wife's cousin, Ana Hamilton, had arrived at the airport and intended to visit them. It was normal for an alert to be sent to the palace when a prospective guest arrived, but Saif frowned at that news, questioning why the woman had chosen to fly to Alharia when only months earlier she had run away as fast as she could sooner than marry him. Was it possible that Ana's parents had already been arrested? Could their daughter be here to plead their case? What else could she be doing in Alharia?

Saif appreciated that it was his task to tell his wife what he had learned several weeks earlier because he could not let her meet with her cousin while still in ignorance of his recent discoveries.

'Have her brought to the palace,' he told Dalil. 'But drive her around for a while—take her to see some tourist sight, or something… I don't want my wife to be taken by surprise or upset and I need some time to prepare her for her cousin's arrival.'

'Of course,' Dalil agreed earnestly. 'The Princess must be protected at all costs from anyone who might seek to take advantage of her.'

Tati was enjoying mint tea and a savoury snack in the courtyard when Saif strode down the stairs into the courtyard to join her. He was breathtakingly handsome in an Italian wool-and-silk-mix suit that was exquisitely tailored to his lean, powerful frame. Her wide blue gaze clung to him and then pulled free of him again, her soft mouth tightening as she told herself off for being so susceptible. *That* kind of nonsense, that mooning over him like a silly sentimental schoolgirl, couldn't continue.

'First of all, I bought these for you in Paris, but after your mother fell ill there didn't seem to be a right time to give them to you,' Saif intoned, setting a jewellery box down on the table. 'This seems the appropriate moment to express my happiness about the child you are carrying and present you with this small gift to mark a special occasion.'

'You must've had to dig deep to find that happiness,' Tati opined tartly.

'You took me by surprise, but once the news sank in, I was thrilled,' Saif asserted defiantly in the face of her dubious look. 'Everything changed for me when you told me that you were pregnant. When my mother walked away from me when I was a baby, it made the whole topic very emotional for me. I tried not to dwell on her abandonment. I suppressed the sadness that that awareness inflicted because I believed that that is what a man must do to be a man...'

'Oh, Saif,' she whispered, her body stiffening as she fought the pressing need to go to him, to comfort him, to soothe the hurt he had felt that he had to deny as an adult man. But that was no longer her role, she reasoned. Furthermore, it was becoming ever more clear to her as he talked that Saif was not driven by love to wish to remain married to her for their child's sake but by fear for their child's hurt in the future. She couldn't fault him for that, she decided heavily, but that he should only want to be with her to be a father for their baby pierced her deeply.

Brushing off those emotional responses, Tati flipped open the box on a superb pair of emerald earrings in the same design as the magnificent pendant she wore. 'Wow,' she whispered without being prompted because it was yet another exciting gift that no sane woman could fail to appreciate. 'They're beautiful—'

'Perhaps you could wear them for dinner tonight,' Saif proposed. 'We have a surprise guest joining us.'

'Oh…and who would that be?' Tati gazed at him enquiringly as she twirled the emerald earrings in the sunlight. She put them on with the kind of defiance that denied that there was anything special about the occasion while reminding herself that she ought at least to enjoy the frills while she still could.

'Your cousin, Ana, is about to arrive here,' Saif imparted. 'Of course, you may be grateful for the company of a female friend at the moment.'

Utterly taken aback by the idea of Ana visiting Alharia, Tati stiffened, wondering if it was crazy to suspect that her cousin might be turning up to give Saif a belated opportunity to see what he had missed out on on his wedding day. When Ana got an idea into her head, it was hard to shift, although even Tati was a touch disconcerted by her cousin's lack of embarrassment at visiting the home of the same man she had refused to marry only weeks earlier. 'Why would I be grateful?'

Saif breathed in deep. 'Because of the discovery you have recently made and the complications—'

'I'm not going to share any of that with Ana!' Tati protested. 'That's *our* business and much too private.'

'I think that is for the best, but before she arrives there is information about your family which I have to share with you,' Saif proffered heavily.

Tati became tense, noting the grave expression he wore. 'What information and about whom?'

'Your uncle and aunt. I'm afraid I genuinely do not know if your cousin was aware of what's been going on for the past few years.'

'Going on?' Tati interrupted. 'What do you mean by "going on"?'

'Three years ago, after your grandmother died, your uncle and her solicitor worked together to deprive you of your inheritance. Your grandmother not only set up a trust to cover the cost of your late mother's care, but she also left the Fosters Manor estate to you.'

'That's impossible,' Tati broke in afresh. 'I wasn't left anything! My uncle told me that.'

Saif ignored the interruption. 'You were to inherit the estate when you reached twenty-one, but you were supposed to enjoy the income from it immediately. In effect your uncle was disinherited in your favour. Your uncle had made continual financial demands on your grandparents during their lifetime and your grandmother apparently believed that he had had his fair share before her death. Unfortunately, she appointed both your uncle and the solicitor, Roger Sallow, as executors of the will. The solicitor was corrupt. Your uncle bribed Sallow to remain silent and at the official reading Sallow read an invalid will that had been written years earlier. Your uncle has since made regular very large payments to the solicitor. The size of those payments probably explains his continuing financial troubles because Sallow became increasingly greedy.'

'I can't believe this…' Tati massaged her pounding forehead with her fingers. 'Granny Milly actually chose to leave it all to *me*?' she exclaimed in disbelief. 'How did you find all this out?'

'The day I married you, I asked a private investigation agency to do a report on you,' Saif revealed tautly. 'At that stage, I knew nothing about you and I wanted the facts. The investigator met with an old friend of your grandmother's who had witnessed the will without actually seeing the contents and she chose to share her concerns with him.'

Tati frowned. 'Her concerns?'

'She knew what your grandmother had originally planned and was very surprised when she saw that nothing changed at the manor after her friend's death, but she didn't come forward because she decided that it was none of her business and she didn't wish to offend anyone. She could, of course, have *asked* to see the will, which was on public record, but she didn't know that,' Saif recounted wryly. 'Basically, she is an elderly woman who didn't want to risk getting involved in what she suspected could be a crime.'

Tati parted bloodless lips. 'A crime?'

'You have been defrauded of your rightful inheritance and that is a crime,' Saif pointed out grimly. 'The investigation agency consulted me as soon as they uncovered the irregularities and I told them to find the evidence and put the whole matter in the hands of the police.'

If possible, Tati turned even paler. *'The police?'* she whispered in horror.

'Fraud has been committed, Tatiana,' Saif asserted grimly. 'How else may such wickedness be handled?'

Tati lifted her aching head high and looked back at him with icy blue eyes of condemnation. 'I don't know, Saif. You would need to tell me because, even though this concerns me, *I* wasn't consulted.'

'I imagine the police will seek some sort of statement from you, but they have all the evidence they require for a prosecution.'

Tati nodded, in so much shock that she was barely

able to absorb what she had been told. She couldn't quite credit her hearing. She had never liked her uncle, but that he could act so basely and deliberately defraud her, while still treating her like a despised poor relation who was a burden, took her breath away. As for the trust that Saif had mentioned, the trust set up to care for her poor mother's needs, the knowledge that that information had been withheld filled her with nauseated rage on her late parent's behalf. She had been controlled and threatened with lies when all along her uncle had had little choice but to keep on paying those care home bills because stopping payment could have drawn dangerous attention to him.

'*When* did you find all this out?' Tati prompted sickly.

'The first week we were married…well, I didn't know the whole story then, but I was informed that there was every sign that your uncle had committed fraud and that he was being blackmailed by the solicitor for his misdeeds.' Saif studied her anxiously because she was very pale even if she was handling the whole business more quietly than he had somehow expected. 'I didn't want to make allegations against your relatives without adequate proof, which is why I remained silent about my suspicions.'

'And why are you finally telling me now?' Tati enquired stiffly, a glint in her unusually bright gaze, resentment and bitterness and anger all flaring at once inside her.

'Only because your cousin is about to arrive and, if the police have made a move against her father, she could be visiting with a plea that you intervene…although, to be frank, I doubt that you have the power now that the police are involved and have the evidence of his crime.'

'I gather you think that Ana must know about this!' Tati commented stiffly.

'I imagine she does,' Saif said very drily.

'I doubt that very much. Ana is spoiled, selfish and materialistic but she's never been dishonest or cruel. There's no way *she's* involved!' Tati told him with firm emphasis.

'Since you are so fond of her, I can only hope that you are correct.'

'No, my belief is that Ana is visiting to subject you to a charm offensive,' Tati mused, grimacing a little at having to voice that opinion because it mortified her.

'*Me?* A charm offensive?' Saif repeated blankly. 'What are you saying?'

'The man Ana ran away from you to marry let her down and now she has regrets about not marrying you.'

'A little late in the day,' Saif remarked as dry as the desert sand.

'As far as Ana's concerned, I'm only a substitute for her and not a very good one at that,' Tati explained as she rose from her seat. 'You're rich, generous and good-looking. She's probably hoping you'll be willing to consider a swap.'

'A *swap*?' Saif sliced back at her in sheer disbelief.

Tati gave him a long, considering appraisal, ticking all the mental boxes he occupied in her head. It was no wonder she had fallen for him like a ton of bricks when he was gorgeous and capable of immense charm when he wished to utilise it. 'Ana isn't particularly intelligent. But, you know, you would still have done much better with her than with me,' she told him ruefully. 'I doubt that my cousin would ever have become accidentally pregnant.'

'I *am* pleased about our baby,' Saif countered fiercely, displeased by the sarcastic tone of words that hinted that her cousin was welcome to him.

Tati flung up her head, blond strands rippling back from her troubled face, her eyes full of newly learned cynicism. 'So you say…'

CHAPTER TEN

ANA LOOKED STUNNING, her golden hair a silken swathe, her brown eyes beautifully made up, her silky short dress showing off long shapely legs. Initially full of peevish complaints about the 'old boring ruin of a castle' she had been dragged to view by some palace official, she soon switched to a playful smile when she realised that she was being rude. She then embraced Tati without hesitation and pouted in disappointment when Saif excused himself to make a phone call.

'Good grief,' she muttered as the door closed behind Tati's husband. 'Saif's even better looking in the flesh! Those cheekbones, that amazing physique!'

'How's everybody at home?' Tati enquired rather stiffly.

Ana sighed. 'Much the same as usual. Mum's nagging Dad about this autumn cruise she fancies and Dad's saying he doesn't want to miss the start of the shooting season. I'm so sorry I was rude when you came to the manor. Everything just got on top—George, the change in your fortunes…and I missed you.'

'I missed you too.' Warmed by that little speech, Tati searched her cousin's face and was fully satisfied that the blonde had no clue that legal problems could be hovering over her family. *She* herself was still struggling to accept the situation that Saif had outlined. She was outraged that he had kept her out of his enquiries and that only Ana's unexpected arrival had persuaded him to come clean about what was *her* business, rather than his. At heart too she was still reeling in shock at what she had learned while trying not to dwell on what was likely to happen in her marriage in the short term.

Saif didn't love her, and if he wanted her to stay married to him longer it was only because he was keen to protect their child. There was nothing she could do to change that, but she could still act on her own behalf and…walk away. More and more that was what she wanted to do, and she kept on suppressing that thought, reminding herself that her child deserved a father, but still the prospect of escape pulled and tugged seductively at her. Saif had sent her crashing from the heights of happiness down into the depths of despair. If she couldn't have Saif fully and for ever, she didn't want him, and she certainly didn't want some empty, pretend relationship dragging on for years with him, because the pain of that would kill her by degrees.

'Oh…my…goodness!' Ana exclaimed with emphasis, leaning closer to Tati to brush a fingertip against a dangling emerald earring gleaming like a rainbow in a shaft of sunlight. 'Now you have earrings worth a fortune as well!'

'Saif's very generous.'

'Then hand him over,' Ana urged cheerfully, as if she were asking to borrow something quite inconsequential. 'He's the serious type, isn't he? He needs someone more exciting like me in his life. You could go back to England and I could—'

Tati's stomach hollowed out. 'I'm pregnant, Ana. It wouldn't be quite that simple.'

'You mean…' Ana stared at her in open astonishment. 'You mean *you* actually *slept* with him? And you've conceived?' Ana shook her head slowly and took a moment to regroup. 'Well, good on you because I don't want kids until I'm well into my thirties.'

Tati wore an impassive expression. 'I think you'll have to see how Saif feels about that.'

Ana laughed. 'Of course, he'll want me…men always do!' she carolled with enviable confidence. 'I could see that he was working hard not to look at me when I arrived, trying to hide his interest, and now I understand why. Obviously, if you're pregnant, he feels he can hardly jump ship.'

Tati wondered if it was true that Saif had been trying to hide his interest. Ana was beautiful, lively and sexy. Of course, he would have noticed, particularly when Tati was pale and quiet because she was barely speaking to him and their relationship was at an all-time low. 'But doesn't it bother you that he's been intimate with me?' she pressed, striving to turn her cousin's thoughts in a more appropriate direction. 'Doesn't that put you off?'

'Oh, not at all. Men aren't that fussy when it comes to a willing woman,' Ana said knowledgeably just as her phone began playing a favourite tune.

Tati knew instantly what the call was about because Ana was no dissembler. Her eyes flew wide and she said sharply, 'You can't be serious! The *police*? I don't believe you!'

While she was talking and becoming more and more distressed, Tati got up and left the room to trek downstairs to Saif's office.

'Ana's just found out that her parents have been arrested…and *no*, she didn't know anything about it. I want to fly back to England with her.'

Brilliant green eyes locked to her flushed face. 'That would be unwise.'

'I don't care whether it's wise or not,' Tati responded truthfully. 'This is a family matter. You interfered and let me find out the hard way, but it's not your decision or your business…it's *mine*.'

'I was trying to protect you. I didn't want to risk telling you anything false. I don't deal in unsubstantiated stories,' Saif intoned with cool dignity. 'Becoming involved in the fallout from your uncle's actions at this stage could be very challenging for you. You would be in a very awkward position as his victim.'

'I'm not a coward. I can deal with unpleasant things,' Tati told him, lifting her head high.

'If you go to England, I will be accompanying you. We'll fly out in the morning,' Saif announced.

'Even if I don't *want* you to?' Tati snapped angrily.

Saif breathed in deep and slow, his green eyes glittering as bright as the earrings she wore. 'Even then.'

'Well…' Tati stomped back to the door in a temper. 'I'll just ignore you. I'll pretend you're not there getting into business that has nothing to do with you!'

'Everything that relates to you involves me because we're a couple.'

'I wouldn't use that word about us,' Tati said in fierce denial, leaving his office to return to her cousin.

'The police have let them both out on bail and have confiscated their passports like they're *criminals*!' Ana wailed at her incredulously. 'Dad's being charged with fraud and Mum's being charged as an accessory. How on earth could Granny have done this to us? I mean, Dad was the eldest child, everything *should've* gone to him. It's not surprising he went a little crazy and did wrong.'

'Actually, my mother was the eldest by eighteen months,' Tati chipped in gently as she rubbed her sobbing cousin's spine in a soothing motion.

'But the will that they pretended was still current left the estate to Dad. So, Granny must have changed her mind.' And then Ana sobbed. 'Oh, hell, Tati, how could Dad lie and do such a thing to you when you're part of our family as well? I never dreamt he could sink so low!'

'I think his hatred for my mother…and in her absence, *me*…overwhelmed his judgement. But I shouldn't be discussing this with you, Ana. I'm too close to it. Talk to your friends,' she urged.

'I can't tell *them* about this! When this gets out into the papers everybody will think I'm as guilty as my parents are of robbing you blind!' Ana sobbed. 'Oh, Tati, can't you please stop this happening?'

But as Tati discovered, late the following day when she was interviewed by the police in England and had answered their questions, the prosecution had nothing to do with her. Crimes had been committed and the solicitor was in even more severe trouble than her uncle and was suspected of having suggested the substitution of the outdated will to Rupert Hamilton in the first place. His dealings with his other clients were now under careful scrutiny.

When the official business was complete, Tati felt drained and she climbed into the limo that came to collect her and focused on Saif's lean, darkly handsome features wearily. 'Well, you were right, there's nothing I can do.'

'But why would you *want* to do anything to help your persecutors?' Saif demanded in driven disbelief.

'Not because I forgive them, because I don't,' she said quietly. 'I had a hellish time after Granny passed worrying about my mother's security in the care home. I could never forgive them for that or for treating me like dirt. But I pity Ana because she loves them and she's ashamed and mortified and she had no idea what had been done.'

'Then compensate her in some way if you wish to be generous. You seem to forget that you have become a very wealthy woman with considerable sums at your disposal. What your uncle deprived you of was a mere tithe of what you are now worth,' Saif informed her.

Tati fixed dismayed eyes to him. 'How am I wealthy? You may be, I'm not!'

'When we married, I settled funds on you that would make you wealthy by most people's standards...if not mine,' Saif told her coolly.

Tati clasped her hands together tightly. 'I don't want your money. I'm not being rude or ungrateful, but it's not right for me to be taking money from you when we were never truly married in the first place.'

Saif expelled his breath in a sudden hiss and clamped his even white teeth down on a swear word. *'Truly?'* he derided. 'We had the ceremony. We have shared a bed, made love and conceived a child. How is all that *not* a marriage?'

'The intent was missing. You didn't want to marry me,' Tati reminded him stubbornly.

'Is it enough to say that I would have that intent now and would marry you again, given the chance?' Saif shot at her in a raw undertone.

Tati paled and studied her linked hands, reckoning that he was only saying that because she was pregnant and had to be placated. 'No, it's not. Let's stick to our agreement for the moment.'

'Which agreement? The "friends with benefits" idea seems to have died a death,' Saif breathed curtly. 'The agreement to part within months is impossible as matters stand.'

Tati bowed her head. 'I'm not in the mood to talk about it right now,' she told him shakily, feeling terrifyingly close to a bout of overwrought tears.

She was acting like a shrew and an indecisive one at that, Tati mused guiltily, and yet he had been endlessly kind and supportive. Despite her discouragement, he had escorted her to England and had sent a lawyer to the police station with her when she'd turned down his company. She loved him so much and, even when she was angry with him, that love burned like a torch inside her and made her want to do silly stuff like grab him and hug him just for being there when her life was tough. Nobody prior to Saif had ever stood up for her before. He was so loyal, so caring that he made her love him more than ever, but that only made her feel worse and more of a burden to him.

'Your uncle contacted me this afternoon to request a meeting. He and your aunt have moved out of the manor.'

Tati dealt him a startled look. 'They...they *have*?'

'An obvious first move. It's your house where they treated you like a servant,' Saif pronounced with distaste. 'He will now wish to impress you with his re-pentance.'

Tati couldn't even picture a repentant version of her pompous relative. 'What did you say?'

'I said it was your decision as to whether or not you would see him,' Saif murmured grimly.

Tati could tell by the hard slant of his wide sensual mouth what *his* decision would have been, but she appreciated that, for once, he hadn't interfered. 'I'll see him at the hotel this evening if it suits.'

For the first time she was asking herself why she had got so very angry with Saif. She had deeply resented the admission that he had known about her uncle's crime before she had, even though she would never ever have found out the truth on her own behalf. She had spent her adult life being pushed around by people with power over her or her mother and she had often been brow-beaten into doing what she didn't want to do. Saif had decided that he knew better than her even though the wrongdoers were her relatives, and she knew them best. But there was one crucial difference with Saif, she ac-knowledged now that she had calmed and taken a step back from shock and anger: Saif did what he did from an engrained need to protect her, not from a desire to belittle or control her, and that made a huge difference.

Tati slanted a glance at his lean, bronzed face, rec-ognising the hard tension bracketing his mouth. 'I'm sorry I've been so unreasonable about all this,' she told him before she could lose her nerve. 'It's such a nasty, sordid business.'

'And I don't want you dealing with this right now,' Saif slotted in honestly, his stunning green eyes en-hanced by his dense black lashes.

'It's almost over,' she pointed out. 'And I want to go and see the manor again tomorrow.'

'Why?'

'I spent a lot of my time there when my grandmother was still alive. It was a place of happy memories until Mum fell ill,' she admitted stiffly. 'I refuse to let my last few unhappy years there when my uncle was in charge spoil that for me.'

Saif was prepared to admit that Tatiana had a backbone of steel under that fragile exterior of hers, a quiet dignity, which had very much impressed the lawyer who had been at the police interview with her. He had phoned Saif the instant he'd emerged from it, full of praise for the calm, intelligent manner in which Tatiana had dealt with the situation. But Saif was much less fond of that reference to the house that was hers here in England and her attachment to it. He said nothing, however, convinced that he would strike a wrong note if he commented. He had never been in an equal relationship with a woman before, he reflected with a frown. Perhaps that was why he had erred and dictated rather than discussed.

Her uncle Rupert arrived at eight that evening at their hotel. Tati saw him alone, hardening her heart while he recited his woes and excuses, not to mention his embittered recriminations against the grandmother she had loved. It was always someone else's fault, never his when anything went wrong in Rupert Hamilton's life. When she told him of her decision his mask of discomfiture slipped for a second, and his hatred showed. He argued with her until she lost patience because she could not have cared less what happened to her uncle and aunt or where they went, but their daughter, Ana, was a different issue. If she could protect her cousin she would, and she would not apologise for it. The older man left in a very bad mood.

'I almost intervened when I heard him raise his voice,' Saif confided as he strode out of the room next door.

'I'm not scared of him and he no longer has any influence with me,' Tati admitted tightly, very pale, her blue eyes shadowed. 'But it was very unpleasant. He was shocked at what I had to tell him. Even after what he did, he still thought he could talk me into giving him the Fosters Manor estate, but I refused him and told him that when the time came I will be signing the London apartment over to Ana, so that she will still have a home. If she chooses to have her parents live with her there that's their business, not mine. I will warn her that her father is likely to try to persuade her to put the apartment in his name and that she must not agree to that. I can do no more. I understand that my uncle is likely to get a prison sentence of short duration as he has no previous record and that my aunt is likely to get community work. So, that's it now, all done and dusted.'

'You're exhausted,' Saif pronounced, bending down and scooping her bodily out of her chair before she could even guess what he was planning to do.

'I don't know why,' she sighed as he carried her through to the bedroom and settled her down on the bed.

'You're pregnant and the stress hasn't helped. Dr Abaza said that you would probably be unusually tired these first weeks.'

Tati got ready for bed, wondering if Saif would be joining her, because there was another bedroom available. She was thinking that it was far too early for him to even be thinking of sleeping and recalling that the night before he had not come to bed at all when her own eyes drifted shut.

In the morning, she felt strong enough to deal with just about anything. Even leaving Saif? She studied him over breakfast, a clenching low down in her belly as she collided with those spectacular eyes of his, hunger flaming through her in warning. Heat built in her cheeks and flushed through her entire body and she pressed her thighs together, thinking that Saif still mesmerised her. Swearing off him, taking a step back, was horrendously difficult when every natural impulse drew her back to him.

'You're coming down to the manor with me?' she queried in surprise. 'I thought you had work to do.'

'The work is always there. If I didn't ignore it sometimes I would never have any free time at all,' Saif asserted with a flashing smile that was nonetheless distinctly tense to her gaze.

He couldn't actually have guessed what she was thinking about doing…could he? For goodness' sake, Tati scolded herself, he's not telepathic! And yet she couldn't escape the sneaking suspicion that somehow he knew, somehow he had worked out already that she had decided she could not continue their marriage on the basis he had suggested. It might be the sensible, kindest approach for their unborn child, but she was only human and neither a saint nor a martyr and, if he pushed her, she would just tell him the truth so that he fully understood her position.

Tati dressed with care for the visit, donning a pretty polka-dot sundress that matched the summer sky. As she had already discovered to her consternation, pregnancy changes had kicked into her body a lot sooner than she had expected and quite a few items no longer fitted comfortably. Her breasts had swelled while her waist seemed to be vanishing. Luckily, a looser dress hid the fact.

Saif watched his wife's shuttered face begin to light up as they turned into the driveway of the old house. She was happy coming back here, happy that she was going to leave him. He straightened his wide shoulders and breathed in deep as they approached the front door, and she began to dig in her bag for the keys her uncle had handed over.

'Use the doorbell. When I realised you were coming here, I had cleaners and a housekeeper hired to greet you,' Saif divulged stiffly.

'Good grief, why would you do that?' Tati exclaimed, discomfiture claiming her afresh.

'You will not be a servant in your own home,' Saif breathed thinly.

'I'm pregnant, not disabled!' Tati protested. 'I'm not like Ana. I'm very self-sufficient. I can cook, clean, do *anything.*'

'But you will not…today anyway,' Saif completed flatly.

A pleasant older woman welcomed them into the wainscoted hall. It shone with cleanliness and the scent of beeswax polish was in the air. Tati smiled, recalling it that way from her childhood. Wandering into the pretty but faded drawing room, she went straight to the piano to study the photos there, picking up one of her grandparents when they had still been hale and hearty. She wasn't remotely surprised that, while there were a few gaps where her uncle and aunt had removed their own pieces of furniture, they had left behind all the family photos.

Two little blonde girls were in the background of the picture, giggling, and beside them stood a tall, elegant blonde with a bright smile. 'Ana and me,' she told Saif. 'And that's my mother with us.'

Her eyes throbbed and her throat ached as she thought back to those days at the manor before her uncle took over.

'I won't let you leave me!' Saif breathed with startling abruptness into the silence.

In consternation, Tati spun round to look at him, her face as red as fire because he *had* guessed what she was planning. 'You make it sound so emotional when it's not,' she muttered uncomfortably. 'I don't know how you guessed that I was thinking of living here and of not returning to Alharia with you.'

Saif lifted his strong jaw, green eyes glittering. 'I know you and I won't let you do it.'

Regret softened her blue eyes. 'I'm afraid I don't see how you can stop me.'

'I'd kidnap you,' Saif announced, disconcerting her so completely that she simply stared at him with a dropped jaw. 'Maybe after the baby was born. I wouldn't want you harmed by the exercise...obviously.'

But there was nothing remotely obvious in that threat that Tati could understand. She adored him but there was no denying that he was a conventional guy, occasionally even rather strait-laced. Remarkably handsome and sexy and full of charisma, but not the sort who broke rules. Hadn't she watched him freeze before her very eyes when Ana had tried to flirt with him? He had been appalled and he hadn't known how to handle it without being rude. So, for Saif to talk about kidnapping her with apparent seriousness shocked her beyond bearing.

'You wouldn't do anything like that,' she told him gently. 'It just wouldn't be your style.'

'If I am forced to live without you, I can make it my style,' Saif assured her with perfect gravity.

Tati sighed with regret. 'Look, you said a lot of true, logical things when we talked. Yes, it would be better for our child if we stayed together for the first years, but I just can't face a future where I'd be living a lie.'

'I will do whatever it takes to keep you…even if I have to change myself. I will change for you,' Saif swore with sincerity.

Her eyes stung with tears. 'You don't need to change. It's *me* who has the problem. I broke our rules: I fell in love with you…and I want much *more* from you than a fake marriage, and that's unfair to you.'

'You…you love me?' Saif almost whispered, staring at her fixedly as if that were the biggest shock he had ever had.

'I wouldn't have told you if you hadn't been talking that…er…weird way,' she muttered in mortification.

'Weird?' Saif's mouth quirked. 'As in being willing to consider kidnapping you? Doesn't it occur to you that while you were falling in love I might have been too?'

Her blue eyes widened, and she shifted infinitesimally closer to his tall, muscular frame. 'Might you have been?'

'First time I've ever been in love. First and last time,' Saif intoned hoarsely, curving a not-quite-steady hand to the curve of her cheekbone. 'I want you in my life for ever and ever like the stupid fairy tales.'

'Fairy tales are not stupid,' Tati told him tenderly, happiness surging up through her in an ungovernable flood. 'How come I'm your first love? There *must* have been someone else at some stage.'

'Maybe I was a late developer,' Saif quipped. 'I was always very careful not to spend too much time with any woman because I feared falling for someone I couldn't have. I knew that eventually my father would expect me to marry a woman of his choice.'

That caution was so much in his nature that she almost laughed. She turned her head to see the new housekeeper in the doorway offering them coffee. 'That would be lovely but...perhaps, later,' she suggested. 'I want to show my husband round the house first.'

'I suppose we should take a look at the outside first,' Saif remarked levelly.

'No, we're heading for the nearest bedroom,' Tati whispered, amused by his innocence. 'I'm about to jump your bones like a wild, wanton woman.'

'With you, wild and wanton works very well for me,' Saif murmured with a sudden laugh of appreciation. 'I'm more relaxed with you than I have ever been with a woman. I suppose we'll be stuck with visits from your ghastly cousin, Ana, for ever.'

'No, she won't be flirting with you the next time we see her. You withstood her attractions and that hurts her ego and turns her off. Next time, she'll be telling me that she doesn't know how I stand you being so quiet... She doesn't realise that you were only quiet because she embarrassed you,' Tati commented cheerfully.

'I wasn't embarrassed,' Saif contradicted. 'I just don't like women who are all over me like a rash.'

'Like me?' Tati teased, stretching up on tiptoe to kiss him, her hands roaming across his chest beneath his jacket as she pressed into his lean, strong length in an act of deliberate provocation.

'You're the sole exception,' Saif husked as she linked her fingers with his and urged him towards the stairs. 'Would you really have stayed here and left me?'

'If you hadn't said you loved me, I think…yes,' she muttered guiltily. 'I would have been so unhappy believing that you were only tolerating me until you felt it was time for us to split up.'

'I tolerate you with pleasure…that doesn't sound quite right,' Saif husked on the landing as he bent over her, nibbling a caressing trail down the slope of her neck. 'We need a bed.'

'I'm not sure there'll be one made up.'

'I ordered a new bed for the main bedroom and said we would be staying the night.'

Tati gazed up at him, impressed to death by that level of preparation. 'How did you know we'd be here for the night?'

'You've been so distant since we had that discussion at the palace that I knew I was in trouble,' Saif confided. 'I was determined to persuade you to stay with me…*somehow*. But I didn't know how I was going to do it, only that I would need a good few hours to have a chance of accomplishing it.'

'You're so modest,' Tati muttered, tugging him into the main bedroom, relieved to see that, aside from the new bed and bedding, it looked much as it had in her grandparents' day. Thankfully, her uncle and aunt had removed every shred of their presence. 'I can't believe we are here in this house together and that you love me.'

'*Believe,*' he urged fiercely as he flipped off her shoes and unzipped her dress, lifting her to arrange her on the bed like a precious sacrifice. 'I love you so much. You have no idea how it felt to think that I was losing you for ever...and all because I said the wrong things.'

'It took you a while to realise how you felt,' Tati told him forgivingly, stroking a fingertip across one high cheekbone.

'No, it didn't. I started suspecting way back when I kissed you in the street after we got off that Ferris wheel in the Place de la Concorde. I've never done anything like that in my adult life, but I couldn't resist you when you smiled. I knew then that I'd never felt that way in my life...it was *so* powerful,' he admitted. 'But I refused to examine my emotions because it didn't fit in with our plans and I was afraid that you would walk away the way my mother once walked away from me.'

Tati groaned and wrapped her arms round him tightly, touched to the heart. 'I'm not walking away. I'm never going anywhere. Gosh, you were a pushover. It took me much longer because I was working hard at trying not to get attached to you. Trouble is...' she sighed blissfully, sitting up helpfully to make the removal of her bra easier '...you're an attachable guy.'

Saif chuckled. 'You just made up a word. What does it mean?'

Her fingertip traced the sensual line of his lower lip. 'It means that there's a whole lot of stuff I like about you…like how protective you are. I've never had that before and at first I confused that protectiveness with you trying to boss me around, and I'd suffered way too much of that kind of treatment here.'

'You start shouting when I try to boss you around,' Saif pointed out with unholy amusement gleaming in his stunning eyes. 'I like your feistiness and your lack of guile and greed and also…your generosity. I still want to lock your uncle and aunt up and starve and torture them for the way they mistreated you, but I admire and respect your compassion.'

'They're already losing everything they value…the house, the money, the lifestyle, their reputations. That's enough of a punishment, but I will have to watch out that they don't take advantage of Ana.'

Saif winced. 'That will be a lifelong challenge.'

'But I can do it,' she told him gently while pushing him flat and unbuttoning his shirt, spreading appreciative hands over his bronzed hair-roughened skin and lingering with a boldness she had never dared to utilise with him before. 'I'm feeling much more confident since I met you…'

Saif gave her a wicked grin. 'I am more than willing to lie back and think only of the greatness of Alharia for your benefit, *aziz*.'

'I can't believe it only took you a couple of days to start falling in love with me,' she told him happily.

'You're a class act,' Saif husked, winding long fingers into her rumpled blond hair, the warmth and tenderness in his gaze like a sublime caress on her skin. 'An act no other woman will ever match.'

'I think you're pretty special too,' she whispered against the marauding mouth circling hers with unhidden hunger, and then they both forgot to talk and got entirely carried away into their own little world of mutual satisfaction and happiness.

EPILOGUE

Five years later

SAIF GLANCED ACROSS the room to where his wife was seated beside his father. It was the Emir's birthday. He was ninety years old and just months earlier had stepped down from the throne to allow his son to become Regent. Freed from the stress of ruling, the older man had become much more relaxed, in a way his son had never expected to see.

Their children—Amir, who was four, and the toddler twins, Farah and Milly—were playing at the Emir's feet, absorbed in the latest toys he had presented them with. For the first time ever, Saif reflected fondly, his father was enjoying a peaceful family atmosphere and he owed that blessing to Tatiana.

His father adored his daughter-in-law. He was fond of telling people that his own life would have been very different had he had the good fortune to meet a Tatiana. As to his pride in having married his son off to the grandchild of his old friend, that went without saying. But the knowledge that his father was happy and at peace and delighted in his grandchildren made Saif's duties a lot easier.

The Emir had not changed personality overnight, but he had become less authoritarian and more willing to listen to other points of view. On the other side of the room his three older sisters, engaged in their endless embroidery and crochet, were chattering to Tatiana, smiling and laughing, patting the slight swell of her stomach affectionately.

Thanks to his rashness, their fourth child was due in a handful of months, Saif mused ruefully. Strange how he had never had a reckless bone in his body until Tatiana came along, but then he had also never been happier. When Tatiana had learned that she was carrying twins the last time, they had decided that three children were enough, and then Tatiana's amazing fertility had collided with his desire to have sex in their private pool and the result was before them. He smiled abstractedly as he watched his beautiful wife weaving her magic with his family. The pool encounter had been spectacularly worthwhile.

As Tati's mobile phone buzzed she excused herself and walked through an open archway out to a terrace to take her call. The Emir had not noticed the phone ringing and she was relieved. While the old man was a lot less grumpy than he had once been, he still held on to many of what his son deemed to be 'medieval prejudices.'

'George wants a baby,' Ana proclaimed in a tragic voice.

'Well, you knew it was on the cards,' Tati reminded her cousin, who had been married for four years. George had finally proposed and stuck to his word after Ana began seeing another man. A banker, George Davis-Appleton was a clever character, more than equal to the task of keeping his avaricious in-laws at bay, and that had meant that Tati could finally relax and know her cousin was safe from exploitation.

'You love my kids…why shouldn't you love your own child?' Tati asked cheerfully.

'It's not that, Tati.' Ana sighed. 'But when you have a baby you have to grow up and I'm not ready for that yet.'

'But George is, so you have to consider him as well. Look, it's the Emir's birthday party here, so I can't talk for long,' Tati warned her cousin, soothing Ana's fears about motherhood aging her overnight.

Rupert and Elizabeth Hamilton had both received prison sentences after the crooked solicitor had declared that her aunt had been present at his meetings with his client. Within eighteen months, however, both of them had been released and they had moved in with their daughter. With Ana married, they still lived there, and Tati hadn't seen her uncle since their last meeting at the hotel, a situation that she was quite content with.

Saif and Tati regularly stayed at the manor when they were in England and spent every Christmas there. Her mother's cousin, Pauline, had moved in as a sort of caretaker for the property when it was empty. Tati's life had changed radically but very much for the better, she conceded cheerfully, because she was fiercely content and happy with Saif and their family.

She glanced up and saw her husband watching her from the archway.

'Hi,' she murmured softly, blue eyes locking to him, brimming with love and appreciation. Tall, dark and devastatingly handsome, he still rocked her where she stood every time she looked at him.

He closed his arms round her slowly. 'You look tired.'

'It was exhausting trying to explain Father Christmas to your father…because there isn't really an explanation and he doesn't like fanciful stuff.'

'It's what you call an own goal, *aziz*. You persuaded him to join us in England for Christmas this year. He wants to be prepared for some weird old man in a red suit trying to squeeze himself down a chimney…' Saif laughed softly.

Tati mock-punched a broad shoulder. 'Don't you dare tell Amir that version. He's already very excited about Christmas.'

'Relax. It's still summer,' Saif reminded her, bending his dark glossy head to steal a kiss from her soft pink lips and a little flame ignited low in her pelvis, provoking a moan deep in her throat.

His mouth circled and teased hers and she squirmed against him, helpless in the grip of that hunger as he backed her up against the wall edging the terrace, ultimately dragging his lips from hers with a groan. 'We can't leave until my father retires for the night,' he reminded her hoarsely.

Tati chuckled and bumped her brow in reproach against his shoulder before stepping back from him. 'You're like oil on a bonfire for me… I'm not complaining,' she murmured with reddening cheeks as she smiled up at him with adoring eyes that he cherished. 'I love you so much.'

Their little private moment was invaded by clattering feet and noisy voices. Amir pelted out with his two-year-old sisters hard in his wake, shouting at him to wait for them. He was tall and black-haired like Saif with the same wonderful green eyes. Farah and Milly were an identical mix of blond-haired blue-eyed little girls with pale golden skin and as lively as Amir was steady like his father.

Saif hoisted up his daughters in his strong arms and walked back indoors. Amir's hand slid into his mother's and he yawned. 'I was trying to tell Grandpa about Father Christmas, but he got all mixed up,' he complained.

As Saif's keen gaze encountered Tati's, he was smiling, warmth and tenderness a vibrant presence in that appraisal, and happiness that was as solid as gold shimmered through her. She had everything she had ever wanted in life.

* * * * *

BEAUTY IN THE BILLIONAIRE'S BED

LOUISE FULLER

MILLS & BOON

To Larry, Leonard, Neil and Neville.
For forcing me into the fresh air
and occasionally bringing clarity to my thoughts.

CHAPTER ONE

THE TRAIN BURST out of the tunnel into the fading light. Frankie Fox flinched as the carriage jerked sideways.

It had taken just over two years of persistence and hard work, but finally it had happened. Two days ago her social media profile—@StoneColdRedHotFox—had reached the milestone of a million followers.

Better still, the man of her dreams had invited her to spend the weekend at Hadfield Hall, his family's home in Northumberland.

She should have been feeling on cloud nine, but instead she was staring morosely through the grimy window at a darkening landscape.

It was her fault she was feeling this way.

For the first time in two years she had let herself dream, let herself hope that she might be given a second chance to belong. That maybe she had done enough to earn a place in someone's life.

And the day had started so promisingly...

After weeks of rain, she had woken up to a pale March sun in a sky of clear harebell-blue.

Miraculously, she had got to the station with time to spare and, best of all, Johnny had been waiting beneath the clock, just as he'd said he would be.

They'd met just shy of three months ago at a product launch. Technically, she had been working, but that had been quickly forgotten because for her it had been love at first sight.

Johnny Milburn was an actor—the kind described as 'hot' and 'up-and-coming'. He certainly looked like a leading man, with that lean body and clean-cut superhero features, the floppy blond hair, a smile that could power the

National Grid, and the most beautiful meltingly soft choc-
olate-coloured eyes.

She had been the one melting when he'd taken her hands
last Saturday and told her that she was working too hard.
That somebody had to tell her she needed a break, and that
person was him.

She breathed out unsteadily, remembering how his eyes
had been fixed on her face as if there was nobody in the
world but her. He hadn't kissed her, but incredibly—unbelievably—he had invited her to spend the weekend with him
at Hadfield Hall, his family's estate on a tidal island off the
coast of Northumberland. It had all sounded swooningly
romantic. Like something out of a Georgette Heyer novel…

She glanced across the table to where Johnny *should*
have been sitting.

Except romantic novels needed a hero and a heroine,
and right now her hero was somewhere over the Atlantic
on his way to an audition in Los Angeles, and she was on
her way to Northumberland alone.

Slumping back in her seat, she sighed.

She'd tried telling Johnny that she couldn't possibly just
turn up at his family's house on her own, but he wouldn't
listen to her.

'Please, Frankie. It's bad enough that I can't go, but if
you don't go either then I might as well call off the trip to
LA, because I won't be able to stop thinking about how I
messed everything up for you.'

'But what am I supposed to say to your brother?' she'd
asked.

Remembering how Johnny's expression had changed
from pleading to relief, she let her head fall against the
train window. She'd been trying to make him see the im-
practicality of what he was suggesting, but instead she had
simply given him the means to make refusing impossible.

'Arlo?' He'd frowned. 'You won't have to say anything to

him. I thought he was home, but apparently he's on some ice floe in the Antarctic. He probably won't be back for months.'

That at least was something, she thought, gazing up at the rain-spattered glass.

Johnny's brother, Arlo Milburn, was not just a decorated former marine and a renowned expert on all things environmental, he was also a polar explorer. She had been dreading meeting him with Johnny there, but doing so on her own—

She shivered.

It was just lucky for her that he was away, because guilt had made Johnny unusually single-minded.

'Look, it's perfect for you.' He'd held up his phone to show her. 'For starters, it's basically off-grid. Plus, you can have the run of the place. Nobody will be there except Constance—'

'Who's Constance?'

He'd frowned. 'She looks after the house.'

'Won't she think it a bit odd, me just turning up on my own?'

'No,' Johnny had said firmly. 'She hates it when Arlo's away. Honestly, she'll love having you there. And you'll love it too. It'll be like a home from home.' He'd taken her hand and squeezed it. 'Besides, I've already called her and left a message saying you're coming, so you *have* to go now, Frankie.'

He'd been so racked with remorse, so contrite, so very handsome…

And, anyway, what would the alternative have been? Running home with her tail between her legs?

It was getting dark now outside, and for a moment she stared at her reflection.

And then what?

If she went out then she would have to pretend everything was fine, and she just didn't have the energy to do that. But if she stayed in then she would be alone with her thoughts…

No, with or without Johnny, she needed a break—a change of scene. A few days away in Northumberland was exactly what the doctor ordered.

Suddenly her heart was racing, and even though she could feel her hands, could see the jutting bleached-out knobs of her knuckles, it felt as though she was losing substance.

Of course the opposite was true.

She alone had survived.

Her shoulders jerked. Even now it was a physical pain. Knowing that everyone she loved, everyone who had loved her, was gone.

Her family had been coming back from a summer holiday in Provence. Her father had been flying the plane when it had crashed. The crash had killed him, her mother, and her twin brother and sister.

She alone had survived.

And every day she wondered why.

'This train will shortly be arriving at Berwick-upon-Tweed.'

The automated voice broke into her thoughts as she fought for calm.

'Please remember to take all your belongings with you before you leave the train.'

Her fingers tightened on the armrest. After the shock had worn off there had been endless paperwork to fill in, meetings with solicitors, and then finally the inquest.

A shiver ran over her skin.

She had told the truth, but nothing she'd said had made any difference. That was when she'd started blogging and she hadn't stopped since. But working non-stop for eighteen months had taken its toll. She was sleeping badly, had trouble concentrating, and lately she had a strange, disquieting feeling of being erased...like a drawing that wasn't quite good enough—

Jolted back into the present, and glancing around, she saw that the carriage was empty. Standing up, she pulled her suitcase down from the overhead luggage rack.

Everything would be fine. Once she reached the Hall, she could relax and unwind. And if she felt like doing something more strenuous she could go for a walk along the beach or just do some cloud-spotting.

And there were plenty of clouds to spot, she thought twenty minutes later, as she hugged her beautiful but utterly ineffective quilted jacket around her shivering body. In fact, the sky was pretty much one huge, dark cloud, and the half-hearted rain from earlier was now sheeting down in force as she rapped on the door with the huge cast-iron knocker.

She waited, squinting up at the immense grey stone house rising above her, her heart beating in time to the raindrops hitting her face.

In her head, she'd imagined Constance opening the door, smiling warmly. But there was no sign of any housekeeper, with or without a smile, and all the windows looked ominously dark...

Trying to still the jittery feeling in her legs, she pulled out her phone. Perhaps she should call Johnny.

No service.

She bit her lip. So did that mean Constance had never got Johnny's message about her coming alone?

Turning, she felt a quiver of apprehension scamper down her backbone as she watched the taillights of the taxi she'd hired at the station disappear into the rain.

There was no way she was walking back over that cobbled causeway in this weather. And it wasn't as if she would be breaking in or anything...

Turning her back against the thundering rain, she found

the key Johnny had given her, pushed it into the lock, and turned it.

It was toe-curlingly dark inside. Her heart thudding, she fumbled for a light switch.

Oh, wow.

She was standing in a tennis-court-sized entrance hall. Water was dripping down her legs into her trainers, but she was too distracted to care.

Home from home, Johnny had said. Clearly that depended on your definition of 'home', she thought, gazing up at the huge mahogany staircase, the stucco ceiling, and innumerable gold-framed oil paintings on the walls.

She had known Johnny came from money. Not the professionally earned sort, but old money—the kind that came with a small but exclusive circle of acquaintances, a flat in Eaton Square, and a country estate. She knew, too, that he had a cousin who was a lord or an earl or something.

Only she had never really put it into context until now.

Her stomach twisted. What would it be like to live here? To be the lady of the house? But of course ordinary people like her didn't actually *live* in places like this. At most they stayed for a weekend—or, in her case, one night.

Tomorrow she would pay whatever it cost to take a taxi to the nearest hotel. Johnny would understand.

Her heart leapt in her throat as a noisy cluster of raindrops hit the windows.

Maybe in the morning she might take a quick peek around the house. Right now, though, she just wanted to go to bed.

Upstairs, there was an unbelievable number of bedrooms, all awash with heavy fabrics and Persian rugs and paintings of horses. Feeling like Goldilocks, she wandered from one room to another, pressing her hand against the velvet bedspreads to test the mattresses.

That one was too soft, this one was too hard, but this one...

Like all the other rooms, this one was large, but it had a different feel to it. There was an overflowing bookcase, a battered trunk at the end of the bed, and a large shabby wicker dog basket beneath the window.

The mattress dipped as she sat down on the edge of the mahogany-framed four-poster bed.

This one was just right.

She washed her face and brushed her teeth in the large and very austere en suite bathroom. No toiletries. Just dark grey tiles, a bath the size of a boat, and a leather armchair that looked like something from a gentlemen's club.

Oh, and a cricket bat leaning incongruously against the wall, as if someone had just walked in off the pitch.

She stared at it in silence, frowning, and then picked it up. She might be on an island, in a house that looked as if it had been built to keep out invaders from across the sea, but it wouldn't hurt to have a little extra protection to hand.

Back in the bedroom, she peeled off her damp clothes and reached into her suitcase for the old dress shirt of her dad's that she wore to bed.

Instead her hand brushed against something seductively soft and she pulled out the whisper of midnight-blue silk she had packed, in case 'something happened' with Johnny.

Her breath caught in her throat as she remembered the moment when she'd seen it in the shop.

She'd wanted to look cool and confident and sexy. That was who she was, after all. A stone-cold, red-hot fox. Or at least it was who she was pretending to be. In reality, she felt anything but.

Throat tightening, she closed her fingers around the flimsy fabric.

She might as well wear it. Who knew when—*if*—she would have an opportunity to do so again?

Wriggling under the quilt, she gazed up at the heavy

draped tapestry curtains. She felt as if she was in a fairy tale. If only Johnny were here with her, it would be perfect.

But he wasn't.

Grabbing one of the pillows, she hugged it close to her body.

Life was not a fairy tale—at least not *her* life, anyway. And her supposed prince would be on the other side of the ocean by now.

Reaching over, she switched off the light.

Instantly the empty house creaked into life. Pipes hummed, windows rattled, and there was a distant thump like a door slamming.

Rolling onto her side, she yawned. The sound of the rain was making her feel sleepy…

And then she heard it. The sound of footsteps.

She sat upright so fast she thought her spine would snap. Her pulse was racing, her heartbeat bouncing off the walls.

It's just your imagination, she told herself, feeling the hairs on the back of her neck stand up.

Except the footsteps were getting closer.

Her ears pricked, she groped frantically in the darkness for the cricket bat—and then almost jerked out of her skin when the door clicked open.

'What the—?'

There was a crash, and then a thump, as someone—*no*, not someone…a man—collided with something solid in the darkness and she heard him swear explosively.

She felt a jolt of panic. Her heart was thumping uncontrollably, her fear so intense that she was shivering all over, and then sudden light blinded her.

Blinking, she stared across the room.

Her suitcase was lying on its back, rocking from side to side like an upended turtle. A man was standing next to it, his huge shoulders filling the doorway, his face shrouded beneath a hood, a bulky-looking dark leather bag in his hand and a dog quivering beside him.

Terror doused her like a bucket of cold water as he dropped the bag and took a step forward. Edging back against the headboard, she held the cricket bat out threateningly in front of her, tension bunching her muscles.

'Don't come any closer,' she managed.

There was a silence, and then the man reached up and pushed back the hood. Eyes the colour of the storm clouds outside locked onto hers.

'Or what?'

His voice sounded as if it was rolling across shingle.

'Come closer and you'll find out,' she said hoarsely.

He leaned almost casually against the doorjamb, his lips twisting into something halfway between a smile and a sneer, so that she caught a glimpse of straight white teeth.

'Is that an invitation?'

She felt goosebumps erupt over her skin.

An invitation!

Shocked, she gazed up at him, open-mouthed.

Not in a million years was her first response.

He was tall, and even though she couldn't see beneath the bulky jacket he was wearing there was a sense of restrained power beneath the almost languid pose. But she liked her men pretty, and this man was not pretty. In fact, his features were strikingly discordant—part-Modigliani, part-Picasso, part-Border Reiver.

He had a too-big mouth, surrounded by a dark, scruffy moustache and beard. His broad nose looked as if it had been broken at some time, maybe several times, in the past, and there was a scar cutting across his left cheek like the cleft in a peach.

Maybe if they had met under other circumstances, when she was feeling more generous, she might have described him as 'unconventionally handsome'. But, given that he had just broken into the house where she was staying and scared her half to death, she wasn't feeling generous.

And yet...

There was something compelling about him—an uncompromising, unapologetic, raw masculinity that felt real in a way that both shocked and excited her. She could almost imagine him standing on the island's clifftops, his grey eyes narrowed on the foam-flecked sea ...

Blinking out of this train of thought, she glared at him hot-cheeked, her fingers tightening around the handle of the cricket bat.

'Look, I've already called the police,' she lied. 'So if I were you, I'd just leave.'

'You would?'

His cool, dark gaze made breathing a challenge.

'But things are just starting to get interesting...'

She tugged the quilt more tightly around her body as he looked down at her.

'In fact, you should probably give the police a call back. Ask them to bring a ball. Then we can actually make use of that bat you're waving around so enthusiastically.'

What?

Frankie looked at him in confusion. She could count the number of conversations she'd had with burglars on one finger, but surely this wasn't how they were supposed to go.

'Do you think this is funny?' she snapped.

'No, I don't.' His gaze bored into her. 'Do you?'

'Of course not—'

'In that case...' He paused, his eyes narrowing on her face with such a mixture of exasperation and hostility that she had to look away. 'Do you think it would be too much trouble to tell me exactly what you're doing in *my* bed?'

Frankie's head jerked up. She stared at him, her pulse doing some kind of complicated step-ball-change.

His bed.

Her eyes dropped to the bag by his feet—more specifically to the initials embossed on the leather.

A. M.

A.M.

In other words, Arlo Milburn…

She groaned inwardly as a grainy silence filled the room. 'Wh-what are you doing here?' she finally stammered. 'You're not supposed to be here.'

Shifting his weight away from the doorframe, he walked slowly across the room, stopping at the end of the bed.

'I think you'll find that's *my* line,' he said coldly.

Watching the woman's pale face stiffen with shock and panic, Arlo Milburn felt his jaw tighten. The last few days had been some of the most stressful and frustrating in his life.

He'd been on his way from the research station on the Brunt Ice Shelf to speak at a climate conference in Nairobi. It was an important conference. They all were. But when they'd landed at Durban one of the engineers had spotted an electrical fault on the plane, so instead he'd spent eight hours pacing the hangar, missing his connecting flight and his chance to speak.

And then, as if that wasn't bad enough, Emma—his extremely efficient assistant—had called to tell him that she had broken her arm and was going to be off work for at least six weeks.

Thwarted at every turn, he'd randomly decided to come home.

Big mistake.

Thanks to the frenetic arrival of Storm Delia on British shores, his journey had been plagued with even more delays. He was cold, wet, and tired, and he wanted to go to bed.

Only his bed was already taken.

By some unknown female who looked as if she had stepped out of that painting by Titian in the entrance hall. Except she was wielding a cricket bat.

Arlo scowled. 'Well? Why are you here? In my house? In my bed? And make it quick—otherwise *I* will call the police, and unlike you I won't be bluffing.'

He felt a rush of gratification as a faint flush of colour spread over her cheeks.

'Stop interrogating me like some sergeant-major,' she snapped. 'You're not in the army now.'

His gaze narrowed. 'I never was. I was a marine. That's the navy. And I was a captain, not a sergeant-major.'

She gave him a withering look. 'Fine…whatever. I thought Johnny had spoken to you.' She bit her lip, doing a good impression of confusion and dismay. 'He said he'd called you.'

Johnny. But of course—

Arlo's jaw clenched and he swore under his breath, wondering what else his brother had told this woman. He'd been taking care of Johnny ever since their grief-stricken father had retreated to his artist's studio after their mother died, and he loved him unconditionally. But his brother was not without his flaws.

Poor timekeeping. A failure to do what he said he would do. And, last but not least, his refusal to judge a book by its cover—something this scheming little redhead had clearly spotted and mined to her advantage.

'Where is he?' he demanded.

She blinked; her mouth was trembling. 'I don't know exactly.'

Her eyes locked on his, and for a split second he forgot his anger, forgot that he was cold and tired. Instead, he stared at her mutely, held captive by the blue of those eyes.

It was the same blue as an Antarctic summer sky. The kind of blue that almost verged on purple, like the flowers on the fragrant, woody rosemary that grew so abundantly in the Hall's kitchen garden.

Maybe that was why he was having to dig his heels into the faded Afghan carpet to stop himself from leaning over and inhaling her scent.

His breath hitched. Johnny was never without a woman in his life. As soon as he'd become a teenager a constant stream of interchangeable leggy girls had started trailing after him, and that hadn't changed as an adult. But for some reason the idea of his little brother and this particular woman put his back up.

Probably because she was an impudent little madam who had no doubt been bowling men over with that look her entire life.

Not him, though.

His back straightened. 'Look, I've spent the last two days in trains, planes, and taxis. I'm cold and tired and I nearly broke my neck tripping over your damn case, so I'm really not in the mood for a game of hide and seek.'

Her chin jerked up and he knew he was doing a poor job of hiding his frustration—which, of course, only made him more frustrated.

'I'm not playing games. Johnny's not here, he's—' she began, her red curls bouncing in indignation, but he cut her off.

'What do you mean, he's not here? If you're here, he has to be here.' Glancing down, he noticed a lumpy shape beneath the bedding and his temper flared. 'What the—?'

The woman scrambled up the bed as he jerked the quilt free of her hands. 'Are you crazy? What are you doing?'

Arlo gazed down at the pillow, and then back at the woman, and a bolt of heat exploded in his groin. The shock of finding her in his bed had blinded him to all but the most obvious features of her appearance, so that he'd registered nothing much more than those eyes, a lot of freckles, and that hair. Now, though, he was registering a lot more.

His eyes skimmed over her near-naked body.

A whole lot more.

She was wearing some kind of dark blue silky slip. Yes, *slip* was the right word for it, he thought, his heart pounding like a cannon against his ribcage. He felt as though the floor had turned to ice and he was sliding sideways.

Her skin was pale, and he knew it would be stupidly smooth to the touch, but it was what was hinted at beneath the slip that was that was making his body ache. The press of her nipples, the provocative curve of her bottom...

He closed his eyes briefly to compose himself, and then tossed the bedding back towards her. 'He's not here.'

'I just told you that,' she said hotly. 'We were supposed to come up here together, only then he got called back for a part and he had to fly out to LA. Anyway, he gave me a key and told me I could have the run of the place.'

'Did he?' He raised an eyebrow. 'How very generous of him.' He saw her teeth clench.

'He didn't know you were going to be here. He was just trying to do a nice thing for me.'

She left the sentence there, but it was clear from the curl of her lip that she considered such 'niceness' beyond Arlo.

'And you are...?' he said impatiently.

'Frankie Fox.'

What kind of a name was that?

A rush of exasperation collided with a sharp, intense desire to press his mouth against hers and wipe that impudent curl from her lips.

'Hence the hair, I suppose?' He stared at her witheringly. 'Do you change your name when you dye it a different colour?'

'This *is* my hair colour.' Her eyes flashed with undisguised irritation. 'And my name is the one my parents gave me.'

Tilting his head to one side, he sighed. 'I'm guessing you're an actor too. They usually are… Johnny's fangirls.'

He'd wanted to cut her down to size only watching the way she wrapped her arms around herself, as if she was cold, he suddenly felt something pinch inside him.

But it wasn't as if Johnny could be serious about her. Sure, she was pretty, but his brother was swimming in beautiful women.

Her chin jutted forward. 'I'm not an actor,' she said stiffly. 'I'm a social media influencer.'

He frowned. 'A what?'

He knew what social media was, but an influencer…?

'A. Social. Media. Influencer.'

She was speaking each word slowly, as if English wasn't his first language or he was hard of hearing.

'Basically, brands send me clothes and accessories and I get paid to tell my followers about them.'

By 'followers' he supposed she meant a bunch of young men with their tongues hanging out.

'Sounds *fascinating*.'

As payback for the eye-roll that had accompanied her reply, he deliberately made no effort to hide the derision in his voice. His eyes bored into the quilt she was clutching to her chest, then shifted to the thin satin straps hugging her shoulders.

'So who exactly are you expecting to "influence" dressed like that?'

The question ricocheted ominously inside his head as he replayed what she'd told him. Johnny inviting her to the family home on its private island…his last-minute call-back in the States…her decision to come without him. And, last but not least, he took in that teasing scrap of material she was wearing.

All of it could be explained away as either coincidence or misunderstanding. But the way she was biting into her lip and gazing up at him through that forest of eyelashes—that was calculated. It was the swift-thinking, self-serving, opportunistic response of a beautiful, unprincipled woman who knew her charms and was willing to turn them on for the right reward.

'No one. I'm obviously not working.'

Not on the clock, anyway.

He felt anger stir inside him. She might not have an Equity card, but she was one hell of an actress. Only she'd picked the wrong man to hustle.

'Not working. And *not* staying,' he said coolly.

Spinning round, he picked up her ridiculous pillarbox-red suitcase and tossed it onto the bed.

'Pack your stuff. You can spend the rest of the night here, but I want you out of my house in the morning. And out of my bed right now.'

She was staring at him open-mouthed, as if she couldn't believe what he was saying. He couldn't quite believe it either. He certainly hadn't been raised to turf guests out of their beds.

But Frankie Fox was not a guest.

He knew her type and she was all kinds of trouble wrapped up in a silk slip. Maybe another man—a more trusting, less experienced man, like Johnny—might be tempted to unwrap her. He knew better. It was the one, the *only* benefit of his short-lived, disastrous marriage to Harriet. Being able to look before leaping.

'You can't do this…' Her eyes were wide, and her mouth was trembling slightly. 'You can't just throw me out.'

'It's my home,' he said flatly. 'I can do what I like. And what I would like is to go to sleep. It's been a very long day, and tomorrow I've got a series of lectures to write up. Because, unlike you, I don't get paid to lounge around in my underwear. Nor am I running a B&B for my brother's cast-offs.'

Watching her hands clench, he knew she wanted to hurl her suitcase at his head.

'How dare you speak to me like that?' she hissed.

'Oh, I dare, Ms Fox.' He held her gaze. 'You see, I know exactly how this plays out. You came up here to play house with my sweet little brother, maybe "influence" him into something more serious. Only he bailed, so you're switching to Plan B. *Me.*'

'*What?*'

A slow wash of crimson flooded her cheeks as the case slid from her fingers. But he refused to let his gaze drop to the tempting thrust of her breasts.

'Unfortunately, you're wasting your time. I'm on a break from women right now, and even if I wasn't, I would never be interested in some little chancer like you.'

She was looking at him as if he was something the tide had washed up on the beach.

'Let me get this right. You think *I* want to seduce *you*.' Hot colour flushed her cheeks like warpaint. 'As if!' She spat the words at him.

'Then you won't mind leaving my bed,' he snapped, more annoyed than he liked to admit by her emphatic response.

'*Mind?*' She scrambled to her feet. 'I'd rather sleep in the dog's basket than with you.'

'I wouldn't,' he said curtly, pulling his fleece over his head. 'He snores. And you can cut the theatrics. There's a whole other wing of bedrooms. But then I'm guessing you know that, from wandering around playing lady of the manor.'

The flush of colour darkened in her cheeks and with a rush of satisfaction he began unbuttoning his shirt.

'What are you doing?'

He could hear the sudden sharp snag of panic in her voice, but he didn't look over at her. 'I'm getting undressed.'

Unthinkingly, he shifted his gaze to the mirror over the fireplace and watched her snatch jeans and a jacket from the window seat. Her face and collarbone were still flushed pink and that glorious hair rippled over her bare shoulders like molten copper. She was exquisite.

His throat clenched. She was also about as far from his ideal woman as it was possible to get—and that was putting it mildly.

He swung round to face her, his eyes snagging on her bare legs before he had a chance to stop himself. 'Leave the keys.'

Breathing raggedly, she fumbled in the jacket pocket. As she pulled them out, they caught in the lining.

He swore softly. 'Here, let me—'

His fingers brushed against hers as he reached to help and he felt a sharp snap of static.

'Don't touch me.' Breathing out shakily, she jerked away from him.

He felt a stab of anger. He hadn't meant to touch her. Only now, as his eyes jumped from the fierce expression on her face to her soft parted lips, he realised he wanted more than one brief moment of contact. What he wanted was to push her back onto the bed and slide his hands over every inch of that satin-smooth skin...

'Nothing could be further from my mind,' he lied. 'Now, give me back the keys,' he said tersely.

Drawing a jagged breath, she tossed them at him and stalked across the room. As she reached the door she turned, tilting her chin to look at him with over-bright eyes, and he felt something twist inside his chest.

'You know, Johnny talks about you a lot. He thinks you're going to save the world...that you're a hero.' Raising her chin, she held his gaze. 'Some hero,' she said, smiling coldly.

And then, without giving him a chance to reply, she grabbed the handle of her suitcase and spun away into the darkness.

CHAPTER TWO

Shifting against his pillow, Arlo rolled over onto his side and opened his eyes reluctantly. There was a pale frame of light around the heavy curtains, so he knew it was morning. It just didn't feel like it.

He stretched his arms over his head. As he did so, his lurcher, Nero, sat up in his basket and looked wishfully at the four-poster bed.

'Stay,' Arlo warned as he sat up groggily.

Frowning, he rubbed a hand over his face. He'd wanted more than anything to sleep, and normally he didn't have any trouble—particularly during a storm. For some inexplicable reason he'd always found it oddly restful to lie in bed and listen to the weather rage like an impotent warlord against the house's thick walls.

Only last night had been different. He had spent most of the early hours of the morning twitching restlessly beneath the sheets in time to the drumming rain.

But then not much had been normal about last night.

His pulse stumbled. For starters, it had been a long time since he'd come home to find a woman in his bed.

He felt his throat close up. As for a woman wearing next to nothing and brandishing a cricket bat... That would be never.

Reaching over, he picked up the bat, weighing it in his hand. He'd been hit by worse before. The last time had been six months ago, on a field trip to the Yamal Peninsula. He'd tried to break up a fight in a bar in Murmansk, between a couple of roughnecks celebrating payday, and had had his nose broken with a pool cue for his trouble.

It wasn't the first time he'd had his nose broken, but it had still hurt—a lot. As had the cracked ribs. And yet if he had to choose, he'd almost rather be hit any number of times with a pool cue than have to remember Frankie Fox's parting words.

Some hero.

His jaw tightened.

Maybe he wasn't a hero to look at, but he had the medals and the scars to prove his heroism—scars that had come from bullets, not pool cues. Yet those words and the expression of disdain on Frankie Fox's face were what had kept him from sleeping. Oh, and the faint scent of jasmine that still clung to his pillow.

Irritably, he swung his legs over the side of the bed and walked into the bathroom. Turning on the tap, he ducked his head under the flow of cold water.

Why was he letting some ridiculous, utterly irrelevant 'social media influencer' make him question himself?

Straightening up, he stared at his reflection. She hardly knew Johnny and she knew nothing about him. He gritted his teeth. But Frankie Fox had been right about one thing. His little brother idolised him.

They had always been close. It hadn't mattered that there was an eleven-year age gap or that they were very different people. Arlo was the difficult one. The brilliant high achiever with a double first from Cambridge and a doctorate in geology and earth science. Whereas Johnny...

His throat tightened. Everyone loved Johnny. It was impossible not to. He was beautiful, sweet-tempered, generous...

Too generous, he thought, stalking back into the bedroom. Yanking back the heavy curtains, he glared down at the turbulent grey sea outside. And some people—unscrupulous, self-serving people, like Frankie Fox—took advantage of that generosity.

He swore softly. Why was he even still thinking about that woman?

But he knew why.

He flexed his fingers, remembering the moment when their hands had touched. It had been more than skin on skin. It had felt oddly intimate. As if it had been their lips touching. There had been a charge of something electric.

They had both felt it...

Felt what? An imbalance of protons and electrons?

He scowled. It had probably been that silk thing she was wearing.

Great. Now he was back to thinking about her semi-naked.

Gritting his teeth, he reached down and stroked Nero's head, as if the action might erase the way her touch had jolted through his body.

Last night he'd been exhausted...disorientated.

Look at how it had taken tripping over her suitcase for him even to realise someone was in the house. If he'd been even halfway up to speed, he would have sensed that the moment he'd walked in the front door.

He ran a hand across his face, registering the slight resistance as his fingers grazed the scar on his cheek.

It wasn't just tiredness playing tricks with his mind. The truth was that since his marriage had imploded, he'd spent way too long on his own—and by choice.

He should never have got involved with Harriet in the first place.

Love, relationships, women...all of them came under the heading of 'Random, Imprecise, and Illogical'. In other words, everything he distrusted. So, aside from the occasional dalliance, he'd kept women at arm's length since.

And then, *boom*, out of nowhere there was Frankie Fox. Not just in his house but in his *bed*.

No wonder he'd got momentarily knocked off-balance. But whatever he'd imagined had happened in those few seconds had been just that. A figment of his imagination.

His lip curled.

Frankie, though, was real, and she was here in his home. And, despite her capitulation last night, he wasn't totally convinced that she would leave without a little persuasion.

Remembering the look she'd given him as she stalked out of the room, he felt his shoulders tighten.

Maybe if what had happened hadn't happened, he might have let her stay. There was obviously room and it wasn't as if he was in any danger. She might look like a living flame, but he'd put his hand in the fire once and that was enough for him to learn his lesson.

But he was here to work, and he didn't need any distractions. He didn't need to spend any more time with Frankie to know she would be a distraction with a capital D.

Constance could book her into a hotel for a couple of days and he'd offer to drive her to the station…

There was a low rumble of thunder and, glancing up at the darkening sky, he frowned.

He'd best get on with it.

This storm was going to be a big one.

Exactly six minutes later, he strode into the kitchen. He stared with satisfaction at the cream tiled walls and limed oak worktops.

After his father had retreated from the world much of the house had fallen into disrepair. The kitchen had been the first room he had renovated and, despite lacking the glamour and opulence of the drawing room, in many ways it was still his favourite.

'Good morning, Constance.' He glanced into the pan on the hotplate. 'Porridge—good! I'm absolutely starving.'

Constance swung round, her eyes widening. 'What are you doing here?'

Arlo felt a stab of irritation. First Frankie…now Constance. Why did everyone keep asking him that?

Turning towards the table, he frowned. 'Eating breakfast, I hope. Is that yesterday's paper?'

Constance ignored his question. 'I thought you were with Frankie.'

With Frankie!

Two small words. One big implication. Bigger than was necessary or welcome, he thought, as a tantalising image of what being *with Frankie* might encompass popped into his head.

Keeping his tone even, he shook his head and replied. 'I haven't seen her.' He glanced up at the window. 'Storm's picked up.'

The wind sounded like a trapped animal whining and the rain was hitting the window with great wet smacks.

'She said you were taking her to the station...'

The cheeky little...

His jaw tightened. 'And I will. After breakfast.'

'But she left twenty minutes ago.'

It took two strides for him to reach the window that overlooked the causeway. The sky was the colour of a twelve-bore shotgun now, and it was raining so hard that it was impossible to see clearly. But he didn't need to see clearly to spot the blur of red inching along the raised cobbled road.

Gritting her teeth, Frankie gripped the handle of her suitcase more tightly and gave it a small, sharp tug.

Arlo Milburn had to be the rudest, most loathsome man she'd ever had the misfortune to meet, not to mention the most hard-hearted. What kind of host turned a guest out of their bed in the middle of the night? she asked herself angrily, for what had to be the hundredth time.

And as for his accusations—

She felt her heart scrabble inside her chest as her memories coalesced. Her shocked realisation that he was Johnny's

brother... His cold-eyed disdain... That moment when the
key had caught in her pocket and he'd tried to help her...

She replayed it silently inside her head, her fingers flexing involuntarily. His hand had been warm—warmer than
she'd expected—the skin rough like sandpaper, and there
had been a tiny but definite jolt of electricity.

Her mouth twisted. Arlo had been so tense with fury
he could probably have single-handedly powered the entire
coastline from here to John O'Groats.

She had no idea how he could be related to Johnny. But,
then again, look at her and her super-high-achieving siblings. The twins had both been super-academic, sporty,
and had won every prize going. Harry had been head-boy
at school, and Amelie was practically a saint. With her
blonde hair and sweet smile, she'd looked like an angel.
Everyone had always been so surprised to find out Frankie
was a Fox...

And now she was the only one left.

But this was not the time to go there. Right now, all that
mattered was getting back to the mainland.

Screwing up her eyes against the rain, she stared down
the causeway, trying not to give in to the panic rising in
her chest. The wind was blowing so hard she could hardly
keep hold of her suitcase and the rain felt more like hail-
stones. Worse, the waves were starting to slop over the
cobblestones.

Was that supposed to happen?

Her lower lip trembled. This whole trip had been a disaster. Basically, she'd spent five hours on a train to get
shouted at and soaked to the bone. *Twice*. And to top it all,
she'd overslept.

This was all Arlo's fault.

If he hadn't got her so wound up last night she wouldn't
have slept through her alarm, and then she wouldn't have

bumped into Constance, and Constance wouldn't have insisted that Arlo take her to the station…

Obviously she hadn't been about to hang around to be insulted again, so she'd pretended Arlo was waiting and sneaked out through the front door.

And it had seemed fine at first…

Her case slipped sideways again and, scowling, she gave the handle a savage jerk.

No, no, no, no… This could not be happening.

One of the wheels had popped out of its socket and was spinning away from her across the cobbles. She watched in dismay as it was swallowed up in a rush of water. Now she'd have to carry her case.

But as she turned to pick it up she felt something change amid the chaos.

Darkness.

As if the sky had turned black…

Looking up, she felt her heart slam into her ribcage, panic strangle her breath.

A huge, curling grey wave was rising out of the sea, towering over her.

For a moment, the air around her seemed to thicken and slow. And then the wave was falling, and the earth shifted on its axis, and then she was falling too, her feet slipping beneath her, her scream drowned out by an infinity of water…

From an immense, unfathomable distance, as though it had reached through the storm clouds, a hand grabbed her shoulder. Suddenly she was on her feet again.

Spluttering, gasping like a landed fish, she squinted up at her rescuer.

Arlo.

Water was sloshing around his feet, swirling and foaming across the cobbles. She caught a glimpse of dark, narrowed eyes, and then he scooped her into his arms as if she was made of feathers.

'Don't let go,' he shouted into her ear.

He turned back into the storm and the scream of the wind felt as if it was vibrating inside her bones like a shrieking banshee. Ahead, she could see nothing. The rain was like a curtain of water.

Her fingers tightened around Arlo's neck and she felt his shoulders brace. Then he bent his body into the gale, pushing forward, the only solid object in a swaying world. Dragging in a shallow breath, she turned her face into his chest, felt the heavy curve of his arm muffling the noise and the pounding rain.

Salt was stinging her eyes, and it hurt just to breathe, but she was not alone. Arlo was here. And she knew that, whatever happened, he would keep on going until he reached where he wanted to be.

A dark shape loomed out of the rain. It was a car, and as her chest hollowed out with relief, Arlo yanked open the passenger door, tossing her and her case inside.

He wrestled with the door and for a moment the roar of the storm filled the car. Then the door closed, and he was clambering into the driver's seat, and turning the key in the ignition.

'Hold tight,' he muttered. 'This could be tricky.'

They inched forward, the furiously swinging windscreen wipers having no impact on the rain thundering against the windscreen.

She clenched her hand around the armrest as a gust of wind sent the car staggering sideways, and then the car stopped and Arlo jumped out. Seconds later her door opened.

'Take my hand,' he yelled over the howl of the wind, and then he was pulling her forward.

They stumbled into the house. The huge front door crashed shut behind them and the high-pitched shriek of the storm faded like a whistling kettle taken off the heat.

Constance was standing in the hallway, her face pale with shock. Arlo's dark dog was beside her.

'Oh, my dear… Thank goodness you're all right. Come with me. There's a fire in the drawing room.'

Arlo glanced away, over his shoulder, his profile cutting a broken line against the cream panelling. 'I'll get some towels.'

Frankie let the housekeeper lead her through the house. She was shivering so hard her chattering teeth sounded like an old-fashioned typewriter.

'Here, sit down. I'm going to make you some tea,' Constance said firmly.

Frankie sat down obediently on a large, faded velvet sofa and as the dog jumped up beside her lightly, she pressed her hand against his back. He felt warm and solid and, blinking back tears, she breathed out unsteadily.

Outside, in the screaming power of the storm, she had been robbed of the power of thought. It had been all she could do to cling to Arlo. Now, with the flames warming her body, her brain was coming back online.

Her fingers curled into the dog's fur as she pictured the scene on the causeway, her guilt blotting out any relief she might have felt at having been rescued. How could she have been so stupid? After everything that had happened. After all the promises she'd made to herself. To her family.

'You need to get changed.'

Her head jolted up at the sound of a deep, male voice. Arlo had walked back into the room, holding a pile of towels. Folded on top were a green-and-blue-striped rugby shirt and some sweatpants.

'Here.' He held out the pile. 'These are some of Johnny's clothes. Your suitcase got drenched,' he said, by way of explanation.

He was staring down at her intently, and the flickering flames highlighted the hard angles of his face. He was soaked right though to his skin too, she thought guiltily. His shirt was sticking to his arms and body, and water was pooling in little puddles at his feet.

Picturing how he'd swept her into his arms like a knight without armour, she felt her heart beating too hard for her body. He'd saved her life. But, more importantly, he had risked his own.

She was about to apologise, to thank him for what he'd done, but before she could open her mouth, he said abruptly, 'They might be a little big, but they're clean and dry. I'll leave you to get out of those wet things.'

Glancing down at the dog, he frowned, moved as if to say something else, and then seemed to change his mind.

She watched him walk back out of the room, and then she stood up shakily. Her fingers were clumsy with cold, and it seemed to take for ever to peel off her jeans and sweatshirt, but finally she managed to get undressed and into Johnny's clothes. As she was rubbing her hair with a towel there was a knock at the door and Constance popped her head round.

'Oh, good, you've changed.' She was carrying a tray. 'I've brought you some tea and biscuits.' Leaning down, she picked up the pile of wet clothes. 'I'll just take these and run them through the washing machine.'

Frankie shook her head. 'Oh, no, please…that's really not necessary—'

'It is.'

Arlo was back. He had changed into faded chinos and a dark jumper that moulded around the contoured power of his arms and chest, and she had a sudden sharp memory of how it had felt to be pressed against his body.

'The salt will rot them if you don't wash it out.' He turned towards the housekeeper. 'Constance, could you give us a few moments? I need to have a couple of words with Ms Fox.'

As the door clicked shut, Frankie said quickly, 'Actually, I wanted to—'

'What the *hell* do you think you're playing at?'

Her chin jerked up as Arlo spun round, his eyes blazing. She stared at him, dry-mouthed, her heart pounding fiercely. Last night she'd thought he was angry, but now she saw that had been a warm-up to the main act.

'I'm not playing at anything—'

But he wasn't listening. 'So what was that little stunt of yours about?' He shook his head derisively. 'Let me ask you something. Do you know what that is out there?' He gestured to where the rain was slicing horizontally across the window. 'It's a storm *with a name*. Not all storms have names, but if they do that means there are winds of over fifty miles an hour.' His lip curled. 'There's also this thing called a *tide*. And twice a day there's a high tide. That means the sea is at its *highest*—'

'I know what a high tide is,' she snapped, her shock switching to anger at the condescension in his voice. 'I'm not a child.'

'Then why were you out there skipping down the causeway like a pre-schooler?' His cold gaze was fixed on her face, the pale line of his scar stark against the dark stubble. 'Did you think you could *influence* the weather? Make the sun shine? Stop the wind blowing?'

Stomach twisting, she struggled against a surge of humiliation and fury. 'I was doing what you told me to do. I was leaving.'

'What I told you to do—?' He rolled his eyes. 'I might have known this would be my fault.'

'I didn't say that'

'But you thought it.' His eyebrows collided in the middle of his forehead. 'Of course you did—because nothing is ever your fault, is it, sweetheart?'

Her ribs tightened sharply at the memory of a different

room on another rainy day. Not her fault officially, no. But the coroner's verdict hadn't changed the facts. She knew it had been her fault. All of it. That if she hadn't been so selfish, so insistent about getting her own way, then her family would still be alive…

Tears stung her eyes and the effort of not crying made her throat burn. Only she was not going to cry—not in front of him.

'Actually, Mr Milburn—'

The calm, bland expression on his face made her pulse shiver. 'Why so formal? I think we went past the "Mr Milburn" stage when you decided to get all warm and cosy in my bed.'

Her jaw dropped. She felt heat in her face, in her throat. Oh, but he was a horrible, horrible man.

Folding her arms, she took a deep breath. 'It's not my fault, *Mr Milburn*, that you're some boorish oaf who throws his guests out into the rain.'

He gave a bark of laughter. Only she knew he wasn't amused.

'Boorish oaf?'

The air crackled between them, and the snap of current mirrored the lightning forking through the sky outside.

His eyes narrowed and he stalked towards her.

Standing up, she held out a defensive hand. 'Stop—'

But he kept on coming as if she hadn't spoken, and she was struck again not just by his size, but by the sense of purpose beneath the layers of muscle and sinew and skin and by the intent in his eyes.

He stopped in front of her. 'Boorish oaf…' he repeated softly, his expression arctic. 'I just saved your life. Or have you forgotten how close you came to drowning?

Of course she hadn't.

For a few half-seconds she replayed the press of his hard

chest against her cheek and how his arm had shielded her from the storm raging around them.

Her skin felt suddenly hot and tight. He had been so solid, so large. And, as ludicrous as it sounded now, he had seemed as implacable as the storm. As uncompromising and unyielding. She had wanted to burrow beneath his skin. To stay in the endless stretch of his arms with her head tucked under his chin…

Her heart bumped against her ribs. It was because he was implacable and uncompromising and unyielding that she'd been out on the causeway in the first place.

'You wouldn't have had to save my life if you hadn't been so horrible.'

His gaze raked her face like the lamp from a lighthouse.

'I think the word you're looking for is *truthful*,' he said coldly.

He ran his hand over his face, as if he wanted to wipe her out of his eyes, and her breath caught. She hadn't noticed it before but three of the fingers on his left hand looked too short, the tips oddly flattened.

She shivered inside. What kind of man was she dealing with?

'You know…' he spoke slowly, his dark gaze locking with hers '… I thought you were just some clueless airhead who was hoping to get her claws into my soft-hearted brother.' His hard voice echoed around the room. 'But you are a *child*. A wilful, reckless child who wants everything her own way and when that doesn't happen throws a tantrum.'

The expression on his face made her skin sting. 'I— I'm not a child and I wasn't throwing a tantrum. I made a mistake—'

'And mistakes cost lives.' His voice was cold, each word more clipped than the last. As if he was biting them off and spitting them out. 'You're lucky it wasn't *your* life.'

Frankie blinked, tried to breathe, to swallow, but it was as if her heart was blocking her throat. She felt sick. It was true, and part of her had wanted, needed, to hear the truth for so long. Only it hurt so much more that she could have imagined.

'I'm sorry,' she whispered, and even though she was warm she was shivering again.

For months she'd been trying to hold it all together, but now she could feel her control starting to unravel—here in this room, with this stranger.

'You're right. I wasn't thinking about anyone but myself. I just wanted to go home. Only I can't—'

Not back to London. *Home,* home. But she could never do that again.

He was staring at her with those unyielding grey eyes and she took a shaky step backwards. *What was she thinking?* Had she really been about to tell Arlo the truth? Him, of all people? A man who clearly thought she was not worth saving.

And the trouble was, he was right.

Hot tears stung her eyes and the room blurred. 'I'm so sorry.' She gave a sob. 'I'm really, really sorry—'

Arlo watched in horror as Frankie stumbled across the room. He hadn't meant to upset her that much. It wasn't something he did: make women cry. Make *anyone* cry. Even with Harriet he'd been polite—courteous, even. It was only after they've broken up that he'd felt angry.

But that anger had been nothing in comparison to the head-pounding fury that had swept over him as he and Frankie had stumbled into the Hall.

How could she have done something so stupid, so reckless?

Worse than her recklessness, though, was the knowledge that he had driven her to it.

He'd wanted to scare her as she had scared him, so that she would think twice before she did something so fool-hardy again.

His heart contracted as he thought back to the moment when he'd looked out of the kitchen window and seen her red suitcase bobbing jauntily along the causeway.

Those few minutes driving over the cobbles had been some of the longest in his life. Even now, the thought of her slipping beneath the swirling grey waves made his stomach lurch queasily.

'Frankie—'

She had reached the door and her fingers were tugging helplessly at the heavy brass handle. Before he knew what he was doing he had moved swiftly across the room. He thought she would tense as he pulled her against him, but she seemed barely to register him, and he realised that shock at what had so nearly happened out in the storm was finally kicking in. Or perhaps she had been in shock the whole time, he thought, as for the second time that day he scooped her into his arms.

'Shh… It's okay…it's okay.'

He carried her over to the sofa and sat down, curving his arm around her, holding her close as she sobbed into him.

Finally, he felt her body go slack and she let out a shuddering breath.

'Here.' He handed her a handkerchief. 'It's clean. And, more importantly, dry.'

She wiped her swollen eyes. 'Thank you.'

The wobble in her voice matched the shake in her hands as she held it out. He shook his head. 'No, you keep it.'

He watched as she pleated the fabric between her fingers, and then smoothed it flat, so that his initials were visible.

'I'm sorry,' she said shakily. 'For putting you in danger—'

'No, *I'm* sorry.' He frowned, wondering why it was so

easy to say that now, when earlier herds of wild horses couldn't have dragged those words from his lips. 'If I hadn't kicked off at you last night you wouldn't have felt like you had to take that risk.'

Gazing down at her blotchy face, he felt a prickle of guilt. And he certainly shouldn't have kicked off at her just now—not when she was in such a state.

'I was tired, and annoyed with Johnny, and I took it out on you.'

'He did try and get in touch with you to tell you I was coming,' she said quickly.

Possibly... Johnny always had good intentions, and usually he found it easy to overlook his little brother's faults, but for some reason Frankie's defence of him got under his skin.

She looked up at him and the blue of her irises was so bewitchingly intense against her dark, tear-clotted lashes that he almost lost his train of thought.

He shrugged. 'I'm sure he did. Look, when the storm dies down a bit, I can take you to the station.'

She nodded. 'I'm sorry for making such a fuss. I'm just a bit tired. I've been working stupid hours...'

He understood tiredness. Sometimes out on the ice fatigue was like lead in his bones. But there was something more than tiredness in her voice...a note of despair, almost.

His jaw clenched. He understood that too, but Frankie was too young to feel that way.

He felt a stab of anger. Someone should be looking out for her.

Not him, though. Not after Harriet.

Her fingers smoothed out the handkerchief again and he felt her take a breath. Then she said quietly, 'I just want to say that it was really brave, what you did out there. Heroic, actually. So, thank you.'

She hesitated, and then he felt the flutter of her breath as she kissed him gently on the cheek.

The movement shifted her weight and she slipped sideways. Without thinking, he touched his hand against her hipbone to steady her. He heard the snap of her breath as she looked up, and when he met her soft blue gaze suddenly it was as if he'd run out of air. His head was spinning.

A minute went by, then another, and then she leaned forward and kissed him on the lips.

A voice in his head told him to stop her. That this was a mistake. That he didn't know this woman and what he did know he didn't like.

But then her fingers clutched at his shirt, drawing him closer, and he was lost.

It was like walking into a white-out.

There was nothing but Frankie. Nothing but the soft contours of her body and her mouth fusing with his.

His hands skimmed over her back, sliding up through her hair, and he knew that this was not so much an exploration as an admission of his driving need to feel her, to touch every part of her.

He felt her soften in his arms and hunger jackknifed through him as she leaned closer, so that her breasts were brushing against his chest. Blood pounded through his veins as he teased the upper bow of her mouth with his tongue, tracing the shape of her lips, and then he was guiding her onto his lap, pulling her restless hips against the hard press of his erection.

She moaned softly and, parting her lips, deepened the kiss.

He shuddered, heat flooding his limbs. Her mouth felt like hot silk and, groaning, he spread his hand over her back—

The sharp knock on the door echoed through the room

like a gunshot and, peeling Frankie off his lap, he tipped her unceremoniously onto the sofa as he got to his feet.

What the hell was she playing at?

More to the point, what was *he* playing at?

Aside from the unspoken assumption that Frankie and Johnny were involved, this was a road he needed to travel less—not more.

His entire relationship with Harriet had been humbling and short—just under three months from that first kiss to the day she moved out—and he didn't need any more reminders of the idiocy of his behaviour.

Or maybe he did.

She stared up at him dazedly, her cheeks flushed, her lips swollen from his kisses.

Tearing his gaze away, he answered, 'Yes, what is it?'

'Douglas just called.' Constance's voice floated serenely through the door. 'They've issued an orange weather warning. I just thought you'd like to know.'

So the weather was causing road closures, interruption to power, and an increased risk to life and property. In other words, chaos.

Tell me something I don't know, he thought savagely.

Running his hand through his hair, he swore under his breath as his dazed brain finally registered the full implication of Constance's words.

An orange warning also meant being prepared to change plans. In this case, his plans to get Frankie off the island.

Jaw clenching, he glanced over at her.

'Looks like this storm is going to get worse before it gets better. Unfortunately for both of us, that means you're stuck here for the foreseeable future.'

Her eyes climbed up to his, a flush of colour engulfing the freckles on her face. 'Wow, you're a real Prince Charming.'

He held her gaze. 'What? A lovestruck fool chasing after

a woman who can't keep her clothing on? You're in the wrong fairy tale, sweetheart.'

She gave him a look that could have stopped global warming in its tracks. 'You don't need to tell *me* that.'

His mouth twisted. 'Let me explain to you how this is going to work, Ms Fox,' he said. 'I don't want to see you. I don't want to hear you or talk to you. And above all I don't want to kiss you.'

'I don't want to kiss you either.'

She gave him an imperious smile that made him want to instantly eat his words.

'Good.' Stalking across the room, he yanked open the door. 'Stay out of my way. In fact, do us both a favour and stay in your room. Otherwise I might just be tempted to lock you in there until the storm passes.'

CHAPTER THREE

SLAMMING HER BEDROOM DOOR, Frankie stalked across the room, her heart pounding, her whole body trembling.

How dare he?

Her fingers clenched into fists.

Sending her to her room as if she was some child. And saying all that stuff about not wanting to see her or kiss her. As if she wanted to kiss *him*.

Her mouth twisted. Okay, to be fair, she had just kissed him—but it wasn't as if she'd planned it. And he was at least partly to blame…catching her off guard, his gentleness coming so fast after his anger.

Pulse twitching, she let her mind go back to the moment when she had lost her balance, and her brain conjured up his hand on her hip with such unflinching, high-definition clarity she could almost feel his precise firm grip…see the flare of heat in his eyes…taste her own urgent, unbidden desire to kiss him.

Not out of gratitude but out of a head-swimming hunger she'd neither questioned nor understood.

Remembering the noises she had made as his hands had moved over her body, she felt her face grow warm. It had lasted two, three minutes at most. It had been just a kiss…

Except something that had that kind of power—the power to make your heart stop beating—surely couldn't be *just* anything.

Not something, she corrected herself. *Someone.*

Arlo Milburn.

He was like no one she'd ever kissed before. Older, more intense, beyond her comprehension and control. And yet she had wanted him like she had never wanted any man.

And for those two, maybe three minutes she'd thought he wanted her in the same way.

Only then Constance had knocked on the door, and he had jerked back from her as if waking from a daydream.

Or a nightmare.

Her hands felt suddenly clammy. Clearly that was what he'd been thinking. Why else would he have pulled away? A hot blush of embarrassment spread over her skin as she remembered how he'd tipped her onto the sofa and quickly moved to put as much distance between them as possible.

Picturing his expression, she still wasn't sure whether he had been stunned or appalled at what had happened. Probably both.

Her brain froze. But then Arlo thought she was going out with his brother.

The heat in her cheeks made her feel as if her face was on fire. It was a testament to her current state of mind that she had completely forgotten about Johnny.

As Arlo's lips had touched hers, and he had pulled her against his big body, she had forgotten *everything*. It was as if her mind had been wiped clear.

But Arlo's hadn't.

Her stomach clenched.

Did he really believe she was with Johnny? That he was some kind of stand-in?

Oh, she felt awful. But why? Aside from one hug, nothing had happened with Johnny. And nothing had really happened with Arlo.

Just because there was no explanation for their kiss, that didn't make it significant. And perhaps there *was* an explanation. Both of them had just nearly died. Their emotions had been running high and all tangled up, so in some ways it had been almost inevitable that they would kiss.

She breathed out shakily. Hopefully at some point in the future she would be able to laugh about all of this, but in the meantime she was going to have to find a way to get through the next twenty-four hours.

Trying to still the jittery feeling in her legs that thought produced, she walked over to the window. Outside, the rain was still sheeting down, and both the sky and the violently cresting waves were the same dull gunmetal grey.

The weather forecasters had been right. It looked as if this storm wasn't going anywhere any time soon, and that meant she was not going anywhere either. Only there was no way she was going to stay cooped up in this room until the wind blew itself out.

Arlo might be a man of many talents, but even he could only be in one place at once—and as there was both an east and a west wing, the chances of her bumping into him would be minuscule.

Maybe it was time to do a little exploring...

Obviously she had known the Hall was huge, but she was still stunned by the scale of it. There were just so many rooms, and each one seemed to be bigger and grander than the last. Everything was so perfect, she thought, as she gazed around an amazing book-lined library. And so perfectly English. From the plethora of patterns—chintz, checks, muted stripes—to the large, imposing portraits on the walls.

As she left the library and walked down the corridor her footsteps faltered in front of a half-open door. Behind it, a phone was ringing. It wasn't a mobile...it had an old-fashioned jangling sound.

Pinching her lip with her fingers, she hesitated, her shoulders tensing. Surely somebody would answer it...?

But the phone kept ringing, and before she had made a conscious decision to do so she was pushing open the door and walking into the room. It was some kind of office, judging by the two identical imposing wooden desks facing one another like duelling partners. Both were so cluttered with books and papers that it took her a moment to locate the phone.

She found it eventually, juddering beside a snow globe containing a polar bear. Heart pounding, she snatched it up.

'Hello—?'

But whoever it was had already rung off.

Typical. Rolling her eyes, she dropped the receiver back in its cradle. *Why did that always happen?*

Gazing around the room, she felt her breath rise with a rush into her throat. It was definitely an office, and it was equally obvious whose office it was. Her quick glance down at an in-tray overflowing with envelopes addressed to 'Dr Arlo Milburn' merely confirmed her suspicions.

She'd forgotten he was a Doctor of Geography. Or was it Geology?

Feeling as if she had wandered into the lair of some sleeping grizzly bear, she looked nervously round the room. Like the rest of the house, it felt both effortlessly grand but enviably comfortable.

What *was* surprising, though, was how untidy it was.

There were books everywhere. But not neatly stacked vertically on shelves, like in the library. Some were on shelves, but they were wedged in haphazardly. Elsewhere they rose in towering piles like stalagmites or huddled against pieces of furniture like snowdrifts.

Frowning, she glanced down at the paper-strewn desk. She'd expected someone like Arlo to be one of those 'tidy mind, tidy home' types, who thought a pile of letters demonstrated an inability to take command of a situation.

Remembering how he'd barked orders at her earlier, she curled her lip. He certainly liked telling people what to do, and it was hard to imagine him losing control.

Well, not that hard, she thought, her face growing hot

and her lips tingling at the memory of how he'd pulled her against his body...

Quickly blanking her mind, she looked down at the chaos of paper, her gaze snagging on a notebook lying open. From this angle it was difficult to tell, but it looked like a sketch of a bird...a gull, maybe. Curious, she walked around the desk and sat down on the battered leather swivel chair.

It was just an outline—a few pencil marks, really— dated and annotated: *Pagodroma Nivea. Juvenile.* Then what looked like a map reference. Turning the page, she discovered more sketches and, her heart suddenly beating very hard, flicked through them.

They were good. Obviously drawn from life and by Arlo. Only she couldn't imagine him taking that moment of care and concentration to sketch anything. He was so vehement, so fierce. Surely his mere presence would make any self-respecting bird take flight...

This is lovely!

She touched a sketch of a seal pup. It was so lifelike she half expected to feel the fur beneath her fingertips.

Her eyes dropped to the notes beneath it. The handwriting was cramped and unfamiliar, and yet it *felt* familiar, comforting... Curling her feet up under her thighs, she started to read.

She recycled her plastics and tried not to use taxis when she could walk—but, truthfully, the environment had always been just another of those unfathomable, slightly intimidating big-concept words like 'the economy'.

But as she deciphered Arlo's notes she found herself not just curious but engaged. He wrote simply but eloquently, balancing the necessary use of scientific terms with obvious, unapologetic passion, so that she could almost see the frosted fields of ice with their exquisite lace of cracks and crystals. And Arlo, his grey eyes narrowed against the polar winds, his mouth—

His mouth… What about his mouth?

Pushing the notebook away, she picked up the snow globe instead, balancing it in her hands as she leaned back in the chair.

Her heart was still beating fast and out of time, as if she'd been caught in the act of doing something wrong. Which, in a way, she had, she thought, her brain tracking back to what had happened in the drawing room.

Only it hadn't felt wrong. Quite the opposite.

She tipped the snow globe upside down, watching the flakes swirl. Back in London, she had thought work, or rather too much work, was her problem, so she had come up here to relax and get some perspective.

Instead, she had nearly drowned, and then she had kissed Arlo, and now her head was even more overloaded.

Her chest tightened. It was stupid that he affected her this way. What she needed was to keep busy…

Her eyes flickered to the notebook, and she remembered what he'd said last night about writing up his lectures.

Could she work for him?

Her whole body stiffened in outrage at the question.

Absolutely not. Who in their right mind would want to work with Arlo?

He was rude and arrogant and high-handed. It would be like working for a dictator.

But, then again, it would be more a favour than actual employment…and only for a day or so. It would give her something else to think about other than his mouth… Plus, it would mean that he'd have to take her a little bit more seriously. Stop treating her like a cross between a disobedient child and some poor relation who had turned up uninvited for dinner.

And he *had* saved her life…

Pushing away from the desk, she let the chair swing slowly round in a slow circle until she was back where she started.

'Having fun?'

Her chin jerked up. Arlo was standing in the doorway, his mouth a thin line of contempt, Nero at his side.

She felt her stomach flip over.

He was scowling, and his dark hair looked as if he had run his hand through it too many times. A laptop dangled open from his hand.

'I was just—'

'Just what?' he snapped. His dark gaze swept around the room like a searchlight. 'You shouldn't be in here.'

'The phone was ringing.' She tried to smile. 'I came in here to answer it…'

She had been trying to do him a favour. Honestly, she wasn't sure why she'd bothered. But, then again, it probably *did* look as if she was snooping… Likely because she had been, she thought, a flush of heat creeping up to her ears.

'So who was it?'

'I don't know. They rang off just as I picked up.'

'How convenient,' he said coolly.

She glowered at him. 'What's that supposed to mean?'

'It means I don't think the phone was ringing. I think you wanted to have a nose around. Perhaps I can help? Were you looking for anything in particular?' The derision in his voice contorted his features. 'Something of value, maybe?'

Oh, that was low.

Her fingers curled around the snow globe. 'You know, it wouldn't hurt for you to be nice occasionally,' she said coldly.

He was staring at her as if she had suggested he might like to eat the contents of a wheelie bin.

'It wouldn't hurt for *you* to do what you're told.'

Her hands were gripping the snow globe so tightly she thought it might shatter. 'Who are you to tell me what to do?'

His dark grey eyes were like the slits in a castle wall. She half expected to see the tip of an arrow pointing out of each of them.

'Who am I? I'm your worst nightmare, Ms Fox.'

He stared at her, his hard, angular face dragging her gaze upwards.

'I'm a man who's immune to your charms. So I suggest you stop batting your eyelashes at me and go back to your room. And make sure you stay there. Otherwise, next time, I won't be feeling so generous.'

She stood up so suddenly that the chair spun backwards. As it bounced off the shelves behind her, a pile of papers fluttered to the floor.

'You don't know the meaning of the word, *generous*,' she snarled. A beat of fury and frustration was pulsing over her skin. Her fists curling by her sides, she shook her head. 'You know, I can't believe I was actually going to offer to *help* you.'

Now he was staring at her as if she had grown horns or an extra head. '*You?* Help me?'

Trying to remember why she had thought it was a good idea, she glared at him. 'With writing up your lectures.'

He gave a bark of laughter. 'Why? So you can engineer a repeat performance of what happened downstairs?' Now he was shaking his head incredulously. 'I don't think so.'

She drew herself up to her full height. 'I didn't engineer anything.'

His flint-coloured eyes were cold. 'You kissed a perfect stranger. I would have thought that required a little forethought—unless, of course, you do that with every man you meet.'

Her hands were trembling, and she was nearly breathless with anger. No, actually, she didn't. As a matter of fact, she'd only kissed a handful of men—and none with the unthinking urgency with which she had kissed him.

Lifting her chin, she glared at him. 'I'm sorry to disappoint you, Mr Milburn, but you're a long way from my idea of perfect.'

The skin on his face stretched taut, like a drum, and she felt the air grow charged, as if the storm had moved inside.

'As you are mine. I mean, aside from the quite obvious fact that you lack the discipline and diligence I would expect from anyone who works for me, I'm not sure you have the specialist knowledge I need. I mean, what exactly do you know about ice anyway?'

The curl of his lip made her want to throw the snow globe at his head.

'Other than crushing it for frozen margaritas at a "fun girls' night just for you"?'

His words sounded familiar.

Her jaw started to tremble. That was because they were *her* words—from the blog she had posted last summer. She breathed out shakily. The idea of Arlo reading her blog made the anger leak out of her like air from a burst balloon.

Her heart thudded heavily in her chest. She felt stupid and shallow and superfluous. But then that was what she was. It was just that in the heat of their argument she had momentarily forgotten.

Arlo saw her stiffen and swore under his breath.

Finding her in his office, curled up in his chair, had caught him off balance more than he'd ever be willing to admit.

She had been pinching her lip—a habit she seemed to have when she was thinking—and, watching her press her fingers into that cushion of flesh, he had felt a rush of too-predictable heat tighten his muscles.

It had been a shock to discover than he could still be so weak, so hungry for what was so obviously wrong for him, and he'd felt angry and frustrated with himself. Angry, too, with her, for exposing this weakness in him.

Maybe he had been a little brutal, but it wasn't as if he was going to take her up on her offer. The idea was ludicrous.

Or was it?

Gazing over at Frankie, he pondered the question.

Perhaps, in a way, her working for him wasn't such a bad idea, given the facts—which were that he had no idea how long the storm would take to blow itself out, and that Frankie would be here in the house with him until it did. Giving her a job would not just keep her out of mischief, it would put their relationship on a more formal footing and provide clear boundaries.

'What did you mean by help?' he asked slowly.

She stared at him mutely, then said, 'If that's your version of an apology you might want to do a little work on it.'

His eyes locked with hers. *Apologise for what?* She was in his office, uninvited—

With effort, he reined in his temper. Right now, there was enough turmoil outside—he didn't need to add to it.

Unlocking his jaw, he took a breath. 'I'm sorry for what I said.'

He waited as she shifted from one foot to the other, her expression guarded.

'I'm sorry too,' she said finally. 'I shouldn't have come into your office without asking. I wouldn't have done, but your phone was ringing, and I thought it might be important.'

Her apology surprised him almost as much as her offer of help, and for a moment he wondered if he'd misjudged her. But it wasn't easy to get his head around the idea that he might have been wrong—partly because he still thought she was inherently self-serving, and partly because it reminded him that he'd been so wrong about Harriet and was supposed to have learned and moved on from the experience.

Pushing that thought away, he nodded. 'If the offer is still there, I'd like to take you up on it. You'd be doing me a favour,' he added, when she didn't reply.

'I *would* have been, yes.'

'You still could,' he said carefully.

Her eyes widened. 'So you can laugh at me again?'

'I wouldn't laugh—'

Glancing away, she shook her head again. 'I'd be no use to you. Like you said, I'm only interested in the kind of ice that comes in a glass. I don't know the first thing about vertical migration or hydrofracture.'

Vertical migration... Hydrofracture...

Arlo frowned. How the hell did she know about those? Unless—

'You read my notebook.'

She gazed back at him, her chin jutting forward.

'So what if I did? I'm not going to share it with my followers, if that's what you're worried about.'

'No, I mean you can read my writing.'

She looked at him, confusion warring with curiosity, then shrugged. 'My father was a doctor.'

Her tone told him that she was not entirely sure why she was telling him that fact.

'Everyone thought his writing was illegible, but I grew up with it so...'

'Is that why you offered to help me?'

She shrugged again. 'I don't know. It felt like the least I could do. I mean, you did save my life.' She glanced away. 'And I'm not working at the moment.'

What did that mean? He knew almost nothing about the mechanics of social media, but what little he did know

suggested that it was a twenty-four-seven, three-hundred-
and-sixty-five-days-a-year kind of gig.

Not that it was any of his business… And yet he found
himself wondering what it was she wasn't telling him.

Watching her pinch her lip again, he tamped down the
urge to reach over and pull her hand away and then cover
her mouth with his.

His jaw clenched, and suddenly he needed her to agree.
'Look, Frankie, I know we got off on the wrong foot, but
this storm is going to be kicking around for a couple of
days and that means we're going to be—'

'Stuck with each other?' Her eyes met his. 'Not if I stay
in my room, like you told me to.'

'I shouldn't have said that either. I was just—'

Just scared. Scared of what would happen if they came
within touching distance of one another. Scared that he
would give in to that same desperate, urgent desire that
had swept him away as effortlessly as one of those towering grey waves outside.

'Just being a boorish oaf.'

There was a pause.

'Is it just transcribing?' she asked.

He felt a jolt of surprise. 'You've done this before?'

Her eyes slid away from his, and he had that same feeling as before—as if she was holding back.

'My older brother and sister both did dissertations. They
paid me to type them up.'

He nodded. 'Okay, well, there's a bit of an overlap between my notes on the web and the ones I had to write by
hand, but I can talk you through that. It would help, too, if
you could answer the phone. Take messages if I'm on the
other line.'

There was a pause. He could almost see her working
through the pros and cons.

She sighed. 'Okay. I'll do it. But just so we're clear, I'm

working *with* you, not for you.' Lifting her chin, she let her hair fell back from her face so that he could see the curve of her jawline. 'I'm not having you bark orders at me—'

He held up his hands in appeasement.

'There will be no barking. Although I can't speak for Nero.'

A reluctant smile pulled at the corners of her mouth, softening her face, and suddenly it was difficult to find enough breath to fill his lungs. If she kept smiling like that then maybe the dog kennel might be the safest place for him.

'Good. That's sorted. Take a seat.' He gestured towards the other desk. 'And we can get started.'

The morning passed with almost hallucinatory speed. One moment Frankie was walking across the room to the other desk, and the next Arlo was pushing back his chair and telling her it was lunchtime.

Gazing round the beautiful dining room, with its cream panelling, carved wood fireplace and oil paintings, she felt her heartbeat accelerate. Mostly, if she was at home, lunch would be a sandwich eaten at her desk—and then only if she could be bothered to make one. More often than not it was just a bowl of cereal.

This, though, was a sit-down three-course meal, with cutlery and napkins and side plates...

'Everything okay?'

Arlo was staring at her, his face arranged in one of those unreadable expressions.

'Everything's fine.' She glanced down at her starter: a tartlet of smoked roe, tomato, and marjoram.

'It's just that when you said, "Let's grab some lunch", I was expecting something a little more basic.'

'What did you think? That we'd be gnawing on reindeer bones—'

She smiled faintly. 'Something like that.'

Reaching for his knife and fork, he shrugged. 'I've spent the last few months eating polar pâté three times a day with a spork. When I get home, I like to eat real food at a table.' His eyes rested on her face steadily. 'It's one of my rules.'

Her brain picked over his words. *One of his rules.* What were the others?

Picking up her glass, she took a sip of water. Earlier, she'd asked herself who would want to work with him. The answer, surprisingly, was pretty much anyone and everyone, judging by the number of calls she'd answered in the hour before lunch. The phone had rung almost non-stop.

The Smithsonian Institution, the Royal Geographical Society, and Stanford University had all asked him to speak, and after just sixty minutes in his company it was not hard to see why. Listening to him talk, it had become clear to her that Arlo knew his stuff. More importantly—and, she was guessing, more unusually in a scientist—he was both concise and eloquent.

She liked the sound of his voice, the strength of it, and the measured, precise way he chose his words. And he spoke Russian fluently.

Of course, she *didn't* speak Russian, so she had no idea what he'd been talking about when he'd spoken it on the phone, but it had sounded almost like poetry.

He looked like a poet too. Or maybe a cross between a poet and pirate, with his scowl and his messy hair and that complicated mouth.

Although it hadn't felt that complicated when they were kissing...

As if he'd heard her thoughts, Arlo looked over at her, his grey eyes boring into hers. She put down her glass and over the sudden, rapid beat of her heart said quickly, 'I can imagine.'

He shifted back in his chair, his dark sweater stretching endlessly across his shoulders. 'Stop fidgeting and eat something,' he said.

'I'm not fidgeting.'

'Just eat,' he ordered. 'I don't want you passing out on me.'

'I've never passed out in my life,' she protested.

He stared back at her impassively, a comma of dark hair falling across his forehead to match the white scar on his cheek.

'So?' Leaning forward, he speared a piece of tomato on his plate. 'You nearly drowned this morning. I don't suppose that's a regular occurrence, *ergo* there's a first time for everything. Now, eat.'

She stared at him, exasperation pulsing down her spine. 'Have you always been this bossy?'

He hesitated, as though seriously considering her question. Then, 'I would say so, yes.'

Picking up her cutlery, she rolled her eyes. 'I bet you were a prefect at school.'

There was a pause and, watching his lips almost curve, she felt the air leave her body.

'Actually, no.'

'Really? Finally, we have something in common,' she said lightly.

Their eyes locked, hers teasing, his serious, and then he nodded. 'It would appear so.'

Suddenly she felt as if the room had shrunk. Or maybe the table had. Either way, it felt as if they were sitting way too close.

There was another small pause, and then he smiled. 'Now, eat.'

As he turned his attention back to his plate her fingers tightened around the knife and fork. Some people's smiles—Johnny's, for instance—were just a part of them. But Arlo's was miraculous, transformative, softening the blunt, uncompromising arrangement of his features into something far less daunting.

She silently fought against an urge to reach out and trace the swooping curve of his mouth. A mouth that held and delivered an urgency of promise…

As if sensing her gaze, Arlo looked up and, not wanting him to notice her flushed cheeks, she bent her head over her plate.

For a moment they ate in silence.

'Good?' He raised one dark eyebrow.

She nodded. It was melt-in-the-mouth delicious, the pastry literally crumbling under her fork.

In fact, it was all delicious. The main course of silky pappardelle with beef shin ragu was followed by a tart Amalfi lemon sorbet and then coffee.

Leaning back in his seat, Arlo gave her a levelling glance, his dark eyes roaming over her face. 'You were pale before. You have colour in your cheeks now.'

Her heart started to beat very fast.

He had the most intense gaze of any man she'd ever met. It felt as if it was pushing through her skin…as if he was inside her.

Inside her.

Her pulse twitched as the words repeated inside her head and blood surged through her, so that for a moment she forgot what they were talking about, forgot where she was, *who* she was.

Looking away, she cleared her throat. 'It's been a long day and a lot has happened.'

He nodded but didn't reply. A few seconds ticked by, and then he said abruptly, 'Yes, about that…'

Her stomach dropped as if he'd just pushed her out of a plane. She stared at him, the skin on her face suddenly hot and tight. 'What about it?'

'We haven't really discussed what happened earlier.'

No, they hadn't—thankfully.

She glanced out of the window. Outside, the wind was rearranging the trees that edged the garden.

It was unsettling enough having the whole episode playing on repeat inside her head. She didn't need or want to replay it in front of this man with his dark, intent gaze.

Unfortunately avoiding it might not be an option.

Picturing his expression as he had carried her back to the car out on the causeway, the relentlessness in his eyes as he'd pushed back against the wind, she felt a tremor ripple through her.

Arlo Milburn was definitely the tackle-things-head-on type.

Turning her eyes to his, she shrugged. 'There's nothing to discuss. It was—'

'A mistake?' he asked.

'Yes.' She nodded vigorously—perhaps too vigorously, she thought a moment later, watching his face harden. 'Or maybe not a mistake…more a misunderstanding.'

'You think?' He shifted back his seat, his dark brows rising up his forehead. 'It seems fairly unambiguous to me. You kissed me and I kissed you back.'

'I suppose that's one way of looking at it,' she said slowly.

'What are the other ways?'

Goosebumps skittered down her spine as she struggled to put together a coherent sentence, or at least one she could say out loud. In other words, nothing about feeling that he hadn't only rescued her out on the causeway but *claimed* her…

'I think of it as more of a cosmic chain reaction,' she managed. 'You know…when things collide…like stars, planetary forces…'

'And lips?' Her insides tightened as he held her gaze.

'I suppose you believe Elvis is alive too?' He shook his

head dismissively. 'I'm only interested in facts, not half-baked theories.'

'Not everything can be explained by facts,' she retorted, stung by his manner. 'Some things just happen.'

Except they didn't, did they? Everything that happened, however 'accidental' it seemed, was the consequence of a collection of facts, decisions made, paths taken, feelings overruled...

The details of the dining room were blurring around her in the silence. She shivered. And it didn't matter if some of those facts stayed hidden, they were still true. They would always be true.

'Like what?' he asked.

He was staring at her in silence and, momentarily trapped in his gaze, she held her breath. Should she tell him the truth? That he was right. That nothing was random. That there was always a reason, always something or someone responsible—

Pushing back her chair, she stood up. 'Look, Mr Milburn, interesting as this conversation is, I thought we had work to do.'

'It's Arlo—and we do,' he said calmly. 'That's why I wanted to talk to you about what happened in the drawing room. To reassure you. You see, I don't believe in mixing business with pleasure. It never ends well.'

Frankie blinked. She took a deep breath. Just for a moment she had almost liked him. She'd even thought he liked her. And all because of one stupid, unthinking kiss.

But that kiss hadn't changed anything. It certainly hadn't changed him. He was still the same rude, arrogant man who had turfed her out of bed.

'That's sweet of you.' Angling her chin up, she smiled thinly. 'But you don't need to worry on my account. I've practically forgotten it ever happened.'

CHAPTER FOUR

LEANING BACK IN HIS CHAIR, Arlo extended his arm over his back, grimacing as he stretched out his neck. A pulse of frustration beat down his spine. They were back in his office, and as a gust of wind shook the house he stared out of the window to where the waves were flinging up foam.

Usually, he found it easy to work. But not today, he thought, glancing down at the cursor blinking reproachfully at the top of the blank page on his computer screen. Today he'd struggled to find one word that could hold his attention long enough for him to forget that Frankie was in the room.

His eyes narrowed on the halo of auburn curls that was just visible over the piles of books on the other desk. It was unconscionable to let a woman—*this* woman—distract him from work. Work that was, after all, the only reason she was here in his office. Although now he was finding it hard to remember why he had ever thought that was a good idea...

Shifting back in his seat, so that he could no longer see the top of her head, he watched his screen go black.

He hadn't been lying when he'd told Frankie that he was on a break from women. A long break, as it happened—maybe too long. But it was through choice rather than lack of opportunity. He'd deliberately let the expeditions, the lecturing, the research, take precedence over his love life.

It was easier that way...less painful.

Love was for fools. Or maybe it made people into fools. Either way, he'd decided a long time ago that it was too unpredictable to make it the basis of any relationship other than a familial one.

Of course, familial love was no less painful. But at least it played by the rules. It was logical. Naturally, a mother might love and support her child, a father his son, a boy his brother. It was hardwired into their DNA.

Love between a couple was different: dangerous. It didn't matter if it was based on duty or desire, it lacked any real scientific foundation. Lust, on the other hand, was the engine in the juggernaut of life. It was a simple compulsive force—like gravity. Potent. Persuasive. Undeniable.

Thinking back to the uppity put-down Frankie had thrown at him after lunch, he felt anger coil up inside him like a snake. He had felt like running after her and shaking her. Or, better still, kissing her. Kissing her until she melted into him as she had done that morning.

'I've practically forgotten it ever happened.'

Who was she trying to kid?

Unclenching his jaw, he shifted forward.

'Could you please stop fidgeting?' Frankie's voice floated up from behind the desk. 'Some of us are trying to work.'

A rush of heat tightened his muscles. 'Are you talking to me?'

She sighed audibly. 'Well, I'm not talking to Nero.'

As the dog lifted its head from the floor Arlo hesitated and then, pushing back his chair, stood up and walked across the room.

'It wouldn't matter if you were. You see, unlike you, he prefers it when people bark.'

'And I prefer it when people are straight with me.' Her eyes narrowed. 'I thought you wanted my help.'

'I do.'

'Then what's with all the huffing and puffing?'

'I wasn't aware I was huffing and puffing,' he lied. 'It's just transitioning back to working behind a desk...it's hard after so many weeks out on the ice.'

His jaw tightened. She was looking at him as if she thought that level of sensitivity was beyond him. But he could be sensitive when required. In fact, he could be anything she wanted—

His body tensed as he remembered her breathless little gasp when he'd pulled her hips against his body.

'I haven't changed my mind. You're doing a good job.' Clearing his throat, he gestured towards the shelves behind her desk. 'Actually, I need to check something in one of those files. The blue one,' he said, pointing at one at random.

She got to her feet, her eyes travelling over the haphazardly stacked shelves. 'You have really great organisational skills.'

He tapped his head. 'It's all up here. I know where everything is. No, I can get it myself. No, let me—'

Reaching up, he made a grab for the file, but she was already tugging at it.

'Ouch!'

Books and files were tumbling from the shelf, and he swore as one hit him squarely on the bridge of his nose.

'Why don't you ever do what you're told?' The pain was making his eyes water. 'I said I'd get it.'

Frankie glared up at him. 'You know, I'm getting really tired of how everything is always my fault with you,' she snapped.

'Not as tired as I am of nothing ever being your fault,' he snapped back.

'I didn't say that…' Pressing her hand against her head, she winced.

'Are you hurt?'

She shook her head, but as she lifted her hand, he felt his pulse jump into his throat.

'You're bleeding—'

'It's nothing.'

'It's not nothing.' He led her to the sofa. 'Sit.'

She pushed against his hand. 'I'm not a dog.'

Damn, she was stubborn. She was also bleeding. He took a breath. 'Please could you sit down?'

With relief, he watched her drop down onto the cushions. Angling the lamp to see better, he grabbed her chin between his thumb and forefinger.

'Look up. *Please*,' he added as she stiffened against his hand.

He parted her hair. 'Okay, it's a small cut. It's not bleeding much, but you'll probably have a bit of a bump.'

She sighed. 'I don't need a nurse.'

'Lucky I'm a doctor, then,' he said.

Her eyes narrowed. 'Of rocks. And ice. Not people. Now, if you've finished?'

'I haven't.' He fished out a handkerchief from his pocket. 'Press this here. I'm just going to get the first aid box. And don't even think about moving.'

Leaning back against the sofa cushions, Frankie closed her eyes and breathed out shakily. It was Arlo's fault, she thought angrily. If he had organised his shelves like any normal person this wouldn't have happened.

Her head was throbbing and there was a metallic taste in her mouth, and she felt a nauseous rush of *déjà vu*. Clutching the arm of the sofa, she opened her eyes and steadied herself.

That had been her first memory after the accident that had killed her entire family. Eyes closed, her head hurting inexplicably. She hadn't understood at first. She had felt as if she was dreaming, only then she'd opened her eyes and realised the nightmare was real.

'Sorry I took so long. How are you feeling?'

Arlo was back. She gazed up at him, frowning. 'Fine. It's really not that bad.'

'I'll just spray some antiseptic on—'

He was being so nice, and his touch was gentle in a way that made her throat ache more than her head.

'What happened here?' he asked.

His fingers had stilled against her head, and she knew that he had found the thin line of puckered skin.

According to the French media it was a miracle she had survived the crash. Afterwards, when she'd seen photographs of the plane, it had been hard to believe she had not just survived but walked away with just one tiny reminder of what had happened that night in France.

Only one visible reminder, anyway.

Balling the handkerchief in her hand, she shrugged. 'I was in an accident. A couple of years ago.'

She couldn't see his expression, so she didn't know what he was thinking, but she did know she wanted to stay in control of this particular conversation.

'I banged my head. It left me with a healthy respect for safety belts and this scar.'

That was true. Not the whole truth and nothing but the truth. But she had never told anyone that except at the inquest, and that had been an experience that had taught her not to expect justice even from those charged with dispensing it.

'So we have something else in common,' she said lightly. Looking up into his face, she widened her eyes. 'Oh, but you're hurt too.'

'What? This?' Reaching up, he touched the dark bruise at the bridge of his nose. 'It's nothing.' He smiled. 'It's hardly going to mar my good looks, is it?'

'You *are* good-looking.'

His forehead creased into a frown. 'Maybe I need to take a closer look at that bump…'

She bit into her lip and he held her gaze.

'It's okay. Johnny's my brother. I know what beauty looks like.'

Conventional beauty, she thought. Or perhaps it would be better named conformist beauty.

Johnny was Michelangelo's *David*. All perfect lines and symmetry. And yet for some reason she couldn't quite picture his face anymore.

Her heart smacked against her ribs.

There was nothing symmetrical about Arlo. He was a rough draft, formed by a more urgent hand. An Easter Island profile chipped in bone, not rock. A man who corrected the course of everything in his path.

Glancing up, she felt a jolt of electricity crackle up her spine as their eyes met.

'Beauty is God's handwriting. It's not legible to everyone.'

There was a long pause, and then his eyes fixed on her face. 'But it is legible to you?'

Her heart thudded hard. She felt something stir inside her, as if there was a storm building there…

'Doctor's daughter,' she said, breaking the taut silence. 'So, Arlo, tell me—what made you want to go to Antarctica?'

For a few half-seconds, Arlo didn't reply. Not because he didn't know the answer. He had been trying to work out why she had changed the subject, only the sound of his name on her lips seemed to have momentarily stopped his brain working.

Just seconds earlier he'd been trying to remember why he'd thought it a good idea to give her a job.

Something about putting her off-limits—that was it. An imbalance of power.

Now that decision felt premature on so many levels… not least because he felt uniquely and perilously at a disadvantage.

Hoping his silence suggested that he was taking her

question seriously, rather than taking leave of his senses, he dragged his gaze away from her soft pink mouth.

'When I was twelve years old, I read *The South Pole* by Roald Amundsen. I found it gripping. The menace and the mercy of nature. There's a copy in the library if you want to read it. Second shelf on the level as you walk in.' His eyes met hers. 'Don't worry. The books are a lot better behaved downstairs.'

She smiled then, and suddenly it was his turn to change the subject.

'So how are you finding the work? Not too dry, I hope?'

'Not at all.' She hesitated, then, 'Actually, your notes are surprisingly interesting.'

'Thank you. I think,' he said, the corners of his mouth pulling up very slightly.

'It's just that there's a lot of numbers. You know…percentages of this and metric tons of that.'

He frowned. 'In other words, facts.'

'Exactly.' She stared at him impatiently, as if he was missing something glaringly obvious. 'I know you love facts, but most people find them really intimidating, so you have to make them interesting and understandable. And you have. I mean, if someone like me can understand them you must have done.'

'What do you mean, "someone like me"?'

She bit her lip. 'You know… Someone who lacks "discipline and diligence".'

There was a small, stiff silence as he replayed her words—his words, in fact—inside his head. 'Look, I wasn't thinking straight this morning. I was still angry and scared—'

Her chin jerked up. 'Scared?' She screwed up her face as if she didn't believe him. 'Of what?'

He hadn't meant to admit his fear out loud, and now he felt his body tense as he remembered that grey wall of water rising up around her. Remembered, too, the promise he had made to himself all those years ago. Never to let fear overrule facts. Never to let the preventable become the inevitable.

'Scared that you'd be hurt.' *Or worse.*

Frankie was staring at him in silence. 'I thought you hated me…'

They were so close he could see each and every freckle on her face. He wondered how long it would take to count them. And where exactly they stopped on her body.

He cleared his throat. 'I don't hate you.'

He heard her swallow. 'I don't hate you either.'

His breath stalled as her eyes rose to his face. Gazing down, he could see the pulse at the base of her throat beating in time with the blood pounding through his veins.

He was powerless to look away.

Time seemed to soften and then stop.

Their legs were touching at the knee…her hand was just inches from his. Never in his life had he wanted to kiss a woman so badly…

But before he could wrap his hand around her neck and bring her mouth to his, the grandfather clock at the end of the room chimed the hour.

She blinked, as if waking from a dream. 'It that the time? Constance said supper was at a quarter past.'

As she got to her feet Arlo frowned up at her. 'You know what? I've just remembered I need to call a couple of people back. But you don't need to wait for me—in fact, you shouldn't. Tell Constance I'll sort myself out in a bit.' Standing up, he walked over to his desk. 'And take Nero with you, will you? Otherwise, he'll just bug me to feed him.'

He made his calls and then, wanting to prove to himself that he could, he sat down and waded through his notes.

Finally, Nero came padding back upstairs. It was ten

o'clock. 'Okay, then.' Pulling the dog's silky ears, he followed him downstairs, but instead of heading to the kitchen, Nero trotted down the corridor.

He followed him into the library. It was dark, but the fire was still glowing, and opposite the fire Frankie was asleep on the sofa, a disorder of curls framing her face, the Amundsen book open beside her.

His shoulders tensed.

Should he move her? Probably not. She might freak out—and anyway that would mean taking her up to her bedroom.

He felt his body grow taut. He'd been shot, punched, and he'd suffered frostbite, but the idea of sliding Frankie's body beneath the sheets and then having to walk away was a new, excruciating pain.

Leaning forward, he gently added a couple of logs to the fire and then, tugging a throw off the back of the sofa, he draped it over her body.

His jaw tightened. Now what? Sleeping on one of the other sofas seemed like a bad idea, but he didn't want to leave her alone.

He glanced down at Nero. And he didn't have to. 'Up,' he said quietly, watching the dog jump up onto the sofa and curl into a ball. 'Now, stay.'

Body twitching, Arlo turned and walked swiftly out of the library, and away from a sudden, inexplicable desire to trade places with his dog.

When Frankie woke the sky was light.

She had been dreaming of Antarctica, sleepwalking across blue-shadowed frozen oceans, and for a few half-seconds the light pressing against her eyelids felt like the solid white sun shimmering above that endless polar landscape.

Except it was far too warm to be Antarctica.

Yawning, she opened her eyes and sat up.

At the end of the sofa Nero lifted his head, his tail thumping against the armrest. Her body tensed. Nero meant Arlo.

Heart pounding, she glanced over her shoulder. But the library was empty. She was alone.

She felt a flush heat her face. She hadn't been alone last night—at least not in her dreams. Arlo had been with her, always just out of reach and hazy, as if he was walking through mist.

Her stomach did a clumsy little flip. It sounded weird, putting it like that, but dreams told you what you already knew. Her dream was simply proving that she found Arlo baffling.

Satisfied with that explanation, she patted the dog's tousled head, her eyes following his gaze to the windows.

Surprise chased away her unease.

The trees in the garden were no longer bending over like supplicants and the sky was a dirty white instead of battleship grey.

Glancing at the clock above the fireplace, she frowned. It was too early for breakfast.

'Come on, then,' she said softly. 'Let's go and get some fresh air.'

Outside on the slopes a fine mist was making it hard to see the sea, but beneath her feet the short salt-soaked grass was speckled with tiny vivid pink-and-blue flowers.

Up ahead, Nero was bounding around in circles, clearly ecstatic at being able to have a proper run, and he was barking, yelping in excitement at something—

Not something. Someone. Arlo.

She felt a buzz go through her body.

He was walking out of the mist towards her, just as he had in her dream, his dark hair falling in front of his eyes, his long legs making short work of the springy turf.

She stared up at him, her blood turning to air, her vision shuddering in and out of focus. He was bare-chested, with a black sweater tied around his waist and, incongruously, a dark sheep, complete with curling horns, draped over his shoulders.

Her mouth felt as if it had been sandpapered.

He looked like someone from another age and he seemed completely at ease—as if he often stripped off to the waist and carried livestock around. Her gaze dropped to his chest…to the acreage of pale muscle.

When he had picked her up on the causeway, and then again when she had kissed him, she'd had a sense not just of physical strength but of a potent, untapped power.

Now she knew why.

He was not just 'ripped', there was a kind of organic solidity to his physique—almost as if his upper body was made of stone. And yet there was nothing clumsy about the way he moved. On the contrary, he had the same easy, loping gait as the dark dog that was now trotting beside him.

At that moment Arlo looked up, and her stomach clenched as if it was being squeezed by a giant hand. She watched him come closer, nervously trying out various half-finished sentences in her head. And then he was stopping in front of her, and suddenly it was a struggle to fill her lungs, much less think in sentences. Above them, the sky seemed to shrink back on itself.

'Good morning.'

He gave her a slight almost-smile and, even though he was the one who was half naked, she felt herself blushing.

'Are you looking for me or just out for a walk?'

His dark grey eyes rested on her flushed face and, trying to control the hammering of her heart, she said quickly, 'A walk.'

Dragging her gaze away from the thin line of dark hair that disappeared into the waistband of his jeans, she looked up at the sheep. 'What happened to it?'

His forehead corrugated into a frown. 'It's difficult to

say. Either she hunkered down in the wrong place or she got blown over by the wind. She doesn't seem hurt, but she didn't want to move. She's probably just winded.'

'Where did you find her?'

'Just over there.'

She followed his gaze. The mist had cleared, and she felt a kick of horror. Maybe the slope was less steep when you were standing on it, but from this angle the gradient looked almost vertical.

'You went down there?' Her horror morphed into outrage. 'Imagine if *I'd* done that.'

His eyes met hers. 'Why would you? You don't have anything to prove.'

And he did? She stared at him in confusion. He was a decorated soldier, an expert in his field, *and* a polar explorer.

'What do *you* have to prove?' she asked.

He tilted his head back, an impossible to read expression on his face.

'The other day someone told me I wasn't quite the hero I thought I was.'

She stared at him, her heart suddenly pounding so hard against her ribs she thought the force of it might send her flying down the hillside.

Trying to play it cool, she held his gaze. 'Is that right?'

He nodded. 'Unfortunately, there's a major shortage of damsels in distress on the island, so I had to resort to rescuing sheep.'

Watching Frankie's lips curve up into one of those treefelling smiles she seemed able to produce at will, Arlo felt his stomach go into freefall. He had slept badly again, woken early, and even though he'd felt exhausted his body had been twitchy, his mind too restless to let him even try falling back to sleep.

It was only as he'd walked downstairs that he'd realised why he was finding it so difficult to sleep. The storm was passing, any day now the causeway would be safe to cross, and Frankie Fox would be free to leave.

Yesterday morning he would have greeted that statement with relief. But a lot had changed in the twenty-four hours since he'd found her semi-naked in his bed—not least, his opinion of her.

His chest tightened. He hadn't expected her to do so, but she had impressed him yesterday. She'd worked hard, listened, and asked questions where necessary. In another life he might have given her a real job, or he might even have—

Have what?

He stopped mid-thought, but it made no difference. His body was already answering the question.

Gritting his teeth, he stared past her to where the waves were tumbling against the rocks. He had to get a grip. Frankie might not be the flaky little chancer he'd thought she was, but she was not his type.

For starters she was already involved in some way with Johnny, but even if she wasn't, she was only twenty-one— little more than a kid.

Except she hadn't kissed like a kid.

She'd kissed like a woman.

His shoulders tensed as he remembered the soft, breathy moans she'd made as his tongue had parted her lips. He'd wanted her, and he was pretty sure she had wanted him at that moment. But he'd tried living in the moment before, blindly trusting to what Frankie called 'planetary forces', and it had been an out-and-out disaster.

Only it was a lot easier to think that when Frankie wasn't actually standing in front of him, looking ridiculously swamped and yet frustratingly sexy in one of his old jackets.

Conscious of her gaze and needing to do something to

shift the restless energy inside him, he swung the sheep down from his shoulders onto the grass. As it trotted away without a backward glance, he unwrapped his sweater from around his waist and pulled it over his head.

Heart beating fast, he glanced up at the sky. For the first time since he'd returned home there was a tiny patch of blue. By tomorrow, aside from the battered-looking gorse bushes, it would be as if the storm had never happened. The causeway would open. Life would go back to normal. Some parts of it, anyway.

He cleared his throat. 'By the way, you were right about Johnny. He did leave a message—two, actually—but they only came through yesterday evening. He said you needed to have some fun.'

But why? he wondered. She was young and beautiful, and she lived in London. Surely fun was at her fingertips.

Johnny had also said Frankie needed some TLC, but he didn't want to think about that. Not when the only kind of tender loving care he could think of offering her involved both of them naked and in his bed.

He looked down at her, not prompting, just waiting. She shrugged. 'Johnny's a good friend. He worries about me but I just needed a few days away from London. I feel fine now.'

She had chosen her words carefully but the sharp stab of relief he felt at hearing her describe Johnny as a friend was forgotten when he looked down at her.

Her mouth curved up at the corners, but there was something forced about the smile and he felt a prickle of guilt spread out across his skin. Unless TLC stood for total loss of control, he'd massively under-delivered.

'How could I not feel fine when I'm surrounded by all this?'

Now her smile seemed real, and some of the tension seemed to have left her face.

'You like it?'

She frowned at the surprise in his voice. 'Of course. It's beautiful. All nature's beautiful. It's so calming and uncomplicated.'

Smiling, he shook his head. 'Not all nature, I can assure you.'

'Are you talking about Antarctica?'

As she looked over at him, he saw a flicker of curiosity in her blue eyes.

'What's it like?'

It was a question he'd been asked so many times, but for some reason he wanted to give her more than just a generic answer.

'It's exhausting. Terrifying. Intoxicating. And heartbreakingly beautiful. A lot of the time it feels like a dream.' He tilted his face upwards, towards the sky. 'Everything is so extreme out there. The sky is bigger, the wind is stronger, the cold is like nothing you've ever felt, and the sea is this beautiful endlessly changing blue...'

She looked over at him and he felt his heartbeat stumble. *Not as blue or as beautiful as Frankie's eyes.*

Forcing his gaze away from her face, he stared down at the jagged rocks. 'There are icebergs there that are the size of countries. And the air...it has texture. You feel like you could scoop it up in your hands.'

Her face was flushed. 'It sounds amazing. But I guess it would have to be for you to want to leave this place so often.'

He gazed down at the chimney stacks of the Hall. Leaving the island, leaving his home, always filled him with sadness. He loved everything about it. But some things were more important than feelings—his or anyone else's. He'd learned that the hard way.

He hadn't always felt like that. As a child, his parents' adoration for each other had seemed like a mythical power. Only watching that power wither away during his mother's illness had been devastating, and his father's furious grief almost more so.

He should have realised then that it didn't matter what you felt or how strongly you felt it—the power of love was no match for cold, hard facts. But he had been young and desperate, and so, driven by an incoherent need to save an ideal, he'd impulsively married a woman he barely knew.

Now he understood that if you wanted to save something—someone—you needed more than feelings. In fact, feelings were just a distraction.

He shrugged. 'It's addictive. It demands so much of you. And yet in other ways it's so fragile. I think that's what makes it so incredible…unique. There's nowhere like it.' He felt her gaze on his face. 'But you don't need me to tell you about it. Go and see for yourself.'

'Me?'

'Why not? The poles aren't some snow-covered men-only club for boffins or billionaires with frozen beards and thousand-yard stares.'

She burst out laughing. 'Is that how you see yourself?'

It was disconcerting how much he liked making her laugh. 'More importantly, is that how you see me?'

The air between them seemed to thicken and he felt his body tense as she bit into her lip.

'You are a bit intense. But your beard isn't frozen.'

He shook his head. 'You know, having you around is doing wonders for my ego.'

She rolled her eyes. 'I don't think your ego needs bolstering.' Squinting up at the sky, she sighed. 'It's so lovely out here, but I suppose we'd better get back to work.'

For the briefest of moments his disappointment vied with his shock that work had slipped his mind, but then he nodded. 'Yes, we should.'

Constance had seen them coming and was waiting by the back door.

'Apparently the storm warning's been reduced to yellow,' she said. 'So, am I right to assume that this will be the last night of your stay with us, Frankie?'

A small silence bled into the hallway as Frankie glanced up not at Constance but at him.

Was it? Was it her last night?

But before he could open his mouth she said quietly, 'Yes. It's been lovely, but I have to get back to London and I would have been going back tomorrow, anyway. Nothing's changed.'

'No,' he agreed, holding her gaze. 'Nothing's changed at all.'

CHAPTER FIVE

PICKING UP HER LIP-LINER, Frankie stared at herself in the dressing table mirror. So this was it. Her last night at Hadfield Hall.

She couldn't quite believe it, but from the moment Constance had asked about her plans, time had done another of those contortions, so that in what felt like a matter of seconds the day was over and it was time to dress for dinner.

Her pulse quivered and, breathing out shakily, she gazed over to where her suitcase sat on the bed.

Nothing's changed.

Throughout the day, her words and Arlo's response had kept popping into her head. And she was right—they both were. Nothing had changed.

Only it felt as if something had. Actually, it felt as if *everything* had.

Oh, for goodness' sake.

Frowning, she smoothed over where she had jerked the lip pencil upwards. She took a breath. Maybe that was why, for one fleeting, truly idiotic moment, she had thought he was going to invite her to stay longer. Not that she would have accepted, of course. That would be utterly insane. Her flat, her job, her *life* was in London.

This was a lovely place to visit, and okay, she and Arlo weren't at each other's throats anymore, but he was still a stranger.

A stranger she had kissed...

Refocusing with an effort, she glanced down at her cream cashmere jumper and dark red silk skirt, then lower to her high-heeled red shoes, trying to see herself as Arlo would.

But, really, what was the point?

Her pulse stilled. If there was one thing she'd learned about Arlo Milburn it was that it didn't pay to second-guess him.

He was already waiting for her in the dining room, standing by the fireplace looking down at the flames, one arm resting on the overmantel. Her breath seemed to spontaneously combust in her throat as he looked up at her, his grey eyes narrowing admiringly.

'You look beautiful.'

He was looking at her steadily, with total attention, and she felt her face and hands grow warm. 'I thought I'd make a bit of an effort.' She smiled, feeling suddenly shy. 'You look great too,' she added, her eyes skimming his dark trousers and a shirt that was so flawlessly white his upper body looked as if it was made of Arctic ice.

She wasn't just being polite. He really did look great. Both his trousers and shirt were cut beautifully and emphasised his muscular thighs and the wideness of his shoulders.

'Usually I wear this when I win something.' He didn't smile back. 'So it seemed appropriate.'

She frowned. 'What have you won?'

'Dinner with you, obviously,' he said quietly.

His words tingled like snowflakes against her skin. But of course, he was just being nice because she was leaving.

She smiled. 'Some people would probably see that as the consolation prize.'

He held out his hand. 'Not people worth knowing.'

He led her to her seat, and as she waited for him to sit down, she gazed around the room. She had spent such a short time here, but already everything felt so familiar...

Arlo felt so familiar.

Glancing over, she felt her throat constrict. He was changing before her eyes. That tense, angry man whose dark eyes had spilled scorn on her was now reaching over to fill her wine glass.

The food was superb again. Guinea fowl with leeks and morels followed a starter of roasted scallops with sea herbs, and to finish there was a white chocolate mousse with lemon sorbet. And although she'd been expecting the conversation to be a little stop-start, it wasn't at all. In fact, he was surprisingly good company. Intelligent, with that dry sense of humour she had glimpsed before, and happy to talk about practically anything.

Her pulse dipped. But no doubt he was just making an effort because it was her last night.

She laid down her spoon. 'That was wonderful, but I truly couldn't eat another thing.'

'Really?' He frowned. 'Only there's another two courses—'

She glanced up just in time to see the smile leaving his lips. 'Very funny.'

'Don't you mean *hashtag can't stop laughing*?' he said softly.

Now she was laughing and shaking her head. Then she groaned. 'Please don't make me laugh…it hurts too much.'

'Sorry.' He leaned back, studying her. 'You know, when Johnny and I ate too much when we were younger my dad used to take us up to the rumpus room and make us run races.'

'Is that the long room with all the little leaded windows?'

He nodded. 'The windows are like that so you can play ball games up there without smashing the glass. We used to play everything. Rugby, tennis…' His grey eyes met hers. 'Cricket?'

'No, absolutely not,' she said, shaking her head. 'I'm too full to run—and not in these heels. It wouldn't be a fair contest.'

In the light from the chandeliers his features didn't look

so hard, so at odds with each other, as he held her gaze. 'If you keep those heels on, the disadvantage would be entirely mine.'

She felt her skin grow warm. 'What about a game of snooker?' she said quickly. She had spotted the table during yesterday's brief exploration. 'That shouldn't be too strenuous.'

'It's actually a billiard table,' he said as they walked into the wood-panelled room. 'Billiards is a great game, but most people treat it like the dull cousin of snooker and pool.'

'You mean like Mr Collins in *Pride and Prejudice*?'

He shook his head. 'No. Mr Collins *was* dull. Billiards is not. It's simple to learn, but it punishes you far more than snooker or pool when it comes to the fundamentals.'

She bit her lip. 'And that's important, is it? Punishing yourself?'

'Only in as much as it allows you to punish your opponent more,' he said softly.

Their eyes met and then he handed her a cue.

'Okay, then. The rules of the game: billiards is played with one red ball and two white cue balls…'

They agreed that the winner would be the first to reach a hundred points.

'That sounds like a lot,' she said slowly. 'But okay…'

Forty minutes later, Frankie leaned back against the table, biting into her lip.

Arlo laid his cue down on the baize. 'Frankie Fox,' he said quietly. 'Social media influencer and stone-cold, red-hot billiard player.'

She screwed up her face. 'I was going to tell you, but—'

'You thought you'd wipe the floor with me instead?'

Her mouth dried up as he walked slowly towards her.

'No,' she protested. 'You just looked so sweet and serious when you were explaining everything. I couldn't bring myself to stop you.'

'*Sweet?*' He blew out a breath and then he smiled. 'That's a new one. So, who taught you how to play?'

'My brother Harry.' She blinked. It was probably the first time she had spoken her brother's name in more than eighteen months, and it scraped inside her mouth. Fixing a smile to her face, she continued, 'The pub down the road from where he lived at university had a billiard table. If it's any consolation, I used to beat him and all his friends too.'

Sighing, Arlo shook his head. 'I suppose I should be grateful we didn't play for money.'

'I don't want your money—'

He was standing so close she could feel his warm breath, could see the metallic gleam and the urgency in his eyes.

'What *do* you want?' he said slowly.

It was a simple question. The answer was not.

She swallowed, shifted, transfixed by the clashing arcs and clefts of his features. It was like looking at a topographic map, and she wondered what would happen if she ran her finger along one of the lines.

Where would it lead her?

Her body was tingling, her heart hammering inside her chest. Everything looked and felt different—more *there*, more sensuous. The faint scent of woodsmoke…the billiard table pressing into her thighs…the shimmering chandeliers…

Maybe it was the wine, she thought. But she knew that it wasn't, and she felt something stir low down.

She knew that it was Arlo.

He was the answer. She wanted him.

Her insides tightened, the truth accelerating her racing pulse. But everything was tangled, snarled together so tightly that she was incapable of doing anything other than stand there and stare at him.

'I don't know,' she said at last.

He took a step closer. 'Would it help if I told you what I wanted?'

Her eyes found his. He was watching her intently, his face taut, the muscles in his arms bunching beneath his shirt.

'What do you want?' she whispered, clenching and un-clenching her fists.

Reaching out, he ran his finger along her jaw. 'I want you. And you want me.'

The rawness in his voice shocked her so much that she didn't even attempt to deny his words. His dark eyes were trained on her face and the tension inside her was at break-ing point.

She knew that he was waiting for her, that he would walk away without a murmur if she wanted him too. But she didn't want him to. Only she couldn't seem to speak.

She took a breath and said the only word that would form in her mouth. 'Yes.'

He leaned into her, dipping his head so that his lips brushed against hers, and then his hands were pulling her closer, so that it felt as if they were starting where they'd left off last time.

Heart pounding, she slid her fingers over the solid mus-cles of his chest, almost dizzy with the freedom of touching him. His hands slid under her jumper to cup her breasts, and she moaned against his lips as the nipples hardened.

'Open your mouth,' he said hoarsely, and she responded, tightening her fingers around his arms as he deepened the kiss.

Only she wanted more and, pushing him back, she grabbed her sweater and pulled it over her head. His eyes narrowed as she began undoing his shirt, and then, with a growl of frustration, he yanked it apart, the buttons fly-ing everywhere.

She swallowed hard as he dragged the sleeves down over his wrists, and then he was reaching out, pushing aside the fabric of her simple white bra. Her whole body tensed as his callused thumbs chafed against the taut tips of her breasts, and suddenly she was desperate to feel his mouth against them.

Moving her hands over the hard planes of his chest, she leaned towards him, arching forward, then gasped as his lips fastened on her breast.

She heard him grunt, and then he was lifting her onto the billiard table, pushing her skirt up. His thighs were between hers as he drew first one, then the other nipple into his mouth, his teeth scraping lightly over the rigid flesh.

She moaned weakly. It felt so good, so right…she'd had no idea it could feel like this. Hunger was surging through her and, sucking in a breath, she pressed her hand flat against the hard ridge of his erection.

Groaning, he lifted his head. His jaw was clenched, the muscles in his chest stretched tight.

'What is it? Is something wrong?' she asked.

Breathing out shakily, he shook his head. 'Nothing's wrong. It's just I haven't done this in a while.' He grimaced. 'I don't want it to be over before it's started.'

Her eyes dropped from the flushed skin of his torso, moved lower. Half-naked, fully aroused, he looked amazing.

She felt a rush of nerves.

And intimidating.

'Actually, I haven't done it in a while either,' she said slowly. 'In fact, not very much at all.'

He looked at her, eyes appraising her, and then he cleared his throat. 'But you have done it…?'

'I'm not a virgin,' she said quickly. 'Why? Did you think I was?'

His fingers tensed. 'Yes, just now…but only because I thought by "not very much" you meant not at all.'

'I don't want you to be disappointed.'

He was breathing deeply, his chest rising and falling, a dark flush in his cheekbones. Reaching up, he cupped her chin, his grey gaze skimming over her throat, her collarbone, her breasts...

'Listen to me, Frankie, you do not disappoint.'

Her belly clenched as he brushed the thumb across her lips.

'And, just for the record, it's my job to satisfy you—not the other way round.'

She felt wetness between her thighs, and she dragged in a strangled breath as he dropped to his knees and kissed his way down her body, his roughened hands stroking her until she shook with need.

She didn't remember it being like this. He made her want him so much.

Gently, he pushed her legs open, dipping his fingers into her slick heat, and then she felt his warm breath on the skin of her thighs as he parted her with his tongue.

Her head fell back, and she swayed, her fingers tightening around the lip of the table. Heat flared inside her and she dragged in another breath, trying to clear the dizziness from her head.

But his tongue was relentless.

Teasing, taking, tasting.

No one had ever touched her like this.

She felt helpless and hungry. His touch was dissolving her, the pleasure building as his hands slid under her bottom and he raised her up to meet his mouth.

The ball of heat inside her was pulsing in time with his tongue and her hands caught in his hair, holding him steady. She was lifting herself up, the pleasure tipping almost into pain as she rocked faster and faster, and then she spasmed, muscles tightening, tensing...

Heart thudding, she held on to him as he stood up, his

eyes finding hers. Her hand slid over his stomach to the buckle of his belt, freeing him before she wrapped her hand around his hard length.

His breath hitched. 'Turn round,' he said hoarsely, and she felt a ripple of need shiver across her skin.

His hands gripped her waist and she braced herself, head spinning, as his lips trailed down her neck. She heard the sound of something being torn and dazedly realised that she had been too caught up in her climax to remember a condom.

He pushed into her slowly, his breath vibrating against her throat, and then he reached round her to cup her breasts as he started to move.

Her belly clenched as his hand moved to her clitoris, and she felt him accelerate in time to the second climax building inside her. Then he tensed, groaning, his big body engulfing her, his head falling against her shoulder.

For a moment he lay against her, breathing raggedly. and then he pulled back. Glancing down, she saw herself as he did. Skirt rucked up about her waist, bare legs, high heels...

Her breath caught. She felt stunned. She had never done anything like that before. Never felt what he had made her feel.

'I...' she said, searching for words. But there were none.

Their eyes met, and his gaze sent flickers of feeling everywhere.

Was this—? Should they—? Did he—?

She had loved how his body felt on hers, and she was suddenly desperate to touch him. Only she knew that if she touched him it would start up again, and that might ruin everything. This was enough. It had to be enough.

Leaning down, she scooped up her jumper and pulled it over her head. 'I should probably go up now. I've got to pack.'

He stared at her, tall, silent, his eyes dark, his face expressionless.

'Then I'll let you go,' he said.

It was the right thing to do. The only thing to do. But it took every ounce of willpower she had to walk past him into the dark corridor.

CHAPTER SIX

IT WAS GOING to be a beautiful day, Frankie thought, gazing out of the car window.

In London, she never really noticed the weather, except in terms of whether she could legitimately take a taxi. In fact, she was pretty sure she'd never even listened to a weather forecast.

But up here in Northumberland she found it mesmerising. It was like watching a magic show. One moment the sky was conjuring up flocks of grey clouds, like sheep, the next streaks of sunlight that pierced the grey like shimmering, iridescent ribbons.

Right now, the clouds were growing wispier by the minute, while on either side of the causeway the waves jostled one another half-heartedly before turning to foam.

Her pulse shivered. It was hard to believe this was the same sea that had almost swept her off the causeway. Hard, too, to believe that she was going home.

Taking a breath, she glanced furtively to where Arlo sat beside her, his large, powerful hands resting with deceptive languor on the steering wheel, his eyes fixed on the cobbled road.

She felt her body tense. Was he thinking the same thing? Or was he just counting down the minutes until they reached the train station?

Her heartbeat accelerated as she remembered the moment last night when he had leaned forward and kissed her. She'd told herself that their first kiss had been a one-off and that Arlo wasn't her type.

But everything she'd told herself had been wrong.

Everything she'd known about sex had been wrong too. She'd only done it twice before. Both with her ex, Aidan.

The first time had been just awkward, and a little uncomfortable. The second had been better in terms of comfort, but afterwards she had wondered what all the fuss was about.

Now she knew.

Last night with Arlo had been a revelation. *He* had been a revelation.

As his lips had fused with hers it had been like flint striking rock. Everything inside her had been flame and heat. His body had felt so solid, so strong, and as she'd pressed against him, she'd had the sudden intense feeling that she wanted to stay in his arms for ever...

She pressed her hands together in her lap.

It wasn't just intense—it was crazy.

And yet it had been so tempting...

To take it a step further.

To go with him upstairs and do it again, and again, and again...

But something had held her back—some sixth sense that had told her if she went further, she would soon be out of her depth. She'd already gone further than she probably should have.

Arlo obviously felt the same way.

He parked and had her suitcase out of the boot before she'd even taken off her seat belt. Clearly, he couldn't wait to get rid of her, she thought as she struggled to keep up with his pavement-eating stride.

'All right, Mr Milburn. I thought you only just got back. Where you going this time, then?'

'I'm not going anywhere, Alan.' Arlo's face uncreased fractionally as he shook hands with the uniformed station attendant. 'I'm just dropping Ms Fox off. Okay if I see her onto the train?'

'That's really not—' she began.

But Arlo was already walking swiftly along the platform, her now-battered suitcase clamped under his arm.

Trailing behind, she followed him into a carriage, heart thumping as she watched him push her case into the overhead luggage rack.

'Okay, then.' His eyes were as expressionless as his voice. 'Have a good trip.'

Her heart lurched. *Was that it?*

But before she even had a chance to open her mouth he turned and walked away, the hem of his coat curling around his legs like the tail of a panther.

Her head was suddenly pounding so hard that it hurt to stand, and for one horrible moment she thought she might faint. Forcing her feet to move, she sat down in the nearest seat even as somewhere inside her head she heard her own voice telling Arlo that she'd never passed out in her life.

Pressing her head against the window, she closed her eyes. Last night had been an admission of something beyond thought—the raw and inescapable hunger that seemed to have engulfed them both since that moment on the causeway.

It had been a moment of passion. A moment, not even a night. Only something had happened. Something had passed between them...

The carriage doors opened.

'I think she's got a cheek, talking to you like that.' The woman's voice floated over her head. 'You should tell Mary. She'd give her what for—'

'I don't want to cause any trouble...' A second woman, quieter, anxious sounding.

'Frankie.'

The deep voice made her eyes snap open and, turning her head, she froze.

Arlo was standing beside her, his broad, muscular body effortlessly filling the carriage, his face austere and irregular beneath the harsh overhead lights.

She stared up at him wordlessly, her skin prickling with

shock. He looked almost as stunned as she did, as if he wasn't quite sure what he was doing.

'Is this how you want to leave things?' he asked.

There was short, quivering silence as she stared at him wordlessly, stunned by the directness of his question.

'No.' Breathing out shakily, she shook her head. 'No, it's not.'

Something flared in his dark eyes and then he was reaching up and pulling down her suitcase. 'Then come with me.'

This was not something he did, Arlo thought as he reversed out of the parking space and accelerated away from the car park. He did not chase after women and drag them off trains. It was a mistake on so many levels. He knew that logically and unequivocally—and yet here he was doing it.

It had taken two minutes.

Two minutes of his legs carrying his numb body forward before he had turned and headed back to the station past an open-mouthed Alan. And with each step he'd told himself that he could stop, turn around, go back to the car at any point.

But as soon as he stepped into the carriage and seen her sitting there that had changed. He'd spoken before he'd caught up with himself, the question fully formed on his lips, and by the time he'd considered the bigger picture they were walking back, past Alan.

The horse had well and truly bolted.

Or rather the train had left the station.

Maybe Frankie hadn't considered the consequences until now either. It would certainly explain her silence, he thought, staring fixedly out through the windscreen.

He was still staring fixedly ahead as they strode back into the Hall, past an open-mouthed Constance and upstairs.

The enormity, the incredible stupidity of what he was doing, hit him like a wrecking ball as he walked into

Frankie's bedroom. At the station he had simply wanted to stop her leaving. That had been the endpoint. Now, though, he saw it was just the beginning.

Only of what?

Last night he had behaved recklessly, driven by a compulsion he hadn't understood. But in some part of what could loosely be called his brain it had made sense. He had wanted Frankie, wanted to satisfy the hunger that had been eating at him ever since he'd found her in his bed.

If she hadn't wanted him he would have walked away, of course. Only she *had* wanted him. She had turned to flame beneath his fingers and now his body was hard and aching for more.

He didn't know why. All he knew was that they weren't finished. And that it was the pursuit of their unfinished connection that had brought them here.

'There's another train in four hours.' Still holding her suitcase, he swung round to face her. 'If you've changed your mind about coming back.'

'I haven't,' she said quietly.

There was a short, stiff pause and Arlo felt his chest tighten. This was exactly the kind of conversation he hated. Taut, emotional, unpredictable... But, if anything, Frankie seemed even more uncomfortable with it than he did, so that he was more concerned with putting her at ease.

'It felt wrong...you leaving like that.'

Her eyes found his. 'I felt the same. It's just that nothing like this...' she swallowed '...like *us*, has ever happened to me before.'

His heartbeat was drumming inside his head. Nothing like this...*like her*...he thought silently, had happened to him either.

Looking down at her, he felt his shoulders tense. He had nothing to offer her in the long term. Even the idea of permanence induced in him a kind of vertigo, and he needed her to know that.

His eyes found hers. 'I don't do relationships, but I think we have something special. Something I'd like to explore.'

He held his breath. No polar region had ever excited him as much as the idea of exploring every inch of Frankie.

'So when do we start?' she asked.

She hadn't moved, but the room suddenly felt smaller. She seemed closer, and she was breathing as unevenly as he was.

Arlo stared at her in silence, her words turning his groin painfully hard. This was why he'd gone after her: sex. Only it was more than sex. When he looked at Frankie there was fire, heat and hunger on a level he couldn't remember feeling before—not even for Harriet.

His throat felt as if it was clogged with his hot, wet breath, and he was holding his body so tautly it felt as if it might snap.

A minute went by, then another, and then they both moved at the same time—his hand wrapping around her waist and pulling her closer as she leaned forward, her fingers sliding over his shoulders.

As her lips parted against his he forgot to breathe. Her mouth was hot, and the taste of her was making his head swim. Shifting closer, he deepened the kiss, her soft moan instantly taking him to the point where kissing was not enough.

She clearly thought the same.

He could feel her fingers tugging clumsily at the sleeves of his coat, and without breaking the kiss he unzipped the front of her jacket, pushing it off her shoulders and down her arms.

Now her hands were on his chest, pulling at his jumper.

'Easy, Frankie.' He caught her arms, his eyes finding hers. 'We have time. We have plenty of time.'

'Okay…' Her fingers bit into his arm and she began pulling him towards the bed. 'But let's just get undressed…'

Her words were like petrol thrown on a bonfire.

Turning, he pushed the door shut and began to yank his jumper over his head. His T-shirt followed hers onto the floor, and then they both kicked off their boots and socks.

Now they were both just wearing jeans.

Dragging his eyes from the swell of her breasts, he drew her closer, his lips finding hers, and then he kissed her—kissed her until she moaned, and he felt her body start to soften.

Head spinning, he nudged her backwards. As they toppled onto the bed he pulled her on top, so that she was straddling him. Her hands were everywhere, sliding over the skin of his back and shoulders and down his arms, as if she couldn't quite believe he was real.

He understood that feeling. He couldn't believe she was real…that he was free to kiss and touch her…

Capturing her face in his hands, he teased her top lip with his tongue. He wanted more. He needed more. He needed all of her. *Everything.*

Reaching up, he touched her small breasts, cupping them in his hands, grazing his thumbs over the nipples, and then he sucked one tautened tip into his mouth, feeling it swell against his tongue.

Her head fell back and his body tensed as she began to squirm restlessly against him, against where he was growing harder by the minute. He sat up and, using the muscles of his thighs, tipped her forward onto the heavy press of his erection.

Frankie breathed out shakily.

He was very hard and very big.

Heart thudding, she reached up to touch his face, her fingers moving lightly against his beard-roughened jaw.

'I didn't say it last night, but you don't disappoint either,' she said softly.

Abruptly he leaned forward and, wrapping his hand in her hair, lifted her face to his and kissed her—a hard, hungry, open-mouthed, searing kiss that stole the breath from her lungs so suddenly that her head was spinning and she was shaking...

A moan that seemed to come from the hot, molten core of her body rose up in her throat and she rocked against him, her fingers sliding through his hair.

He grunted, and in one motion grabbed her arms and rolled her onto the bed, unbuttoning her jeans and tugging them down her legs, taking her panties with them.

For a moment he just stood at the end of the bed, watching her, face taut, jaw clenched tight, muscles bunched, eyes dark with an undisguised hunger that sent flickers of excitement scampering over her skin.

And then he was pulling off his jeans and boxer shorts.

It was the first time she'd seen him completely naked.

Her mouth felt as if it had been sandblasted. He definitely didn't disappoint, she thought, sucking in a sharp breath.

Then suddenly he was on the bed beside her, pulling her into his arms.

Breathing shakily, she ran her hands over the hard, defined muscles of his chest, her fluttering fingers tracing the line of dark hair down his stomach.

A shiver of need ran through her as she took him in her hand.

Then leaning into him, she drew up her leg, to meet the blunt tip of his erection. He jerked against her, a raw sound breaking from his lips, and, reaching past her, shook his wallet from the back pocket of his jeans.

Pulse quivering, she watched him unwrap the condom and slide it onto his hard length, and then his dark eyes locked with hers as he pushed gently against her.

'Is that okay?'

'Yes.' She breathed out slowly, opening her legs wider, then wider still. 'Yes, like that. Yes,' she said again, curling her hands around his shoulders.

He was pushing up inside her, his hand lifting her bottom so that there was nothing between them but heat and sweat, his thumb stroking her clitoris as she moved. His dark eyes locked with hers and she cried out, her body tensing in release, and then he was thrusting hard into her, pulling her close and burying his face against her throat.

For a moment he lay on top of her, breathing shakily, and then, lifting himself from her body, he rolled off her and got to his feet.

His eyes scudded down her body then back up to her face. 'I'll be right back.'

She stared after him, savouring the broad expanse of his back and the muscular curve of his shoulders. He was so unashamedly male, and she felt so unashamedly satisfied.

She shivered. Without the warmth of his body, she felt cold. Shifting backwards up the bed, she wriggled under the covers.

Moments later he slid in beside her, pulling her against him.

She let her hand rest lightly across his stomach, feeling calmer than she had for weeks…maybe months. Coming back had felt like a risk, but maybe this was what she'd needed all along. Intimacy. Physical contact.

She had read in a magazine that hugging someone produced feel-good hormones, and sex was the most intense kind of hugging. That must be why she felt so good.

Only nothing this good ever lasted.

'Don't overthink it.'

Startled, Frankie looked up. Arlo was staring down at her, his grey eyes steady and unblinking.

'What just happened—don't overthink it,' he said quietly. 'It's not that complicated.'

Isn't it?

She stared at him, a beat of panic pulsing over her skin. Maybe not for him. He could just lie back and enjoy the aftermath of release. But feeling calm and happy carried a different risk for her.

'I'm not overthinking,' she lied.

She let her hair fall forward to hide her face. It wasn't a complete lie, more a half-truth. But she wasn't ready to tell him the whole truth.

'Frankie, look at me.'

His voice was impossible to ignore. Lifting her head, she met his gaze.

'Look, I haven't had a day off in a long time and you need a break,' he said. 'We're just going to spend it together.'

Her heart missed a beat.

Could she? Should she?

But she'd already answered both those questions by coming back. And Arlo wasn't offering something solid or permanent—something that could be lost or broken. It wasn't a contract of commitment. What they had, what they both wanted, was purely physical. So why not let it run its course?

'I'd like that.'

'I'd like that too,' he said, his dark eyes locking with hers.

She felt her body start to melt. It was lucky, she thought, that she didn't have feelings for Arlo. To love a man who made you feel this way would be terrifying.

But then his head dipped, and he pulled her against him, and she stopped thinking and surrendered to a wave of want and need and heat...

Frankie had been slightly worried about facing Constance again, but as it turned out Frankie was not the only person who had returned to the island. Throughout the day more and more staff kept arriving.

Arlo seemed amused by her astonishment. 'What did you think? That Constance did everything on her own?'

She had. But now she thought about it, it seemed ridiculously obvious that that would be impossible. The house was vast, and then there were the gardens, and the island itself...

'There are twelve people working here full-time.'

'What? Even when you're not here?'

He nodded. 'Most of the staff have been here for at least a decade. They're like family.'

Frankie smiled, but inside she felt that familiar ache of loss and envy at the word family. Only she had no right to envy the very thing she had helped destroy, she thought, as Arlo introduced her to Constance's team of indoor staff.

'You can meet everyone else later,' he said as they left the kitchen. 'This way.'

He touched her lightly on the back and she felt a flicker of heat low in her belly. 'Where are we going?'

'Nero needs a run. I thought we could go down to the beach.' His dark gaze rested on her face. 'Work up an appetite.'

It was glorious outside.

The sky was an almost Mediterranean blue, and the tide was out, and to her amazement the beach was sandy. Arlo rolled his eyes as she pulled off her boots and socks, but then he did the same.

'Oh, it's freezing!' She gasped as the sea swirled over her bare feet. But only for a moment. Then it was still cold, but in a good way. 'It's so beautiful,' she said, gazing down the beach. 'It actually makes my heart beat faster.'

Arlo picked up a stick and hurled it a ridiculous distance down the beach. 'Are you sure that isn't me?'

Reaching down herself, she flicked some cold water at him and then started to run. He caught her easily, pulling her against him so that she felt suddenly breathless with his nearness.

'You are going to pay for that, Ms Fox.'

'Big talk, Mr Milburn.'

He laughed then—a genuine laugh that made her go weak in the middle.

'That feels like a challenge,' he said.

She laughed. 'Is that your way of saying you want a billiards rematch? Because we can play for money this time, if you want.'

'Only if you wear those shoes.' He smiled slowly. '*Just* those shoes.'

The slow burn of his gaze reached inside her, pressing down against her pelvis. 'I'm game if you are.'

Grimacing, he shook his head. 'You know, your brother has a lot to answer for. I think at some point I'm going to have a few words with him about unleashing you with a cue on an unsuspecting male population.'

Feeling cold on the inside, she stared past him at the sea. *Answer him. Say something...anything*, she told herself. But her mouth wouldn't move.

After a short, gritty pause, he said slowly, 'It's not a big thing, Frankie. I'm not angling to meet your family.'

She felt her chest pull tight with anger and panic. How dare he throw that at her? This was his fault. If he'd warned her that he was going to start talking about her family she would have prepared herself.

'Not everything is about you, Arlo—' she snapped.

Adrenaline was spiking inside her and her hands were shaking. She could feel it building beneath her skin. The misery. The guilt. The memories she fought so hard to keep at bay. Her heart twisted and she pressed her knuckles against the ache.

'Frankie...'

His voice was gentle—too gentle. It was melting her

anger, melting the barriers she had built, so that the memories were filling her head and the truth was spilling from her lips.

'You can't meet my brother.' Tears filled her eyes. 'You can't meet any of my family. They died in an accident two years ago. They all died. Everyone except me.'

For a few half-seconds Arlo stared down at Frankie in shock and horror, and then he pulled her into his arms, holding her close until she softened against him just as he had on that first morning.

Only this was so much worse.

'It's okay, Frankie. It's okay,' he said, holding her tighter. But obviously it wasn't.

His heart was thudding painfully hard, the last few days replaying on fast-forward inside his head. The things he'd said, the way he'd acted.

'Here.' Pulling out a handkerchief, he gently wiped her eyes and cheeks.

She bit into her lip. 'I'm sorry. You don't need to deal with all this. It's not fair. You lost your parents too.'

He tensed. They hadn't talked about his parents, Lucien and Helena, but no doubt Johnny had told her the basics—that his mother had died young and their father was dead now too. Heaviness was seeping through his chest. He'd known pain and loss, but to lose everyone like that... It was impossible to imagine how that must have felt—how it must still feel, given that it was so recent.

'You don't need to worry about that. I've got strong shoulders.'

He pulled her closer. She needed to talk, but he felt as if he'd cornered her into the conversation, and he sensed that it would be easier for her to answer yes/no questions.

'Was it the same accident that gave you your scar?'

She nodded. 'It was a plane crash. We were coming back from a holiday in France. My dad was flying the plane.' Her mouth trembled. 'He loved medicine but flying was his passion.'

'Do you know what happened?'

He felt her shiver.

'Not really. At the inquest they said he'd fallen asleep. I'd taken a travel sickness pill. The first thing I remember is waking up to this enormous headache.'

Arlo nodded mechanically, but inside his head he was visualising the scene. The wreckage. The bodies. The silence. His chest squeezed tight.

'Does Johnny know?' He hadn't consciously intended to ask that question, but for some reason he cared enormously about the answer.

She shook her head. 'I haven't really told anyone. I did a couple of sessions with a therapist, but I don't know how to tell people. It's stupid, really. I did try a few times, but they were always so horrified, and then I just ended up trying to make them feel better.'

It wasn't stupid. After his mother's death people had wanted to be kind, but mostly he'd found himself having to manage *their* reaction. The idea of Frankie trying to cope with that as well as everything else made the muscles in his arms tighten painfully.

Her eyes found his. 'You're a good listener,' she said quietly, sifting a layer of sand between her toes.

He pulled her closer and kissed her. Holding her, feeling her soft body against his, made his heart contract.

But he ignored it.

This wasn't about him. It was about Frankie. And she needed more than a few days off. She needed someone to fill the family-sized gap in her life. She needed someone to love her and look out for her.

He couldn't do any of those things but he could, and would, take care of her, for now, until it was time for her to leave.

CHAPTER SEVEN

HANDS TIGHTENING AGAINST the ship's wheel, Frankie squinted through the sunlight at the sea, her heartbeat leap-frogging in time to the waves.

She had not been prepared for this. For any of it.

For the patches of shining brightness or the dazzle of spray hitting the bow of the boat. But most of all for where the pursuit of her unfinished connection with Arlo Milburn had taken her.

They were on board his yacht, *The Aeolus*, and she couldn't quite believe that she was here with him.

Remembering her stumbling confession out on the beach, she felt her chest tighten. She still didn't really understand how she had ended up telling Arlo about the accident. She hadn't planned on telling him anything.

Why would she?

They'd promised one another nothing.

But Arlo had been so calm, unfazed—and in a way that wasn't surprising, given how he lived. He must have had to deal with far more terrifying things in Antarctica.

What she hadn't expected was for him to show compassion. Had she thought about it, she would have assumed he would be brisk, practical, detached. Instead, his gentleness had caught her off-guard, and she had been telling the truth when she'd said he was a good listener. He was the first person who had given her space to find the right words. Or maybe to realise that there *were* no right words.

He hadn't just rushed in and tried to fill the void with his pity and shock, and crucially he hadn't made it about him. And that was the most incredible part, given that he had lost both his parents too.

He had understood that in that moment there had been

no room for his experiences, even though they were relevant. He was the first person who had seemed to know that she was in a dark place and that what she needed most of all was for him just to join her there.

So instead of telling her that he knew how she was feeling, or giving her advice, or trying to be positive, he had let her talk. He had listened—really listened—so that it had been easy to tell him the truth.

Her stomach muscles tightened. Not all of it—not the fact that she had caused the accident…that it was her fault that her family had died.

Just for a moment or two she had thought about it. A part of her had wanted to tell him. But she had tried telling the truth before in France, first at the hospital, with the *gendarmes*, and then again at the inquest, but both times it had made no difference.

She allowed herself a brief glance at the man with the intense focus and formidable craggy profile at the other end of the boat.

At the hospital she'd thought it was because she was speaking English and that something had got lost in translation. But at the inquest there had been a translator, and it was then that she'd realised it wouldn't matter what language she was speaking, because telling the truth couldn't change what had happened.

It was her punishment not to be heard or understood, for to be understood would mean to be forgiven, and she didn't deserve that. And that was why she hadn't told Arlo about the part she'd played in the accident.

'Bear off a touch.'

Arlo's level voice came to her across the deck, and she looked over to where he was working the boat with the crew. She knew nothing about sailing, but it hadn't taken more than ten minutes at sea for her to understand that Arlo knew a lot.

Her pulse beat in her throat.

Like the rest of the crew he was wearing a dark T-shirt and buff-coloured chinos, but he still stood out from everyone.

Partly that was his height and breadth, but the human race had evolved sufficiently not to blindly follow someone simply on account of their strong thighs and wide shoulders. There was something else that drew her gaze. Something not actually visible. A certainty and authority that was both self-contained yet infinitely subtly responsive to those around him. An energy that thrummed from his core…that was tangible with your eyes shut. Or in the darkness of a bedroom.

Her face felt suddenly hot. She stared, dry-mouthed, her heart thumping against her ribs.

His hair was blowing in front of his eyes and her breath caught as he raised his hand and pushed it back from his angular face…

Their skin might be callused, and he might have lost the tips of two of his fingers, but she loved his hands. Their shape, their size, the dark hairs on the back of his wrists… They were so expressive of his mood, moving constantly while he spoke.

Watching them now, as he demonstrated something with a rope to one of the crew, she felt almost dizzy with hunger, remembering how they had moved over her body.

As if sensing her gaze, Arlo looked up. She felt her face grow warm as their eyes met, and then her heartbeat accelerated as he excused himself and began walking towards her.

'Everything okay?'

He'd stopped in front of her and, gazing up at him she felt a hum of pleasure. If not for the presence of the crew, she would have reached up and pulled his mouth onto hers.

'Yes, everything's fine.' She glanced past him to where

the huge white sails swelled in the wind. 'Actually, it's incredible. But then I've only ever been on a ferry before, so...'

That morning, when Arlo had rather offhandedly suggested they go out on his boat, she had imagined some kind of dinghy, maybe even something with oars, but certainly nothing like this.

At over sixty metres long, *The Aeolus* was no rowing boat. She was a single-masted sloop-rigged superyacht. Although, truthfully, the expensively smooth contours reminded her less of a boat and more of a huge white gull—the kind Arlo had sketched out on the ice floes.

The Aeolus moved like a bird too, skimming fluidly and silently over the waves, following some invisible flight path that seemed to have more to do with the natural rhythms of the wind and the sea than the actions of the crew scurrying about the deck or the high-tech navigation system.

His dark gaze rested on her face. 'Well, they both float,' he said drily. 'But it's a bit like comparing a mule to a steeplechaser.'

She laughed. 'I wasn't actually comparing them.' A warm feeling settled in her stomach. His mood seemed lighter today, his gaze less shuttered, so that without giving it much thought she asked, 'So who taught you to sail?'

For a moment he didn't reply, and she wondered why. It wasn't exactly a contentious question. But then she realised that he wasn't weighing up his answer, but how much to say.

A bit like me, she thought, confused by this sudden small connection between them.

'My Great-Uncle Philip,' he said finally. 'He was in the navy. He loved sailing and—' his mouth flicked up into one of those stiff, almost-smiles '—he expected his entire family to love it too.'

He glanced past her to where the sails arced, winglike, above the unbelievably dark blue water.

'He had a beautiful boat. But before he'd let you on board you used to have to go out with him in a dinghy—prove yourself ready and worthy.'

Frankie shuddered. 'Like a test?'

He gave another of those careful almost-smiles. 'Exactly. It was pretty stressful. He was exacting, and relentless when it came to attention to detail, but he wanted you to be the best sailor you could be, and he thought that experience was a gift to share. It wasn't all hard work. We had a lot of good times too,' he said, almost as an afterthought. 'We'd sail all day and then we'd go back to the house, and the whole family would be there, and we'd have this huge meal, and me and my cousins would get to stay up late…'

Her throat tightened with a mix of pain and envy. She missed her family so much it felt as if someone was squeezing her chest in a vice. And yet she liked hearing Arlo talk about his family. It made his face change, grow handsome, almost…

Glancing up, she found him watching her and, feeling suddenly self-conscious, she said quickly, 'I don't think any boat could be as beautiful as *The Aeolus*. I feel like I'm in *The Great Gatsby*, or something, but she's not vulgar. There's something organic about how she looks…as if she's in harmony with the sea.'

He looked pleased, and she felt something wobble inside her. She didn't know why, but she liked watching his grey eyes lighten at something she'd said.

'You like her?' he asked.

'I do.' She nodded slowly, then frowned. 'Why are boats always female?'

He thought for a moment. 'Historically, I think it's because a lot of boats used to be named after women. *The Aeolus* isn't, so I don't know why I say "she" and "her". I suppose I'm a little traditional.'

Tilting her head to make his eyes meet hers, she smiled slightly. 'I wouldn't say that.'

There was a beat of silence as their gazes locked and she felt a shiver run over her skin, knowing that he, like her, was picturing the many and various ways they had made love last night—some of which she hadn't even known existed, all of which had made her forget how to breathe.

Her breath caught now as he took a step forward, moving behind her so that she could feel the press of his body, slipping his hands past her waist to close over her hands.

'What are you doing?'

'You were drifting,' he said softly.

His skin and the bristles of his beard were cold against her heated face and she felt her heartbeat lose its rhythm.

'I'm just correcting your course.'

It wasn't just the boat that was drifting, she thought helplessly. She could feel her body melting, her insides turning liquid and hot, limbs softening and if he hadn't been holding her she would have slid to the floor.

'I don't know where we're heading,' she said hoarsely.

In her head, she'd meant literally—as in their destination—only it had sounded different when she'd said the words out loud.

Her heart bumped against her ribs.

It was something they hadn't discussed—how and when this would end. When they were in bed, with her body still ringing like a tuning fork and his body so warm and solid next to hers, it had been easy to do as he said and not 'overthink' things.

So don't start now, she told herself. *Stop thinking about what you told him yesterday and just enjoy the ride.*

'I meant with the boat,' she said quickly.

There was a short, pulsing silence, and then slowly he raised his head and drew her chin around, so that she was looking at him. His face was completely expressionless.

'We're going to drop anchor just up the coast. Constance has fixed us some lunch, and I thought you might enjoy a picnic on dry land. Or we can just stay on *The Aeolus*.' His fingers softened against her skin. 'But it's your call. Just tell me what you want, and I'll make it happen.'

Frankie had chosen a picnic, as he'd known she would, Arlo thought, glancing up at the flawless forget-me-not-blue sky.

Who wouldn't want a picnic on a day like this?

As if trying to make amends for the storm-force winds and slanting rain of a few days ago, the weather was perfect. Just the shimmering sun and a soft, Gulf-Stream-warmed breeze that barely lifted Frankie's dark red curls from her face.

A part of him was still reeling from her revelation yesterday. He hated to think that she'd been so hurt and lost, that she was still hurting.

That was what today was about.

Distracting her from the pain and hoping that it eased a little in the meantime—just like when Johnny had been teething and Arlo had carried him around the Hall, showing him the paintings in the early hours of the morning.

They had dropped anchor near one of the small uninhabited islands on the outer Firth of Forth. They'd taken the tender between the jagged rocks, and now they were sprawled on rugs on the heather-topped cliffs, picking through Constance's peerless picnic.

A loaf of homemade bread and a simple cold dish of thinly sliced slivers of chicken breast, dressed with a refreshing yoghurt sauce, were joined by baby beetroot with chutney, spiced aubergines, and some superb cheeses. To follow there was a rhubarb fool and a fruit and marzipan panforte, accompanied by a chilled bottle of Mâcon Blanc.

'I can't…' Frankie protested as he leaned forward and filled up her glass.

'On the contrary—you can. I'm the one who can't.' He dropped the bottle back in the ice bucket.

She screwed up her face. 'But that's not fair. You organised all of this and now you have to stay sober.'

Arlo stared at her in silence, a pulse ticking below his skin. It didn't matter that most of his crew were experienced sailors, or that it was a beautiful calm day. Alcohol and boats didn't mix.

But that didn't mean he was sober. On the contrary, being with Frankie made him feel as if he'd drunk a cellar full of wine. Although probably that was just the ozone. After a day at sea, he often felt that way. It was just a co-incidence that he was here with her.

His heart thumped against his ribs.

He couldn't deny, though, that he liked knowing he could make her happy. That it was in his power to make her happy.

And unhappy.

Here, out in the sunlight, basking in Frankie's smile, it felt suddenly more important than ever to remember that— to remember how it had ended the last time he'd sought out that power.

He felt a twinge of guilt, as he always did when he thought about his blink-and-you'd-miss-it marriage.

His marriage…the divorce.

Harriet was part of a past he'd intentionally buried deep, deep down, so that he didn't have to think about it. And it had been working just fine until Frankie had arrived with *her* past, and *her* questions, and now suddenly memories kept pushing to the surface.

He gritted his teeth. Not just memories. Feelings too. Only it was going to stop now. Whatever it was he was feeling for Frankie had nothing to do with the past.

She needed a friend. It didn't mean anything. All he was

doing was trying to make a few days of her life feel like a picnic. There was nothing more to it than that.

'I've been meaning to ask—what are the other rules?'

He glanced up at her. 'Rules?'

She waved her fork in the air. 'The other day you said that when you came home you had to eat real food at a table because that was one of your rules.'

Had he said that? How unbelievably pompous of him. He didn't have any rules.

Or rather he did. Unfortunately, he had broken both of them for Frankie.

His chest tightened. She wasn't the first woman he'd dated since Harriet, but with those other women he'd always been, if not happy, then ready and willing to part company after one night. And he'd never taken them home. Those were his unspoken rules.

But not only had he spent more than one night with Frankie, she was also staying at the Hall.

Sleeping in his bed.

An image of her as she'd looked that morning, pale limbs sprawled against the sheets, whipped at his senses and he felt a mix of resentment and relief at his ever-present hunger.

Feeling her gaze on his face, he shrugged. 'Nothing that exciting, I'm afraid. Just what everyone tells themselves after being on their own in a cold, brutal world. You know… the usual rules about not taking things, people, for granted.'

He'd said the first thing that came into his head but, glancing over at her pale, set face, he suddenly wished he had told her the truth. Silence stretched away from him, sweeping down to the sea like the great, granite cliff, and he swore softly.

'Frankie…' Reaching out, he took her hand. 'I didn't mean to—'

'It's fine.' Her fingers tightened around his. 'I know you

weren't talking about me, but you're right.' She glanced down, her dark lashes fanning out over her cheeks. 'We all take so much for granted. I know I did.'

His heart squeezed at the bruised ache in her voice. That was the difference between them. She couldn't control her pain. She hadn't learned how to block it out. But then it was all so new for her.

'It's a problem most humans have,' he said slowly.

Before his mother's illness he had taken so much for granted. He felt his chest tighten, remembering those days out on his great-uncle's boat. They had been long, tiring days, but being surrounded by his family every hour he had felt magical, blessed. Bulletproof.

It was hard to believe now, but back then he had genuinely thought that they were invulnerable, that his parents' all-consuming love offered them some magical protection against hurt and injustice—even illness and death.

It hadn't helped that the bohemian world they'd created had felt so far removed from 'normal' life. The life lived by his cousins and his friends from school.

Nobody else's mother played her cello on the beach. His friends' fathers didn't let their sons have a day off school to practise making the perfect martini.

In their enchanted cocoon of love and laughter, anything 'real', like letters from the hospital, had got ignored or forgotten.

But cancer didn't go away just because you ignored it.

It still burned in him now, the memory of his parents' life together. It was a dull, red fire that he purposely kept smouldering—but not because he was waiting for the right woman to come along and rekindle it. His jaw clenched. No, it was there as a reminder of what happened when you let someone become your whole world and then you lost them and your whole world crumbled.

And that was another difference between him and Frankie.

She was still a believer—still looking to replace like with like, still hoping for something, or someone, to fill the gap in her life.

That someone wouldn't—couldn't—be him. What had happened with Harriet had only happened because he, like Frankie, had been young and alone and lost in grief. Yes, he had loved Harriet, but in a couple of months he would have probably loved someone else. And then someone else.

Only his life had just imploded, and his feelings for her had got mixed up with all the loss and the loneliness, and ultimately everything had been a disaster.

But it hadn't been without purpose. At least he could make sure that Frankie didn't make the same mistake.

He looked down at her hands, turning them over. They were so small and soft. *She* was soft—he knew that now. Too soft for a world where you didn't need to be in Antarctica for life to be randomly brutal and harsh. Too soft to be in that world alone.

And one day she would find someone…someone special.

Blocking out the nip of jealousy at the thought of the faceless, nameless man who would one day hold Frankie close, he tightened his hand around hers.

For now, she just needed support.

'I find it helps to live in the moment,' he said slowly. 'To focus on the real and the present.'

Her eyes found his. 'Is that why you like sailing so much?'

He considered her question. 'I've never looked at it that way, but maybe yes.' Lifting her hand to his mouth, he kissed it gently. *'In vino veritas.'*

She grimaced. 'I haven't drunk that much.' Reaching for the bottle, she giggled. 'Oops… Perhaps I have. I don't normally like wine, but this is so delicious. All your wines are.'

He laughed then—not just at the wonder in her voice but at his own sudden and startling joy in the 'real and present' moment he was living. A moment he could enjoy in good faith, knowing that he was back in control.

'My father would have been deeply gratified to hear you say so. Wines were one of his three great loves.'

He saw the flicker of curiosity in her blue eyes—eyes that changed from moment to moment like the sea shimmering beneath the cliffs, so that first they were silver, then a dark indigo, and then the colour of amethysts.

'What were the other two?' she asked.

She had done it again. Resurrected the past so that he was thinking about his mother. Her face was clearer than Frankie's, the absence of her no less unthinkable and punitive now than it had been in those terrible first few days after her death.

He let a minute or two of silence tick by, but he could hardly ignore her question.

'That would be painting… And Helena. My mother,' he said slowly. 'Unfortunately for my grandfather.'

Frankie frowned. 'Why unfortunately?'

'That's how my parents met. My grandfather hired Lucien to paint my mother's portrait for her twenty-first birthday—'

'And they fell in love!' She ended his sentence triumphantly, excitement lighting up her face.

He nodded. 'Correct. And then they eloped. Over the border to Scotland. They planned it all in secret for months. Nobody knew anything about it until they called from Gretna Green.'

Frankie's eyes were wide and soft. 'That's so romantic.'

Leaning back, he studied the play of expressions on her face. Her excitement made him feel old and jaded. But that was a good thing. It meant he was back in control. It meant that moment earlier, when it had felt as if he was losing his footing, had been just a momentary lapse.

Holding her gaze, he shook his head. 'My grandparents didn't think so. They were furious. Understandably. Helena was only twenty, and Lucien was hardly ideal husband material.'

'He was a famous artist,' she protested.

'A forty-five-year-old artist with two failed marriages under his belt. And he wasn't that famous—not then. Plus, they'd already lined up a far more suitable husband-to-be. So, my uncles went and found her and brought her back home, kicking and screaming.'

She blinked. 'They did?'

He nodded, swept along by the familiar glamour of the story despite himself. 'And then Lucien turned up at the house with a shotgun, threatening to shoot my grandfather, and got himself arrested.'

'Then what happened?'

The dazzle of eagerness in her eyes caught him like a punch to the solar plexus and he shrugged. 'Me. I happened.' He paused, staring at her steadily. 'My mother was already pregnant by then, and my grandparents realised they were fighting a lost cause.'

Watching her expression turn hazy, he felt a rush of vertigo. He could see it in her eyes. She was falling in love with the story and it sliced something open inside him.

'It's like a real-life fairy tale,' she said slowly.

His chest tightened. Most fairy tales ended with a wedding, not death and despair.

'You think?' He couldn't stop the note of bitterness from creeping into his voice.

'Of course.' She frowned. 'What could be more romantic?'

Her softly worded question pulled at his senses and, glancing over at her face, he tensed. She wanted to believe in happy-ever-after. Like most people, the aftermath—what happened when the happy-ever-after ended—didn't interest her so much.

He shrugged again. 'I suppose that would depend on your definition of "romantic".'

There was a small beat of silence and then Frankie looked him straight in the eye. 'Love conquers all. Every time.'

Turning his head, he glanced away from the open blueness of her gaze. 'Then I'd have to disagree with you.'

Frankie stared at him in confusion, separately and vividly aware of both the pulsing tension in his jaw and the distance in his eyes. She'd been having such a wonderful day. And it wasn't just the excitement of sailing on a real boat or the picnic which had taken her completely by surprise, it was Arlo.

Maybe it had been the freedom of being out on the boat, or perhaps if had been her opening up about her family yesterday, but he had talked more about his life in the last half-hour than he had done over the previous four days.

And that had been the sweetest surprise of all.

Only now it felt as if he had retreated into himself again.

She bit her lip. 'I don't understand…' she said slowly. 'How can you tell me that story and not believe in love?'

He shook his head. 'I'm not saying that.' His grey eyes held hers briefly, then flicked away again. 'My parents' love was mesmerising—like watching a magic trick. It was impossible to look away, not to be dazzled.'

She watched mutely as he stared up at the sky, his face expressionless.

'Their love was so intense and beautiful. It flooded the world around them and the people around them, like me, with this incredible light. It was like standing next to the sun.'

His mouth made a brief curve, painful to watch.

'But at the end of the day the sun is just a big star. All stars collapse, and when they do, they pull everything into the darkness with them.'

Frankie swallowed. She knew all about the darkness. The terrifying plummet into the abyss. But even though she knew that he'd lost both his parents, she hadn't thought that Arlo felt that. He seemed so in control, so invincible.

But what did she really know about his life...his past?

She hesitated, and then she took his hand and held it, feeling his tension against her thumb. 'How old were you when she died?'

He didn't reply, and for a moment she thought he wasn't going to, but then he said stiffly, 'Thirteen. I'd just started my first term at Eton. I didn't go back. I couldn't. Lucien was in such a state and Johnny was only two years old.'

Which was why Arlo hadn't ever been a prefect, she thought, her heart contracting.

'Didn't anyone help?' she asked.

'Lots of people tried. Family, friends... And the staff were all fantastic.' He sounded tired. Almost as if he was back in that huge, grief-filled house. 'But my father didn't want help. He wanted her. And when he realised he could never have her back he stopped crying and started raging against the world.'

Frankie shivered. He spoke as he wrote, each word chosen with a measured precision that only added pathos to his story.

'What did he do?'

Arlo's expression was bleak. 'He drank a lot. Smashed up his studio. Burned his paintings. Not all of them. Constance rescued some. Then he just gave up. He stayed in his pyjamas...he barely ate.'

'But who looked after you and Johnny?' Her voice sounded brittle—accusatory, even—but she didn't care.

All she could think about was Arlo, all alone in the Hall with a tiny brother and a raging, unhappy man.

'Nannies on and off, at the beginning. They loved Johnny, but my father terrified them, so they never stayed long. Constance helped a lot. Mostly Johnny wanted me, and in the end we just muddled through.'

Her heart felt too big for her chest. Johnny had told her that Arlo had raised him, but she hadn't really believed him. 'What about you?' she whispered.

He shrugged. 'I didn't need looking after.' His beautiful, misshapen mouth twisted. 'And I wasn't easy to look after. Not like Johnny.'

Frankie nodded. She could all too easily imagine the awkward, brooding teenage Arlo, silent and trapped in his grief. Of course any nanny would prefer a beautiful, uncomplicated child like Johnny. She gritted her teeth, pushing back against the pressing weight of misery rising in her throat. Why did the world have to be so cruel? So unfair?

'I'm sorry,' she said quietly. 'I'm so sorry there was no one there for you.'

His face tensed. 'No, that's not how it was, Frankie. My uncles and aunts were fantastic. They sorted out all the financial stuff and the running of the Hall. But I wouldn't let them help with Lucien or Johnny.'

He looked up at her, his mouth twisting into a smile that made her hand tighten around his.

'As you know, I can be pretty stubborn when I want to be.'

'Why wouldn't you let them help?' she whispered.

For a moment he seemed lost in thought, and then his smile twisted tighter. 'I suppose I was trying to make amends.'

His voice was flat, dull, as if all the emotion had been ironed out of it.

She stared at him numbly. 'I don't understand…' Why would he need to make amends?

His eyes found hers, hearing the question even though she hadn't asked it.

'I knew she was ill. We all did. But my parents lived in this fantasy world of love and beauty and art. They ignored anything that was too "real". And I didn't want to face the truth on my own, so I let myself be persuaded to do nothing as well.'

The emptiness in his voice made the afternoon feel suddenly cool.

'I wanted to believe that their love could conquer everything, even though I knew unquestionably that it couldn't—that it was just a beautiful story.' He glanced over to where *The Aeolus* swayed against the tide. 'I made a choice, and it was the wrong one. I let my feelings override the facts. After the funeral, I made a promise never to do that again.'

And he had kept his promise.

'So that's why you became a scientist. And why you don't believe in love.'

For some reason it hurt, saying those words out loud. Hurt more than it should. Almost more than knowing he'd been so lost and alone.

His eyes found hers, the clear sunlight touching the grey with silver. 'I didn't for a long time. But I do now.'

She couldn't speak. Suddenly her whole body was taut like a bowstring, and even though there was no reason to do so she was holding her breath. The beat of her heart hovered like a diver on the top board as she waited for his next sentence.

'For other people. Not for me. I could have done something—*should* have done something…told someone—but I didn't. I was like a child, watching the fireworks while the house burns down. And I know you're going to say I *was* just a child, but—'

'You were,' she said hoarsely, watching the tension in the tiny muscles around his mouth.

His jaw was taut, his eyes distant. 'I don't expect you to understand.'

But she did. She understood completely.

Love had let him down, failed him. No wonder he had turned his back on the world and chosen to spend his life wandering the icy extremities of the Arctic and Antarctica, putting his trust in science and data and brutal, honest facts.

It all made horrible, painful sense.

He had failed to save his mother so now he was trying to save the world. She understood that feeling. She felt the same the way—felt the same need to do penance and the urge to share that common chord—and her guilt was almost irresistible—

Her chest tightened. *Who was she trying to kid?* Nothing about her self-interested behaviour that night in France had anything to with the way Arlo had acted. And she wasn't about to burden him with her guilt.

Reaching up, she stroked his cheek. If she closed her eyes she could barely feel the scar. But scars were like icebergs: the damage ran deep.

'I do understand,' she said slowly.

If only that understanding came with some unique power to help his invisible scars heal, but she had nothing to offer him.

After they'd climbed back aboard *The Aeolus* Arlo turned towards the deck, but Frankie tightened her grip on his hand.

He frowned. 'I was just going to check in with the crew. Make sure everyone's okay.'

'They can manage without you.'

His eyes fixed on her face. 'Is this a mutiny?'

'Yes, it is,' she said softly and, feeling as if her heart

was dropping away from her body, she pulled him to her and kissed him softly.

She had been wrong. There *was* something that would soothe the pain. His and hers. Something that was in her power to give.

'You took care of me yesterday.' Her eyes locked with his and he breathed in sharply as she slid her hand between his thighs. 'Now it's my turn to take care of you.'

And, turning, she led him away from the deck and down to their cabin.

CHAPTER EIGHT

ROLLING ONTO HIS SIDE, Arlo stared across the room at the open bathroom door. Frankie was in the shower, and over the sound of the running water he could hear her singing. He couldn't make out the words of the song, but people only sang in the shower when they were happy and that was what mattered.

His shoulders tensed. Although after his performance yesterday she might be forgiven for not believing that.

Gazing unseeingly across the room, he thought about the things that he'd told Frankie out in the heather on the cliffs.

It shouldn't have happened. Ordinarily it wouldn't have. She was by no means the first woman to ask him about his parents, and he'd never had any trouble deflecting questions. But yesterday he hadn't been able to stop himself talking. And not just talking. It had been practically a full-blown confession. He had talked about everything.

Except Harriet.

But why would he mention his ex-wife?

It all seemed so long ago now.

He'd met her at university, just weeks after losing his father, when he had been desperate with grief. It shamed him to admit it now, but she had been a shoulder to cry on.

Except, of course, he hadn't cried.

Maybe if he had he might not have married her.

But he'd been young, and the impulsive flamboyance of marrying someone he barely knew had seemed like both the right way to honour his parents' love and a chance to give Johnny some kind of normality and stability.

But his marriage had been over before it had started, its only purpose seemingly to confirm what he'd already known. That love required a blind, unquestioning faith he'd lost.

His stomach tensed. Maybe it was no bad thing to remind himself of that—especially after last night. He wasn't made of stone or ice. Even if they hadn't been sleeping together, he cared about Frankie, and her story had broken his heart.

Not that there was any *real* risk to his heart. This was only about sex. Anything else was just a completely understandable impulse to look after someone who needed help.

He stared at the indentation in the pillow, where Frankie's head had been. Last night, after she'd fallen asleep, he'd looked up her family's accident on the internet, and the photos he'd found had left him feeling nauseous. There had been wreckage everywhere. A wing had been torn off and the plane looked as if it had been twisted like a wet cloth.

His chest tightened. Those pictures would stay with him for a long time. But not as long as that look on her face when she'd told him about the crash.

She had seemed so small and young and lost.

A dull ache spread out slowly inside him like spilt wine. He knew how that felt. Even now he could still remember it: the months spent watching his mother shrink in on herself, and then the years after her death, when his father had stopped being the huge, exuberant bear-like man of his childhood and became instead a child…a lonely, angry child who locked himself away with his pain.

But he was lucky. He'd had Johnny, and his family had always been there when he'd let them.

Speaking of family…

He shifted up the bed and, opening his bedside cabinet, pulled out an envelope. Inside was an invitation to his cousin Davey's tenth wedding anniversary party. And a request for him to say a few words.

He wasn't planning on going. He'd already hinted as

much, pleading work, and by rights he wouldn't have even been in England if there hadn't been that problem with the plane, so…

He felt a stab of guilt. Davey wouldn't make a fuss about it, but he knew his cousin would be disappointed. But not surprised. And that made him feel even more guilty. Not that he was going to do anything about it. Much as he loved his family, he didn't do the big family events. They were just so full of an energy and emotion he couldn't handle.

Davey would understand. He'd call him and let him know…

The shower had stopped and, tossing the invitation to the top of the cabinet, he rolled on his back as Frankie wandered into the bedroom and instantly he forgot all about his cousin and the party.

Her hair was tied into some kind of bun thing, and she had a towel tied over her breasts so that her shoulders were bare. Staring over at her pale, damp skin, he felt his fingers itch to tug the towel loose.

'Nice shower?' he said softly.

She nodded. 'The best. Honestly, the water here is amazing. It's so hot and it's literally never-ending.'

Smiling, he reached for her hand and pulled her towards the bed. 'We use hydropower.'

'You mean like waves?'

'Sort of,' he said, pulling her onto his lap. 'There are caves under the island. When the sea floods them, we use three Archimedes screws to capture the energy of the flow, like a kind of reverse positive displacement… What? What is it?'

Frankie was staring at him, her expression soft, almost hazy.

'Nothing. I just—'

She steadied herself against his shoulders and he felt his body harden as her fingers splayed over his skin.

'Is there anything you don't know?' she asked.

Lots of things, he thought. *Like how she could look so beautiful with shadows under her eyes.*

Or how she had walked away from that crash alive.

Pushing that thought away, he looked into her eyes. 'Plenty, but if the subject interests me enough I make it my business to find out everything there is to know.'

I see.' She shifted against him in a way that made his hands clamp around her waist. 'So what kind of subjects currently interest you?'

'Well, just lately I've grown very interested in social media.'

He watched as she let her hair down, shaking it loose so that it tumbled over her shoulders.

'Anything else?'

'Billiards.'

'Really?'

This time as she shifted the towel flared around her hips and a tingle of heat tightened his muscles as he caught a glimpse of red-gold curls.

'Anything else?' she asked again, softly.

'Foxes.' He sucked in a breath as she leaned forward and ran a finger down the dark line of hair bisecting his abdomen. 'Female foxes in particular.'

The small smile tugging at the corners of her mouth made a complex mix of heat and tension spike inside him.

'And how do you plan on finding out about female foxes?' she asked.

He cleared his throat. 'I'll start with a thorough and exhaustive examination of any previous research.' As her hand slid beneath the bedclothes, his hands tightened around the edges of the towel. 'Although I'm guessing that sounds a little academic and dry.'

'Maybe a little academic…' Raising her hips, she tugged the towel loose and let it fall down her body. Their eyes met and he moved his hands up her back, caressing the indentation of her waist as she lifted her hips and then lowered herself onto him. 'But definitely not dry.'

He sucked in a sharp breath. She was warm, slick, tight. 'That's good,' he said through gritted teeth. 'That's so good.'

'Then what will you do?' she whispered.

She was shivering as if she was cold, but her skin felt hot and smooth, like sun-baked sand.

'I'll go out into the field…do some hands-on research of my own.'

He cupped her breasts, his thumbs grazing her nipples so that she arched forward, her mouth forming a long, slow amorphous syllable. He felt his control snap. Reaching up, he brought her face down to his and kissed her fiercely, his groan of pleasure mingling with hers as he rolled her beneath him and surrendered to the impossible need building inside them.

Later, tucked against his warm body, Frankie lay with her head against Arlo's chest, listening to his heartbeat.

She was still trying to catch her breath.

Each time it happened she kept expecting it to be different. For the spell to be broken, the magic to have gone. But each time was the same.

Not the same, she corrected herself. That made it sound boring, and in bed, as in life, Arlo was adventurous and passionate and tireless.

He felt so good. Big and warm and strong, so that even in the eye of the storm, when his hard body was driving into hers, she could sense the solid core of him. And afterwards, in his arms, she felt so calm, so safe.

Closing her eyes, she turned her face into the hollow beneath his shoulder, breathing in his scent. She could feel body softening against his. Except it wasn't just her body that was softening. The last few days had turned everything she'd thought to be true on its head, so that it was hard to believe she had once found him horrible and rude and arrogant.

And it wasn't just the sex. Yesterday, he had been kind to her, and gentle—tender, almost—and it was making her feel tender towards him. Particularly after what he'd told her about his parents.

And it was okay to feel that way, she thought defensively. There was no need to overthink it. It wasn't as if she was in love with him or anything.

'What are you thinking?'

She blinked. Arlo was looking down at her, his eyes resting on her face. Hoping very much that he couldn't read her thoughts, she said quickly, 'Just about how beautiful it looks outside.'

His hand touched her hip bone and he ran his finger lightly along the curve of her bottom. 'Not as beautiful as you.'

Her eyes met his. 'So, do you have anything planned for today?' She wriggled away from his hand, laughing. 'Aside from *that*.'

'No, nothing. I'm entirely at your disposal.'

She breathed out shakily. In one way it was a relief to feel that stab of hunger, to be reminded that this was all about sex. But it was starting to scare her how much she needed him.

And it *was* a need. A requirement like air or water.

She couldn't imagine life without him. Only at some point she was not only going to have to imagine it, but experience it for real.

She couldn't stay here for ever. Her life was in London and that wasn't going to change, however good the sex or however momentarily kind Arlo was, and there was no point in imagining anything more permanent.

'Let me see what time it is,' she said, needing to move away from the heat of his body, or at least to prove that she could.

Leaning past him, she grabbed his watch.

'Oh, sorry.' She reached down for the card that she'd knocked to the floor. Unthinkingly, she glanced at it. It was an invitation to a wedding anniversary party.

'Who's Davey and Serena?'

'My cousin and his wife. It's their tenth wedding anniversary.'

Arlo's voice was clipped and, glancing up, she saw that the easy intimacy of moments earlier had faded. Now he looked guarded, wary.

'That's wonderful. And they're having a party.' She gave him a small stiff smile. 'Don't worry—I'm not angling for a plus-one. I'll be long gone by—' She broke off, her eyes widening as she read the date. 'But it's today.' Looking up, she frowned. 'I don't understand. Why didn't you say something?'

'Why would I? I'm not attending.'

Even without the sudden coolness in his voice she would have sensed that as far as Arlo was concerned this particular topic of conversation was over.

'But why? It's a special occasion.' Her stomach clenched. 'It's not anything to do with me, is it?'

He frowned. 'I'm sorry to break this to you, Frankie, but very little in my life is anything to do with you.' His eyes were hard now. 'We're not overthinking this. That's what we agreed, remember?'

Frankie stared at him, mute with shock, feeling a chill slide over her skin at the starkness of his words. 'I remember.'

'Good.' He rolled off the bed and stalked past her naked. 'And, just so we're clear, I'm not going to be running my social diary past you any time soon.'

'I'm not expecting you to. I just thought it had to be me…the reason you aren't going. I mean, what other reason could there be?' she persisted. 'It's not as if you're doing anything else…and it's your cousin's anniversary party.'

Pulling on his trousers, he shook his head. 'My reasons are my business, and this conversation is over.'

She held her breath, hanging on to her temper. 'Why are you being like this? I was just trying to be nice.' Turning, fists clenching, she took a step towards him. 'What is the matter? I don't understand—'

'Then let me make it plain.' There was no emotion in his voice. 'What I do, where I go or don't go, is nothing to do with you. And that goes for my family too.'

She stared at him, her anger fading, giving way to a savage, wrenching pain that made tears choke up in her throat.

'You're right. It isn't my business. Nor is it my family. I think I just forgot that for a moment.' She balled her hands, trying to contain all the chaos and emotion inside her. 'I was thinking about *my* family and how I'd give anything just to see them again—'

The room swam.

'Frankie—'

She held up a defensive hand. 'It's fine. I don't need you to comfort me. I can deal with it on my own.'

'Please— Please!' He took a step closer. 'Please don't cry. I never want to make you cry.'

Her eyes burned as he caught her, his hands gripping her shoulders.

'I'm sorry,' he said. 'I didn't mean what I said. I don't know why I said it. It's not even true, and now I've upset you—'

She breathed out shakily. His misery was palpable— as was his remorse. 'Not everything is about you, Arlo. I'm upset because I lost my family. And, yes, you made me think about them. But I've spent the last two years not being able to do that, so that's a *good* thing.'

And it was true. She didn't feel trapped or alone with her loss anymore; in fact, she actually felt more, not less, in control.

'I don't mind getting upset, but I do mind you talking to me like that. I don't deserve that—'

'No, you don't.' He pulled her against him, his thumbs tightening around her wrists. 'I'm sorry,' he said again.

The features of his face were so familiar, but his expression wasn't. He looked troubled, young, unsure of himself.

'It's just the idea of a party... I'm not like you. I'm not a people person.'

Wasn't he? She stared at him in confusion. Arlo seemed to have good relationships with everyone at the Hall, and Johnny adored him.

'But they're your *family.*'

He nodded. 'Yes, and I love them. It's just being with all of them all together is hard for me.' He hesitated. 'But you're right. It's a special occasion. I should be there. I *need* to be there.' Looking down at her, he clasped her face, stroking her hair. 'And I'd like you to be there with me.'

Her heart bumped. 'Arlo, you don't need to... That wasn't why—'

'I know it wasn't. And I don't need you there—I want you there.'

'Are you being serious?'

He nodded slowly. 'Of course.' His hand found hers. 'Please, Frankie. I really do want you to come with me. Davey's home, Stanhope Park, is an amazing place. There's a pool, and horses, and Davey's organised a clay pigeon shoot for the morning after.'

She bit her lip. 'It all sounds lovely, but I don't have anything to wear to a party.'

'Wear what you wore the other night,' he said softly. 'I promise not to strip it off you this time.'

Their eyes met and her fingers twitched as his words sent a current of heat from his hand to hers, so that she was suddenly vibrating inside.

Why not go? It would be fun to dress up and dance. And, despite having recovered his composure, Arlo clearly found this kind of event hard. Her eyes snagged on a puckered scar on his chest. He had helped her so much…maybe it was time for her to help him.

She screwed up her face. 'You're sure your cousin won't mind? Me just turning up?'

'I'll call him, but he won't mind. Davey's not like that. He's a good man. Kind. Loyal. A little bit cautious.' He smiled one of those almost-smiles that made her world tilt off its axis. 'But then he's spent years being the son and heir.'

She pinched her lip, feeling suddenly nervous. 'So what do I call him?'

'His full title is Viscount Fairfax, but in person he's just Davey.' He rubbed at the worry lines between her eyebrows. 'Look…straight up, the house is a bit full-on. But they're very normal people who do very normal things, like have lunch with their family.'

Frankie nodded. It would be all right. In London she met all kinds of people all the time for her work. But then she hadn't ever cared what they thought. Arlo was different. She didn't want to let him down.

She didn't want to let her own family down either.

A knot was forming in her stomach. That *she* should have survived was the cruellest cut of all. So many times she had wondered why she alone had been spared, and she was still no closer to knowing the answer… All she knew was that she had to make her life count and make them proud.

His dark gaze roamed her face. 'You don't believe me?'

Glancing up, she tried to smile, tried to hide the conflicting emotions swirling inside her.

'I do. I just don't want to mess up,' she said slowly.

'I wouldn't worry about that.'

'But you're not me,' she said slowly. 'You don't have anything to prove.'

He hesitated, and she wondered if, like her, he was hearing an echo of that moment out on the hillside above the Hall. Only that had been teasing, rhetorical... They both knew Arlo had nothing to prove. Whereas she...

'Everyone has something to prove,' Arlo said quietly. 'Look at Davey. He owns a twenty-thousand-acre estate, but he didn't earn the money to buy it.' His hand touched her cheek. 'He inherited it from his father, along with his title. That was the easy part. Now he has to run it well enough so that it will be there for *his* son to inherit. He wants to do the best he can.'

'I want that too.' She could hear the emotion in her voice but didn't try to stop it. 'After the accident, I made a promise I'd do everything I could to make my family proud of me.'

'I'm sure they were proud, Frankie...' Frowning, he tried to cup her chin.

But, batting his hand away, she shook her head. 'Proud of what? The fact that I spent all my time on my phone? Messed up my exams? Dropped out of university? It's not exactly most parents' outcome of choice for their child.'

'Did they say that?'

She made herself look at him. He was watching her calmly. 'Of course not. They weren't like that. They weren't like me.'

They were like Arlo. High achievers. Top of everything they tried.

'My dad was a paediatrician. My mum was a barrister. Harry was a junior doctor and Amelie was a solicitor. But they weren't trophy-hunters they were good people...'

Better than good. They'd been decent, dependable, far more deserving of life.

Suddenly she was unbearably conscious of her guilt.

His brows drew together. '*You're* a good person, Frankie. And I don't believe for one moment that your family would want you thinking like this.'

The vehemence in his voice made her breath catch in her throat, but it was his hands, with their firm, unwavering grip, that steadied her. She felt a lightness inside her that seemed momentarily to reframe the choices she'd made.

He didn't have to do this, she thought. Take time to reassure her. Leaning forward, she kissed his cheek, her lips soft and warm against his skin. 'You're a good person too,' she said slowly.

As he let his head rest against hers she felt her heart contract. Since losing her family, the idea of getting close to someone, caring about them, had been too terrifying to contemplate. She couldn't risk it happening again. To love and then lose someone again was beyond her. That was why she kept people at arm's length, built emotional barriers between herself and the world.

Until Arlo. Seeing him so vulnerable had made something crack open inside her. But she had to keep things straight in her head. Maybe one day she would be able to love and be loved, but not here, not now, not with him.

This could only ever be temporary, and these feelings of tenderness were just the result of her loneliness and her desire to belong somewhere.

And besides, Arlo didn't even believe in love.

He let his head rest against hers. 'You'll have fun, okay? I promise. Now, get dressed and pack whatever you think you'll need. I've just got a couple of calls to make.'

* * *

'I got Robert to bring the car round,' Arlo said, turning to Frankie as they walked downstairs. 'But I thought I'd drive myself.'

Glancing discreetly at his watch, he felt a ripple of astonishment as he saw the time. Incredibly, it had taken an hour and a half for Frankie to pack, but he'd waited patiently, sensing that to rush her would be counterproductive.

She had been nervous before, but now she seemed excited and he was the one feeling jittery.

No, not jittery so much as conflicted.

He wanted to go, for Frankie's sake, but he was still dreading it. Partly that was because he'd never been as extroverted as Johnny and his parents, and he found spending time with his family *en masse* hard. But mostly the reason he didn't want to go was because celebrating Davey and Serena's tenth anniversary would remind him of his own failed marriage.

His stomach clenched. It was so unbelievably petty and shameful that he could barely admit it to himself, much less Frankie. Only she'd said that thing about her own family and he'd had to pull himself together.

She shook her head. 'I still can't believe I know someone who has a chauffeur.'

He shrugged. 'It's not that big a deal. It's just a useful option if I need to take my hands off the wheel.'

Watching her bite into her lip, he felt his insides clench.

'You have a one-track mind,' he said softly.

Her blue eyes locked with his, wide and teasing. 'So do you.'

'You carry on looking at me like that and I'm going to have to put you in the boot,' he warned.

She laughed. 'Empty threats, Milburn. The Land Rover doesn't have a boot.'

'We're not going in the Land Rover, Fox,' he said, holding open the front door.

Turning, she clamped her hand to her mouth. 'Oh, my goodness. Is that a Rolls-Royce?'

The note of excitement in her voice was strangely satisfying, and he let his gaze follow hers to where the huge golden convertible crouched like a lion in the drive.

'So this is the car Robert drives.' She giggled. 'I couldn't imagine you being driven around in state in your Land Rover. But this makes more sense.'

Reaching out, she slid her fingers over the silver figurine crouching on the bonnet and he felt almost light-headed. It was dizzyingly easy to imagine those same small, delicate hands caressing his body.

'Does she have a name?' she asked.

'She does.' He cleared his throat. 'The Spirit of Ecstasy.'

Her eyes met his, a small smile tugging at the corners of her mouth. 'I'll bear that in mind.'

'Are we here?' Only a little while later, Frankie was glancing out of her window. Up ahead, a pair of huge wrought-iron gates rose up between the high brick walls edging the road.

He nodded. 'This is it. Stanhope Park.' Leaning over, he punched a number into the keypad set into the wall and waited as the gates swung open.

As the big car swept up the driveway Frankie suddenly sat up straighter, her cheeks flushed with excitement and awe. 'Oh, wow,' she said five minutes later, as he pulled up in front of the beautiful house.

Switching the engine off, he looked over at her. 'Okay?'

'Yes.' She nodded, and then she froze, her blue eyes widening with panic. 'But what have you told them? About *us*?' She stumbled over the word. 'I mean, about who I am... what I am to you?'

He stared at her in silence, his heart beating against his ribs, stunned by her question and by his own idiocy. It was the first question everyone would ask, only up until now he hadn't thought to classify their relationship. It hadn't seemed necessary. In fact, naming what he and Frankie shared felt wrong, for some reason.

But this was going to be hard enough as it was. He didn't need to complicate matters by questioning what was, in essence, just a fling. He should follow his own advice and not overthink things.

'I think it'll make things simpler if we stick as close to the truth as possible. Why don't we just say we met through Johnny and you're up from London for a couple of days?'

She didn't say anything for a moment, and then she nodded slowly. 'That would work.'

'Good,' he said brusquely as the front door opened and a trio of Labradors came cantering out, followed by a tall blond man. 'Now, come and meet Davey.'

Arlo had been right about his cousin, she thought, as Davey led them into the house. He seemed like a really nice, normal man. But, despite what Arlo had said earlier, it was difficult not to be intimidated by Stanhope Park.

It was as big as a hotel, and if it hadn't been for the fact that Davey was wearing a Tattersall check shirt, moleskin jeans, and tan-coloured brogues she would have felt as if she'd slipped through a looking glass into the seventeenth century.

Lavish gilding, Rococo tapestries and jewel-bright festoon curtains were perfectly offset by a neutral colour palette of French grey, buff, and pale green. In fact, everything was perfect, she thought, gazing round their vast bedroom.

'I'll leave you to get settled in.' Davey smiled at Frankie. 'Lunch is at two.'

Lunch. She walked slowly the length of the room, trailing her fingers over the smooth velvet and polished wood, then walked back to where Arlo was watching her calmly.

'So…?' He tilted his head back questioningly.

'It's a little intimidating.' She met his gaze. 'Should I change for lunch?' She looked down at her jeans and sweater.

He shook his head. 'But, speaking of clothes, I have something for you.' Taking her hand, he led her past the gloriously over the top canopied bed and into the dressing room. 'I hope you like it.'

Frankie stared past him, open-mouthed, at a curaçao-blue silk dress. Except that dress was too basic a word for the confection hanging from the rail. Thin, fragile straps, a flowing skirt… Turning the dress, she felt her pulse accelerate. And a devastating neckline cut low to reveal the length of her back.

'Where…? How did you…?' she stammered.

'Bond Street. I had them courier it up.' His eyes were fixed on her face, examining her reaction. 'I took a punt at your measurements, so I hope it fits.'

'Oh, Arlo.' She breathed out shakily. 'It's lovely…but I can't accept this.'

'Of course you can. I invited you, remember? And after I spoke to Serena I realised the party was going to be bigger and grander than I thought.'

'Grander!' Her head was spinning. 'You mean, like crowns and things?'

Shaking his head, he brushed her hair back around her ear. 'No, it's just that the guest list is a bit of a roll-call of the great and the good. They like to dress up and I want you to feel at home.'

There was no dress on earth that could do that, she thought dully.

'Who are they?' she heard herself say.

'There's my other cousins, Jack and Arthur. Jack runs

a very successful hedge fund and his wife Charlotte co-owns an art gallery in Knightsbridge. Arthur owns an estate over the border in Scotland, and his wife Jemma is a model. Then there's Tom—he set up a literacy charity…'

She felt hot and shivery, as if she had a fever. Maybe she did have one. It would certainly explain why she wasn't thinking straight…why she had agreed to this. What had she been thinking? It was hard enough to pretend to herself that she was good enough. She couldn't possibly spend an evening trying to convince people like Arlo's friends and family.

'I'm sorry, I don't think I can do this.'

'Do what?' Arlo looked straight into her eyes. He sounded confused.

'Be here. In this house. With these people.' Her hands were tingling now, and she felt a rush of panic, cold and swirling and unstoppable, like the waves rising up over the causeway. 'I thought I could, but I don't fit in here. I don't own an estate. I'm not a lady.'

'So what? I'm not a lord…' The confusion in his eyes had darkened his irises almost to black.

'But you're related to one. And you own an island.' Her heart was crashing in her ears. 'You've walked to the South Pole alone. Everyone at this party will have done something amazing, won't they?'

'And so have you.' His hands caught her wrists. 'Look, Frankie, I get that you're still grieving, but you have got to stop this. You've got to let go.'

Her heart squeezed. 'Of what?'

'This need you feel to be worthy of life.' He was looking at her, his face implacable. 'Look, I understand. You see it all the time in the military. Survivor's guilt. A belief that you did something wrong by surviving. That being alive makes you guilty.'

In a tiny voice, she said, 'But I *am* guilty.'

'Of what? Surviving something that was completely random?'

'Not just surviving.' She drew a breath, trying to maintain control. 'It's my fault they're dead.'

Heart hammering, Arlo stared at her in silence. Her voice sounded as if it was sticking in her throat. She looked frightened, angry, *helpless*.

It was like seeing himself at thirteen.

Pushing that thought away, he shook his head. 'It wasn't your fault, Frankie. It was an accident.'

She pulled away from him, her anger rearing up like a riderless horse. 'How would you know? You weren't there?'

'No, I wasn't,' he agreed. 'But there was an inquest. People must have looked into what happened—'

'Other people who weren't there either.' The skin was taut across her cheekbones. 'They don't know what happened. What I did.' Her face contracted.

'Then tell me.' He looked at her, waiting. 'Tell me what you did.'

The anger that had flared up so fiercely flickered and died. 'I made my dad fly that night. He was tired, and he said it was too late, but I made a huge fuss about getting home because I wanted to go to some stupid party. I knew he didn't want to fly, but I made him—'

The despair in her eyes made his skin sting. This was more than just grief, and the crash had robbed her of more than just her family. It had taken away her trust. Not just that childlike faith shared by everyone that nothing bad could happen to good people, but faith in herself, in the person she'd thought she was.

Shaking his head, he kept his voice gentle but firm. 'Your dad was the pilot, Frankie. And he decided to fly. It was his decision. Not your mum's. Not yours. His.'

'So what are you saying? That it was *his* fault?'

The anger was back and he caught her wrists again.

'It was nobody's fault. Including yours. But you want it to be. Because your guilt is a way of holding on to the people you've lost.' She stared up at him mutely and, loosening his grip, he reached up and stroked her cheek. 'Or you think it is. But you end up losing them anyway, because you can't bear thinking about them, talking about them.'

She took a small shuddering breath and, watching her press her hand against her mouth, he felt his throat constrict. But he carried on relentlessly.

'And I know that's not what you want. But if you want to remember them you have to accept that what happened wasn't some sort of cosmic *quid pro quo*. They didn't die so you could live. You have to accept that and forgive yourself for not dying.'

Her small, white upturned face was like one of the anemones that grew beneath the walls of his kitchen garden.

'I don't know how,' she whispered.

'But I do, sweetheart. Trust me.' His fingers tightened around hers. 'You do trust me, don't you, Frankie?'

'Yes,' she whispered. 'I do.'

'Then you've taken the first step.'

Her face dissolved into tears and, wordlessly, Arlo pulled her against his body, his own eyes burning, his whole being focused on the aim of making the infinite expanse of her grief measurable.

Stroking her hair, he talked soothingly, and finally she breathed out shakily.

'I'm sorry. I always seem to be crying all over you.'

'You need to cry.' Lifting her chin, he kissed her softly on the lips. 'And I have plenty of shirts.'

She folded her body against his trustingly and he tensed inside. He had asked her to trust him, but why? He didn't want her trust. He didn't need that burden. He knew he should move, only his hand kept caressing her hair, and he could feel her soft warmth taking him to a place where cynicism and loneliness didn't play any part.

But even if that place existed it was not for him, and he lifted his hand as she tilted her head back to look at him.

'You'd better go and change, then, before we go down to lunch,' she said, her fingers lightly touching the front of his shirt. 'I seem to have covered this one in mascara.'

'Are you sure you want to stay?'

The shaky smile that accompanied her nod was something he couldn't bear to look at, and he pulled her closer.

'You're not responsible for what happened. No one is. Life is cruel and random, but you're not alone. I meant what I said. I'm here.'

Not for ever, of course. But that was a given. They both knew what this was, and how it would end. And it *would* end…

CHAPTER NINE

TAKING A STEP back from the mirror, Frankie held a breath, her eyes meeting her reflection with silent satisfaction.

She'd kept her make-up simple—just smoky eyes, mascara, a pinkish lip tint—and her hair was pinned up with just a few loose curls framing her face. It was the dress... the beautiful blue dress...that was the star of the show.

It was a dress that managed to be revealing and subtle at the same time. A dress that made her look sleek, sophisticated, and wholly unfamiliar.

Turning, she glanced over her shoulder at the back of the dress. Her pulse jumped like a startled frog.

What back?

She was naked from the top of her spine right down to the twin indentations above the curve of her bottom, and yet she didn't feel exposed. In fact, she had worn far less revealing dresses and felt more vulnerable.

Breathing out shakily, she ran her hand over the smooth, shimmering silk. In part, that was down to how the dress hugged her body, almost protectively. The other reason—the main reason, of course—that she didn't feel vulnerable tonight was Arlo.

Her pulse twitched.

'Trust me,' he'd said, and then, 'You do trust me, don't you?'

And there had been no doubt, not even an atom of hesitation, in her reply. Her trust in him was as unwavering and unequivocal as the man himself. How could it not be? After everything he'd done and said.

Her throat tightened. After the inquest she had stopped talking to people about the accident, about the part she felt she'd played. Instead, she had kept her guilt close, preferring it to the alternative, more crushing pain of loss.

Only she could see now that hiding the truth had meant also hiding who she was, so she'd created Frankie Fox the social media influencer with a million friends—none of whom knew her, all of whom were easy to keep at arm's length.

But she hadn't kept Arlo at arm's length, and in his arms the truth had come pouring out. Today, though, he hadn't just listened. He had forced her to confront the whole truth, made her see that her guilt wasn't just trapping her but condemning her family to exist only in those few terrible, fractured moments.

He had made it possible for her to move past that terrible night in France and it had been like a weight lifting. The pain of losing them was still there, it always would be, but she could live with that now that the other terrible, relentless ache was gone.

Her head had been so fuzzy with adrenaline and emotion that she still didn't really know how he'd done it. But one fragment of memory was diamond-bright.

Arlo had rescued her. *Again*.

Not from a swirling sea, but from herself.

And she wanted to say something—only what? *Thank you* seemed too anodyne. But she didn't know how to express the complicated mix of emotions she was feeling. Maybe the right words would just come to her after a glass of champagne…

Wondering if Arlo was ready to go, she turned and headed back into the bedroom.

She stopped in the doorway, her heart skipping a beat.

He was slumped on the sofa, reading a book. His hair was still a little damp from the shower, but he was more than ready, in a dinner jacket that accentuated his broad shoulders, matching trousers, another snow-white shirt, and, finishing it off like a ribbon on a birthday present, a perfectly knotted bow tie.

Her stomach did a slow backwards flip.

If only she could spend the evening slowly unwrapping him.

But, taking a second look, she felt her breathing slow. Despite the casual arrangement of his limbs, there was something about how he was sitting…an almost unnatural stillness that hinted at the coiled tension beneath his skin.

Remembering his agitation earlier, she felt a fierce protective urge, cold and potent like a shot of vodka. He was on edge—not that he would admit it. He'd said all he'd wanted to earlier—probably more than he'd wanted, in fact. But she knew. And more importantly, she knew what to do about it. He had given her this beautiful dress, but she would take care of him tonight—that would be her gift to him.

As though sensing her scrutiny, Arlo looked up. Clearing her throat, she took a step forward and did a little twirl. 'How do I look?'

He got to his feet, his grey eyes sweeping admiringly over her body. 'Like a goddess,' he said softly.

He closed the distance between them in two strides and the iron strength of his arm anchored her against him as his lips found hers. Sliding her hands up over his satin lapels, she breathed out shakily against his mouth. Her body was softening…her skin was growing warm, too warm. In another few seconds the small amount of resolve she had would melt away…

'Arlo—'

He broke away. 'I know. I know…'

His smile was rigid as she reached up to wipe her lipstick from his mouth. 'That's better,' she said lightly. 'I'm just going to touch up my lips.' She was back in less than a minute. 'Okay, I'm ready.'

'Not quite.' He was holding out a slim black velvet box.

Her heart felt suddenly as though it was trying to beat a path through her ribs. 'What's that?' she croaked.

'Open it and see,' he said quietly.

Speechless with shock, she stared down at a beautiful diamond bracelet. 'You shouldn't have—' Her lower lip was quivering. 'No, I mean it. You've already given me this beautiful dress.'

'That was a necessity. So is this, actually.' Lifting the delicate band, he opened the clasp and slipped it onto her wrist. 'Don't you know, darling? It's the accessories that make the dress.'

That wasn't true, she thought, glancing down at the smooth blue silk. This dress had been perfect as it was. This was generous, thoughtful, *personal.*

She felt her heartbeat accelerate. Arlo had wanted to see her reaction, to make her happy. *But only because he did things properly*, she told herself firmly. And probably that was how he'd been raised. It wasn't personal.

'Arlo, you can't keep buying me things,' she protested.

'Why? It gives me pleasure.' He stared down at her, his grey eyes intent and enveloping. 'You wouldn't want to stop giving me pleasure, would you?'

'No, but I don't have a gift for you…'

Her voice trailed off as he leaned forward and she felt his lips trace the pulse down her neck. The room blurred and a ribbon of heat uncurled inside her. Would it always be like this with him? So instant, so intense, so annihilating.

More importantly, could it ever be like this with another man?

Arlo lifted his head and the room slowly stopped spinning. 'We should probably go…'

His hand was warm and firm around hers. She smiled. 'Then let's go.'

* * *

Frankie could hear the party as soon as Arlo opened their bedroom door. Downstairs, guests were spilling out of the rooms, and it didn't take long for her to realise that not only did most of them know Arlo, many of them were surprised to see him.

Clearly he'd been telling the truth about not enjoying big family events.

He hid it well. His face was blank of expression, aside from the occasional stiff smile, but his arm was rigid beneath hers and she could feel his discomfort.

Only, somehow, knowing that he found it so difficult made it easier for her to step forward and smile and talk and laugh.

This was something she enjoyed—something she could do well, she realised. But, more than that, it was her chance to do something for him. Her chance to make him feel as safe and protected as he'd made her feel out on the causeway.

As they made their way to the ballroom Frankie caught her breath. In daylight, the house was astonishing. Now, though, it looked magical. Like an enchanted fairy tale palace.

Canopies of tiny lights hung down the walls behind huge displays of pink and cream roses, and beneath their feet an immaculate checkerboard marble floor gleamed beneath rows of glittering chandeliers.

The guests were pretty impressive too, she thought, her eyes leapfrogging over the men's immaculate monochrome evening wear to the sparkling dresses and plunging necklines of their wives and girlfriends.

Everyone looked so relaxed and happy.

Everyone but Arlo, she thought, her eyes darting to the man beside her and the lines of tension around his eyes.

'Here.' Plucking two glasses of champagne from the tray of a passing waiter, he handed her one.

'Thank you—oh, wow!'

Gazing up at the soaring ceiling, Frankie felt as if she'd already drunk the contents of her glass.

Arlo leaned into her, his body warm against the cool skin of her back. 'My great-great-great-great-grandfather is the one in the middle.'

'You mean the one kneeling in front of that woman wearing a sheet? I guess he does look a little like you from this angle,' she said softly.

Looking up at him, she was struck again by his size and his austere, uncompromising features, but most of all by his intense maleness. Other men might be prettier, more symmetrical, more elegant, but Arlo was magnificent. And half a head taller than everyone else.

She felt a slight fluttering pressure against her pelvic bone as he stared down at her, his eyes dark with heat. Taking a breath, she said quickly, 'So why did he get to be painted on the ceiling?'

Arlo glanced upward. 'He actually got more than a ceiling. This estate was a gift for his military successes against the French and the Bavarians.'

'And you followed in his footsteps?'

He met her eyes. 'Not quite. Although I did get into a fight with a French geologist out at Svalbard a couple of years back.'

'What happened?'

'He was uncomplimentary about my sledge.'

Frankie burst out laughing. Watching some of the tension leave his face, she felt her happiness grow brighter than the light from the polished chandeliers.

'Oh, there you are!'

It was Serena, glamorous in silver *lamé*, and the warmth

in her voice matched her smile. Beside her, Davey was handsome in his dark suit.

'Davey was worried you'd got lost. He was about to send a search party.'

Arlo shook his cousin's hand. 'As if I'd miss the chance to razz you in public.' He turned to Serena and kissed her on the cheek. 'You look lovely as always, Lady Fairfax.'

'Never mind me.' Turning, she gazed admiringly at Frankie. 'Look at you. You look absolutely gorgeous. Doesn't she, Arlo?'

Frankie felt her blood lighten as his eyes rested on her face, his head tilting slightly towards her. 'Yes, she does.'

Frankie was more than gorgeous, Arlo thought, pressing his hand flat on her back to steady himself. She was captivatingly lovely. He literally couldn't tear his gaze away from her.

The *crème de ciel* blue silk not only matched her eyes, it seemed to ripple over her body like water, and he had to concentrate hard on keeping his hands from sliding aside those thin straps.

Later, he told himself firmly, as his cousin Arthur bounded up to greet him. Later in their room, when they were alone, he would strip her naked and take her in his arms and let his body flow into hers.

Right now, he had to get through this.

Although with Frankie by his side it was proving less painful than he'd anticipated. Her excitement was infectious and, standing beside her, he was struck by how easily she got on with people. She made it look so effortless. Considering she didn't know anyone, she was relaxed and natural and warm—in other words, everything he wasn't. And it was obvious that she accepted people for who they were.

Just as she had accepted him.

But he could see, too, that she loved being part of a

family again—and she *was* a part of it. She fitted into his world like a hand in a glove.

As if sensing his gaze, Frankie glanced over at him and he felt his heartbeat accelerate. The skin was taut over the curves of her cheekbones, her eyes glittering with a curiosity and eagerness for life. *For him.*

His breath caught. When she looked at him like that it was tempting to think beyond the here and now, beyond this evening, beyond tomorrow...

Tempting, too, to think of choices made and yet to be made, of tantalising possibilities that had nothing to do with cold and danger or hardship and isolation, so that suddenly it was easy to imagine an alternative, hazy, sun-filled world, where the sky was always the colour of curaçao and Frankie was always in his bed.

But he'd chased that dream before, and all he'd succeeded in doing was breaking Harriet's heart and proving to himself what he had already known. Feelings could not be relied upon.

So why go there? Why ruin what they had?

This was perfection. A flawless moment frozen in time. It was not for everyone, but for him it was the only way.

From across the room, he heard someone call his name. Glancing over, he saw Arthur holding up his wrist and pointing at his watch.

It was time. The moment he'd been dreading was finally upon him.

Right on cue, a waiter appeared by his side and, picking up the glass of champagne from the tray, Arlo tapped it imperiously with a spoon.

Instantly the conversations around him subsided into silence and, moving purposefully through the crowd, he made his way over to the stage that had been set up for the band.

'Thank you. Most of you already know me. But for those

that don't my name is Arlo and Davey is my cousin. I know pretty much everything there is to know about him. But today isn't just about Davey. As you all know, today is Davey and Serena's tenth wedding anniversary.'

There was a small smattering of applause and a few cheers and he waited until they died away.

'And I was there, as most of you were, ten years ago, when they made their vows. Vows they have kept faithfully.' Turning towards his cousin and Serena, he forced his mouth to soften into a smile. 'As we all knew they would. Their vows were the real deal. Made with love.'

A love he envied and feared in equal measure.

He cleared his throat. 'The kind of love that is an ever-fixed mark—that hasn't changed and won't change with the passing of time or be shaken by storms.'

As he looked out across the mass of faces his eyes connected with Frankie's and he felt as if his heart was dropping away from his body, remembering what he'd said about love to her.

'And that love is why we love them. Why we love spending time with them. Why we're all here tonight.'

The words tasted bitter on his tongue. Each one a reminder of how he'd failed in his own marriage—a marriage that had served only to prove that his parents' rapturous, unfettered joy in one another was beyond his reach.

Someone coughed and he returned his attention to his audience.

'To sum up: money might make the world go round, but Davey and Serena are proof that love is the coin of the realm. Their love for one another, for their beautiful son Bertie, and for all of us.' He raised his glass. 'And now we have a chance to honour that love. So please raise your glasses and join me in a toast to Davey and Serena. For making it all look so easy.'

Everyone chanted out the names and then there was a

huge cheer. He felt a relief that was more intoxicating than any champagne flood his veins.

It was over.

'Thanks, mate.' It was Davey, his face trembling with emotion. The two men hugged.

Beside him, Serena was wiping tears from her eyes. 'I knew you'd make me cry.'

Pulling her closer, Arlo kissed her forehead softly. 'Then you can tick that off the list.'

Serena was a legendary list-maker—particularly when it came to organising events.

'Now, go and enjoy your party. Take Davey out on the dance floor. That'll put a smile back on your face.'

'Great speech.'

It was Frankie. The relief he'd felt moments earlier faded as he looked into her eyes. She looked happier than he'd ever seen her, and somehow sadder too.

'Thank you.'

She hesitated, seemingly on the point of saying something, and then changed her mind. He felt a sudden, overwhelming urge to hold her close, to steady his body against hers. Maybe that would stop this feeling of everything slipping beneath his feet.

'Would you dance with me?' he asked abruptly.

Her eyes found his and she nodded slowly. Taking her hand, he led her onto the dance floor. He held her close, letting the scent and the softness of her skin envelop him, so that by the end of their second dance his body was rock-hard.

She felt it. Of course she did. And, watching her blue eyes widen and flare, he leaned forward and nipped the soft skin of her throat.

'Can we go upstairs?' she whispered. 'I need you now.'

He didn't bother to answer. Instead, he took her hand and led her off the dance floor. He was dimly aware of people's faces. Dimly aware that their hunger must be visible to anyone looking. But all he cared about was getting across the ballroom and up to their bedroom as quickly as possible.

This was what he wanted—what they both wanted. It was all they needed from one another.

As they stepped out into the hall she tugged at his arm. 'Are you sure you want to leave?'

'I've never been more sure of anything,' he said hoarsely and, sweeping her into his arms, he carried her up the stairs.

When they reached the bedroom door his body was straining for release and, kicking it shut, he loosened his grip, bringing his mouth down on hers as her hands locked in his shirt and she dragged him towards her.

Tightening his arm around her waist, he pushed her back against the door, flattening her body with his. Her fingers were tugging at his waistband and he almost lost his footing as she pulled him free of his trousers and gripped him in her hand, and then he was lifting her and jerking up her dress in one swift movement.

She shifted against him as he yanked aside her panties and, breathing raggedly, thrust inside her. Opening her mouth to the heat of his kiss, she wrapped her legs around his waist, arching against him, panting out his name as he surged into her with hot, liquid force.

Frankie lifted the shotgun, her heart pounding as she closed her right eye and tried to visualise the path of the clay. It was easy to pick up the basics of shooting, Arlo had told her. But actually to hit the target...

'Weight on your front foot, bend your knee, stick out your bottom, fire when it's almost at the top of the curve...' she muttered to herself, and then, 'Pull!' she shouted.

The tiny disc spun into the air and—*bang!*—disintegrated with a satisfying crack.

Grinning idiotically, she turned to where Arlo and Davey stood watching her. 'I did it!'

'Well done,' said Arlo softly.

Holding the gun upright, she flicked the bolt so the gun broke. 'I did everything you said and it worked. It actually worked.'

He held her gaze. 'Yes, it did.'

She did a little dance on the spot. 'I didn't think I'd enjoy it that much, but it's so satisfying.'

Arlo grinned. 'My turn.'

Frankie watched dry-mouthed as he walked away. He had an enviable air of calm that made it seem as if he was moving at a slower pace than everyone around him. But then he tucked the gun into his shoulder and she felt suddenly weak in the middle as both his body and gun swiftly followed the four clays through the air with smooth, lethal accuracy.

She sighed. 'Has he always been like this? You know...'

'I do—and, yes. He's one of a kind.' Davey smiled. 'Last night he was being generous. He's the one who makes everything look easy.'

He did, Frankie thought, picturing Arlo giving his speech. Look at how he had just stood up in front of all those people and said those beautiful things about Davey and Serena. *And love.*

Her heart skipped a beat.

He had sounded so genuine.

But then he was hardly going to say what he really thought.

She knew that he didn't believe one word of it. He couldn't have made it clearer that he had given up on love. Only hearing him talk like that made it hard not to wish that he hadn't.

But only for a moment.

She felt a faint flush of heat wash over her cheekbones,

remembering how he had carried her upstairs last night. She didn't need to complicate what was already perfect.

'So tell me? Did you have a good time last night?'

Serena gave her a one-armed hug. They were back at the house, where Serena had laid on a mouth-watering brunch.

'It was better than good.' Frankie smiled. 'It was the best party I've ever been to.'

She had really enjoyed herself—and yet, truthfully, she had preferred lunch yesterday, when it had been just the four of them. In fact, what she liked best of all was just lying on the sofa with Arlo in the library at the Hall...

Now that she thought about it, she'd only really started going out a lot at secondary school—and mostly that had been a kind of pushback against Harry and Amelie's glittering success.

And after the accident, her partying had been a way to fight the loneliness and the guilt and had ended up being her career. Now she couldn't imagine living like that. Only she was going to have to return—and sooner rather than later.

Blanking her mind to that unwelcome thought, she said quickly, 'I had a great time at the shoot as well.'

'I'm sorry I couldn't come down, but Bertie had me up before dawn with his teeth.'

Frankie glanced over at the small blond boy clutching at Serena. She had met Bertie yesterday, and he had been like a jumping jack. Now, though, there were smudges under his eyes and he seemed listless and quiet.

'Would you like me to take him for you?' Frankie asked as Serena attempted to pick up her coffee cup.

Stifling a yawn, Serena shook her head. 'He won't go to anyone when he's feeling like this—'

'Except his favourite godfather!'

Watching Bertie's face split into a huge, gap-toothed smile, Frankie felt a sharp nip of pleasure as Arlo reached forward and lifted him into his arms.

'I'm just going to grab some food,' he said, leaning in to kiss Serena on both cheeks. 'Do either of you want anything?'

Serena shuddered. 'No, thank you. I can still taste that last tequila.'

Arlo made a tutting sound. 'Frankie? Any preferences?'

'Surprise me,' she said softly.

His gaze locked with hers and she felt the air between them snap like an elastic band.

'I'll do my best.'

Watching him walk away, Serena sighed. 'He's so good with Bertie. I suppose he would be—I mean, he practically raised Johnny by himself.' She rested her elbows on the tablecloth. 'But never mind that now. What I want to know is how did you two meet?'

Frankie felt her mouth open and close as she tried to remember what she and Arlo had agreed, but before she could answer Serena waved her hands excitedly.

'No—no, wait a minute. Let me guess. Your car got a puncture and he pulled over to help? Or maybe you were lost—?'

'No, it was nothing like that.' Frankie shook her head. 'I know Johnny from London, and he introduced me to Arlo.' *That was almost true.* 'We hit it off and he asked me to stay.' *That was also almost true.*

To her astonishment, Serena looked delighted. 'Oh, I'm so happy you said that. It sounds so normal. I *knew* you were different from the others,' she said triumphantly.

The others.

Frankie felt something twist beneath her ribs. Not that long ago she'd found it hard to imagine anyone wanting to work with Arlo, let alone share his bed. Now, though, it hurt to imagine his body overlapping another woman's…

Leaning in conspiratorially, Serena lowered her voice. 'I was watching the two of you together and you can't keep your eyes off each other. I told Davey you must be the one—'

What? She stared up at Serena in shock and confusion. 'No, no… I don't think… That's not…'

Serena touched her hand. 'It's okay. I'm not going to say anything. I know Arlo's a very private person,' she said gently. 'But I know love when I see it.'

Love? No, that was wrong. That wasn't what was happening here. She and Arlo didn't love one another.

Her head started to spin. Around her, the room seemed to be blurring at the edges.

No, they didn't.

But she loved him.

She felt a rush of panic and confusion, then denial. That couldn't be true. It just couldn't. Surely you couldn't fall in love so quickly. But she knew that it was true. She *loved* him. Loved him with every frantic beat of her heart.

Her breath caught. But if that was true…

Gazing across the table at Serena, she felt her throat contract. She seemed so certain, and she and Davey knew Arlo better than anyone. But could Serena be right? Could Arlo have fallen in love with her too?

That question kept popping into her head during the rest of the day, but thinking it was one thing. Asking it…

Part of her wanted to. Another part—the part that didn't want to rock the boat—feared the consequences of demanding more when everything was going so well, and she was still dithering later that day, as the Rolls-Royce convertible rumbled back over the wet cobbles on the causeway.

'So, do you want to eat something?' he asked.

'I don't think so.' She thought for a moment. 'Actually, what I'd really like is a bath.'

Dipping his head, he kissed her softly on the mouth. 'Great minds think alike.'

It was lovely to have so much endless and guilt-free hot water on tap, Frankie thought as she lay back in the water, gazing through the spirals of steam to where Arlo lounged, his arms resting along the rim of the bath.

Looking at the heavy muscles bunching, she felt her pulse accelerate. It had always been easy to admire his solidness. But now she found it just as easy to admit that she loved everything about him that wasn't visible. In fact, she loved everything about him.

Only now that it was easy to admit that to herself, she could feel herself wanting to tell Arlo.

Striving for calm, she picked up the soap and began rubbing it between her hands. 'Thank you for taking me to Stanhope Park. I had a really nice time.'

'Well, you were a huge hit. Davey thinks you're wonderful, and Serena is raving about you too. They've invited us over on Saturday for lunch.'

His grey eyes rested on her face and, thinking back to her conversation with Serena, Frankie felt her stomach flip over. 'They're both lovely. And they loved your speech.' She hesitated. 'I loved it too. I thought it was beautiful. But—'

He stared at her steadily. 'But what?'

'I don't know how you could say all that stuff about love and not want it for yourself.'

Sitting forward, he scooped up some water and dribbled it over her bare breasts.

'I thought we'd talked about that,' he said after a long silence.

'We talked about your parents. But how do you know

it would be the same for you? I mean it's not the same for Davey and Serena, and if you met your "for ever" person everything might feel different.'

His face stilled and she felt her heart start to thud against her ribs.

'I'm not the marrying kind—'

'How do you know? How *can* you know? You've never been married.' Her fingers bit into the soap. 'You talk about data and facts, but you're not basing your opinion on fact.'

There was another immeasurably long pause, and then he said coolly, 'Actually, that's exactly what I'm doing. You see, I have been married.'

She stared at him, mute with shock.

When? For how long? Who was she?

He flicked her a glance, hearing her questions even though she hadn't asked them. 'Ten years ago, for just under three months. Her name was Harriet and she was someone I met at university.'

Her heart was still thumping and she counted the thuds, trying to steady herself. 'What happened?'

'I didn't love her. I told her. She left. It was not my finest moment.' His face was bleak. 'I wanted to love her. I wanted to have what my parents had. I wanted to believe. But it was a disaster. All I did was end up hurting her.' Reaching out, he prised the soap from her fingers, his hands covering hers. 'And that's why we can never be more than this. I don't want to hurt you, Frankie. I can't risk that.'

Her eyes were stinging but she made no move to touch them. There was nothing she could do. The flat, uncompromising edge in his voice left her nowhere to go.

'So what are you saying?' she said stiffly.

'I suppose I'm saying...is this enough for you?'

His jaw was locked tight, the skin stretched taut across his cheekbones, and she could hear him breathing.

No, it wasn't.

She felt so much…wanted so much more.

She was on the verge of taking his hand and pressing it to her lips, telling him that she loved him. And she might have done it if he hadn't just told her what had happened with Harriet. But she couldn't unknow what she knew… couldn't unsee the weariness in his eyes…and she couldn't bring herself to tell him the truth.

Not now.

Not if it might mean losing this…losing him…

That was a risk she couldn't take.

She nodded slowly, her stomach lurching at the lie. 'Yes, it is.'

His face relaxed a little and she leaned forward and kissed him softly. She felt his hand touch her cheek and he deepened the kiss, and then she was kissing him back and surrendering to the tide of hunger rising inside her, letting it sweep aside her pain and her love.

CHAPTER TEN

THE NEXT MORNING they woke late. After days of bright sunshine the weather had turned and it was raining again. Not the deluge of last week, but enough for them to retreat to the library after a long, leisurely breakfast.

Now they were sprawled against each other on the rug in front of the fire. Frankie's head was in his lap, his hand was in her hair, and they were watching the flames as they curled sinuously over the logs.

Correction: Frankie was watching the flames.

He was watching her.

A couple of days ago at the party he'd thought she could never look any more beautiful, but he'd been wrong. Today, wearing jeans and some old jumper of his, with no make-up and her hair curling loosely over her shoulders, there was a kind of radiance about her that had nothing to do with the symmetry of her features or the luminous clarity of her skin.

It was about who she was as a person. And Frankie was a beautiful person.

His ribs tightened as he remembered the hours running up to the party.

To say that he'd been dreading it was an understatement. Being surrounded by his family was just so difficult, so painful. It stirred so many beautiful, precious memories, and it hurt to remember all that he had lost.

At three-line whip events—the ones he couldn't legitimately avoid—he usually just watched from the sidelines and left as early as possible. But Frankie had drawn him in, made him a part of every conversation, so that instead of brooding on the past, thinking of what he'd lost, he had found himself talking—not expansively, maybe, but talking just the same—and it had been fun.

She had made it fun.

She was so full of energy and curiosity about life, about people. He loved that about her.

To an outsider, his family might appear insular and cliquey and a little bit clueless about how the rest of the world lived. And they all knew each other. It would be daunting for anyone to be parachuted into such an environment, and he knew how nervous she had been.

But not one person there would have guessed. She had talked to everyone, laughed at Arthur's terrible jokes, and listened patiently while Davey explained the intricacies of his new biomass boiler.

She drew people out of themselves—and drew them together. Not in some stage-managed, artificial way, but naturally.

No wonder everyone had loved her.

And she had loved them.

His heart felt suddenly heavy inside his chest as he remembered the dazzle of happiness and excitement in her blue eyes. She had loved being a part of a family again, and he had loved being able to gift her that.

He felt his shoulders tense. That, though, was all he could give her.

What stopped him going further—what made it impossible for him even to indulge in thinking about going further—was Frankie herself.

She needed more than he could give. No, it was more than that. She needed more than he'd *shown* her he could give.

Talking to her last night in the bath, he'd made it sound as if hurting her was a risk. But 'risk' implied that there was another option where he *didn't* end up hurting her, and that wasn't true.

Memories of his short, unhappy marriage stirred and shivered inside his head.

Had he felt this way with Harriet?

Definitely not. He'd been too young, too desperate.

This time, though, he had no excuse to ruin a young woman's life.

And Frankie deserved better. After everything she'd already been through, she needed someone who could complete her life, not cause it to unravel.

His chest tightened.

And yet he couldn't seem to stop himself from wanting to rearrange the world so that it would offer up a space where he and Frankie could be together. Although at the same time he needed it not to involve any kind of contract or commitment that could be broken.

In other words, he wanted something that didn't exist. Only he didn't have the first idea how to explain any of that to Frankie—which was why he'd ended up telling her about Harriet.

He'd never had to do that before. In the past, with other women, he'd found it easy to stick to his rules without needing to justify or explain himself. But right from the start Frankie had been different. Somehow she had sneaked under the tripwire, and before he had known what was happening she'd upended everything that had previously seemed so certain and inviolable.

Yesterday, she'd left him with no option. He'd had to tell her about his marriage to prove to her once and for all that it didn't matter what worked for other people. It hadn't worked for him.

'What is it?'

Frankie was looking up at him. She felt soft and warm against him, but it was the questioning look in her blue eyes that made his fingers still against her hair.

'Nothing.' He forced a smile as her gaze travelled over his face.

He had to stop this pointless back and forth. It was like trying to move forward in a whiteout.

But probably he was only feeling this way because he'd churned up the past, muddying the waters of the present.

'I was just thinking about maybe going for a dip.'

'You mean, in the sea?'

She wriggled upright, her eyes bright with the adventure of it. Leaning forward, she looped her hands around his neck so that he could feel the tips of her small pointed breasts against his chest.

'But won't it be freezing?'

'It'll be bracing.' He smiled. 'Don't worry. I'm not expecting you to come with me.'

She frowned. 'But I want to. Unless you're planning on swimming around the island or to Denmark?'

It hadn't occurred to him that she would want to join him. He thought she'd opt to stay by the fire. But now, gazing down at her eager face, it seemed blindingly obvious she would never do that.

He shook his head. 'I wasn't planning on being in for more than a couple of minutes,' he lied.

He'd actually been planning on swimming up to the rocks. But he was used to swimming in chilly seas. Frankie wasn't. And without a wetsuit it would be just too dangerous for her to do anything more than take a quick dip.

'Did you bring a costume with you?' he asked.

She nodded. 'I did.' Her mouth twitched. 'Why? Are you saying I don't need one?'

Their eyes met and he felt tiny curls of heat break like waves over his skin as he imagined Frankie coming naked out of the sea like Botticelli's *Venus*.

Feeling his body harden, he shook his head again. 'No, I'm not,' he said firmly, tipping her gently off his lap.

Another second of this and he would be in danger of losing both the power of speech and any desire to move. What he needed right now was to clear his head—and that wasn't going to happen when the soft press of Frankie's body was playing havoc with all his senses, including his common sense.

'Come on.' He held out his hand. 'Let's go and get changed—before I change my mind or you change it for me.'

The sea was glorious. Just how he liked it. The water was drawing up lazily and then hurling itself against the stretch of golden sand like a steeplechaser clearing the final fence.

It was cold—bracingly so—but not enough to stop Frankie from joining him with a shriek as the surging waves sloshed against her body.

They spent a few minutes plunging through the water and then, hand in hand, made their way back to the beach. Grabbing towels, they ran, shivering, up to the Hall.

'Not too hot to start,' Arlo warned her as she unwrapped her body from its crimson swimsuit and stepped into the shower.

As she tilted her head back he joined her, gasping as the water hit his skin. Leaning forward, he let the warm stream soak his hair before smoothing it back against his skull.

Once they were done, and had stepped onto the tiled floor, he wrapped one of the huge plush towels around her and another round his waist, then pulled her closer, fitting her body snugly against his.

'Are you warm enough?' he asked.

Tipping her head back, she nodded. 'I should probably dry my hair…'

'Let me.'

He grabbed another towel and led her into the bedroom. The fire had been lit earlier, but it had died down, so he tossed another log into the gleaming orange core.

Turning, he felt his body harden. Frankie was sitting on the end of the bed, gazing up at him, her hair curling damply over her shoulders. She had let the towel fall away from her body, exposing the slim curves of her breasts, and he watched, mesmerised, as a droplet of water trickled all the way to the tip of her right nipple.

When she looked up at him, he reached down and began rubbing her soaked hair.

'That was fun.' She smiled. 'I thought the sea would actually be colder.'

'You're lucky. It's usually coldest in April.'

Their eyes met, and there were two, maybe three beats of silence. Then she reached up and pressed her hand against the front of his towel.

'That's not the only reason I'm lucky,' she said softly.

Abruptly, his body redirected the flow of his blood with such force that he had to put his hand against her shoulder to steady himself. His mouth dried and he was suddenly conscious of the hammering of his heart as she peeled the towel away from his body and let it slip onto the rug.

There was another beat of silence and then she wrapped one hand around his hard length, cradling him underneath with the other. Without releasing her grip, she pushed him back onto the bed, slipping between his legs as he shifted backwards. He breathed in sharply as she began stroking the taut, silken skin, moving his hand to grip her hair as she flicked her tongue over the blunted head of his erection.

Her hands found his thighs, her fingers splaying against the muscle, and he groaned with helpless pleasure as she took him deeper into her mouth, then deeper still, so that he was powerless to move.

Only he wanted to taste her too. To give her pleasure. Not out of obligation, or a need to prove his virility, but because her pleasure was essential to his enjoyment.

Tugging on her shoulders, he pushed her gently back-

wards and sat up, his mouth finding hers. He'd lost count
of how many times they had kissed before, but as he felt
her hands touch his face his heart began to race.

Her fingers were so light, so gentle. *So loving.*

Gritting his teeth, he fought against the sudden tenderness and, tearing his mouth away, pulled at her hips, kissing her stomach as he turned her body so that she was
above his face.

His head was swimming. Breathing in her scent, he
parted her damp flesh, dipping inside her, seeking the tight
bud of her clitoris. Teasing her with his tongue, he felt her
quiver, and she arched against his mouth, moaning.

'No, no—'

He felt her jerk backwards.

'I need you inside me.'

The hoarseness of her voice made him move more than
the words she'd said.

Lifting her gently, he tried to pull her round to face him,
only his leg got in the way. It would have been awkward
if it had happened the first time, but they had nothing to
prove now, he realised, and when she started to laugh it
was the most natural thing in the world to bury his face in
her hair and laugh too.

She sat up. 'Sorry, I didn't mean to kill the mood.'

'You haven't.'

She was straddling him, with his erection pressing
against the slick heat between her thighs, and he couldn't
remember ever feeling such an ache of longing. It went beyond want. This was need. A vast, untapped seam of need
that was infinitely more powerful than desire.

His stomach tightened and, reaching up, he cupped her
breasts, his thumbs grazing the nipples. 'I don't think anything could do that,' he said slowly. 'I want you all the
time, Frankie.'

His hunger was like a burn, or an itch beneath the skin

that no amount of scratching could satisfy. Her touch did something to him…made him want more and more.

'I want you too. I want you so much.' She sucked in a breath, her voice suddenly scratchy with emotion. 'I want—'

'Shh, Frankie, shh…' He placed his finger against her lips. 'It's okay, it's okay,' he said soothingly.

But, her eyes were so blue, so clear—too clear. He felt as if he could see into her soul, feel what she was feeling vibrating in his chest.

Only the fact that he was feeling anything other than desire was wrong. He didn't do feelings. That was why he couldn't offer her a real relationship—why this could only ever be about sex.

Heart hammering, unable to face the emotion in her eyes, he raised himself onto his elbows and kissed her desperately, passionately, fiercely, needing to wipe out the emotion churning inside him.

Pulse throbbing, he cupped her buttocks, taking her weight in his hands as she lowered herself onto him.

He gripped her hips and began to move slowly, wanting to take his time, to give her pleasure that would eclipse any he'd ever given her before.

His hands found her nipples and he tugged them gently, squeezing the taut tips, feeling a hot rush of satisfaction as a sound that quivered with pure sexual need broke from her lips.

Dropping his hands to her belly, he stroked the smooth skin and then, as she started to rock against him, slid his fingers between her thighs.

Her hands caught his wrists and, looking up at her face, he felt his body tighten so swiftly and strongly that he was afraid he would come there and then.

His body shuddered. *Yes.* This was what he wanted: heat and frenzy and release.

Blood roaring in his ears, he reached up and kissed her

again, his fingers tightening in her hair as he felt his muscles start to tense, his own wave of pleasure building inside him, rising up, dark and unstoppable.

He felt her body lock around his as she cried out against his mouth, and then the wave hit him with full force, curling over him and pounding through him as he thrust into her.

Heart raging, he wrapped his arms around her body and buried his face in her hair. 'Frankie—'

Breathing out, he stroked a tangle of curls away from her face. His body was aching, almost hurting from the intensity of his orgasm, but then his eyes met hers, and the depth of emotion he saw there blotted out that pain with another kind of pain that made him look away.

His ribs felt too tight.

He didn't want to see that softness for him there. That was a need he couldn't meet. He'd tried once before, and failed, and nothing had changed.

He hadn't changed.

He might not be young and naive anymore, but he was still that same man. Still intense and unapproachable, uncommunicative and uncompromising. A man defined by his limits.

He could never be full of fire and drama like his father, or vivacious and beautiful like his mother and Johnny.

Out on the huge expanses of polar ice he was a hero. Here in the real world he felt awkward and inelegant. The idea of someone like him with a woman like Frankie was not just stupid, it was absurd. He might as well try and capture a flame in his hand.

Only last night, for the first time in his entire life, he had felt as if he was standing in the flames with Frankie.

He knew that it had never been like this with any other woman. Never been so easy, so intimate. *So personal.* But then before it had never mattered who he was with. This time it was all about Frankie.

'Hey,' he said softly, seeing her faraway expression. 'Where have you gone?'

She smiled. 'No, I'm here. I was just thinking…'

He was torn, caught between the need to know more and the fear of what he might hear.

'About what?'

'I was just thinking how strange time is when I'm with you. Sometimes it seems to stretch on for ever, and then other times it feels like everything has sped up.' She bit into her lip. 'Does that sound stupid?'

Staring at her steadily, he shook his head. 'When I'm with you everything feels so much sharper. Colours, sounds…'

There was a glow to her now, like the halo of light around the sun, and it would be so easy in the post-coital haze of intimacy and tenderness to step into that light.

He tilted her face, and the fragility of her neck and the delicate bones of her shoulders felt like a warning—a reminder of how easy it would be to hurt her by promising something he couldn't give.

So there would be no *Perhaps if…* or *Maybe some day…*

But he could be honest. He wanted to be honest.

His thumb stroked the upper bow of her mouth as he looked into her eyes. 'It's not been like that with other people. It's never been like this for me before.'

She breathed out shakily. 'Me neither.'

'But it works, doesn't it?'

Her expression was hazy, and then she nodded, and he knew that she was everything he wanted in the world right now.

And then he was pulling her closer, telling himself that when the time came he would let her go without a backward glance.

It was the only way.

* * *

They were eating lunch in the kitchen. Frankie was telling Constance about her dip in the sea, and he was half listening, half watching the play of emotions over her face, when he felt his phone vibrate in his pocket.

Since that day on the beach, when Frankie had told him about the accident, he'd left it on silent, and he was all ready to ignore it until he saw the name on the screen.

Johnny.

'I'm just going to get this,' he said and, pushing his chair back from the table, stood up and walked out into the hallway.

'Arlo.'

At the sound of Johnny's voice he felt a rush of relief fill his chest. Like most siblings, he knew the tell-tale signs of distress in his brother, but there was no breathless note of panic.

'Hey, little brother. Nice of you to get in touch.'

Johnny groaned. 'I know… I know. I'm useless. I really was going to call—'

The line was so clear that if he closed his eyes it would be as if Johnny was standing beside him, and he felt a sharp stab of longing to reach out and hug his brother.

'It's just been completely mad. Honestly, Hollywood people are crazy.'

Suddenly Johnny's voice sounded muffled, and Arlo could almost picture him, head bent over his phone conspiratorially.

'They never seem to sleep. It's like there's no difference between day and night. They just keep on going.' He laughed. 'You'd fit right in.'

Arlo felt his heart contract with love. Hollywood was the last place on earth he'd fit in, but his brother's partisan adoration knew no limits.

'On that basis, so would about twelve million penguins.'

Johnny laughed again. 'True.' There was a pause, then, 'I'm really sorry I haven't called.'

'It's okay. I know you're busy—'

'So are you. And that's one of the reasons I wanted to call. To thank you for letting Frankie stay at the Hall.'

Arlo felt his chest tighten. 'You don't have to thank me, Johnny, it's your home too.'

'I know. But I also know how busy you are, and you weren't expecting her...' He paused again, then, 'So has it been okay?'

'Of course.' It was suddenly hard to speak. To find words that could describe how 'okay' it had been. 'It was Davey and Serena's anniversary party, so we went over to Stanhope, and she's helped me with some of my notes. Oh, and she's trounced me at billiards.'

He heard his brother chuckle. 'Yeah, she's pretty good, isn't she?' There was another pause. Then, 'I'm glad she's had some fun. That's actually the other reason I'm calling.'

Arlo frowned. 'What is?'

'I wanted to do something to make up for letting her down, so I've bought her a ticket to LA.'

His head felt as if it was not connected to his body. 'A ticket?' he asked slowly.

'Yeah, for Saturday. It's a surprise. I thought she could do with a few days in the sun and I think she'll adore LA. It's got everything she loves. Sandy beaches, shopping malls. *And celebrities!* I mean, Frankie was made for this place.'

No, she wasn't, he thought, his forehead creasing into a frown. Frankie was made for family brunches and swimming in the sea.

Arlo stared across the beautiful empty hallway, listening to his brother's voice, feeling a dark, heavy cloud swelling inside his chest.

What was it he'd said earlier to Frankie about their 'arrangement'?

It works, doesn't it?

He felt his whole body tense with fury and disgust. What the hell had he been thinking? Did he really think that was all she deserved? Some open-ended affair with a man who could essentially offer nothing more than sex and his own shortcomings?

She needed sunshine and cocktails and people her own age—like Johnny.

He cleared his throat, making his voice level. 'It sounds like you want her to stay for more than a few days.'

'Yeah, I do.' Johnny hesitated. 'She could really make a go of it out here, Arlo. She's got something about her… I think everyone is going to love her.'

Of course they would, Arlo thought, his fingers tightening around the phone.

The anonymous ache in his chest was no longer nameless. Only it had taken the thought of losing her for him to understand what it was. To understand that it was love.

His heart felt as if it would burst.

He loved her.

And he knew that Frankie loved him. She was too scared to say it out loud, but earlier, upstairs in the bedroom, he had felt it in every touch and kiss.

So what was he waiting for?

Hang up the phone. Go and tell her.

He felt euphoric, adrift with love. The need to find her and declare his feelings rose up inside him and he half turned, his body filling with lightness.

And then he stopped.

He couldn't do it.

He couldn't do that to Frankie—not if he loved her.

Suddenly he was terrified, almost breathless with the

fear that he would give in. Terrified of what would happen if he did.

Because he knew what would happen.

He knew Frankie.

She would leap wholeheartedly, loving him, trusting him to catch her…

But her trust would be misplaced. He couldn't trust himself not to fail, and if he failed he would hurt her more than he was already going to have to hurt her. And he *was* going to hurt her. It was the only way, even though the thought of doing so tore his heart in two.

'Would you like another cup of coffee?'

Glancing up at Constance, Frankie shook her head. 'I'm fine. But could you leave the pot?'

Arlo would want one. When he returned. She glanced over at the doorway, wondering who had called him. Not work. He would have ignored it.

He *had* ignored it—for her.

Her heart squeezed. He had put his life on hold for her and showed her how to live again. He had held her and comforted her and filled her with his strength—metaphorically and literally.

Look at this morning. Arlo had still been inside her, his arms anchoring her to his body, and her love for him had been so complete, so devastating, that the room had started to spin and she hadn't been able to see him clearly.

Not that it mattered. He was so familiar to her now that even if she closed her eyes she could see every minute detail of his appearance.

Her fingers trembled against the handle of her coffee cup. He was so beautiful, and the lines on his face and the scars all over his body didn't diminish that beauty—they just made his beauty unique. More than unique. It was essential. He was essential to her now. She needed him more than she needed her next breath. He was everything. Her always and her for ever.

Only she couldn't tell Arlo that.

That wasn't what he'd signed up for and no alteration in her feelings could change that. She was already out of her depth, but at least there was still a way back to shore. She couldn't allow herself to get in any deeper. She couldn't let herself care even more for Arlo than she did. Not when she knew what it felt like to lose someone you loved. She couldn't go through that again.

Her pulse skipped. And she didn't need to. He had acknowledged that what they shared was different...special.

'It's never been like this for me before.'

Those had been his exact words, and right now that was enough.

'Anyway, I'll talk to you soon.'

She glanced up. It was Arlo. He was still on the phone, and as she looked at him, he pointed at it.

'Yes, I'll hand you over to her now.' He held out his phone. 'It's Johnny. He wants to talk to you.'

'Johnny—oh, my goodness! How's it going? I can't believe you're actually going to be in a *film*!' she gushed.

Johnny laughed. 'Don't blink or you'll miss me. I think one of the palm trees is on screen longer than I am.'

It was strange, hearing his laugh. A week ago it would have left her feeling weak. Now, though, she felt nothing except a kind of sisterly affection.

'Are there really palm trees?' she asked quickly.

She didn't care if there were or not, but she could feel Arlo's eyes on her face and felt suddenly self-conscious.

'Loads. Would you like to see them?'

'Of course.' She was momentarily distracted as, smiling stiffly, Arlo got up and walked over to the window.

'You would? Because that's why I'm calling. I've bought you a ticket to LA. You'll fly out on Saturday.'

She blinked. *But Arlo wasn't in LA.*

'Frankie! Are you still there? Did you hear what I said?'

'Yes, I did. That's amazing.' She forced a note of excitement into her voice. 'But you shouldn't have—'

'Yes, I should,' he said firmly. 'And Arlo thinks so too.'

'He does?' Her heart began hammering inside her chest.

'Yeah, he thinks you need a proper holiday. And besides, he's going to be in Svalbard at the end of the month.'

Her stomach felt as if it was filled with ice. She felt stunned, stupid, small.

Turning her head, she stared across the room to where Arlo was gazing at the sea. There was tension in his body and she knew he was seeing a different blue sea—one dotted with sharp-toothed icebergs.

'It's addictive,' he'd said.

She'd thought he'd been talking figuratively. But how could she compete with such beauty and majesty?

'Look, I know it's short notice, Frankie, but I also know I let you down.'

Johnny's voice broke into her thoughts and she gazed down into her cooling cup of coffee. 'It doesn't matter,' she said quietly.

'It does to me. So please let me make it up to you. Come to LA.'

She sucked in a steadying breath. 'I'd love to.'

As she hung up Arlo turned to face her, and the cool distance in his eyes left her in no doubt as to how he was really feeling.

In his head, he was already there on the ice. Maybe he'd never left. No wonder he couldn't promise anything in the way of commitment.

'So you're off to LA.'

It was a statement, not a question, but she still nodded.

'It's for the best, Frankie.'

'For whom?' She stood up abruptly and walked towards him.

'For you, of course. You're twenty-one. You have your whole life ahead of you, and that life isn't going to start here—'

With me.

He didn't say those words, but they both heard them. But he hadn't heard what *she* had to say. What she needed him to hear…to know.

She was done with hiding the truth. It hadn't stopped her losing everyone she loved and needed before, but it might stop her losing the man she loved and needed now.

She moved to his side. 'But what if I told you I loved you? Would that change anything?'

Only even before he shook his head, she knew that it wouldn't. That he already knew, and it didn't matter.

And knowing that he knew, and that it hadn't changed anything, gave her the strength to pull back and not leap unthinkingly with her eyes wide open.

It was over.

She couldn't do what she suspected Harriet had done—just hope that this difficult, conflicted man would change over time, for her. Maybe she might have done before the accident, but not now. Not knowing what she did about the agony of loss.

It was just so hard to let it go—to let *him* go.

'I don't want your love. And I don't want to hurt you. I want to be honest with you.' He glanced away from her. '*This*…what we had…was amazing. You're amazing.'

Had. There had been no moment of decision but already he was talking in the past tense, as if the choice had been made.

She stared at him in silence. 'Just not amazing enough,' she said slowly. She felt as if someone had punched her in the stomach, and her fingers curved protectively against the ache.

'No, that's not true.' His eyes narrowed on her face. 'This isn't about you.'

She stared at him, her heart breaking. 'You're right. It is about *us*. And I think you're not giving us a chance.'

Say something, she willed him. *Ask me not to go to LA.*

But a distance had opened between them now that seemed impossible to bridge and he said nothing.

Disbelief thudded inside her head.

After everything that had happened, surely it couldn't end like this?

As the silence lengthened, grew weighty, she could bear it no more. 'I don't think there's any point in me staying, so I'm going to go upstairs and pack. Can you call me a cab?'

'I'll take you to the station.' His voice was hard and flat.

Turning, she walked back across the kitchen, stopping in the doorway. 'You know, you saved me, Arlo—not just on the causeway, but here.' She touched her head. 'And here.' She touched her heart. 'You made me trust myself and I'll always be grateful.'

Her heart was aching, as if it had been torn in two, but she was going to leave nothing unsaid.

'I know that if anyone can save the world it's you. But I just hope that one day you meet someone who can res-cue you.' She took a breath, pushing back against the pain of imagining that scenario. 'Someone who can make you trust in love again…make you trust yourself. Someone who will make you see that love is a risk worth taking and that a life without risks that aren't to do with cold and ice and danger is no life at all.'

There was nothing more to say. The weight of misery pressing against her heart was unbearable and, turning, she walked swiftly out of the room.

CHAPTER ELEVEN

THE TRAIN BURST out of the tunnel with a rush of warm air and a high-pitched squeal of brakes that filled the platform at Covent Garden underground station.

Frankie joined the crowd of commuters and shoppers jostling one another into the carriage. There was nowhere to sit so she grabbed hold of a hanging strap, leaning her head wearily into the crook of her elbow. She felt exhausted, although there was no real reason why she should. She'd hardly left the flat since getting back to London.

In fact, today was the first day she'd actually bothered to change out of her pyjamas, and it was a shock seeing herself reflected in the grimy window. A lot of the time over the last three days she had felt as if she was slowly being erased.

As the train started to judder forward she mechanically tightened her grip, shrinking into her coat. Her shoulders tensed. Even the thought that she might accidentally be thrown against someone made her feel queasy.

It wasn't personal.

Except it was.

She just couldn't bear the idea of touching someone who wasn't Arlo.

Or maybe it was the knowledge that she would never touch Arlo again that was making her feel so unsteady.

The train rumbled into the next station and she watched numbly as people got on and off, remembering those final few minutes they'd shared.

It had been almost a second-by-second replay of the first time he'd put her on a train. He had lifted her bag up onto the luggage rack and told her to have a good trip, and then turned and walked away.

Gazing at the window, she let her reflection blur. The difference was that Arlo hadn't come back for her. She had sat in the empty carriage, waiting, hoping, praying... But two minutes later the train had pulled out of the station.

In many ways it had been unremarkable—just a train leaving a station. To her, though, it had been as if day had turned into night.

Her eyes burned. She hadn't cried then. She still hadn't cried. The tears were there, but for some reason they wouldn't fall.

It was raining as she walked out of the tube station. It had been raining ever since she'd left Northumberland—a steady grey drizzle that made people hurry home.

Home.

Her throat tightened. It made no sense to think of the Hall as home, and yet it felt to her more like home than the flat.

Turning into the street where she lived, she plodded through the puddles uncaringly.

But, of course, home was where the heart was—and her heart was with Arlo...would always be with Arlo.

Only he didn't want her heart.

He couldn't have made that any plainer, but it had taken her until this morning to finally accept that as one of the unchangeable, absolute truths that Arlo so loved.

Her heart contracted. How long was this going to last? Her every thought beginning and ending with Arlo?

Glancing up, she felt her breath catch. A tall man was standing by her front door, face lowered, shoulders hunched against the rain.

Her feet stuttered and then she was stumbling forward, breaking into a run, a trace of hope working its way through her blood, flaring into the light.

'Arlo—'

He turned, and disappointment punched her in the diaphragm. It wasn't him.

'Thank goodness. I was worried you'd already left.'

It was her neighbour Graham. Beside him was a huge cardboard box.

'They tried to deliver this earlier, but you were out.'

She forced a smile. 'That's so kind of you, Gray, thank you.'

'No worries. Do you need me to take it inside?'

'No, it's fine. Honestly.'

He looked relieved. 'I'll see you when you get back, then. Have a good time.'

Upstairs in the flat, she dried her hair with a towel and frowned at the box. It was probably just some designer, sending her stuff to promote.

But when she tore off the parcel tape and stared down at the suitcase a lump built in her throat. She replayed the moment on the causeway when the wheel on her old suitcase had broken, snapping the thought off before she got to the part where Arlo had scooped her into his arms.

Because, of course, Arlo had sent the parcel. He had a pile of exactly the same suitcases in his bedroom.

There was an envelope with her name written on the front, and heart pounding, she opened it. Inside was a plain correspondence card, and written in Arlo's familiar slanting handwriting was a message.

I'm sorry.

The pain made breathing impossible. She curled over, clutching the card, and finally did what she had been unable to do for the last three days.

She wept.

'Come on, then.'

Patting the sofa, beside him, Arlo breathed out unevenly as Nero jumped up onto the velvet cushions. He didn't normally let the lurcher up on the furniture, but there was something comforting about the dog's warm fur against his hand.

His throat tightened. Not that he deserved to be comforted after how he'd acted.

Picturing Frankie's stunned, pale face, he tensed his fingers against Nero's head. He had been so blazingly certain, so smugly convinced that he was in control…that he had got it all worked out.

Now all his assumptions seemed at best naive and at worst inhuman.

She had told him she loved him and the stark honesty of her words had unmanned him. Coward that he was, he had thought she would leave that unspoken, so that he could keep on pretending that he didn't know how she felt.

How *he* felt.

He gritted his teeth.

So many times out on the ice he had been faced with a crossroads—a moment in his journey when a decision had to be made. A choice that could mean either life or death. And each time he'd made a choice.

It was what he did. He spoke about it at schools. In lecture theatres at universities. The great explorer Arlo Milburn, talking about risk…about how every step in any direction was ultimately a leap of faith.

But he hadn't made that leap for Frankie. He loved her and he had let her leave, and this time tomorrow she would be on her way to LA.

And in a week's time he would be out on the ice, living the life he'd told her he wanted. A life he had chosen over her. A life that suited someone like him—someone who found the prospect of having a woman who loved him too risky. A life where risk was confined to sub-zero temperatures and blizzards.

In other words, not a life worth living.

* * *

There. It was done. Finally she was packed.

Letting out a breath, Frankie got to her feet and stared down at her plush new suitcase. She had dithered about taking it, but in the end it had seemed churlish not to—and anyway her old suitcase was ruined.

She glanced at the clock by her bed. The taxi would be here in a minute, but that was fine. She just had to get her coat and then she would be ready to go.

She was going to get to the airport hours before she needed to, but that was what she'd decided to do last night, after she'd finally finished crying. She had cried a lot. About the accident and her family and about Arlo. At one point she had thought she might never stop crying, but at one minute past midnight she had run out of tears.

And that was when she'd made up her mind that today was going to be the first day of her new life.

Obviously, she wasn't going to just forget all her problems. But there was no future in living in the past and she wanted to start living again.

That was what Arlo had given her. He had helped her take that first step. More than anything she had wanted him to join her on the rest of her journey, only that wasn't to be.

But she wasn't just going to mark time and blog, like she had after the accident. She was going to go out into the world and live her life. Do some travelling. Make some new friends—real friends. Reconnect with old ones. Learn a new skill.

The intercom buzzed and, shrugging on her coat, she took the handle of her suitcase and glanced slowly around the flat. Maybe when she came back she would finally make this into a home.

She always used the famous black London cabs for work. The cabbies were always fun to talk to, and it looked cool arriving at events in one. Now, she found the familiar beetle shape of the car comforting.

As she buckled up, the cabbie turned round. 'It's Heathrow, isn't it?'

Frankie nodded. 'Yes, please.'

'Going somewhere nice, are you?'

'Los Angeles.'

'Lovely. Me and the wife went there last year. Then we did a road trip to New York.' He laughed. 'I know! I spend all day in the cab and then I do three weeks driving across America for my holidays. But I loved it. Every day felt like an adventure.'

Frankie smiled. 'This is a bit of an adventure for me too. My friend moved out there a few weeks ago and out of the blue he called up and invited me to stay.'

'Already? He's keen!'

'Oh, it's nothing like that. We're just friends.'

'Course you are.'

Looking up, she could see the cabbie grinning in the rear-view mirror.

'Just so you know, I'm going to shoot right at the traffic lights. I wouldn't normally, but there's roadworks on Woodley Road.'

She nodded. 'Okay.' Frowning, she pulled out her phone. 'Or you can try Mercer Street and then Warwick Park—'

Her voice stalled in her throat. The phone in her hand felt suddenly leaden. Or maybe that was her limbs.

Heart thumping, she stared down at the screen. She had been planning to check the route, but instead she was looking at the last journey she'd searched.

To Northumberland.

She'd thought she couldn't cry any more. But now tears started to roll down her cheeks.

Turning her head towards the window, she took a breath. The rows of terraced houses had given way to shops and banks and cafés. Already the streets were starting to buzz with life.

LA would be bigger, brighter, busier.

But it would still seem empty to her.

Everywhere would always be empty if Arlo wasn't there.

'No, no, no… Now, don't you go getting upset.'

Glancing into the mirror, Frankie saw that the cabbie was looking at her in horror.

'You don't need to worry,' he said. 'I know a detour that'll get you to the airport in plenty of time. You'll have your adventure, I promise.'

She felt her heartbeat accelerate.

Not if she went to the airport, she wouldn't.

Wiping her eyes, she leaned forward. 'Actually, we're going to have to take a slightly bigger detour…'

Arlo woke late on Saturday morning. He had been awake for most of the night, willing the morning to come so that he could get the day over and done.

He'd expected it to be grey and dull, but the weather forecasters had got it spectacularly wrong and after days of rain the skies had cleared and the sun was beaming above the horizon.

But it wasn't the sudden upturn in the weather that had got him out of bed.

It was Frankie.

His mouth twisted.

Only not quite Frankie.

She had been there in his dreams, and just as he'd begun to wake her soft body had pressed tightly against his. He had felt her warmth, and relief had spread through his limbs. And then he had woken properly, and her absence had been like a crushing weight on his chest, so that he'd had to get up and move about.

He should be packing. But that would mean going into

his bedroom, and he had been avoiding it for days, choosing instead to sleep in one of the spare rooms.

Downstairs, the house was silent and still, and he made his way into the kitchen, Nero padding lightly after him. It would all be over soon. Just this last day to get through and then she would be gone. In a week he would join the expedition at Svalbard and lose himself in the fathomless expanse of the Arctic.

His phone rang, the noise jolting him, and he felt a sudden rush of raw, unfiltered hope. But as he glanced down at the screen it swiftly drained away.

He hesitated, debating how to swipe, and then he made up his mind. 'Davey. How are you?'

'Oh, I'm fine. But apparently you have lost your mind.'

Arlo frowned. He could count on the fingers of one hand the number of times he and Davey had fallen out, but on those rare occasions his cousin had always been placatory—apologetic, almost.

Now, though, his cousin's voice was shaking with either anger or frustration or both.

'What are you talking about?' he asked.

But he didn't need to ask the question. He already knew what—*who*—Davey was talking about.

'I'm talking about Frankie.'

Arlo felt his heart twist. Hearing her name out loud hurt more than he would have thought possible. Hearing it out loud seemed to make her absence more vivid, more real. *Too real.*

Rubbing his eyes with the heel of his hand, he said stiffly, 'I don't want to talk about Frankie—'

'Well, I do.' He heard Davey take a breath. 'Serena called her. Just to find out if she wanted to ride before lunch on Saturday. Apparently, she's going out to LA to see Johnny.'

Arlo swore silently. He'd forgotten all about lunch. 'I should have called. I'm sorry—'

'I don't care about lunch. *We* don't care about lunch. We care about you, and why you ended things with Frankie.'

'I didn't end anything,' he said flatly. 'It wasn't that kind of relationship.'

'What kind? You mean the kind where you can't take your eyes off one another?'

Arlo bent his head, struggling against the truth of Davey's words. 'Exactly. It was a physical thing, and it burned out.'

He had never lied to his cousin before, and the lie tasted bitter in his mouth.

There was a long silence, and then Davey said quietly, 'It didn't burn out. You snuffed it out. Like you always do. Only it never mattered before. But Frankie's different. She loves you—really loves you.'

'I know—' The words were torn from his mouth.

His heart contracted as he remembered the moment he'd given her the bracelet and how she'd been upset for giving him nothing in return.

She *had* given him something. She had given him her love and her trust. She was a gift—beautiful, unique, irreplaceable.

'And you love her.' The anger had faded from Davey's voice. 'I know you don't want to admit it, and I know why.'

Picturing the moment when he'd rejected Frankie, Arlo felt a pain sharper than any physical injury he'd ever endured. He had told her he wanted to be honest and then he had lied to her face.

'I can admit it, but it doesn't change anything. I tried marriage, commitment, love—whatever you want to call it.' His chest tightened, and remembered misery and panic reared up at him. 'It was a disaster.'

'Yes, it was. Because you were young and you were grieving and you made a mistake. And if you'd been like everyone else on the planet—like me and Johnny and Arthur—you would have known that was *all* it was.'

He heard Davey sigh.

'But you hadn't ever made a mistake. You were always so smart, and so in control, and you didn't like how it felt. And when you got divorced you didn't just walk away from Harriet. You walked away from love.'

Arlo felt his throat tighten. His eyes were burning. He hadn't walked. He had run. He had turned and run away from love and kept on running until some cosmic force had put Frankie in his path...or rather in his bed.

Frankie, with her fiery curls and freckles, her permafrost-melting smile and her teasing laughter, which trailed a promise of happiness like the tail of a kite high in the bluest sky.

More than anything he wanted to turn and follow her, but—

'I have to keep on walking because nothing's changed,' he said slowly.

He couldn't change his past.

Davey cleared his throat. 'Everything's changed. Frankie is not Harriet, for starters. But what's changed the most is you. You're different with her.'

Different *because* of her, Arlo thought, his fingers tightening around the phone.

'And you don't need me to tell you what to do. Just to tell you that it's not too late,' Davey said softly.

But Davey was wrong, he thought, his heart swelling against his ribs. It had been too late from the moment he first saw Frankie. All this panic and doubt was just him struggling to catch up with the truth.

For so long he'd been so fixed on the idea of absolutes that he'd been blind to the beautiful potential of a life where random events simply challenged you to take new directions. Like down a causeway in the middle of a storm. Or to a crowded family party.

He swallowed past the lump in his throat. 'Then I should probably get going if I'm going to stop Frankie catching that plane.'

Hanging up, he glanced at his watch. If he left now, he could catch her at the airport...

It took him less than ten minutes to grab his jacket, find the keys to the Rolls, and more or less run outside to where the huge gold car sat slumbering on the warm driveway.

His heart was leaping.

Three days ago the past—his and hers—had felt like insurmountable obstacles to a future where he and Frankie could be together. But she had been right. Love conquered everything, even the obstacles around his heart, and now nothing would stop them being together.

He knew now that he didn't need or want to chase what his parents had shared.

He wanted and needed Frankie.

Together, they would make a life that was rich and enticing and joyful—but not perfect. Why would he want perfect? It was their flaws, their failings, that had brought them together, and it was in failing that they'd found strength in themselves and one another.

Turning the car around, he began rumbling over the cobblestoned causeway, tensing his muscles to stop himself from just putting his foot down on the accelerator pedal and flooring it.

There was plenty of time.

He had a full tank of fuel so he would only need to stop once.

He frowned. *What was happening?* The steering wheel was turning in his hands like a dog pulling on its lead, and there was an ominous choking sound coming from the engine.

His hands clenched around the wheel, urging the big car on. But he could feel the power dying, and he watched as with slow, agonising inevitability the Rolls slid slowly to a standstill.

Switching off the engine, he yanked up the handbrake and threw himself out of the car. He flipped open the bonnet and stared down at the engine. He had no idea what was wrong with it. The alternator, maybe?

But that wasn't something he could fix right here and now. He needed another car.

He began to run back to the house. He would take the Land Rover.

His footsteps faltered. Except he couldn't. Constance had taken it to go shopping in Newcastle. Even if he called her it would take her at least an hour and ten minutes to get back and that was too long.

The train would take even longer.

What he needed was a taxi—only of course there was no phone signal out here, and it would take him twenty minutes to run back to the house…

Heart hammering against his ribs, he squinted into the pale sunlight. He must be seeing things.

Except he wasn't.

There really was a London black cab rumbling slowly over the cobblestones.

It stopped in front of the Rolls and he stared in shock—not at the car, but at the woman stepping into the sunlight.

'Do you need some help?' she asked.

Frankie was standing there, her red hair gleaming in the sunlight.

'What are you doing here?'

He watched without blinking as she walked towards him, scared to blink in case she disappeared. His throat tightened with love and longing as she stopped in front of him.

'Oh, you know… I was in the area.'

'But you'll miss your flight.'

Frankie nodded. 'That's the plan. Although it only really became a plan this morning, when I was on my way to the airport.'

Arlo swallowed. His mouth was dry, and he felt breathless with shock and hope. 'I was on my way there too.'

Her face tensed. 'To go to Svalbard?'

'No.' He took a step forward. 'I'm not going to Svalbard. I was coming to find you. To stop you from leaving.'

She took a step forward too, and now he could see his love and longing reflected in her beautiful blue eyes.

'And why do you want to stop me from leaving?' she said shakily.

Lifting his hands, he cupped her face. 'Because I love you and I need you. And I want to spend my life with you.'

'You love me!' Frankie echoed, and then she started to cry. All the way up in the taxi she had been picturing Arlo's face, imagining what he might say, but the simple, absolute truth of his words were more than she could have wished for.

'I want to spend my life with you too. More than anything. I love you so much.'

'Not as much as I love you.'

His face creased and she saw that he was crying too.

'I can't believe that I let you go. Or that you came back—'

'Of course I came back. Everything else in my life is optional. But you—you're like air to me. I can't breathe without you.'

Arlo pulled her closer, his mouth finding hers. 'I can't breathe without you either.'

He could hardly believe what was happening. Not just

that she was here, and that she loved him and he loved her, but that love had come so simply and completely.

'I made everything a struggle,' he said softly. 'I fought the past, my family, and most of all myself, because I was scared of being proved right. But I've never been happier to be proved wrong.'

He felt her hands slide around his body and they looked into each other's eyes, both of them certain that here in each other's arms they were in the right place—the only place they would ever want to be.

* * * * *

COMING SOON!

We really hope you enjoyed reading this book.
If you're looking for more romance, be sure to
head to the shops when new books are
available on

Thursday 2nd September

MILLS & BOON

THE HEART OF ROMANCE

A ROMANCE FOR EVERY READER

MODERN — Prepare to be swept off your feet by sophisticated, sexy and seductive heroes, in some of the world's most glamourous and romantic locations, where power and passion collide.

HISTORICAL — Escape with historical heroes from time gone by. Whether your passion is for wicked Regency Rakes, muscled Vikings or rugged Highlanders, awaken the romance of the past.

MEDICAL — Set your pulse racing with dedicated, delectable doctors in the high-pressure world of medicine, where emotions run high and passion, comfort and love are the best medicine.

True Love — Celebrate true love with tender stories of heartfelt romance, from the rush of falling in love to the joy a new baby can bring, and a focus on the emotional heart of a relationship.

Desire — Indulge in secrets and scandal, intense drama and plenty of sizzling hot action with powerful and passionate heroes who have it all: wealth, status, good looks…everything but the right woman.

HEROES — Experience all the excitement of a gripping thriller, with an intense romance at its heart. Resourceful, true-to-life women and strong, fearless men face danger and desire - a killer combination!

To see which titles are coming soon, please visit

millsandboon.co.uk/nextmonth

MILLS & BOON

Coming next month

REDEEMED BY HIS NEW YORK CINDERELLA
Jadesola James

"I'll speak plainly." The way he should have in the beginning, before she had him ruminating.

"All right."

"I'm close to signing the man you met. Giles Mueller. He's the owner of the Mueller Racetrack."

She nodded.

"You know it?"

"It's out on Long Island. I attended an event close to it once."

He grunted. "The woman you filled in for on Friday is— *was*—my set date for several events over the next month. Since Giles already thinks you're her, I'd like you to step in. In exchange, I'll make a handsome donation to your charity—"

"Foundation."

"Whatever you like."

There was silence between them for a moment, and Katherine looked at him again. It made him uncomfortable at once. He knew she couldn't see into his mind, but there was something very perceptive about that look. She said nothing, and he continued talking to cover the silence.

"You see, Katherine, I owe you a debt." Laurence's voice was dry. "You saved my life, and in turn I'll save your business."

She snorted. "What makes you think my business needs saving?"

Laurence laughed incredulously. "You're a one-person operation. You don't even have an *office*. Your website is one of those ghastly pay-by-month templates, you live in a boarding house—"

"I don't need an office," Katherine said proudly. "I meet

clients in restaurants and coffee shops. An office is an old-fashioned and frankly completely unneeded expense. I'm not looking to make money off this, Laurence. I want to help people. Not everyone is like you."

Laurence chose not to pursue the insult; what mattered was getting Katherine to sign. "As you like," he said dismissively, then reached for his phone. "My driver has the paperwork waiting in the car. I'll have him bring it round now—"

"No."

It took a moment for the word to register. "Excuse me?"

Katherine did not repeat herself, but she did shake her head. "It's a kind offer, Laurence," she said firmly, "but the thought of playing your girlfriend is at least as absurd as your lie was."

Laurence realized after several seconds had passed that he was gaping, and he closed his mouth rapidly. He'd anticipated many different counteroffers—all that had been provided for in the partnership proposal that was ready for her to sign—but a refusal was something he was wholly unprepared for.

"You're saying no?" he said, to clarify.

She nodded.

"Why the hell would you say no?" The question came out far more harshly than he would have liked, but he was genuinely shocked. "You have everything to gain."

She tucked a lock of dark hair behind her ear, and he was momentarily distracted by the smooth slide of it over her skin. The change in her was truly remarkable. In her element, she was an entirely different person than the frightened teenager he remembered, and she carried herself with a quiet dignity that was very attractive.

Continue reading
REDEEMED BY HIS NEW YORK CINDERELLA
Jadesola James

Available next month
www.millsandboon.co.uk

LET'S TALK
Romance

For exclusive extracts, competitions
and special offers, find us online:

f facebook.com/millsandboon

🐦 @MillsandBoon

📷 @MillsandBoonUK

Get in touch on 01413 063232

For all the latest titles coming soon, visit

millsandboon.co.uk/nextmonth

JOIN US ON SOCIAL MEDIA!

Stay up to date with our latest releases, author news and gossip, special offers and discounts, and all the behind-the-scenes action from Mills & Boon...

 millsandboon

 millsandboonuk

 millsandboon

It might just be true love...